AMY COLLINS

A BOSTON ADVENTURE

Kevin Mullin

Written Words Publishing LLC
P.O. Box 462622
Aurora, CO 80046
www.writtenwordspublishing.com

Published by Written Words Publishing LLC January 30, 2024.

ISBN: 978-1-961610-11-8 (paperback)
ISBN: 978-1-961610-12-5 (eBook)

Library of Congress Control Number: 2023917496

This is a work of fiction. All events and characters in this story are solely the product of the author's imagination. Any similarities between any characters and situations presented in this story to any individuals living or dead or actual places and situations are pure coincidence.

Cover designed by Written Words Publishing LLC

Manufactured and printed in the United States of America

<u>**AMY COLLINS BOOK SERIES**</u>

Finding Home (Book 1)
Amy Collins: A Boston Adventure (Book 2)
Amy Collins and the Marsh Matron (Book 3)

<u>**OTHER BOOKS BY KEVIN MULLIN**</u>

Dagda: House of Horrors

PROLOGUE

When she was 92, my Gramma Amy took my sister Maggie and me to visit Boston. It was to be a reunion with her sister Millicent, who was 94. They were the last two family members of their generation. We all knew this would be their last visit together. Gramma Amy was thrilled to be able to see her sister again after so many years.

Her doctor recommended we take the train. That way, Gramma Amy could get up and walk to encourage her blood flow. Blood flow is very important for older people. It can also be quite beneficial to young people. The journey was uneventful, although I loved watching the scenery breeze by. The tall pine trees of northern Michigan were soon gone, replaced by unwholesome looking cities dressed in gray and brown. It was hard to imagine these places were once thriving towns that swarmed with contented adults and playing children.

One dying city replaced the next. Although, one or two downtown areas did seem to be clean and bright, with towering skyscrapers guarding its residents, just not the ones who lived near the tracks. I decided that towns along the Great Lakes weren't desirable places to live.

Boston's train station was loud, crowded and overwhelming when we arrived. People were everywhere, looking for arrivals or saying good-byes. Others were sleeping on the platforms and benches or begging for money. It was not at all a fun place.

"Millie is sending a car for us," Gramma Amy said as we walked off the platform into the station house.

I looked out the window into a sea of automobiles.

"How will we know which one?"

"He'll tell us," Maggie said, pointing to an older man in a gray uniform holding up a sign that said *Amy Webb*.

He escorted us to a stretch limousine while whispering to Gramma Amy. It was my first, and so far, only time I got to ride in such a grand vehicle. It had a television, wet bar (though I only got to drink a ginger ale), phone charger, and seats that massaged. It only lacked a bathroom. We drove for maybe half an hour, until we reached the Dorrance Hill neighborhood, where the houses were bigger than some hotels.

We zigzagged through the old streets until we came to Ellsworth Lane. We followed an off-white brick wall for a minute or two and turned into a driveway. The driver pressed a button on the dashboard and the wrought iron gate slowly side-stepped open for us.

"You'll be meeting my sister Millie, her daughter Elizabeth, and her two daughters, Elaine and Doreen," Gramma Amy repeated for the 100th time, "If America had royalty, they would be highly regal. True aristocrats. Be on your best and most silent behavior."

The driveway was lined with tall dogwood trees that blessed us with their pink blooms. The trip ended in a circular drop off point, where we were deposited. Three women were waiting for us. An elderly woman who was obviously long retired, and two younger specimens of matronly elegance. They all wore long black dresses with pearl necklaces decorating their throats and gloves covering their forearms. The younger two had fake smiles surgically plastered on their lips while their bleached blond hair brilliantly reflected the sun. Their plasticized faces were designed to make them look youthful, but they both forgot to fix their desiccated and wrinkly necks.

"Elizabeth," my grandmother called out and the older woman hugged her warmly. She turned to the other ladies and greeted them by name and hug as well, "Elaine, you still look like you're in your 20s."

I suppose, but you'd have to add two 20s together to be accurate.

"You're too kind, Aunt Amy," the woman replied.

"And Doreen," Gramma Amy went on to the other woman, "You will always be a beauty."

Maggie and I glanced at each other with the same thought:

If that was true, it's time for us to start wearing paper bags over our heads.

But we smiled politely as we were introduced. If there was only one thing I learned from Gramma Amy, it is this: Silence is golden.

The chauffeur came up behind us and carried our luggage to our rooms, two stories up and down a long hallway to the end. I felt like we had walked all the way to Vermont by the time he opened our doors and set our luggage down.

Our rooms were almost as big as our house in Michigan. Well, one floor, maybe. I got a queen-sized lace trimmed bed with fluffy blankets. Shelves of books and dolls were neatly arranged around the walls. The room was painted a pastel pink with lime green trim. Maggie almost gagged when she saw the color combination.

"Never mix pink and green in the same room," she informed me, "It looks like this."

I didn't think "this" was so bad. Maggie simply shrugged and told me that when I got older, I would develop aesthetic appreciation. Right now, all I had was childish infatuation mixed with gauche tastelessness.

Whatever.

After our debate, we went downstairs to join the adults. They weren't hard to find. All we had to do was follow the laughter. An extremely old woman sat in a wheelchair next to Gramma Amy. They were holding hands and giggling at old reminiscences.

"Maggie and Jenny," our grandmother called out, "Come meet your great grand-aunt Millie, my oldest living relative and best friend."

We politely hugged her and sat at the far end of the table. She smelled of canned beets and rancid perfume. A side effect of her medicines, Gramma Amy told me later.

Sadly, Aunt Millie didn't have much longer to live. That was obvious, even to a child like me.

We eventually moved to the large dining room for dinner. A flower arrangement in a green and gray glass vase shaped like a mermaid with very human exposed breasts centered the 24-seat table. Gramma Amy stared at it with distaste.

"I have never liked mermaids," she said, "Even when they were properly dressed."

The offending vase was removed by one of the servants instantly.

We then sat down with Aunt Millie at the head of the table. Our places were set with elegant extravagance. We had multiple plates and bowls, fancy wine glasses, tumblers for water, and approximately a dozen forks, spoons and knives.

I'm going to use the wrong fork and spoon for every bite.

My insecurity must have shown because everyone laughed.

"Just eat, Jenny," Aunt Millie told me, "No one notices or cares what fork you use."

And so, we ate. Since we were in Boston, it was no surprise that dinner was fresh caught fish broiled in butter. Small boiled red potatoes and broccoli completed the meal. Desert was Boston Crème pie, of course. The adults drank Riesling while my sister and I sipped iced tea.

"I set up an appointment for you at my clinic," Aunt Millie told Gramma Amy. "It'll be tomorrow. It's so good to know we can find the truth."

"Why?" my grandmother shook her head sadly, "Are we less sisters, less friends?"

"No, not at all. But haven't you ever wondered? Hasn't something got you so curious that you just had to find out, no matter what? Can you understand that?"

"I can," I said, and all eyes turned to me with eyebrows raised to impossible heights. "It's in all the fairy tales. The husband tells the wife she can go anywhere in the house except one room, and sooner or later, she goes in that one room."

"And gets killed," Maggie added helpfully.

"Have some more pie," Aunt Millie said darkly.

Elizabeth and her two daughters were pleading for the cause as well. Finally, with an eye roll, my grandmother nodded. Everything was set. Whatever *everything* was.

Before going to sleep, I went down to her room to say good night. She smiled and let me in. Her room was bigger than my sister Debbie's apartment, maybe even bigger than her apartment building.

I flopped on her bed and we talked for a bit.

"What's tomorrow?"

"Tuesday."

"I mean at the clinic? Are you testing to see if you can be a donor to her for something?"

"No, Jenny," she replied slowly, "We're testing to see if we're sisters by name or by blood."

"You don't know?"

"Until DNA testing came along, we could never know, just make educated guesses. Remember, I have two stories about who I am. Two families that claimed me. I didn't care really where my blood line came from. I felt unique because I had two families."

"But I thought—"

"Let's get away from what we think. I'll tell you what we know."

And so began her story of her life in Boston. Of course, Gramma Amy was very proper and her reminiscences were heavily edited to leave out the vulgar language and names people used so prevalently in her youth. She thought it made the world a better place when people spoke civilly to and about each other. It was an opinion I certainly agreed with. This is Amy Collins Webb's story as she herself told it.

CHAPTER ONE

THE DREAM

Although I couldn't have known it at the time, I think it all started with that nightmare, the one I always remembered. I was in the Malmort River again, near the bottom. An enormous and thoroughly evil alligator attacked me and dragged me down there for dinner. Most of us thought it was eighteen feet long, though after it was caught, the hunters decided it was a bit smaller. To a ten-year-old girl fighting for her life, the size was unimportant. It was big.

My only weapon against this horrible reptile was an oar from the boat he destroyed. My original intent when I saw it lurching towards me was to swat its snout and swim away, but the paddle was reversed. I was holding the wide flat part while the handle was facing my predator. I grabbed both ends of the blade and pushed it at the creature's snout, thinking if I caused it enough pain, it would go away. My first father from New York told me that the best strategy in winning a fight quickly is to smash your opponent's nose.

In this case, it was even better. I missed. The current swerved the handle so that the oar plunged downward, deep into its mouth. I felt it shudder and swim off to clear its throat, allowing me time to escape while it was distracted. I'm sure all it did was bite down and swallow the oar, but maybe that killed its appetite for little girls. Whatever happened, I got away.

This part of the dream was a simple remembrance. It was natural for a person to dream of her traumatic experiences. It was the next portion of the dream that was memorable. I swam up to the surface for air. But I wasn't in The Malmort River in Louisiana anymore. I surfaced in The East River in New York City. My Aunt Mary and Uncle Gio were there, along with my sister Julia and brother Patrick. My stepsisters were there too, Sophie and Isabella. The day was hot and the sky was a vivid, unnatural blue. The water was gray, and rather dry (I was in bed dreaming, after all). Everything was painted in unnatural colors, except Uncle Gio, who was a stark black and white. Silent and unsmiling.

"It's time to go home," he said.

I shook my head. I didn't want to go home with him. They sent me away and I was happy in my new home. I wanted nothing to do with them. I swam away as fast as possible.

"You can't run from home, Amy," Aunt Mary called out. She was frightened. Not for me. Never for me. She was afraid of her husband, and I was her sacrifice to keep him happy. I had to swim away.

"Come back here," Gio the Giraffe called out to me while pulling out his revolver, "Or I'll shoot you dead."

He repeatedly shot at me while I swam away, missing every time. I didn't even hear the bullets hit the water. When I felt I was far enough away, I turned back. The pistol shot backwards and the rounds struck him instead of me. His bullet riddled body fell forward.

"Amy," a new voice called to me from far away, "Amy, over here, I need to talk to you."

A large outcrop of boulders appeared nearby. I saw a young woman waving, motioning me to come to her. I swam over her way while the others bickered. It was a short swim. Effortless. But then, reality is different in a dream. I reached the rock and she lifted me up with ease.

"Well, hi, Amy Collins," she said politely. She was pretty, with white hair and eyes as blue as the ocean.

"Hello Miss—"

"Endora. Here, sit, look around. The ocean makes a fine home for us all."

Her hands firmly turned me around to where I had just swum. The New York skyline was gone. A rocky coast was there now with a pebble strewn beach maybe five hundred yards distant.

"This is Tarrelahuesett," she told me, "The people who lived here call it The Still Waters That Kill. The settlers shortened the name to Tarrelsett: The calm waters."

"That's quite a difference," I said looking back at her.

"It is. Everywhere you go, things can seem peaceful and quiet on the surface, but underneath, you will find evil people and whirlpools of animosity. You don't see them until it's too late. It's all part of dealing with people. They think they're entitled to what they want, and you don't know what they'll do to get it."

I nodded, and that's when I noticed she didn't have legs. From the waist down was a gray and silver tail, just like a fish. My eyes jumped up to her face.

She smiled brightly at me. "It's a matter of getting what you want," she repeated, "People don't want to eat people, but they do want to eat fish. Fish want to eat fish *and* people. So do mermaids."

Her eyes transformed into fishy globs while her teeth grew into gigantic fangs and she lunged towards me. I jumped back, lost my balance and fell off the rocky cliff back into the ocean with her laughter echoing in my ears as I swam to the shore.

"Don't be in a hurry my sweet," she croaked out in an inhuman voice, "We have much to talk about."

I woke up with my heart thumping hard against my ribs. After a while, I was back asleep. The nightmare forgotten but not entirely.

We have much to talk about.

Chapter Two

Rest and Recuperation

In January of 1930, I was sent to live with my Aunt Cassie in Faucette, Louisiana. Within the first two months, I received a concussion from a kick in the head, slipped and fell when a bullet grazed my temple, and then the gigantic alligator attacked me in the river, which gave me a great story to tell. I think I preferred the concussions to the alligator attack. Doctor Gannon, our local physician, was worried about the bite wounds on my leg so I was kept out of school for several weeks with my foot propped up and my head in a book.

My adventure earned me a few newspaper stories, both nationally and in *The Faucette Local*, our daily paper published by the Harmon family. I never actually met the Harmons or their children. They were sent to boarding school and the parents went to the Methodist church on the Atchafala River. If I saw them around town, I wouldn't recognize them. They were familiar with me and my family though. My mother's family used to share the same church with them, but when my unmarried mother was pregnant with me, they led that congregation in convincing my family to find another church.

After I arrived in Louisiana, Mom put me in public

school, but soon I obtained a scholarship of sorts to a private Catholic school. My teacher, Sister Barbara, faithfully sent me my homework assignments and called once a week to see how I was progressing. She was a dedicated and wonderful teacher. My classmates also would come calling on me and I was able to maintain passing grades that year.

Although we were not Catholic, I was granted special permission to attend by Father Cassidy at the request of Governor Huey P. Long. Mr. Long gave Father Cassidy two options that day. Either accept me as a new student as part of a community outreach or watch the church be razed to the ground in search of 'evidence' of criminal activity.

I found out later that Father Cassidy not only accepted me into the school, he made clear that I was a part of the school. No one was to make me feel unwanted at St. Linus. Not only was I not unwanted, I made friends with my Catholic classmates and we went treasure hunting down a particularly dangerous river called *The Riviere de Mal Morte*. Malmort for short. It meant *The River of Bad Death*. It was there that I met that gigantic alligator, the biggest ever to swim in North America, at least to my mind. Of course, I'd have preferred to find the chest of gold coins instead.

Although my leg ached a bit because of the bite, Mom (the name Aunt Cassie told me to use for her) still expected me to contribute to the household. Thus, after I completed my schoolwork, she gave me chores that a wounded young girl could easily handle. I especially loved shelling pecans and prying up the soft nut from the hard shells, which I quickly threw into the fire for heat and disposal. Sadly, Mom got the not-entirely-incorrect idea that I was eating the pecans as fast as I shelled them.

My next job was polishing the silver. She correctly decided that I wouldn't eat any of the tableware. Luckily for me, Mom was seven months pregnant. She snacked all day long on strange things. Her favorites were popcorn loaded with mustard and ketchup or pickles in cream. Given that she seemed prone to eat anything, I suspected that if a spoon or two went missing, I would not be the prime suspect.

One day after the silverware was shiny and bright, Porky, our hired hand, came to the house with an ice chest filled with freshly caught perch. Mom had him put it on the table while she got out the cutting utensils.

"Have you ever cleaned a fish before?" she asked me casually.

"No, but I can get out some cleanser from under the sink if you want."

She laughed and hugged my shoulder.

"Amy, I just don't know how we ever survived without your wonderful sense of humor. However, on a serious note, I know you've *seen* them getting cleaned before."

She put a cutting board in front of me with a big mixing bowl and platter to the side.

"Just like with a chicken, we turn a fish into food. Now, you like fish, right?"

I nodded. "But will I still like fish after we're done here? They look so sad with their little dead eyes staring at me."

She picked up a viciously sharp cleaver and chopped down with lightning speed, cleanly decapitating one of the unfortunate perches. She picked up the head and examined it for a moment.

"Doesn't look sad to me," she said, "Appears to be happy to feed us. Rest in peace, my tasty little friend."

She tossed the head into the bowl and picked up a smaller knife.

"After the head comes the scales. Start at the tail and scrape forward to get him good and clean. No one deserves to get a mouthful of scales."

"Are you sure? Maybe that's how the scales of justice work."

"Ha-ha," she flipped the denuded fish over and scooted the cutting board and knife over to me. "Let's see Amy work now. Remember, you have to learn to be useful. A woman can't make it in the world if she's only a decoration."

I held the tail down and started scraping. It was not a pleasant job. The dead fish smell instantly made me a little queasy. Not sick enough to get me out of my fish cleaning lesson, but enough to wish we gave the little perch a bit more mercy. The tail was not exactly slimy, but moist in an unwholesome way, leaving my hand sticky and smelly.

"You are doing so good with this project. So much better than with the chickens."

I had to agree. Last month, before my fight with the alligator, she taught me how to 'turn a bird into food.' I felt quite a bit more empathy with the birds. They were fluffy, clucked a bit and gave us eggs. Fish just aren't sympathetic animals. Their whole purpose in life was to be eaten. If not by us, by something else. I'm glad we got to them first.

I'm really on my way to being a country girl.

One quick slice down the underside then more scrapping as the digestive parts oozed out. On second thought, this was just as bad as the chicken. The guts made a nauseating plop in the bowl and the fins and tail quickly followed. What was left was a fish as I knew it. Soft, white and ready to be battered and fried. We placed the now edible fish on the platter and we went to the next one.

"I'll be glad when we're fin-ished," I told Mom, making a weak pun.

She gave me a sideways glance and said, "Don't tell me this is worse than plucking chickens."

"No, the chickens are higher on the SCALE of disgusting, but they gave me a TALE to tell."

"I'll be glad when you outgrow the bad jokes," she shook her head.

"Then things will go swimmingly?"

My first father was a wonderful Irishman named Michael Collins. Back when I lived with him, we told each other puns all the time, much to the annoyance of my Aunt Mary, who I was raised to think of as my mother. Papa, as I called him, was not my father, he just happened to marry my Aunt Mary at the right time. Mom was a young woman "in trouble," a wonderful euphemism for pregnant without wedlock. Mom gave birth to me in New York and left me for them to raise as their own. That way the stigma of being illegitimate wouldn't follow me. And in those days, it was a big disgrace, for both of us.

Things went well in New York at first. We had a wonderful neighbor who took me in and taught me all kinds of things that led to my being a star student at school. Aunt Mary was always distant to me, but I was loved enough by my younger sister and brother, along with Papa. Then one winter day, my first father was gunned down while delivering illegal booze to the city.

That sad news was followed by another dreadful turn of events when Aunt Mary married her second husband, a thoroughly repugnant and oily hoodlum named Giovanni Corelli, known as Gio the Giraffe. I had to call him Papa Gio and refer to him as my second father. Disgusting Pig would have been my more accurate, if socially unacceptable, name for him.

He had two daughters who absolutely despised me. They resented me being in the new family. So did Gio. Eventually, he decided he would become Uncle Gio at the same time Mama became Aunt Mary.

The Giraffe worked for a man named Antonio Dragucci at a 'gentleman's club' in Manhattan. They decided that I would work there as penance for breaking Gio's daughter's nose after she smashed my violin into pieces. Aunt Mary stole some money from her evil husband that night and whisked me to the train station with a ticket to Faucette, Louisiana to be with her sister, my real mother.

Mom was a bit embarrassed to tell me about my birth but after a few weeks it became clear who she really was. For one thing, she did not let me call her Aunt Cassie. It was Mom almost from the first day, even though I thought she was my aunt.

"I'm your real mother," she would say, "And even if I wasn't, I would be."

That sounded so good to me. She had the same rule for my two new brothers and four sisters. None of them were my *full* brothers or sisters by blood, but that didn't matter because Mom made it clear that we were all full family, even if we didn't share the exact same lineage.

However, I was the only one who loved to play on words. Mom considered that kind of humor to be God's punishment for sins of the past. Her sideways glance made me aware it would be wise to let them go for a while.

I remember that day we cleaned the fish vividly. After they were put in the icebox, Mom received a letter from the postman that required her signature. She read it, threw it on the table, and waddled over to the phone to call New York.

Chapter Three

Family

I continued to the next fish while she waited for the connection. I was thinking about my Louisiana family. Mom's husband was Paul Villians (pronounced vee-YAN), a local widower. That made him my third father and I called him Dad. He was a barrel-chested tall man with a ruddy complexion and a wooden leg. No one in town was fooled by that handicap. Dad could still handle himself in a fight. Everybody knew it and respected that fact.

In his youth, he was part of a gang of bank robbers led by a ne'er-do-well named Antoine Nye. They robbed banks from the end of the Civil War to the beginning of the Great War. When they were old enough, Dad and his five brothers joined that gang. Antoine believed that most of the outlaws of that time wanted money and fame. It was the fame part that got them killed. So, he recruited a large gang but only had a few bandits rotate from raid to raid. That way, their descriptions were always different. The law agencies of the day never knew that just one gang was doing all the raiding. Because the gang was so big, each robber's share was small. It never raised suspicions when they blew through their loot.

It was a perfect operation until 1917, when Antoine got

greedy and went for a giant haul in a little town in Arkansas called Edgewater. The whole gang was shot to pieces. Dad only survived because he didn't go. He was in jail at that time becoming acquainted with his half-brother Vincent. The raid went on without him and only two survivors rode back to town. Dad had a low opinion of them because he thought they should have fought harder to save the others.

One of the survivors was Angus Nye, Antoine's son and Dad's former brother-in-law. He was a charming older man who searched for me after I received a concussion at school and wandered off. He called me a mermaid because he found me sleeping on a flat rock in the middle of the creek that ran behind the school.

I liked Angus and his wife Brigitte, though they seemed mismatched. Angus was a young 52, though grizzled from his rough life. Brigitte was 30 but seemed 10 years younger. She gave him love and laughter. He gave her security. They always seemed happy. She was occasionally sad they had no children, but she accepted that fact and went on with her life. Although Angus and Dad patched things up outwardly, Dad never tried to conceal his dislike for the man.

The other survivor was Durrell Kaker, a dour man in his early 40s, only slightly older than Dad. He was a widower with two grown and married daughters who lived in Atlanta, as far away from him as possible, or so I suspected. Although he wasn't exactly mean, he was unpleasant. When I arrived in Faucette in January, he wouldn't let me wait in the warm train station for Dad to pick me up. I had to wait outside in the winter wind. Dad, wooden leg and all, walked up to him and thumped his head. Kaker made such an issue of it that they both spent time together in jail. They talked about Edgewater and Dad decided there wasn't anything that could have been done to save his friends and family. The days of robbing banks on horseback were over. They were just the last to find out.

While I was thinking, Mom got through to New York. She was talking (screaming, really) when the rest of my family came home from school, escorted by my Gramma Morris, who only deposited them before hurrying to the outhouse. Annette was my oldest stepsister (she was Dad's eldest daughter from his first marriage) and had just turned 17. She had light blonde hair and blue eyes which made her quite attractive. She was nice to me but spent most of her time either reading mysteries or enjoying the company of Guy Thomas, her boyfriend. Recently, she seemed to be more distant. She had been complaining of not feeling well.

My other stepsisters were their usual perky selves. Michelle was 15 and as pleasant as could be. She was big boned with thin brown hair. She may have been the least pretty of us on the outside, but I suspected her soul was as beautiful and bright as the sun. The room was always better when she was in it. Anna Marie was 11 and was already a beauty with luscious brown hair tied in an expertly done braid. She was tall for her age and I was small for my ten years so there was a five-inch difference in height. She didn't smile much but made up for it by scowling a lot. It would take a few years for us to get close. The youngest one to come home was Holly. She was my seven-year-old half-sister from Mom and Paul and by far my favorite. From my first day, she was always by my side whenever possible. She was my special friend. The first one from my Louisiana home to make me feel like family.

"You won't believe it," Michelle said, practically shouting at me with breathy excitement.

"What?"

"Guess who just got married?"

"Who?" My eyes widened with delight. Weddings were big things out here and I was immediately excited. Little did I know.

Anna Marie jumped in, "We were on our way to school and you know those old buildings next door to the schoolyard?"

Old ruins would be more accurate, but I nodded, not understanding the connection.

"We were on our way to school and there were dozens of Foyts fixing up the roof and covering the windows with black tar paper," she told me.

The Foyt family was well known in these parts. They were big, mean, and rather dull. They showed signs of severe inbreeding. Good people to stay away from was the prevailing opinion.

"'Whatcha doing?' I asked, 'Nobody's lived here in years.' And they said, 'We're fixing it up as squatters for Noreen and her husband.'"

"Noreen Foyt got married? She's only thirteen," I was surprised.

"What difference does that make?" Anna Marie asked.

"I don't know. Seems kind of young."

"That's just the Yankee in you," she replied, unaware that she sounded kind of hostile, "We have different ways down here. There's no age limit on how old she has to be. Besides, her family thinks she turned fourteen last week."

Thinks?

"Who'd she marry?" I asked, shaking off her strange explanation.

"Huck," both Michelle and Anna Marie shouted.

"Finn?" I was shocked and appalled.

Huck was a farmhand Dad had fired two months ago for trying to get too familiar with me. He wanted us to pretend we were married and do the things married people do. Dad also told him to leave town. Huck might have forgotten that part since Dad's fist slammed into his jaw. Now, he was going to live next door to the school?

They all nodded.

"But that's okay," Michelle said, "We can just walk on the other side of the street to keep away from him."

Mom's conversation on the phone got a few decibels louder and apparently woke up Jason, our youngest family member. He was almost four and tolerated me well enough, but Michelle would always be his favorite. Those two would get on the piano together and decimate any song they played. Sometimes, I thought I heard something familiar in the notes but more often they sounded like feral cats screaming in a New York City back ally. As the school year was coming to a close, Michelle had too much homework to do to abuse our piano. I commiserated with her and Jason, but deep down I was happy.

"What's going on?" Annette asked, hearing the high-pitched rage in Mom's voice.

"I'm not sure," I replied, "She got this letter in the mail and went straight to the phone."

Annette picked up the letter and read it.

"Oh dear," she said, looking at me.

"What?"

"Aunt Mary wants you to return to New York. She hired a lawyer."

Chapter Four

A Conversation at Wentworth Founding

While Mom was talking to Aunt Mary and Uncle Gio, another conversation was happening in Pennyton, Massachusetts. Pennyton was an exclusive village north of Boston where wealthy families, descendants of the original settlers, lived. "Old money" families with prestigious names and large bank accounts.

William Jarviston, the butler and head of staff at Wentworth Founding, was having a conversation with Matilda Langston Wentworth, the lady of the house. Tilly, as her friends called her, was in mourning. Her husband Joe, known to the world as Josiah Pierce Wentworth III and son Joey, Josiah Pierce Wentworth IV, Fourthy to the family, both died in a boating accident the week before. The ocean can be unforgiving when sailors make mistakes.

Jarviston was a nondescript middle-aged man, maybe 50, maybe older, who was bald on top with neatly trimmed sides and a goatee. His blue eyes twinkled as he gazed down at Tilly. She was the love of his life. Her light brown hair was slowly becoming gray and her face was showing the start of permanent smile lines. But at 48, she was still an attractive woman with clear blue eyes and perfect teeth.

She remained in bed, even though the shadows of afternoon were getting long. It was proper for a grieving woman to avoid people, especially when she lost her husband and her only son. But Jarviston suspected her grief was more of an act to meet the expectations of proper society. After all, she told him several times that she despised her husband and was afraid of her son. Act or not, the doctor, as usual, prescribed morphine to help her sleep. Women of her social standing were delicate and needed help to cope with the tragedies of life. And Tilly Wentworth always needed help. If she had nothing to cope with, then she would have to forego her occasional dose of morphine. And that, she would never do.

She lay in bed watching him with dry eyes while he poured tea for her and put it on a bedside tray. Four months earlier, when her infant daughter Rosemary was found dead in her crib, Jarviston saw real grief. The tears flowed freely and there was no consoling her. Her six surviving daughters tried, but her grief could only run its course. She suffered the greatest loss a mother could bear.

On the other hand, the loss of her husband and son was no cause for weeping.

"Do you judge me harshly, Willie, because I grieved for Rosemary, but not Joe or Joey?" she asked in a matter-of-fact voice.

"No, Ma'am. I knew them, too."

She snorted out a mirthless hiss.

"That's why Joe hated you so much. You tell the truth. Sometimes, I wondered why he didn't try to fire you."

"Because I know all the secrets, Ma'am."

"What secrets?" she was curious.

She had known Willie for over 25 years. He never struck her as a man her husband of 30 years would confide in.

Josiah Wentworth was a man of his class and his class would never allow a servant to know any information that could be damaging.

"Where he bought his ties? Or shoes? Where he planned our next vacation?"

"Well," he replied with an obvious show of courage, "I know one about your daughter."

She giggled a bit. The morphine was making her giddy.

"Which one? I have six daughters, not counting Rosemary."

"Seven."

"Seven?"

"Not counting Rosemary."

She looked at him with uncomprehending eyes.

"A forgotten daughter? You think I could go through nine months of sickness and bloating, the pain of birth, and forget about it? That must be some secret."

"Oh, it was. Until now that is. I'm sure you remember the pregnancy but not the birth. You were drugged for the pain."

"Go on," she said thoughtfully. She was drugged for all the births.

"You may remember you were in New York at the time."

"For my sister Hyacinth's wedding when Joey was born. I remember it well. Lovely wedding. Odious husband. But my son just had to be born at that time. Far away from home. I do remember Joey's birth. It's the kind of thing a woman doesn't forget. Are you saying there was a twin? One with some kind of defect Joe wouldn't tolerate?"

"No," Jarviston soothed, "Nothing like that. You may remember as well that since you announced the blessed event was coming, Mr. Wentworth said you would have a boy, even if he had to invade Heaven and bribe God to get one. He never acknowledged the mere possibility that you would give him another daughter."

"I know. He had no use for the ones he had."

"I wouldn't say that."

Actually, he would say that, but it was unkind, so it wasn't really necessary. J.P. Wentworth was not a doting or loving father to any of his daughters. His son received all the fatherly attention he had to offer, which wasn't much, since he had a business empire to run and a parade of mistresses and evening acquaintances that filled up his spare time.

Several of these women also presented the elder Wentworth with children. Given J.P. Wentworth's reckless love life, children were always expected but rarely appreciated. Some of the women opted to have the child and Wentworth provided for them, in his typically miserly way. The majority of the unwanted pregnancies were terminated. Many young women left Wentworth Crossing with tears in their eyes and cash in their purse.

"The doctor gave you opium to help ease the birthing pains, you remember," he guided the conversation back.

"I remember. I was in pain and then I woke up the next day with news I had a son. I was so happy. I thought maybe a son would make Joe love me again…"

"If you really look back at it, I think you know he never loved you, just your inheritance," he replied, "But he was generous that night. He paid for the anesthesia for all the young ladies. Four girls and one boy were born. Specifically, there was one unmarried hillbilly girl from Louisiana in the charity ward. She had a nasty fall which started her labor. She was quite a handful. She was screaming in pain and sick with worry. He made sure she got sedated first."

"She must have been very pretty."

"Very loud is more like it. She had a little boy that night. A couple of hours before you had your daughter."

He watched as her confusion slowly morphed into anger. She sat up and adjusted her position on the bed, spilling most of her tea onto the tray, which Jarviston gracefully whisked away.

"You mean that monster just switched babies in the hospital and no one stopped him? Where were you? You just let him and didn't tell me anything for over ten years? You let me think that little monster was my fault?"

The little monster was Fourthy, the family's problem child. He was quite vicious. At seven, he poisoned the family dog in a scientific experiment to monitor its death throes. He loved throwing stones at unsuspecting birds in hopes of injuring them enough to watch the life exit their bodies when they died. He wanted to see if the escaping soul could be visible. He killed things (mostly insects) in the morning, afternoon, and night, from dawn until dusk.

His father described it as a phase he was going through. The phase went on until last autumn, when he decided he liked touching girls. All girls—his sisters, their friends, the hired help. The servant girls had to repeatedly push him away or slap him. A few resigned, saying he threatened to tell his father he saw them stealing things from the home. And they all knew that J.P. Wentworth III always believed his son.

"The father's bad enough," one young housekeeper said to the cook, "But what's that little beast going to be like when he learns what else he can do besides touch?"

"What more can he do?" the cook responded soothingly, "He'll just be like his father."

And then Baby Rosemary died in her crib. She just

stopped breathing, which sometimes happens. The problem was that Millicent and Lisa, two of his older sisters, saw the boy leave the nursery that day. They went into the room immediately and discovered the lifeless body.

Neither of them actually *saw* him do anything. There was no evidence of foul play. The only thing that could be said with certainty was that he was where he should not have been. But it was one broken rule too many. Young Wentworth would be suspected of sororicide for the rest of his life. He would also be sent away to boarding school, though his accidental death spared the unsuspecting school of his mischief.

"No one thinks the little monster was your fault," Jarviston soothed, "Probably he was damaged somehow when his mother fell. Plus, your husband didn't correct his early misdeeds, perhaps thinking he'd get better. But he got worse. No one blames you. Your husband chose to let him run wild like that."

She was mollified. Yes, how could any of it be her fault?

"I didn't want to talk to you about Fourthy," he went on, "I wanted to tell you about your daughter. The one Mr. Wentworth traded for."

"Traded for? What a way to phrase it. Makes it sound almost like slavery. So, Joe kept track of her? That is a surprise."

"*I* kept track of her," he replied annoyed, "With his permission. And resources, of course. Would you like to know about her? She means a lot to me. And you as well, I would think."

"Well, of course." It was her turn to be annoyed. Why should she mean more to the butler than her own mother? For a moment, she had a memory of a long-ago dream, but it vanished as Willie pulled an envelope from his suit pocket.

"Well, to start with, she lives in Faucette, Louisiana, just east of Baton Rouge. Her mother left her with her sister and brother-in-law to raise. His name was Michael Collins…"

"Michael Collins?"

"Not *that* Michael Collins," he said, "Her Michael Collins was a low-level bootlegger and enforcer, known for his ability to cold-cock people he didn't like. It seems he didn't like many people. Regardless, he was shot to death a few years back. Her mother or aunt or whatever you want to call her remarried another gangster named Giovanni Corelli, sometimes called Gio the Giraffe. It seems that little Amy cold-cocked her stepsister, Gio's daughter. Like father, like daughter. Her aunt got her out of town to Faucette the next day. That was in January. We have an informant who keeps us up to date on the girl. Our person sent these clippings."

She looked down at three yellowed newspaper headlines.

Young Girl Shot While Preventing Robbery.
Alligator Attack! Young Girl Missing.
It's a Miracle! Amy Collins Found Alive!

She read through the stories with growing interest. Obviously, hillbilly girls from the south led much more adventurous lives than the proper children of Patrician New England.

"And you are sure that this girl is my daughter?"

"No doubt. We bribed two doctors, seven nurses, and four staff members to say that Fourthy was your son. It was important to your husband that the Wentworth name be carried on."

She snorted.

"Do you know how many Wentworths there are in the world?"

"None from your husband's line."

"Good thing," she muttered, "Does this spy of yours still send us information?"

"Occasionally. Nothing recently. She's been staying home to recover from the alligator bite. She goes to a Catholic school and the nun who teaches her class comes by her home with her the schoolwork and to help keep her grades up."

"Her new family can afford a Catholic school with that kind of special attention?"

"Not really. The governor told the priest in charge to accept her on a scholarship or he would tear down the church and school to the ground."

"She knows the governor?"

"She met him once. That we know of. Our informant hasn't sent us anything else about that. But apparently Gio and Mary want her back in New York and are drafting a legal challenge for custody."

"Why?"

He sighed. "Gio runs a gentleman's club. Some of the customers like their dancers young. They fetch a lot of money."

"Young dancers?" she snorted derisively, "I imagine you mean the kind that dance horizontally. This Gio the Giraffe sounds like a two-legged cockroach."

"Which brings us to why I started this conversation," Jarviston went on, "I was thinking that while their lawyers are distracted, we could flex a little legal muscle of our own and have her come up here to visit you and meet her real family. I think it would be quite nice if she could come up for the summer. I can't think of anything more beneficial to the child than to have a bit quieter existence. We certainly don't want her to be a…dancer at that club. It'll be a short and brutal life for the child."

"Why just the summer?" she replied thoughtfully, "Why not permanently? I'm sure you can handle all the arrangements."

"I can. And permanently does sound better."

Chapter Five

A Surprise Wedding

The legal process had begun. Aunt Mary apologized to Mom over the phone, but Gio was adamant that I return. My sister Julia and brother Patrick (my cousins, actually) missed me and the house wasn't right without me. The family was broken apart now. My stepsisters, Isabella and Sophia, wanted to start over and make everything right. I could have violin lessons again. Besides, they have better financial resources. Their house had electricity. New York was just a better place for a child with my talent and ability.

Of course, I knew Isabella and Sophia would continue to make things wrong, not right. I was already taking violin lessons. We had enough money. Electricity was overrated. And Louisiana was the better place for me to be.

Gramma Morris, who was my great grandmother, had returned by now and snorted at the thought of me leaving. "Horse manure. All they can do is offer a colder climate and bolder gangsters. How much love and attention did they give her? None."

"Gramma Morris is right," Michelle said, "We can't let those people take her away. This is her family. Right, Amy?"

"I never want to leave here. New York will never be home for me again," I said adamantly.

"Don't let them take her," Holly was starting to cry already and nothing even happened yet.

"And if they threw her away once, what's to stop them from doing it again?" Anna Marie made a valid, if harshly phrased point. It was rather nice though, that she was taking my part.

Annette nodded in agreement, but her heart wasn't with us. Her eyes were puffy and red. The conversation went on, but nothing new was added. My family wanted me to stay. That made me happy.

Michelle and Anna Marie made dinner for us that night. Fish and collard greens. Greens were not my favorite food at all, but they were much better than anything my Aunt Mary ever cooked. I read some *Wizard of Oz* book to Holly and Jason for a while, and Mom and Annette went into the master bedroom to talk for a bit.

When Dad came home, Mom called him into the room as well, even before he could say anything more than 'Hi' to the rest of us. Whatever was going on with Annette was serious. We hoped she wasn't ill. We soon found out that *ill* wasn't quite the word for it.

They all came out, grim faced and determined looking. Dad just glared at Annette for a second or two then nodded to the phone. She picked it up and rolled the handle to let the operator know she needed a connection.

"Hi, Guy," we heard her say, so we knew she called her boyfriend. She invited him over for dinner that night and to do homework. Guy already graduated but still knew a lot about school stuff.

"He'll be here by six," Annette said, sounding more sad than happy.

"Good. It's always a good thing to have your boyfriend over. I rather like Guy. He doesn't annoy me."

"No one annoys you," Annette responded, "Or you'll punch their face in."

"Not everyone," Dad replied, his voice becoming a bit of a growl, "I never punched him in his face. And a little damage might make him better looking. A scar here and there gives character."

He smiled innocently at her as he sat down and adjusted his wooden leg on the couch. Annette accepted the loss and went to the kitchen to help prepare dinner. While I was reading to Holly, I glanced up and noticed that as Annette was preparing the greens, Mom quietly went to the phone and made another call. She had a satisfied smile on her face when she hung up. For the rest of my life, when I hear the term the-cat-that-ate-the-canary smile, that's what I envision.

Guy arrived at six, almost on the minute. Annette let him in and stood on her toes for a second for him to kiss her. I was taken aback since I never saw such a display of affection from either of them. Guy seemed pleasantly surprised also.

Dinner went well. Dad was downright courteous to Guy. Normally, he ignored him or made snide little remarks, which ratcheted up the tension in the room. It was so good to have a nice, relaxed dinner with just family and friends.

Guy came from a colorful family of lawyers and judges, although his own father was a successful dairyman. The original Thomas was a carpetbagger from the north who came south as a government official to squeeze what little food and money there was out of the poor inhabitants. His plans changed rather drastically when he married a local girl. After making some amends, the Thomas family thrived in Faucette.

"So, how's business been?" Dad asked.

"Well, it's been kind of slow. The orders are getting smaller. Grain and expenses stay the same."

"Times are tough."

"You know," Mom said, "Speaking of hard times, when I was pregnant with Amy, I was in the roughest patch of my life. Hugo not only wouldn't marry me, he married Estelle Beaufort. So, I had a real problem here. Tommy, that's Hugo's younger brother, told everyone in town that there could have been other fathers, so my whole reputation was demolished."

"Their father sent Tommy away for that, in fact," Annette added, "Because it was not the right thing to do. He's in Georgia now."

Guy nodded, obviously disinterested, though I was fascinated.

"The only people who stood by me were Gramma Morris and Mary. And Mary was having her issues with my father. He sent her a letter from Europe, this was right after the Great War, telling her he met a man he wanted her to marry.

"Well, no one was going to tell Mary De Montfort who to marry. Not long after our parents got back, Mary eloped. I caught a train to be with them. Amy was born in the charity wing of the Manhattan Lutheran Hospital. I was so lucky. Some millionaire's wife was in labor too, and he paid for all of us expectant mothers to get morphine for the pain. I didn't even see Amy until the next day, when I sent her home with Mary and Michael. I couldn't stay there anymore because I would be heartsick every time I saw my precious little girl. So, I got some jobs bookkeeping and waitressing, until Gramma Morris asked me to come back to help her in the restaurant."

"Yep," Gramma Morris said, "Couldn't ask Mary to help. She had her own family and she's useless in a restaurant, especially the kitchen."

"So, I heard," Guy said.

Annette must have repeated some of the stories I brought back from my first home. Dinner was over. We started clearing the plates while Mom started a pot of coffee. Guy and Annette whispered contentedly at the table.

"I never want to see anyone else go through that," Mom continued, "Especially family."

As if on cue, someone knocked on the door. Michelle was the closest and opened it. Paster Seth Josephson was on the other side, smiling at her with a Bible in his hand.

"It's Pastor Seth," Michelle called out.

"Oh, good," Mom called back, "Come on in."

Dad greeted him with a handshake and motioned for him to go to the table, while he went into the master bedroom. Mom had a cup of strong coffee set out for him with honey next to it.

After he settled into his chair, Pastor Seth innocently asked, "So, what is the emergency that I can help you with?"

"Good question," Dad said from behind us.

We all turned and he had just come out of the bedroom with his Browning 12-gauge shotgun. He cocked back the hammers, which added some seriously dramatic tension to our situation.

"What we have here is a 'wife or death' situation. Young Mr. Thomas is about to propose to my daughter, who is going to be the mother of his baby."

"I already did," Guy said, looking to Annette to confirm his statement.

"I told him," she said helplessly.

"And I'm proud of you, boy," Dad said sarcastically, "Now, we just need to seal the deal, so to speak. Love is always a gamble and I don't gamble if there's a chance you'll run off."

"Mr. Villians," the pastor cried out, "This is outrageous. I'm not going to perform a ceremony under these circumstances."

"Oh, no?" Dad said, with an evil smile forming, "You mean these sweet young girls will have to watch me kill this poor boy right in front of them and then they'll have to clean up all that blood and gore just because you don't like the circumstances?"

"But if he already proposed—"

"Then we moved the date up a bit. They're obviously eager to get into each other's arms. They already proved that. And he's either leaving this house a married man or a dead man."

Pastor Seth tried to reason with Dad. He pleaded. Both he and Guy explained that there would be nothing for Annette to worry about. He would do right by her. But Dad held firm, with Mom beside him nodding her support. Annette just looked miserable.

Finally, Dad and his shotgun won over the pastor and his Bible. Pastor Seth nodded his head sadly. I remember hearing a lot of sighs. Relief, contentment, resignation, resentment. The wedding was on. Jason was picked to be the best man. He stood by Guy while Pastor Seth groused through the ritual. When it was time for the ring, Gramma Morris put one in Jason's hand and nodded towards Guy.

They kissed and we applauded. Dad put the gun back in the bedroom.

Mom hugged Annette but got no response. Dad also hugged her tight and lifted her off the ground. He was happy and laughing. She was angry and embarrassed. Dad shrugged and limped over to Guy, grabbing his hand and shaking it. A might too hard by the looks of it. Guy just glared at him.

"Now, boy," Dad said with obviously false joviality, "Don't let a bad start keep things bad."

"Bad start? You were going to kill me."

"I was not," Dad said, trying to look wounded, "If I was going to kill you, I would've loaded the shotgun."

That broke the tension as we all laughed, even Holly, who seemed almost traumatized by the events of the evening. Now everyone relaxed, even the bride and groom, though they remained hostile but not overtly disrespectful to Mom and Dad. Annette even called us all over to show off her ring. It was tastefully done. Curved lines engraved the sides with crescent shaped sapphires surrounding a small diamond.

"My aunt's wedding ring," Gramma Morris told us, "I want it kept in the family. If you decide at some point that you want something more modern, please give it back to me or one of your sisters. I'm sure one of them will want it."

"I want it," we all shouted. Clearly, there would be competition for it if it ever became available again. I was impressed by the gift. Annette was not Gramma Morris' blood kin, but she was still family. If anyone said anything different, they'd get a tablespoon thump on the back of the head.

"I think it's perfect," Annette said, hugging Gramma Morris.

"I'm glad. The diamond represents enduring love and faithfulness. The sapphire is a protection against anyone who tries to interfere or destroy your love. That's why there are two sapphires. One for the man, one for the woman protecting your holy and eternal love."

While the girl-talk was going on, Dad ushered Guy and the pastor to the kitchen and opened a clay jar of moonshine and poured each a shot.

"Nothing symbolizes a man's friendship and loyalty more than having a drink together. Father-in-law and son-in-law. To hell with the in-law stuff. Father and newly minted son! You know, now that you're married and the baby has his daddy's name, we don't need you. We just want you anyway. A toast on it."

If ever there was a worse toast, I never heard it. Neither did the groom, judging from his face. Poor Guy had to drink. No telling what his fate would be if he rejected Dad's offer of friendship.

Pastor Josephson tried to demure. "I don't drink. I'm a man of God."

"That's okay. Tonight, you can just be a man."

The party, such as it was, ended soon after. Guy called home to tell his parents that he was a married man now. It was a long discussion, but we only heard the things he said. Was his family happy for him? Disappointed? Who knows. They did seem to be angry that he got himself into the situation.

We girls slept downstairs that night so the newlyweds could have the whole upstairs all for themselves. I couldn't think why they needed more than a bedroom and a door but thought better to ask any questions. However, even from downstairs, I could hear them argue and grouse at each other. Annette cried for a bit, then there was some soft cooing and sighing. Soon I heard the bedsprings slowly squeak and creak. I knew things would be all right. I also figured out why we were all sent downstairs.

CHAPTER SIX

THE NEW FAMILY MEMBER

At breakfast the next morning, it was cheerless and quiet. Guy was obviously upset about the situation and maintained a stony silence. Annette was very solicitous and understanding to him. We girls were quiet and observant. It was awkward and no one really knew what to say.

Dad laughed with a false joviality and called Guy, "My newest and most favorite son-in-law." At least he was making an effort.

"I am so happy you're really part of the family," Mom said, also making an effort, "I was so happy you proposed."

"My first proposal was more romantic. Besides, I never gave a hint that I wouldn't do right by her. You overreacted."

"You overreacted to Annette's beauty and charm. I only reacted to your overreaction," Dad said, his voice lowering a bit to a warning growl.

"Now, wait a minute—"

Annette covered his mouth with her hand. "It's done," she said sadly.

"That's right. It's done, boy. You're part of the family, like it or not. But everybody will be happier if you like it. I will be." Dad's words obviously closed the subject.

Guy nodded.

"And you can always stay here until you're on your feet. You can work with me if you want," Dad said as he brought the rolled-up paper over to Mom.

"Robbing banks?"

Dad whapped him with the paper, not playfully. "I dare you to show me any article about a one-legged man robbing banks."

Guy obviously figured this conversation was going nowhere. "Annette and I are going to go home. My home. We'll talk to my family and I'll introduce my new bride."

"You never met his parents before?" Mom asked.

"Not as Mrs. Guy Morris."

Dad guffawed a hearty fake laugh. Breakfast was over. My sisters quickly ran out of the room to finish getting ready for school and left early. Dad, an expert trapper, left to check his snares. I think he was a bit confused how he should act towards Guy now. After a bit, Annette and Guy also left. Mom walked them to the door. If she was expecting a hug goodbye, she was disappointed.

"I wish she had finished high school," Mom sighed, "But sometimes life just throws you for a loop. We can only do what we think is right. I hope they forgive us. I especially hope Annette forgives Paul. He only did what he thought was right."

Only? I would think that forcing two people to get married at gunpoint would rate something stronger than 'only.'

"I'm sure they'll forgive and forget," I said diplomatically, "If nothing else, they'll always have a story to tell."

An hour later, the phone rang. I only heard Mom's side of the conversation. It was Annette. Guy's father gave him $20 for a wedding present and they were going to

California. Guy had an elderly great aunt who was all alone and needed some help. She was offering them a place to live in exchange for housework and gardening. As Faucette didn't really offer anything except farming, they decided to accept the offer and see how it went. If nothing else, they could come back home after seeing the world. Guy was an heir to the dairy farm, after all.

Mom was very supportive, even though at twenty-six, she was only nine years older than Annette and Annette never thought of her as a mother figure and only called her 'Mom' at Dad's request. But Mom still wanted to meet her grandchild. Annette promised to write and call when they got there. I could hear the excited tone in her voice as she was launching her life in an entirely unexpected direction. There wasn't a trace of anger. We were happy for her, but there was an emptiness in the house now.

"And that emptiness will grow bigger and bigger as each of you leave. We can only hope for grandchildren to fill in the holes. But you know, your dad and I are filling them in anyway."

"I can see that. Looks like you already started," I ventured with a smile.

We laughed, and I started my school assignment. I was walking around without a limp and would go back to school the following Monday, the first week of May.

Chapter Seven

The New Story

My first day back at school was a busy day for us all. There was a big "WELCOME BACK, AMY" banner hanging above the door and I received a huge round of applause. Sister Barbara smiled a welcome and my classmates gathered round me in a group hug. Meredith Baxter, my best friend, who insisted that I be included on the river trip was there with Elizabeth Farrell, another dear friend as well was the prettiest ten-year-old I had ever seen. Carmen Birnardo, who rode in the front of the boat to be our lookout, was all smiles. Ron Faucette and David Terrell also came along, sharing their zany ideas, along with Jonathon Prejean, our leader, who should never be allowed to lead anything, anywhere, ever again.

The first hour was about our adventure on the Malmort. It turns out the 18-foot alligator that attacked me was only 16 and half feet long. It was stalked relentlessly through the swamps until it was caught. They knew it was the one because part of the oar was still in its stomach.

"So, if you're having nightmares," Merry told me, "You can rest easy now."

"I wasn't having nightmares," I replied not entirely truthfully, "Well, maybe about all my missed homework, but not that thing."

"Well, good," Jonathon said, "We can fix up the boat and try again."

He had to be joking. The boat was totally destroyed.

"Oh, no," the rest of us cried in unison while Sister Barbara laughed.

"Perhaps a less adventurous adventure," she advised.

"Well," I replied, "maybe something not on the Malmort."

"Or any other river," Elizabeth Farrell added, "Or anywhere with mud. I lost my shoe walking back to get help. And it was cold. And raining. And wet—"

"Rain usually is cold and wet, dear," Sister Barbara said gently, "And forgiving is warm and pleasant."

"Yeah," added Carmen, "We should all forgive Jon. He can't help it if he can't lead. Or make plans. Or read a map."

"I was reading the map. We just stopped before we came to the sand bar."

"We did," I hated having to agree with him, "I swam to it just as the rain started."

"You see?" Jonathon gloated, "I had us going the right way."

"The gold was an old broken still," I finished.

"A gold still?" he asked, refusing to admit defeat.

"No," I said firmly, "Just an *old*, rusty still by an abandoned house."

It really wasn't a broken still or an abandoned house. They belonged to our friends the Farley sisters. They found me and brought me back home on their houseboat. They made wine in that still and it was their only source of income. I had no desire to cause them trouble with the law after they saved my life.

"Oh," he said downheartedly.

And with that, we got to the business of learning. Sister Barbara's visits to the house paid off and I felt up to date with the other kids. The final tests were coming up and I wanted to do well. I started the year in fourth grade but my grandmother, who ran the schoolboard, had me promoted to fifth shortly after I moved to Faucette due to the hostile and violent reception I received from the children in the public school. I didn't want to let her down.

An ancient carriage was waiting for me at the gate when school was over. I had a violin lesson with the Countess, an elderly woman who freely admitted she wasn't nobility, but the people of Faucette liked to think of her as an aristocrat anyway. She was 87 and set in her ways. As far as anyone knew, she never even sat in a motorcar and would never give up her coach for anything modern. It kept Killy, her driver, employed. He waved hello to me as I stepped inside the coach.

"It's good to see you again, Miss Amy," he called out, "House ain't the same without your lessons. Too quiet."

This was my first lesson since the attack, so it had been a while.

"I can imagine."

The house was quiet as a tomb even when I was playing there. It needed children to bring it to life. But then, all houses do.

The Countess lived alone in a magical looking antebellum home, filled with memories, stories, love, and above all, dust. Our arrangement was that I cleaned for an hour and did other light housekeeping chores and then I'd get a lesson on my instrument. And one unique aspect of her house was its ability to replenish dust. I truly believed I removed a small mountain of lint since we started our arrangement. And there was another one waiting for me.

We talked while I cleaned. She was amused at my adventure in the swamp.

"I suppose you might think twice about going on the Malmort River after telling your mom you'll be canoeing on the creek."

"Well, yes," I said, while soaking a cloth in vinegar and lemon juice, "It was a last-minute surprise."

"It was to the rest of us as well," she said tartly.

I winced. I wasn't used to harsh words coming from her.

"But oh, well," she continued, "I guess you learn from your mistakes, sometimes. Provided they don't kill you."

I nodded. The sills sparkled and the cloth was putrid black. I swirled it around the basin, wrung it out and attacked the wing chairs and tables.

"You did survive, so maybe it was a part of the plan. Sometimes, our mistakes lead to the best things in life. I was reminiscing, before you got here. You know, you remind me of my adopted sister, Donna Lynn. She danced a bit as part of our show."

The Countess was also an orphan, adopted into a family of travelling musicians who taught her how to play the violin. She became part of the Johnson Family Troup and performed all across the Midwest before the Civil War. Most of the other children were also adopted but the Johnsons were a loving couple and turned the Troup into a home for them all.

"Donna moved in with us for a bit after we got married. She went to the dances and socials until she met a man. Efraim Deveraux. He was a landlord of what was once a nice sized estate. He rented out plots to sharecroppers and freedmen. She wanted to be swept off her feet, but he couldn't do that with an industrial sized broom. But he came calling and they got married. Of course, he was already married to his booze. She was more alone with him than if she was just alone. Well, there was a new teacher in town. Terrance Benson. Your great-great-grandfather. He was handsome and single. So, she went to him for consolation. What she got was in a family way.

"Well, Efraim knew he wasn't the father and he threw her out. Benson wouldn't take her in because he figured a woman who cheats on her man is a woman who cheats on her man. He wasn't interested. She went to Baton Rouge and had her son. She named him Ichabod. It comes from the Bible. It means without honor. Whatever happened to her, I'll never know. She and Ichabod kept Efraim's name, even though he had nothing to do with either of them.

"Well, Efraim died young. And drunk. And alone. And despised. Ichabod came in and claimed his inheritance, as the surviving son. After all, his mother was married to Efraim when he was conceived and born. Who cares about the speculation? He was the legal and solitary heir.

"He set about evicting the tenants so he could grow sugar cane for rum. That put him in direct conflict with my father-in-law. But the De Pilord family always came out ahead. He bought the young man out, giving him in cash roughly half of what the land was worth.

"Ichabod was thrilled and bought a house on the other side of the Atchafala River. Then he built a small theater and dance hall for shows and entertainment. Just what any town needed. It became the movie theater we have today. All that from Donna Lynn's mistake.

"Ichabod married well. My niece by marriage. So, my unrelated nephew married my unrelated niece. They had two sons and a daughter before she died. The younger son and daughter are stories for another day. The older boy was

Lamar Devereux. His daughter is the town seamstress."

"Betsy Devereux," I said. She was my best friend of all the adults in Faucette. "So, Betsy and I are not all that distantly related. I thought she was my mother's fourth cousin."

"Close. She is your third cousin, once removed. Many people don't understand the difference, you know."

"I don't."

"Well, imagine two sisters. One has a son. One has a daughter. Those children are first cousins. Now the son has a son. He and the original daughter are first cousins once removed. Now the daughter has a son. They are second cousins. They both are second generation from the original two sisters."

"And Grandpa Terrance treated your sister terribly. That's why you don't like him," I said. I rather didn't like him now.

"It's one reason."

I finished dusting the furniture and turned to the baseboards.

"You know," she went on, "Terrance Benson came home after the war. The real war. Between the states. That would be 1865 or early 1866. Either way, it was before my arrival here. There was some kind of to-do over there. The whole family left. Just packed up and walked away. No one saw them on the roads or river anywhere. Just gone."

"Maybe they took a train," I guessed.

"They weren't running yet. The Yankees tore up all the rails. Then they heated and twisted them so they couldn't be reused. Rail traffic wasn't fully operational out here for a number of years.

"No, they just vanished. The last to go was Terrance Benson himself. His sister just had a baby and left it with him. Maybe he took it with him when he left town. Rumor had it he went west and left the land for his friend Black Jack Morris to farm. Morris got all the crops and kept the house livable for Benson's return. Apparently, there was a wine cellar on the property that Benson locked up good and tight. He told Morris to never go in there. You know why?"

I shook my head.

"Because he found a family of three wandering down the road. Sickly lot. He let them stay in the cellar until they got better. When he brought them food and water, two were dead and the baby girl was extremely ill. They had smallpox. So, Benson left in a hurry and locked the place down. Told Morris if he entered the cellar, he could get smallpox. Then he headed west. Said he needed to clear his head.

"The day he left, a baby girl was put on the church doorstep. She had a note pinned on her blanket. 'Please take care of her. Her name is Spring Waters.'"

"Spring Waters? That almost sounds like an Indian name."

She shook her head, "Green eyes and blond hair. Her full name was Spring Waters De Pilord. Not long after we married, I convinced my husband we should take her in. She captured my heart when I arrived here. She was four or five by then and selling flowers at the station, trying to raise money for her orphanage.

"And she was such a help after my own children arrived. She was a doting older sister. She loved all my children, especially Fiona. She was her favorite. They had some kind of spiritual bond I didn't understand. Spring knew when Fiona was hungry, cold, needed a change, just everything. Even after Fiona could talk, she didn't need to say a word to Spring. Spring just knew. Poor Spring was more brokenhearted when Fiona died than I was."

"What happened?"

"She was learning to ride the horse and fell off. Hit her head and died instantly. It was such a horrible thing." Her eyes were tearing. "She just turned ten. Your age." She shook off the invading memories. "Get out your violin before you rub the wood down to nothing."

"But what happened to Spring Waters?"

"She met the most evil man in the world. Then she left and never sent word home of her whereabouts. She was just gone."

"And the other baby?"

"Gone," she shrugged, "Probably dead by now. All we know is there were two baby girls with that man. One was his niece and no one knows about the other one."

That story left me with more questions than answers, which was usually the case since moving down south. Who was Spring Waters? Where did she come from? Did Mr. Benson, my great great-grandfather leave her at the church? What became of the two babies? There was such a mass migration after the war, anyone could have left behind an unwanted mouth or two to feed.

Chapter Eight

Our New Lawyer

Dad was waiting for me in the wagon, his wooden leg casually pointing forward. I felt bad that he had to pick me up because he looked uncomfortable. But since storm clouds were gathering overhead, I decided feeling bad was preferable to walking in the rain. I sat next to him after securing my instrument and homework in the back. He surprised me by reaching around my shoulder and squeezing me next to him. Although there may have been an inadvertent touch occasionally, he never hugged me like that before.

"We'll be going to the courthouse next week," he told me, "We got us a fancy lawyer to help make sure we keep you." Then he glanced over at me. "You *do* want to stay here, don't you?"

"More than anything. I found home here. I don't ever want to leave. How could we afford a lawyer?"

"Guy has a cousin who just passed the bar a couple of weeks ago. He's going to represent us for free. Kind of like a wedding present."

"Well, that's nice. I kinda thought the Thomases would be mad."

"No, nobody's mad. Things just happen. Besides, they

got the better end of the bargain. My daughter. We got stuck with Guy."

"Guy? But I like Guy."

"So do I. He's my favorite son-in-law."

Only son-in-law.

The rest of the ride was silent until we got home.

Our 'fancy' lawyer was already there. Mr. Louis Thomas wore greasy overalls with a white tee shirt underneath. His hair was cut in the classic bowl style and his straw fedora was hanging on the coat rack. One of several uncles he shared with Guy was Judge Mark Thomas, the man who would oversee the hearing. That was a good thing.

Mark's siblings consisted of six brothers and two sisters. Mark was the oldest, while David, Louis' father, was the next in line. David hadn't spoken to Mark in almost 30 years because of a legacy dispute. Louis never spoke to him at all. The issue derived from their father's estate being divided into eight parts, due to the Napoleonic code. All children received an equal share. The code overruled any will that stated otherwise.

One of the shares contained the old Thomas house, which their great-grandfather built just after the war. Both brothers wanted that house. It was the largest in the parish and quite a status symbol. At first, they just argued and bickered over it, but then they became so bitter that David challenged Mark to a duel. That was a bad thing.

He proposed a swordfight. He would wear an old Confederate uniform with bright brass buttons while Mark would sport a union coat with equally large buttons. Whoever cut off all his opponent's buttons first would be the winner and the dispute would be resolved. Mark wisely declined as such an incident would forever brand him as an unreliable oddball. That seemed sensible.

Instead, they armed themselves with thick cypress staffs and charged each other on horseback. They flailed and attacked one another like medieval knights. The one who got unseated would give up his claim. They thought such an action would make them look less eccentric, although no one else in the parish thought so.

By the end of the third charge, Mark had two broken fingers, a sprained wrist, and a severe cut on his left bicep that had to be bandaged. His brother had a bruise high up on his chest and a sprained knee. Mark tied his almost useless arm around the horse's reins and was ready to charge again. He may have been tired and in pain, but he would never willingly surrender to David, who by now was his mortal enemy. David watched this last act with a mixture of amusement and contempt.

The last charge began and the two brothers rode toward each other in a great fury. Mark had his weapon in his left hand almost perpendicular to his horse, while David had his high overhead, waiting to strike a vicious and possibly fatal blow to the head. Mark swung his staff first with all his might and struck a strategic blow. He hit David's horse right between the eyes and it went down, smashing into his own steed and both duelists fell on top of each other.

The battle was stopped by the sheriff at that point. A neutral committee was called in to decide how the inheritance would be divided. The house wound up going to a younger brother, Jared Thomas, who went on to become one of the richest men in the state, by virtue of not being stupid.

By the way, Judge Thomas did not escape the reputation of being an eccentric. Neither did his brother, who wisely moved to Hammond to practice law.

"I'm sure you're a good lawyer," Mom said to Louis

sweetly, "But with your family history being what it is, would it be a good start for your career to plead a case in front of your uncle? He might hold a grudge, you know."

"Uncle Mark? I don't think we have to worry about that. The opposing attorney is a Yankee. I'm sure he hates Yankees more than he hates family."

That was certainly reassuring.

He explained how the court would handle the case. His uncle had a reputation for placing little value on intangibles, like family bonds, love or belonging. He believed the children were better served under the family with the higher balance sheet. Therefore, if both families want the child, then money and position would be the first item he would consider.

But the judge was also a firm believer in the law. The Giraffe's criminal past was well documented and criminals don't make good parents, as far as he was concerned. However, Dad's own past, although not as well documented, was known to be less than law abiding. His temper led to rash decisions and he initiated several fights, even after he lost his leg in the Great War. Judge Thomas knew all about that, since Dad stood in front of him on several occasions.

The judge also frowned upon shotgun weddings. However, the Giraffe had a history of forcing several American girls of Italian descent to marry an immigrant for residency purposes, which was news to me. Not a surprise, just news. Our lawyer figured that the rap sheets would probably cancel each other out.

He also figured the birth certificate could be our biggest problem. Mom registered as Aunt Mary so I would have a name and not be seen as illegitimate. That meant that Aunt Mary was my legal mother as far as the court was concerned. In order to overcome that disadvantage, we had to convince the judge that I was better off here, where I was loved and wanted, not in New York where Aunt Mary neglected me.

"I don't want to go back there ever again. She wouldn't even let me call her Mama or anything," I protested.

"The judge will take that into consideration," our lawyer replied, "But intangibles like that really aren't going to have much effect on his ruling."

Wonderful.

Mom had one more question for Louis. "You *are* planning to wear something a little more formal to court, aren't you? Appearances can mean so much."

"Yes, ma'am. I have a new five dollar suit I just got from the Salvation Army store."

Mom smiled weakly. There was nothing more to do but wait. Louis politely left and we had dinner. Nobody felt like doing anything afterwards, so we just went to bed.

CHAPTER NINE

FAMILY HISTORY

Sister Barbara was very serious and stern the next day. We students never saw her without a friendly smile before and kept relatively quiet while she straightened things on her desk.

"I have good news today," she said, "Though how good it is depends on the Lord. Because we had no hurricanes, floods, tornados, or thunderstorms, we can use those banked off-days to speed things up and go to our final exams this week. There will be no games, talking, interrupting, or daydreaming. We have a lot to cover and I want it done."

"Does that mean we won't have to come back until next year?" Jon asked hopefully.

"No, it means we will be done with schoolwork and we can talk about what you'll be doing in sixth grade. But fifth grade will in essence, be over. I will need your full cooperation. This is a golden opportunity for you all."

None of us could quite see how this was an opportunity, but as there was no choice in the matter, we worked as we never did before. No unrelated stories or questions, no jokes, no side conversations. Nobody knew how Sister Barbara would react if we didn't work up to her new expectations, but no one really wanted to find out. Tests would begin tomorrow.

I was required to read to Grandpa Terrance after school that day. I still called him Mr. Benson most times as that was how I was introduced to him. I was a little bit upset with him over what he did to the countess' sister. It seemed so sad to think Donna Lynn died all alone and abandoned.

He was waiting for me on the porch. His white cataract ruined eyes fixed on my feet as they strode up to the door.

"You're stomping rather fast today," he observed, "Something on your mind?"

"Yes, there is," I retorted, "The Countess just told me what you did to Donna Lynn. You seduced her and left her to die. I don't know how many commandments you broke. Adultery, lying, murder by…something, I'm sure, abandoned your own son, all while teaching at the school. How could you do such a thing?"

"Something like that wouldn't be easy. Lucky for me, that's not what happened. I wish you'd stop talking to that old witch. Speaking of liars, she calls herself a Countess but she can't tell you who her own parents were. She got lucky marrying into a family of lunatics who thought they were displaced aristocracy."

"That has nothing to do with Donna Lynn."

"Truth has nothing to do with Donna Lynn." He settled back in his chair. "But you want to know what happened, I can tell you. She wasn't very pretty, but she was blessed with being clever. Downright sly. She married a useless drunk who was touched in the head. He'd row his canoe down the Malmort to the heart of the swamp and said he visited the Marsh Matron. She'd tell his fortune and give him strange elixirs and he brought her fresh food. Said she lived in some old one room house that's been there for centuries. Never got flooded. Never got blown away.

"Now, there were tales of the Marsh Matron going on for years. Efraim was the only one stupid enough to brave those waters to see if they were true. Once he met her, he went back weekly for a couple of years. It was the matron who told him to pursue Donna Lynn. She thought being a husband and father might be good for him. So that's what he did. But after he got her, he didn't want her.

"So, the poor neglected wife came to me. I'd been alone for a while now that my wife Eva was gone and fell for her charms. But you see, she didn't come to me for love. She came for revenge and she knew I had a reputation with a gun. She tried to get Efraim and me to have a good old western shootout, like there ever was such a thing. That one read too many books. She wanted him dead and me the killer. We were both too smart for that. He told her to leave and I told her not to come back. And that's what happened."

"And she moved to Baton Rouge."

"Some say," he agreed, "Others say she went south to live with the Marsh Matron. Whatever happened, Ichabod came to claim his inheritance right when Efraim passed away. Like he knew it happened. And he never said a word to me."

Why would he?

"What did you mean when you said you had a reputation with a gun?" I asked hesitantly.

"After the war, I came home and threw everyone out. Didn't want them around. But after a couple of days, I didn't want to be around. I left the place for Blackjack to farm and headed west. Went as far as Colorado. Found a place called Hopeful Hill and ran into an old friend named Tom Moran. The first settlers there were looking for gold, only found tin. But it was enough, everyone was happy. Then Ned Stark found copper underneath the tin.

"It was a disaster after that. People lost their farms because Stark bought out the mineral rights. Those dumb farmers thought the company would tunnel under their farms. Turns out he just tore the farms down to the minerals, including the houses. It became a mine town after that.

"Well, come payday, we had an explosive situation. We had young miners with money, who filled themselves with booze and walked around with loaded guns. Now *that* makes a bad combination. Tom got himself elected sheriff and made me his deputy. Well, that set something off in old Tom, and he was quick to kill. They called him Murdering Tom Moran because if he had a complaint, he'd rather kill the culprit than arrest him."

"I heard of him," I said with excited disbelief, "He had another deputy named Killin' Jim Killebrew. And Killin' Jim went all over Texas, shooting anything that moved. You were lucky you lived through that job."

"Not quite accurate. I was Jim Killebrew. Never appreciated the nickname 'Killin' Jim Killebrew.' Now Mike was deadly with a gun. They fired him real quick like. Me too, even though I was the one who was always restraining him. He stuck around. Ned Stark hired him to 'encourage' the other miners to sell. Those who didn't sell, he killed. He ran up quite a death count until a posse hanged him. Me? I just left. Why stay in a dangerous place if it's not home?

"I was a saddle tramp for a bit. Then I got another deputy job, but it was boring. Nothing much happened. Everyone was well behaved," he sounded disappointed, "But I guess when the deputy has a name like 'Killin' Jim,' not much *is* going to happen. I wandered around a bit more until I got homesick and returned. And the rest you know."

"I saw a movie about you where you chased down a bad man and killed a dozen people who got in your way and you shot him in the head in a church pew during benediction."

"That was a movie. You shouldn't watch movies like that."

I was relieved. "You mean it didn't happen?"

"No, it happened. They just shouldn't have made a movie about it."

He seemed finished with the story, so I changed subjects. "Did you put Spring Waters on the church steps that day?"

He turned and looked right at me, as if he could see me clearly. "Spring Waters De Pilord was my half-sister's baby. When I came home and killed my father, she got all hysterical and went into labor. Well, since you know my father was the baby's father, I wasn't going to have anything to do with it. I did the right thing. My sister didn't want her. She said she'd throw it in the river as soon as she was on her feet."

I was thinking back to a previous conversation we had.

"I thought you chased her and the baby away with the others. Along with your wife," I accused.

"Well, you might as well know the whole story then, I reckon," he said sadly, "After the war, I came home to that mess. My mother beat senseless. My brother totally hooked on Laudanum. My wife and sister both pregnant by my father. My wife married to my brother, though I'm sure nothing happened after the ceremony. My children were already dead."

"Why did your father kill them, really?" I was rather

tired of his stories always changing.

"I got a job in Neuville on the Vitriol Plantation. Before the war, you know. I met Eva and we fell in love. She was a slave there, but as white as you and me. We figured she was 1/512th African and the rest white. She was smart, pretty and had hair about your color, kind of fawn brown. But she was a slave. It was a forbidden love. The law wouldn't let us marry because of her black blood. But it was still a real love. People who make up these laws don't know what kind of effect they have. It was our love and our lives and we were going to live the way we wanted to.

"So, we ran away and came back home. We figured no one would suspect. But the Vitriol family followed us and caught up to her after I went to war. They wanted her back, but my father just beat them into the ground and told them he'd kill them if he ever saw them again. That was something in those days. Even though I married her, the miscegenation laws annulled it. And she still belonged to the Vitriol family as a slave which meant that my children were illegitimate and part slave and owned by the Vitriols. My father wouldn't tolerate that kind of taint on the family."

"But he and Eva—"

"Yeah, kind of strange. Anyway, getting back to your question. I named the baby Spring because it was late spring when she was born and Waters because I saved her from drowning. No one would know her family history. Who'd want to know? Certainly not her. Of course, all she did with her life was move to the swamp and live like a witch in a second-rate story book."

"You mean Spring Waters is the Marsh Matron?"

He shrugged, "There were more than one of them, I reckon."

"What happened to the other baby? The one you found in the cellar after its parents died?"

"That's how I met the Marsh Matron. That baby was sick and I didn't know how to handle it. I dropped Spring off at the church and canoed down the Malmort until I found her shack. She took the baby. Maybe she raised it, maybe it died. I never bothered to find out.

"Weren't you going to read me a story?"

There's a lot to a family's history.

CHAPTER TEN

OUTSIDE THE COURTROOM

At school the next day, Sister Barbara told me privately that the real reason we were testing early was so I could prove I finished fifth grade. That way, I could start sixth grade anywhere when the next school year started.

That afternoon, I walked to the courthouse after school. Just as I approached the steps to the old building, the door opened and a strange and frightening woman came out.

She stood tall and thin with white hair mostly tucked into her head scarf, although quite a few locks and strands were blowing free in the warm breeze. I found it an odd way for an obviously middle-aged woman to wear her hair. She was dark but light enough that she could have passed for white if she wanted to. She obviously didn't want to though.

She wore old and tattered clothes. Small blotches of blue survived here and there on her blouse, but it was mostly faded to gray. Her tan skirt hung down mournfully with a frayed hem sliced with slight tears, as though she climbed over a barbed wire fence. Her earrings were simple rose quartz crescent moons. A distinctive gold-plated necklace glittered from her neck. Little squirrel skulls with rose quartz crystals stared at me through their tiny eye sockets. I would never forget her appearance or her first words to me.

"Amy Collins," she said imperiously, almost an order, "I have wanted to meet you for a while now. Come sit with me for a moment. We have much to talk about."

I followed her to the top of the stairs where we sat. We couldn't sit on the benches. She was black and I was white. There was no bench for 'all.'

"My name is Noxolo Amilee Greenough. You may call me Mother Greenough," she commanded, "You know my sister, Cecilia Carter."

"I do?"

She stared hard at me.

"Pay attention to what surrounds you. You know her as Cici."

"I do know Cici," I said, getting excited, "She's our cook. But I thought her sister died."

"Pay attention to what surrounds you," she repeated, obviously annoyed, "A person can have more than one sister. You have no true sister, but more half and stepsisters than you will ever meet."

"I do?"

"You do," she confirmed, taking my hand gently and tracing my palm with her fingers, "And you will go to a faraway place where fantastic things will go on all around you. And you will meet all kinds of people. Not all of them will be what they seem. Some will be dangerous. You see these creases here?" She pointed to the center of my hand, but I only saw one line. "The hazards seam crosses your lifeline. Danger awaits you. Danger in the form of a...mermaid?"

She seemed confused by her own reading. Then she nodded. "Mermaids call out to sailors with songs of love and drown them. Make them think they love and want them. Never your friend. Always dangerous. Always evil. Always beware of the mermaid."

"I had a dream."

"Oh?"

"A girl was on top of some rocks in the ocean. She called to me to talk and when I got there it was a mermaid and she tried to eat me."

"Yes. We live in the real world. The spiritual world is walled off to us, but you hit your head. It weakened that wall. You see more than you understand. You will learn. There are worlds within worlds. And when we enter them, strange things can happen. Some things we can control. Other things control us. Some destroy us. We are always destroyed by what we want.

"Did you ever hear of Edward Dupree, the famous sculptor? He came from Neuville. His father runs a shoe store here in town."

I nodded. "I met his father. He's a very nice man."

"To some. Not to me. But Edward was not nice to anyone. He had a gift with stone. He could carve a hummingbird's wings and make them look real. Without a chisel. Or so it's said.

"When you look around all the towns, you see his works. Men on horseback, orators standing like they're speaking. But he also sold to private collectors. You know what they wanted? Women with no clothes on. They call them allegories. Great symbolic art depicting great symbolic ideas. They're women with no clothes on. Nothing more. They represent lust.

"Edward knew he was gifted. He had a market for his work. He could be great in the right place. Not here. He set up a studio in Flowerton, just north of Boston with his favorite model, a local girl named Gisette Gagneux. They thrived up there. He became quite rich selling statues of his wife with no clothes on. The last one was life itself. So, they say. Life itself.

"One day, Gisette got sick and died. Very sudden. Poor Edward. He went mad with grief. After her funeral, he took the train back here. He spoke to Mama Louviere, my older sister. She is a high mistress of the *Hai-tak-Koo,* the spirit arts."

"Voodoo?"

"Different. *Hai-tak-Koo* calls on creatures of the other realms for assistance. Healing, mending, repairing broken hearts. Sometimes darker things like making the world a better place by removing an evil soul. But Mama Louviere was kind. When Edward came to her, she tried to turn him away."

"What did he want?" I was afraid to ask.

"To bring his lady love back."

"From the dead?"

"It's been done. Never with good results. She told him it would be dangerous. It would be disappointing. It would not work and he would curse the day he went against God's law. The dead must stay dead."

"But he insisted. Even though she was dead and buried. So, she gave him a charm, the symbol of eternity with the spell of life imbued in it. He was to clasp it on her neck and she would come to life."

"You mean dig up her grave and—"

I lived in the country long enough to know the horrid smell of decomposing flesh. I came across many dead animals while walking along the roads. The stench was nothing less than sickening.

"Be still and pay attention to what surrounds you. The statue. He was to put the necklace on the statue and she would come to life. And that is what he did. And that is what she did."

"She came back to life?"

"Not as a woman. The statue came to life. No flesh. No blood. No bone. Just marble. Stone cold rock."

"He must have been disappointed."

"He was angry. It wasn't her fault he called her back from the dead. He yelled and screamed at her. Called her bad names I won't repeat to you. He was furious. She was getting angrier listening to him. Then it ended. She slapped him hard across his face. Broke his neck. He was dead before he hit the floor. She started crying when she saw his lifeless body and kissed him. Then she went back to the pedestal and pulled off the chain. You can see a bit of the gold chain hanging out from her clenched fist. It's in a museum in Flowerton. His old studio.

"The police never found a killer, of course. But now that he was dead, the critics found America's premier sculptor. 'Even the sculpture's tears are lifelike.' That is what they said. He got what he wanted and it ruined him. By luck, it was just him. Imagine if someone else was there. Sometimes people destroy themselves and others when they pursue what they want. You just be wary."

She stood up. Our conversation was over. She put a hand on my shoulder and said, "Be strong."

I watched her step down the stairs and away.

Strange conversation.

I turned around and went into the building. Mom and Gramma Morris were there waiting for me. Gramma Morris was strict and stern and tolerated no nonsense. She also had a sharp tongue that more than once hurt my feelings, but always apologized when she realized that I wasn't used to her kind of criticism. Her way of showing love was to make sure I was safe, fed and comfortable, and to include me in family events. I was glad she was there.

In we went to start our depositions for my custody. The courtroom smelled like stale furniture polish and floor wax. A few benches stood empty and a couple of tables sat in front of the judicial bench. We started to sit next to Louis, who was wearing a gray suit and off-white shirt today. Depjim, the deputy who was assigned to Faucette, pulled Dad aside and advised him to not lose his temper.

"A New York lawyer can be worse than the deadliest water moccasin," he said.

Dad nodded his agreement.

Louis smiled at us as we sat down. He was nervous because it was his first case. I was nervous because it was my future.

We all stood when Judge Mark Thomas entered the room. He was a small man with gray hair and a moustache who coolly appraised the room as he sat down. His glasses had the thickest lenses I have ever seen that magnified his eyes and gave him a scholarly appearance. A black glove covered his ruined left hand which had never healed from the injuries of that long ago duel.

The lawyer at the other table was representing Mary and Giovanni Corelli. Two men I never saw before sat in the spectator section. One was taking notes and glancing through papers, while a bald, middle-aged man with twinkling blue eyes and pointed beard spotted me and gave me a friendly wink. I assumed they were with Mr. Tremble.

Since Aunt Mary was the plaintiff, her lawyer went first. He had a high-pitched voice with a Brooklyn accent so thick it could be scooped up in an ice cream server. It was all we could do to make out his words.

"Your honor," he began, "My name is Richard Tremble and I work for the law firm of Robb, Swindell and Cheatham, located in Manhattan—"

"What a delightful name for a law firm from New York. Leaves your opponents with little doubt of your intentions."

"I am aware of the unfortunate names the partners were born under—"

"And when you make partner, it will be Robb, Swindell, Cheatham, and Tremble. Quite an image."

"It is the contention of the plaintiffs," Tremble continued, ignoring the judge's humor, "That young Amy Collins was sent to visit her aunt for a limited visit, but when it came time to send her back home, where she belongs, the defendants, Paul and Cassandra Villians (he deliberately mispronounced the name so it sounded like Vill-ans, not Vee-yon) refused to send her back. She has remained kidnapped and in fact has been placed in harm's way several times through sheer neglect and indifference by her aunt and uncle."

Dad stood up and backed his chair away, like he was going to walk over to Tremble, but Depjim and Louis each put a hand on his shoulder while Judge Thomas looked on, disapproving. Tremble smirked. It was obvious that he was trying to get that kind of reaction.

He continued, "The disappointment and betrayal my clients felt about her abduction by people they so trusted is tragic. It is our duty to return this poor unfortunate girl to her home with the kind, decent and caring people who will raise her with the love and affection any child needs to thrive."

"You must live in a stable to be able to pile on that

much horse manure in so short a time," Gramma Morris commented.

Everyone laughed, even Judge Thomas, but he still had her removed from the court for being a disruptive presence.

My part of the process was easy enough. I simply stated that I was neglected by my Aunt Mary and felt uncomfortable around the Giraffe and Isadora, his sister. There were a few eyebrows raised at my referring to him by his gangster nickname. My two stepsisters were nothing short of vicious to me. And most importantly, I did not want to go back. I belonged here with the people who really loved me. After that, the judge smiled at me and had me sit down.

A hearing was set for the following Wednesday.

"Will you be the presiding judge?" Tremble asked.

"Yes."

"It seems their lawyer has the same last name as you do."

"Yes. It's been that way all his life. You see, when children are born to a couple, they retain their father's name. His father, who is also named Thomas, just happens to be my brother. And we carry the name of our father. That's how names work."

"Thank you for the lesson, Judge Thomas," Tremble said sarcastically, "But I'm sure you will agree with me that it is unusual for a judge to be trying a case when his nephew is counselor for one of the parties."

"No, I would not. What's unusual is having sisters go to court when the issue can be resolved in a more friendly atmosphere. If you're worried about impartiality, I can assure you that I consider my nephew there to be just barely competent as a lawyer but highly successful as an irritant.

And I haven't spoken to my worthless brother in almost thirty years and have no intention to ever again. If there is any favoritism, it won't be towards him. But it also won't be for a scallywag Yankee lawyer who is capitalizing on other people's problems. Rest assured I find you both to be equally disgusting.

"But if you prefer a different judge, there's Quentin Davis. His daughter-in-law is the girl's aunt. Or you can go to Neuville, just north of here. Judge Beaufort is the father of one of the girl's aunts by marriage and his other daughter is married to her biological father. The choice is yours, but you'll have to wait a week or two to get a hearing scheduled. And remember: Everyone related to Amy is related to her mother and aunt. That means there's blood on both sides of the argument."

"I'm sure you'll be a fair and honorable judge. No need to move." He looked defeated already.

Good.

Chapter Eleven

Inside the Courthouse

Of course, I wasn't allowed to go to the actual custody hearing. I had school and we were taking our finals. Besides, most of the adults thought there would be things said that I was too young to hear. Luckily for me, Dad didn't think I was all that delicate and believed it was important that I should know what was happening since the final decision would have a monumental effect on my future.

Richard Tremble stood up and read off a list of things designed to make the judge think Aunt Mary and Uncle Gio were better parents. The first thing he mentioned was the birth certificate. It showed Aunt Mary as my mother, ignoring the fact that Mom simply didn't want the certificate to say illegitimate. That was unprovable.

He then brought up my various injuries. The concussion from the school fight was glossed over, but the night I was waitressing at the restaurant and was shot in a robbery was discussed in greater detail.

His point was that I should not have been working at night, should have known what to do in case of a robbery, and there should have been an adult with me. Lila, our waitress, was there but she was in the kitchen, which didn't count, as far as he was concerned.

There was also the excursion down the Malmort without an adult. That was serious neglect. He argued that Mom and Dad just didn't have what it takes to be parents of a large family. I would be better off in New York which had superior schools, more educated people, and my talents would be appreciated. I was not in a healthy environment down here.

Judge Thomas was unimpressed. "I'm so sorry our little town doesn't meet your approval, but as ignorant, uneducated, talentless, bores maybe her family can offer her something you never mentioned. Love. Ever hear of it?"

"Yes, Judge Thomas, I have. It is love that had her parents send me down here to bring her back to her home."

"Why you?"

Mr. Tremble looked confused.

"Why didn't one of them come down here with you?"

"Well, Mr. Corelli works and Mrs. Corelli has other children to take care of."

"What does Mr. Corelli do for a living?"

"He runs a club. Music, dancing, meeting people."

"Drinking?"

"Of course not. That's illegal."

"So is lying to a judge. You want to tell me what he really does? Or should I tell you? You know, running a speakeasy is not exactly something a responsible parent would do."

Score one for the judge. Zero for the sophisticated Yankee lawyer.

When it was our side's turn, Louis went into full character assassination on my New York parents. His first target was my first father, Michael Collins. He produced several police reports and criminal complaints against him. Mostly just fighting and cold-cocking people, but also several incidents of lewd behavior.

"Lewd behavior?"

"Your Papa was injured in the war. He had trouble with his natural abilities. He was just angry all the time afterwards."

Only Dad, being Dad, said it in a more graphic and disrespectful way. I certainly got the point as well as a lesson on the variations of human desire. Certainly, I was shocked. It explained why we never heard the bedsprings sing when he was home with Aunt Mary. They sounded like a symphony after she replaced him with Gio.

"But what does that have to do with anything?"

"Your Aunt Mary is attracted to violent lawbreakers who live dangerous lives. Your papa was eventually murdered. Corelli lives the same lifestyle. What happens if he comes to the same end? And if she marries another gangster? Then what? What kind of danger will she put you in?"

"But Michael Collins lived the way he did and we were never in any danger. And why did Aunt Mary ever marry him?" I asked.

"I'm coming to that. Remember that your grandfather was forced to retire from the army after the war?"

I nodded. Major James De Montfort was Mary and Mom's father.

"The army was discharging men because the war was over. It was keeping some senior staff, of course, and he wanted to be retained. His service record was good, but he was competing with younger and smarter men, with the latest in medical knowledge. He was a 52-year-old Major with a mediocre record and 25 years of service. He also had

Parkinson's disease, which is career ending for a surgeon. He wanted to stay in the army and be a staff officer, but he had little to offer at his age.

"He did have one hope. Captain Marshall Faulkner. He was a career officer who lost his wife to the flu. Well, your grandfather was pushing Mary to be friendly to him. Get him to know her, like her, maybe fall in love with her, marry her. Captain Faulkner had the ability to keep your grandfather in the army."

"How?"

"Major General Howard Faulkner was his father. A two-star General can pull a lot of strings."

"But Aunt Mary eloped," I said thoughtfully, "That ruined his last hope. That's why he disowned her. She must really not have liked that Captain."

"Rumor had it he was violent with women. I heard he killed a prostitute in Paris. That was covered up by the General. It's why he was still a Captain. At his age and during a war, he could easily have been a Lieutenant Colonel. Certainly, a Major. It's been said that his wife didn't die from the flu. He may have accidentally strangled her. Not a great husband. Add in his vicious little she-wolf daughters and no thinking woman would want to be married to a man like that."

"And my grandfather wanted her to marry him?"

"He did. She didn't. So, she ran off at the first chance. Not much later, your mom announced she was going to have you and your father wouldn't marry her. The Major's career wasn't just over. It crashed to the ground in flames. The army didn't need a man who couldn't control his teenage daughters."

"So, he and Gramma De Montfort disowned them both."

"And he never met you. Never spoke to his youngest two daughters again. He died less than a year from his discharge. Let's hope it was worth it to him."

The stories got even worse. It turned out that Aunt Mary never worked at a doctor's office as I had been told. She was too lazy and disinterested to be able to handle a job that required a responsible person. No, she was a "kept woman," which meant that she slept with her boyfriend and he paid for her apartment and living expenses. Since Aunt Mary lived in her own home with a husband who didn't touch her, she was a highly desired diversion.

"Since she had a home already, she just needed to be available to the man who provided for her. He paid the rent and gave her an allowance for food. Provided for their children, Julia and Patrick."

"Excuse me, Dad," I asked has a heavy feeling of dread possessed me, "Did they say who the boyfriend was?"

"Can't you guess? Gio Corelli, your stepfather. His wife died about a year before your Papa was murdered. Apparently, they didn't get along too well. Things just worked out nicely for Gio the Giraffe. Almost like it was planned."

I learned a lot about things that happened in my childhood. The club Uncle Gio ran was a gambling and drinking establishment where the dancers were really prostitutes. Much was made of the Giraffe's association with Antonio Dragucci, who owned the establishment, since he was a famous gangster. I wasn't sure how famous he was, I never heard of him until Gio and Aunt Mary got married.

"And they want me back there?"

"Our lawyer reminded the judge that it wasn't a healthy environment."

"So, I'll get to stay?"

He shrugged. "It's all in how the judge is thinking that day."

"But it wouldn't be right to make me go back." I had tears in my eyes.

He shrugged but squeezed my shoulder. "If lawyers and judges cared about doing the right thing, they wouldn't be lawyers and judges."

It seemed that neither set of parents looked particularly competent when the hearing ended. It was now up to Judge Thomas to sort through the information and make his final decision.

That Friday, after finals were over, we waited in the courtroom to hear the decision. We were all wearing our best clothes. Dad had on a tie that he couldn't get to look right. I remember I wore my Sunday dress that Betsy made for me. It was a beautiful dress and I felt pretty when I wore it.

The bailiff came out and called us to order and we rose when Judge Thomas entered. When we were seated, he banged his little gavel on his desk to indicate he was ready to begin.

At that moment, the door opened and the middle-aged man who I saw on the first day of the hearings came in. He had a confident look, as though he knew every courtroom in the country. The shorter, bald man with the twinkling blue eyes and pointy beard followed him. Today that beard made him look a bit like the devil.

The tall man coolly scanned the room. I could tell he didn't miss a detail. His wandering gaze focused on me when he saw me slouched over in my chair and he smiled smugly. I could tell I was his reason for being here by his cold-hearted expression. I don't know if he saw me as a person or some blob of meat to be retrieved and eaten.

"Amy Collins?" the well-dressed man asked the judge. Judge Thomas nodded back, obviously annoyed.

"My name is Newell Davis from the Schultz, Brown, and Van Pelt law firm out of Boston. We represent the interests of Mrs. Matilda Langston Wentworth. Mrs. Wentworth has recently found out that her late child had been switched at birth and that Mrs. Wentworth is the true and biological mother of Miss Collins. As such, I have a court order from the Boston Federal Court for the custody of Miss Collins. It is our intention to return her immediately to her mother."

Chapter Twelve

The Surprise

Switched at birth? My head was swimming. Everyone started talking at once in the ensuing chaos. My family and I were ordered out of the courtroom while the judge sorted through this new development with the lawyers. Depjim had to gently guide Dad out of the courtroom, since he looked like he was ready to hit someone. And I don't think he was particularly concerned with just who he punched. There were certainly enough possibilities. But we went out like we were told to and sat on the hall bench.

"Don't you worry now, Amy," Dad told me, "Nobody's taking you anywhere."

"Exactly," Gramma Morris agreed, "And by the way, do we have to deal with any more surprises or people who want to pry you away from us?"

"I hope not. I mean, I don't think so, anyway."

Dad muttered, "I wish now I brought my shotgun."

"And do what? Make the two lawyers marry each other?" Mom was exasperated.

"Be fun to watch them consummate their marriage."

"Paul!"

We were soon called back into the courtroom. Judge Thomas and all the lawyers seemed unhappy. The bald man smiled at me when we entered. He seemed nice enough, unlike his lawyer friend.

When we were seated, Judge Morris lightly tapped his gavel.

"Mr. Davis has with him a ruling from the Federal District Court of Boston. As a parish judge, I have no power to rescind or send back the ruling."

Mr. Davis was as smug as a well-fed snake. To be truthful, I have never seen a smug, well-fed snake before because I don't get anywhere near them, but I always liked that phrase from the first time I heard it.

Mr. Tremble was not happy and interrupted, "But Judge Morris, you know this isn't right. Mary Corelli raised this young girl from her infancy until January. It is her name on the birth certificate. This interloper has no business even being here! And since when do federal courts get involved with custody hearings?"

Bang! Went the gavel.

"I just love it when one interloper complains about the other," Judge Thomas exclaimed, "If it was a different time, I'd have you horsewhipped, tarred and feathered, and run out of town.

"As it is, I have confirmed with the federal court and the order is valid. My biggest concern was that the school year is so close to being finished but the school informs me that Miss Collins has completed the grade and passed all her tests. This court has no choice but to remand immediate custody of Amy Collins to Mr. William Jarviston, who will escort her to Pennyton, Massachusetts."

The bald man stood up.

"Sit down, you pretentious scallywag," the judge ordered, "I understand that Mr. Davis has business further west?"

The lawyer nodded.

"Off to destroy some other poor family, no doubt."

"That's unfair, Judge. I'm just doing my job."

"So were the Russian revolutionaries when they slaughtered the Tzar's children. I allow that it's your job, but what you don't seem to know is it's not the right thing to do."

"The child belongs with her legal and natural mother," he said obstinately.

"And you belong in jail. Court is dismissed."

The gavel pounded down on the desk one last time. The judge got up and looked at us all before leaving for his chambers, shaking his head.

Chapter Thirteen

Reactions

Mr. Jarviston stood behind us with a pleasant smile and relaxed demeanor, but I still didn't want to go anywhere with him. I didn't know him. He wasn't family. He sensed my shyness and bent down so his eyes were at my level.

"A lot of information all at once," he commiserated.

I nodded. I had no idea what to say to him or how to react.

"You know, I understand there's a little café not far from here. We can get a little snack before we go. I was hoping to catch the five o'clock train home. You'll just love the house in Boston. I just adore living there."

"I'll be living with you?" I was confused now.

"You'll be living with your family at Wentworth Founding. I'll be living in the servant's quarters. But it's the same house."

Mom was crying now.

"Can't she at least come home for one last night? Her sisters will be heartbroken if she doesn't even say goodbye. Besides, we have to pack her things."

"Things?"

"Her clothes."

He looked down at me and tried to hide his obvious

distaste for my outfit.

"She'll be provided a whole new wardrobe when we get to Pennyton."

"Pennyton? I thought we were going to Wentworth Founding."

He smiled. "Wentworth Founding is the name of the house. Pennyton is the name of the town. It's a tiny ways north of Boston. You'll love it there." He turned to Mom. "You know, these courtroom situations can take a lot out of a person. Maybe we should have her get a good night's sleep at her home before we go. There's a seven o'clock tomorrow morning we can catch."

The lawyers had emptied the tables of their papers and gathered round us by now.

"You know, little girl," Davis said in a not unfriendly way, "Regardless of what Judge Thomas may think of me, I sincerely believe I did right by you, if only to keep you out of New York."

"What do you know about it?" Tremble sneered, "This is just a little roadblock. Mary Corelli is her rightful parent and she *will* get her back."

"Why?" Gramma Morris asked with a venomous glare, "She was in such a hurry to get rid of her that she sent her down here alone with hardly a stitch of clothes. Certainly nothing for winter. Now she wants her back. Why?"

He shrugged. "Sometimes families overreact to things. Given a little time they regret it. Regardless, Mary Corelli is legally her mother. *And we will get her back to her.*"

"Not legally," our lawyer said calmly.

"She will be in New York soon enough and that's where we will appeal. The federal judge overstepped his bounds today. She'll end up where she belongs."

In less than a heartbeat, Dad grabbed Tremble by his

lapels and lifted him up and over the swinging gate, tossing him down the aisle. Dad started down the aisle towards the stunned lawyer, but Louis stopped him.

"We all saw him trip over the gate, Paul," Depjim said softly, "But if you put a fist shaped bruise on his face it won't matter what we say."

"Just helping him get to his train."

"I don't think he needs help," Davis said, then he said to Tremble who was getting up, "By the way, if something happens and that little girl ends up in New York, I will do to your law career what my shoe does to cock roaches."

"Thank you for your concern," Dad said with a mixture of gratitude and sarcasm, "But if anything happens to Amy, I'll just shoot him."

"Paul," Mom was exasperated.

Tremble left in a hurry which was probably beneficial to his health.

"You know, Willie," Davis said to Jarviston, "Instead of catching a train tomorrow, you may want to consider waiting a day. Tremble knows you plan on catching the seven o'clock. If he plans anything nefarious and you're not there, then what can he do? In the meantime, Amy here can have some more time with her family while getting to know you. Maybe have a little goodbye party."

"I'd like that," I said.

"Hmm," Jarviston said suppressing a smile, "Would I be invited to this party?"

"You'd be the guest of honor," Gramma Morris told him.

"I think we can delay our departure then."

"I wonder how the judge would have ruled if Mr. Davis didn't show up," Gramma Morris thought out loud.

"That I can answer," Louis said, "My uncle told me I

did as good as he could have expected, but it came down to one thing—the birth certificate had Mary's name as the mother. She would have gotten custody. Along with Gio the Giraffe."

"You'll love Boston," Jarviston repeated, "If nothing else, we have a better class of criminal. Well, I'll be at the hotel. Let me know if you need me for anything. I do enjoy setting up parties. You'll have six older sisters in Boston, you know. We were always setting up and taking down party décor."

"That would be wonderful," Mom said quickly before Dad could reject the idea, "Can you be at Faucette Park by noon?"

"I can indeed," he said with a smile and he left us.

"Why are you letting that northern scallywag help? He's an outsider," Dad complained.

"Because I don't want him getting lonely at the hotel and regretting his decision to let us have our send off. He could always change his mind, you know," Mom replied, "Why give him a reason?"

Chapter Fourteen

The Last Lesson

It was a sad day. We went to our little restaurant on Faucette Avenue, not to eat anything but to invite Cici and Lila to the goodbye party. Oddly enough, they both heard about the verdict and the party before we got there.

Cici was a big black woman with Anglo features who was teaching me to cook Creole style. One day, I deliberately gave some customers beans that I knew would give them painful intestinal gas. She was furious and didn't speak to me for over a week, but I helped her reconcile with Fredrick, her nephew, and all was forgiven. Her eyes were tear stained as she gave me a near fatal bear hug.

Lila was also crying and gave me a gentler embrace. She was with me the evening some local boys robbed the little café that ended in a gun fight. I was slightly winged by one of the bullets and slipped and hit my head. It was an adventure we would always share.

"Ain't there nothing we can do?" Cici asked between hesitant breaths.

"Prepare for the best party this town ever did see," Mom replied.

"At the park," I added.

"Be a big party," Cici mused, "But isn't there some kind

of second opinion we can get?"

"It's called an appeal," Lila added helpfully.

"I don't think so. He showed an order from a federal judge," Gramma Morris replied, "I guess they outrank a parish judge. He just looked at the documents and said, 'Take her.' That was that."

"But she's so little to be going all that way," Cici said, forgetting that I rode from New York to Faucette by myself, "And a little girl needs her Mama."

"That's where she's going. To her Mama," we turned to see Gramma De Montfort, my maternal grandmother (or not, now that I thought about it). "I read the court documents. Cassie, what do you remember about that night?"

"Well, it was pleasant enough at first. Michael had just gotten a jar of popcorn down for me to pop when Mary got in. She was in a mood. Asked him if he found a job yet or just lounged around the house all day. That got him all worked up."

She lowered her voice to imitate a man and affected an Irish accent, "'It so happens I helped an old gentleman this morning and got a dollar tip for it,' he told her. She scoffed, 'A whole dollar. Now we can buy a cabin in Vermont.'

"'Woman, I put up with nagging when I don't bring in anything, but I earned some bacon today and you're still nagging at me.'

"And with that, he grabbed the jar of popcorn right out of my hand, tore the lid off and started throwing the kernels at her. 'You like me throwing popcorn at you? As much as I like you throwing your little barbs at me?'

"Well, she screamed a bit. A cross between a laugh and annoyance, I think. She ran around the room while he chased her, throwing seeds at her. She whirled around the couch and out the front door while he was right behind her, tossing those kernels, none too softly. I closed the door to keep the heat in. New York winters are cold, you know."

Gramma De Montfort nodded, obviously impatient.

"So, I watched them from the window. They were running down the street, both laughing a bit. She was trying to act scared but failed. He was even worse at trying to look fierce, although his size did help. They had to be freezing but you wouldn't know it by watching them, her dodging popcorn and him throwing it.

"She found a policeman and hid behind him, catching her breath while Michael stopped and stood up straight with one of his charming smiles.

"'Why hello, officer. We were just feeding these poor hungry little pigeons. God's creatures, they are. They look so starving, they do.'

"And they did. A half-dozen birds sat pecking up the castoff food. A couple of others stared at them with their best 'starving bird' expressions. 'I hate these disease-ridden unclean devil birds. You get out of here and back to your home. It's cold out here and if you don't get somewhere warm, you'll be feeding these little beggars' cousins. The *buzzards*. Now, go back to your home,' said the policeman."

"And so, they returned home, cold and shivering and looking very sheepish. Well, we were out of popcorn, so I decided to go to the store and get some. I found out during my pregnancy that popcorn mixed with mustard and cinnamon was just God's gift to the mouth. Don't care for it today though."

"Imagine that," Gramma De Montfort said dryly.

"It's good with mayonnaise and raisins too," she added.

"I can sure tell you and Mary are sisters," Cici said through a frown.

My Aunt Mary was known as a spectacularly bad cook who simply mixed ingredients together without worrying about whether the final result was edible or not.

"Cassie?" Gramma De Montfort was growing impatient.

"Well anyway, I just got out the door but slipped in some water and fell hard. I was screaming because I was in pain and just knew I hurt my baby. I was bleeding. Mary and Michael got me to the hospital right away. The baby was coming. I was terrified and hurting but no one cared. Then one of the nurses came in and told me to hush up and she gave me a shot. I woke up the next day and they said I had a daughter."

"I see. That matches up with the affidavits that Boston lawyer gave Judge Thomas. You had a boy and J.P. Wentworth the third wanted him. He got him and left you with Amy."

That stung.

"So, I was the booby prize."

I heard a thumping noise then came a serious pain on the top of my head. Gramma Morris hit me with a teaspoon.

"You said it wrong. You were the prize. Not a booby prize. And you will always be family. Always."

She was crying. And I was crying (the pain from the utensil assault didn't help). So was everyone else in the room, except Dad. Big strong men don't cry. But tears were in his eyes. He just refused to let them fall. We trudged home to give the news to the rest of the family.

"But that's not *fair*," Holly whimpered with tears already flowing, "Papa, you're not going to let them take her away, are you?"

Poor Dad. He couldn't say anything. If he did

something, it would only make it worse. As Depjim said a few times, 'When the law speaks, it may not be right, but it's the law and you'll have a better life if you accept it.'

Holly melted into my shoulder, crying her heart out. Michelle and Anna Marie had tears in their eyes and we all embraced in one of those awkward looking group hugs. The adults soon joined in and for a minute we all felt each other's warmth.

The clopping of hooves interrupted us. A peek out the window revealed the old seventeenth century carriage rolling up the driveway. The Countess had come to visit.

"How ironic," she said, "You came here unwanted, now you leave here with three families claiming you. The only wonder is how your Aunt Mary let you go in the first place. And what you can do with a violin at only ten. It's a shame you were born a girl. You could have been the best violin player of your generation."

She shook her head sadly. "Oh, well, at least we will know it. And you're getting a going away party. Every young girl should have at least one party where she is the center of attention. Will I still see you in the morning for your lesson?"

Mom nodded. She wanted me to be surprised when I saw the party decorations at the park when it was all set up. That meant that after my violin lesson, I would have a last reading session with Grandpa Terrance. That way, I could say goodbye to them both privately.

I was going to be sad after that. I loved my conversations with them. I learned so much about my family from their different perspectives. But whatever happened, they would always be in my heart.

Even though it was getting late, there seemed to be a great reluctance for anyone to leave. So, we planned the party. Faucette Park was just south of the café. It was a big 30 acre spread of pristine grassland and live oaks covered in Spanish Moss that lay at the end of Faucette Avenue. There were statues of great Confederate generals and local heroes facing the Malmort river. It had a playground for the smaller children. Picnic tables sat lopsided beside a large fountain that sprayed water twenty feet into the air. Large grills stood by for cookouts, though we never used them.

"Good food don't taste like smoke," was a family motto.

Hugh Landacre, who until recently I thought was my grandfather on my father's side, pulled in for a short visit. Hugo Landacre, his son and my father (we thought), was in Baton Rouge and would miss my departure.

Grandpa Hugh agreed that the park was a splendid idea. He would see to it the Landacres would come. Mom thanked him with a smile, but I knew it hurt her inside to even speak to him, much less tell him she appreciated anything he did. She believed a good part of the blame for Hugo not marrying her lay with him.

Hugh smiled back at her, but he soon got ready to leave. It was obvious he felt the lack of desire for his company. His family was unpopular these days and not just with Mom. The Landacre Sawmill and Timber Companies, Faucette's largest employers, just laid off a sizable portion of the town. Hugh Landacre was no longer the beloved employer he once was.

I hugged him goodbye. I thought he was a good man, even though he was the one who insisted that his son not marry my mother. That made me illegitimate, which was an unforgivable crime here in the south. Even some of his relatives were still hateful to me, mostly the women.

"Well, goodbye, Grandpa Hugh—" I stopped, "I don't

know." My eyes filled with tears. "What do I call you all now?" I looked around at all the faces who gave me home and security.

"Dad," that wonderful man said.

"Mom."

"Gramma Morris."

"Gramma De Montfort."

"Grandpa Hugh."

"Holly."

We all laughed. The tears were gone.

"Takes more than blood to make a family. Takes love. Takes belonging. Takes knowing there's going to be a hole in this family without you," Gramma Morris said.

"Just like when Annette left," Dad said, "It'll hurt, but the Lord wants it this way. Otherwise, I'd get my shotgun out and set things right."

"Paul." Mom never knew when Dad was serious or joking about his weapon. Of course, neither did I, but I thought it was the right thing to say.

"I'd go with you," Grampa Hugh said with a smile.

"Don't you go encouraging him," Mom snapped, exasperated. But he was already leaving.

We decided to wait until the next day to start preparing for our party. We would go light and just have hamburgers and sausages with fries and coleslaw. Everyone loved Cici's coleslaw. I liked it too, but I think I would have preferred it with lettuce instead of cabbage. Cici laughed for hours when I made that suggestion. I figured that meant 'no,' even if the party was for me.

It was warm enough for us to sit out on the porch that evening. Holly and I squeezed together on an ancient wicker love seat, Anna Marie and Michelle in chairs, Gramma Morris on a small stool with the wall for her back support, and the large, cushioned swing for Mom and Dad with Jason sleeping between them. Mosquitos rested on all of us until we swatted them away.

"Won't be much longer we'll have to stay inside unless we get a breeze," Gramma Morris said, "These skeeters will eat us up."

"Breeze?" I asked.

"They only come out when it's still. Wind blows them away."

"They sure do bite a lot," Anna Marie complained.

"Wait till summer," Dad said, "When they get big. You know why there's no vampires in Louisiana? They can't compete with these things."

"They get bigger?" I asked. Maybe going back north wouldn't be so bad.

"My brother Matt told me once he saw two of these skeeters pick up a cow. While they were flying away, he heard them talking to each other. 'Where can we go with this?' said the one. 'Somewhere where our big brothers won't take it away from us.'"

I thought it was funny, but apparently, he told it multiple times before, judging by the rolling eyes and stone faces.

"What were our uncles like?" Michelle asked and Dad grew serious.

He was very close to his brothers who died in that disastrous raid just before America entered the Great War. It wasn't called World War I in those days since World War II hadn't happened yet.

"They were good people," he responded firmly, "They always had a smile and a dollar for anyone who needed it. 'Ceptin' Yankees of course. My dad would roll over in his grave if he knew his sons helped out a Yankee. He spent four years in Tennessee fighting those devils. Kept losing, too.

"Anyway, my dad was an angry man after the south lost. He was on his way to Texas when he saw my mother and they fell madly in love. Her father disapproved of my dad, so he had to work to prove he was worthy of her. Then they got married and lived happily ever after."

This was not the way I first heard this story.

"My brothers were just like Dad from what I understand. Easy going and fun to be around. Just don't rile them up." He slowly moved his hand down his bicep and slapped a mosquito. "Or you wind up like that guy." He flicked it away into the night.

"They were all good young men. I remember on my sixteenth birthday we went to Crosby's saloon down River Street. We sat at our table real quiet-like when Sherriff Woodson came in to cause us trouble. Said I was out past curfew. Had to be in by ten in those days if you were school age, even when I wasn't going to school. Dumb.

"So, Sheriff Woodson tells me to leave my beer behind and go on home. 'I ain't leaving my beer,' I told him, 'I paid good money for it.'

"'You'll leave it and go or get yourself arrested. Disobeying a peace officer and breaking curfew.'

"'You think I care about your curfew?'

"'That's it. You're under arrest.'

"'You know, Paul,' my brother Matt said in a nice slow voice, which anyone with a lick of sense would know was a warning, 'I don't think you're doing anything wrong just being here. You don't have to be arrested if you don't want to be.'

"Now Sheriff Woodson was not known for his thinking ability. He was smarter than a rock but dumber than a carrot. He decided he was going to arrest Matt. When we all stood up, he thought he was going to arrest the whole family.

"But not for long. Matt didn't need any help. By the time it was done, Old Woodson had a broken nose and bloody mouth and two black eyes. But he did some damage. Matt seriously hurt his knee. That sheriff had a hard skull. Then we tied him to his horse and sent him into the swamp to think it over for a while. Pastor Josephson and a couple of others went in to get him out before he did something even more stupid and got himself killed."

He laughed a bit at his memory, but no one else did.

"Well, point is, you girls would've loved your uncles. They were good people."

"That's not how I would define good people. And they were bank robbers," Michelle persisted.

"Just taking back some Yankee money. Lord knows them Yankees bled us dry for years. Still doing it. Even with Huey P. Long on our side, those Yankees want everything we have but the skeeters. We were just getting back some of what's ours."

"So, you did ride with them," I stated.

"Not after Edgewater."

Robbing banks was not a conversation Dad liked. We all stayed quiet until it was time for sleep. Tomorrow would be a sad and busy day.

Cici and Lila were waiting for us at the café. Cici and I had a good friendship, even though she was nearing sixty and black and I was ten and white. She always acted like we were close family. While the others gathered the food, we walked out the back door together to look around one more time. She took off her head scarf and shook it a few times before tying it back on her head.

"I understand why you cover your hair when you're in the kitchen, to keep hair out of the food, but why do so many black women wear coverings all the time?"

"Those are called tignons," she replied, "Long ago, white people thought black women were too pretty. When the settlers came, most of the white women stayed back. The black slaves and freed people of the islands were who they socialized with. White men were all over us with gifts and poems and whatnot. It was the plaçage system, where white men had arrangements with black women just like marriage but no church. They wouldn't marry outside their race so that was the system they thought up. As more white girls came to this country, they got jealous. Didn't like all the competition. So, the Spanish government passed the Tignon Laws. All black women had to wear covers on our head to make us look plain. Didn't work none. Those laws are all gone now but we wear them anyway. Sometimes, folks wear them real fancy-like. Tall and wide. Shows off their social status. But nowadays, most of us just wear them cause we always did."

"Spanish government?"

"Oh, yes. This land was discovered and claimed by Spain years ago. Then France conquered Spain and took it all away."

She leaned down to my ear. "Don't matter what country. All you white folks think you need an advantage, you know. So many of you think you're better than us but you ain't got no proof of that except your words. Always doing something to keep us down. And the law punishes those who talk about it. We just smile and keep our mouths shut. That gives us the advantage. Too bad so few people know that."

I had no words to respond, so I nodded my head. I was

happy she shared her wisdom. We soon went back inside to prepare the coleslaw. Even though it was a depressing day, we found things to keep us laughing and pretended to be happy.

"Now don't be sad because you're leaving," Cici told me after all the cabbage was shredded, "Be happy you were blessed to meet everyone here. Of course, knowing some of the folks hereabouts are bigger blessings than others."

After that, I had to rush over to the Countess' home for my last violin lesson. For some reason, Killy didn't pick me up at the café. But it was nice outside and I rather enjoyed the walk. Frederick answered the door with his eyebrows raised. I wasn't expected.

"Mom and I thought I was supposed to be here." I held up the violin.

"That's wonderful, Miss Amy," he said, "Come in and I'll tell her you're here."

I waited for at least a half hour until she came down holding onto Killy's arm. She was disheveled and looked confused, like she didn't recognize me. I was surprised at her appearance. Usually, she dressed meticulously with never a hair out of place.

"Well, hello, young lady," she said slowly. She gave me a confused smile.

"Good morning, Countess," I replied with a curtsy.

She laughed haltingly, "Oh deary, I am not a countess. Just a governess. You must want Mrs. De Pilord, but she's terribly ill."

"You are Mrs. De Pilord," Killy said kindly, "And this here is Little Amy. Remember her?"

"Come into the light, dear," she commanded.

I stepped forward and she gasped.

"Fiona," she cried, "It's my little Fiona. She came back to me!"

She stumbled over to me and hugged me tightly. I vaguely remembered she had a daughter named Fiona who died. I had no idea what to say. If she was confused, I was bewildered.

"No, no," Killy said quietly, "This is Amy. She plays violin for you these days. You teach her."

"Violin? Yes, I love to hear music," She looked at me with blank eyes. Her right eye was almost completely shut, while the other was bloodshot, "Play for me, Fiona. Play *Shenandoah*."

"I don't know it," I stammered.

"You will," she said imperiously. She nudged Killy and he helped her over to the ancient credenza I dusted so many times. In a second, she pulled out the printed sheet music.

I nodded and prepared my instrument to play. Usually when I learned a new song, she helped me with the timing and notations. She would also play it for me so I could get a feel for the music. Now, I was on my own. Killy had her seated in her chair and she was waiting, her head cocked a bit to her side, like she was having trouble keeping it erect. Killy nodded to me like it was all right.

I played. After the first few bars, the song sounded familiar. *Shenandoah* is a classic American song with a haunting melody. I would remember that day forever. The Countess staring ahead with a blank look and proud smile. Killy nodding encouragement. And the music filling the room.

When I was done, they both applauded. I curtsied and put my instrument away.

"Fiona," she called softly.

I looked up.

"Never stop playing and always keep your violin close," she coughed for a second and looked tired and drawn, "And keep that music. I never heard *Shenandoah* played like that before."

I was touched. That compliment meant a lot to me.

"Hansel," she said to Killy, "I need to have a nap now, please."

"Yes, Miss," Killy said, obviously confused at her calling him by the wrong name. He worked for her for 30 years.

I walked over and hugged her and escaped. I didn't want her to see me cry. I was afraid for her.

Chapter Fifteen

The Last Story

"What's upsetting you today?" Grandpa Terrance was sitting on his rickety porch, a pitcher of iced tea on the table next to him. "I think it's more than just going away."

I looked at him, with his staring eyes. I hadn't even said a word yet. I stepped up on the porch and flounced in the chair opposite of him, after brushing it off.

"How would you even know that?" I asked.

"You're not breathing in an I'm-excited-but-not-happy sort of way. More like a something's-wrong-and-I-don't-know-what-to-do way."

I scowled for an instant. Obviously, blind people are much more aware of things than people with sight.

"It's the Countess," I said, making a point to take deep breaths so I could be understood, "She forgot me."

"She forgot your lesson? That's not unusual for a person that age. It's unusual to remember things when you're that old."

"No," I cried, "She forgot *me*. She forgot my name. She called me Fiona."

"Fiona," he repeated slowly, "Now it's been years since I heard that name. Fiona De Pilord. It could have been

Fiona Benson if things were different."

"Fiona…Benson? Oh my God."

"Please, don't take the Lord's name in vain. You're breaking one of the commandments."

Like 'Thou shalt not commit adultery?'

"Sorry," I said begrudgingly.

"It's been a secret forever."

"But I thought you two didn't like each other."

"Well, we don't. But you should have been able to see that we hated each other too much for it to be anything less than true love."

"Huh?"

"You'll understand when you're older. You only love the one you hate."

"I'm not quite sure that's entirely true."

"It was for us."

"Mr. Benson," I was exasperated.

"What happened to Grandpa Terrance?"

"We're not related anymore. Judge Thomas ruled for me to leave."

"Judge Thomas is a dolt. Riding around on a horse like he was joisting in Old England. Of course, we're related. I can see it." He tapped on his temple. "Right in here." He pointed to his clouded white eyes. "Don't need these to see that much.

"Anyway, it was complicated. She was married to Henry. Henry was in love with Carmen Monroe. She was married to Davey Monroe. The Monroes were black. Carmen was mostly white. She couldn't pass, but she had the best of both worlds. As beautiful as they come. Davey was really black. And as big as they come. Bigger than your dad and uncles. And that's big.

"He was a sharecropper. Worked the fields and shared

the crops with the owner. Tough life. So, his wife slept with Henry, one of the last wealthy men in the parish. Henry played the field, as rich men so often do. Carmen and Davey had to adopt any extra black children that Henry created. So, they had a big family. Carmen had quite a few kids of her own and I might add that Davey also played the field and brought home his pups. And for a price, they adopted unwanted babies from careless women.

"Anyway, poor Susan only had her husband's touch when Carmen was too pregnant to do anything. That's how she had her children. And here she was, a poor orphan girl. If she complained, Henry would've thrown her out. No woman anywhere would feel sorry for the little ingrate. That's just how it was.

"I was kind of a vagabond in those days. I didn't move back here for good until 1872. I continued my deal with Blackjack because I didn't need to farm. I had money, jewels, gold, you name it, and I didn't have anyone to spend it on. I was aware of the De Pilords, of course. Them and the Thomas family owned three quarters of the parish.

"By then, my lawman career was over. I was just an old man with a reputation. Good way to get killed in those days. I was aware of the 'Count and Countess' but kept a distance. Until Donna Lynn came to town. She had some kind of charm that let her get her way with men. You know what happened there.

"Well, through Donna Lynn, I really got to know Sue. She may have been unhappy about how I treated her 'sister,' but she eventually understood my point of view. While Henry was going out and running around, I was coming in and staying put, if you get my meaning."

"I do," I said. I was fascinated and repulsed at the same time.

"Well," he continued after a sip of tea, "One day she found out she was going to have Fiona and Henry was going to throw her out. I paid a little visit to him and convinced him that he really didn't want his kneecaps shot off, so they stayed together. I promised to stay away after that unless he got stupid. And Fiona was born, about 1874, I'd say. You know how that ended.

"Sue and I had a falling out after that. She became quite bold with the men. Slept with Davey Monroe this time and had his child. When the girl was born, the Monroes took her in.

"She was a model citizen after that. Nobody knew Henry wasn't the father of her last daughter. Everyone in town thought her last baby was stillborn. Nobody saw the body. Henry died soon afterwards and she was just some lonely old crackpot lady who rides around in a seventeenth century carriage and lives in a gingerbread home. She still lives in that run down house with her husband today."

"I thought you said Henry died."

"I did," he scoffed, "Henry died forty-five years ago. She married a former slave named Achilles."

"Killy?"

"They got married in a black church in New Orleans. I found out about it by chance. I went up to see her one day and went right in. I thought it was time for us to reconcile on Fiona's birthday. I wanted to see if she needed any comfort for our loss. I saw her clothes were in the closet neat as a pin next to his. I turned to go and he was there.

"Well, what could I do? I certainly felt foolish and embarrassed. I wanted to shoot him then and there, but that would be messy.

"'My mistake,' I told him politely.

"'Don't let it happen again,' he said, not so politely and

that rankled me. I pulled out my pistol and pointed it right at his chest.

"'You're standing where I want to walk,' I told him. That was going to be his only chance. He stepped aside just as Sue came out of a room down the hall. So, we three went down to the kitchen and had some tea. I promised no one would ever find out about them from me. I never spoke to her again, but I kept my word, until now. I expect that secret to be kept by you."

"I'll never say a thing," I told him.

"Sad thing for her," he went on, "Somehow, her children found out about her being married to a former slave. They all completely disowned her. Except for one daughter and maybe Spring. Some of her grandchildren still visit her, but they're only looking for inheritances.

"By the way," he said, "One more thing you may want to know. Sue's baby with Monroe was born in 1876. They named her Cecilia."

"Cecilia?"

"They call her Cici."

CHAPTER SIXTEEN

THE GOODBYE PARTY

Of course, I promised not to talk to anyone about anything he told me. When people have skeletons in their closet, they need to be hung neatly on hangers and scooted out of sight. I hugged Grandpa Terrance goodbye. I was happy he still considered me family. Even though I spent a great deal of time being angry with him, or exasperated by him, or scared of him, I would always love him. Blood or not.

"Blood don't mean that much when you get older," he said as I left, "I'd rather you be in my family than a whole lot of others I'm stuck with. You, I like."

"I like you, too," I said.

I loved him, really, but I was afraid it would embarrass him if I was that blunt. Besides, it was safer for me to say it that way. The women who loved him all seemed to wind up unhappy, abandoned, or dead. I might as well be practical.

I dabbed at my tears as I walked away. He stoically sat there on his porch looking in my direction as I made my way back to the café and a wagon trip back home. It was time to get ready for my party.

One bath and a change of clothes later, we were on our way. Mom insisted I wear some old clothes so we could play without worrying about grass stains or dirt. I would wear my Sunday dress on the train with Mr. Jarviston. And that made sense since we all played tag and hide-and-go-seek and other games that required running around and maybe crawling through mud.

The park was green and clean, with a dozen statues of old Confederate generals staring at the river. There was a battered seesaw and some swings. The slide was rusty and simply didn't work. We could sit on it but never actually slip down. The boys used it to play pirate ship with the one on top being the captain.

An impressive fountain fed by an artesian well was the centerpiece. It was two-tiered and stood maybe ten feet tall with that small tower billowing out cold water another 20 feet into the air. The base stood at a 25-foot diameter and was over four feet deep. A fountain like that needed lots of liquid in order to spew a geyser so high in the air.

The picnic tables sat together in three rows, decorated with paper table clothes held down with bowls of wonderful smelling food. The main dish was shrimp gumbo, made especially for the occasion as a surprise for me. It was Cici's specialty and tonight would probably be the last time I would taste it. Above the table, the live oaks held out a homemade sign on a long sheet of brown butcher paper. 'Goodbye Amy. We'll always love you.' The second 'a' in 'always' was missing, but someone wrote it in with a little arrow pointing to where it belonged.

Mom ordered me to thank all the people who created this wonderful set-up. She really didn't have to, I wanted everyone who came to know I appreciated them. Some more than others.

Laura Sauveterre was there with her family. Before Judge Thomas' decision, I thought we were cousins. I was glad we were not related now. Laura was mean and her mother encouraged her to be hateful to me. Most of the folks of Faucette were not at all friendly to me when I moved here, but some of them warmed up after a while. Laura did not. She was told to be polite to me after a couple of incidents between us. So, she was polite, in a sarcastic, mean sort of way. We would never be friends and we were both quite happy that way. It was certainly better for me since she had years more experience of being hateful.

"How fun it must be to see the world," she said in a taunting sort of voice, "I'm sad to see you go." Her word was 'sad,' but her tone indicated 'joyful' was really accurate. "But at least you're not a bastard anymore."

I wanted to slug her, but I already knew she would win in any kind of a fight. She had four inches and fifteen pounds on me. Not only that, she had dozens of boys in her family who taught her how to fight. I only knew how to punch.

"Yeah, and you didn't have to hate me at all," I said through clenched teeth, "I was always legitimate, just kidnapped. I could have been treated like anyone else."

"Not really. You're still a Yankee. There's no cure for that either."

I had no answer for that, so I dazzled her with my best fake smile and walked away, glancing around to find someone I really wanted to talk to. Mother Greenough was there at a distance with some other black people. I don't think they were there for my party. Paster Josephson from our Baptist church was talking to Father Cassidy. They were both, no doubt, trying to convert each other.

Pierre Dupris was throwing a football to some of my

former classmates from the public school, Louis Lemieux and Chucky Landacre. Chucky used to be my half-brother. Estelle Landacre, his mother, was also there helping Gramma Morris while avoiding Mom. I was surprised she was there at all, but I found out later on that Hugh wanted the family to be there. His goal was to get our families to like each other, or at least hate each other a little less.

That would be a tall order. Hugo, obviously a smooth talker, got both Estelle and Mom pregnant at the same time, with neither one aware that they were being played with. Hugo could only marry one of them and he chose Estelle.

So, Estelle won the husband and Mom got the stigma of having a child out of wedlock. Estelle hated Mom anyway. She still considered Mom a rival. Mom just smiled and ignored her. She would never have an interest in Hugo again.

Mom once told me that Hugo would always be happy, carefree, and useless. Estelle would always be bitter and miserable. It would be that way for any woman who married Hugo. He had the body of a man but the soul of a boy. She blamed Grandpa Hugh for that. He constantly fixed Hugo's messes until Hugo created this one. Even Hugh couldn't help everyone in this situation. So sad.

Holly and her friends were having a kangaroo jumping contest on the other side of the fountain. Anna Marie and Michelle were helping set up the food and Jason found some boys his age to play with. I think they were playing 'who can get their clothes the dirtiest.' Jason was winning.

Merry and Elizabeth were just getting out of their families' cars. I started to greet them, but I was stopped when I heard my name called.

It was Betsy approaching with her boyfriend, Rob. "I

wanted you to be the first to see this." She pulled on a gold chain around her neck and produced a lovely little silver ring.

I inspected it as best I could, not knowing anything about jewelry.

"It's beautiful," I said, "but isn't it supposed to have a diamond in it?"

"It's a friendship ring," she explained, "It means that we promise to not see anyone until I'm certain that he's the one."

"I'm already certain she's the one," Rob said quietly.

Betsy nuzzled up to him, finding his wrists and wrapping them around her.

"Keep talking like that and we can skip the engagement ring," she teased.

"Take her up on it," I encouraged, "You'll never do better."

She shifted her head on his shoulder to look up at him. "Well?" she laughed.

"Good idea. Very practical. We can save some money skipping a ring, I suppose," he said thoughtfully.

"Hmmf," she scowled and freed herself from his grasp. "If I wanted *practical*, I'd live alone."

"You have to want practical. You're with me."

Even at ten, I thought this was not a good thing to say. My suspicions were confirmed when I saw Betsy's scowl.

"What if I want romantic? What do you think a ring means?"

"I'm willing to invest in you."

"Invest?"

"You're a wonderful investment. How could any man look at you and not want to merge his assets with yours?"

"Is that the best you can do for a proposal?"

"What could be more practical than realistic speculation on how beneficial it will be after we get married?"

"I want *romance*, not 'realistic speculation.' I want to be a wife, not some unpaid bookkeeper. Can't you learn to be romantic?"

"How?"

"How do you think?"

I could feel the temperature drop a few degrees, so I said my goodbyes and left them. That conversation went downhill quickly.

Angus and Brigitte Nye were with Mom. They were laughing at something. I went over to see if I could help now that Estelle was gone. Whatever the women were laughing at was now past.

The food was ready. My sisters and I were sent out to round up the guests. It was a nice sized crowd for such short notice. Maybe 50 people showed up, including the children. That was a respectable turn out since our family was not popular or highly regarded here. Mom's reputation in town was forever destroyed by having me. Dad's inability to control his temper, added together with his criminal history, did nothing to improve our status. I suppose we were lucky anyone talked to us at all.

However, I did meet Governor Huey P. Long and he promised to rebuild the bridge that connected our town to the rest of the state. That raised my status quite a bit, but most of the people of Faucette still tended to avoid us. That was a shame for them. They wouldn't get to find out what kindhearted and forgiving Christian people we truly were.

After most of us were done eating, Beauregard Porter walked up to me with Calvin Foyt at his side. Beau was about to graduate from the public school. Although I knew his face and name, we never really talked. He was quite a bit older than me. Calvin had dropped out earlier that year after he helped start a schoolyard brawl that resulted in several injuries. Since he was defending me from my nemesis, Billy Kaker, I thought he was heroic, in a dirty, ignorant sort of way. I always tried to be kind to him, but from a distance.

If the Villians family was scorned by the residents of Faucette, the Foyts were downright sneered at. They were rather different than the rest of us. Their heads were slightly too big for their necks and seemed to sway a bit. The Foyt men were all muscular and carried themselves in a guarded sort of way, like they were ready to take a swing at anyone they saw.

They always wore dirty clothes and seldom bathed. I had heard it said that they could never sneak up on anyone with a nose. I was assigned to tutor Calvin in January and was aware he had noticeable body odor. Now that spring was here and the temperature was warmer, his smell could make a skunk jealous.

My eyes and nose were already watering when they approached. I tried to position myself upwind from them, but for that to work there had to be wind. I had no idea how Beau could stand to be near him.

"So, you're leaving right around the same time we are," Beau said while I was breathing quietly through my mouth.

"Oh?"

"My uncle runs a boxing gym down in New Orleans. He's going to look at Calvin here and get him trained to fight. I'm his agent. I'll be booking the fights and getting the transportation and things like that. You're looking at a future welter weight champion."

I looked at Calvin. He wore a dopey smile, like he was proud he was going to go get pounded into the ground. He, like all the Foyts, could handle himself in a fistfight, but I had doubts about how well he could stay within all the rules of professional boxing.

"I'm so happy for you both," I said, trying to look enthusiastic while my eyes were tearing up, "I hope you do well."

That hideous stench of pure filth and body odor will give him an unfair advantage.

"Please don't cry. I'll be back," Calvin said slowly, "When I'm in the ring, I hope you'll come and watch. It'll be great."

"She's too young," Beau said, "And she's going to be too far away."

Thank God!

"Well, I'll always root for you," I said politely.

Martin Thomas, the junior paster of our church, stopped by to wish them well on their new adventure and I made my escape to fresh air.

"The 'Foyt fog' almost kill you?" asked Michelle, "I almost threw up in his face before I escaped. I can't believe Beau partnered up with him."

"Why not?" We turned to see Margaret Landacre, who until recently was my aunt. "It's the perfect arrangement. Calvin takes the beatings. Beau gets ten percent of the earnings without doing any real work. Beau's never going to do any real work."

Her voice was sad and I realized that she loved him and resented his lack of ambition. Her moist eyes said it all. She was a woman who realized the man she loved would always disappoint her.

"It'll be okay," Michelle told her, "The sooner you know, the less the hurt."

I asked, "Why isn't it 'The sooner you know, the sooner you can get away?'"

Margaret surprised me with a hug. I didn't think we were that close even when we thought we were family.

"It's so sad that you'll have to find out that answer," she said.

I think she was trying to impress us with her deep philosophy but failed.

"Oh look," she exclaimed, "It's the Harmons from our church."

"The ones who own the weekly paper?"

"They're the ones."

I glanced over at the humorless couple in their fifties. He wore a suit with no tie and she had on a light blue print dress and black shawl topped with an old-fashioned floppy hat with ostrich feathers and fresh flowers. I probably had seen them before but wasn't sure. I certainly never spoke to them. They intercepted Gramma De Montfort in front of the fountain. It didn't seem like they were having a friendly conversation.

"Well, hello, Amy," came a voice from behind me.

It was Jenny Du Lin, the town's new teacher. She replaced Mrs. Porter, who was quite unfriendly to me when I arrived. I already transferred to Catholic school when Jenny took over and didn't really speak to her often. I was introduced to her when she arrived because I was expected to go back to public school the following year, before everything changed.

"Hi, Miss Du Lin," I said, "I'm glad you could come."

She seemed very nice, although I knew most of the other girls hated her for some reason.

"Hi, Jenny," Margaret said curtly and walked off with Michelle without saying anything more to me. Obviously, they didn't like her.

"I know you'll miss everyone here," she told me, "But keep an open mind. Boston is a wonderful city, just filled with museums and places to go and be. And it's right on the ocean. You'll love it."

"Oh? You've been there?"

"No, but I've read books. I feel like I've been there. Sometimes, I so want to escape the small-town life and the only way is by reading."

"Oh, I read a lot, too. In New York, it was nicer to read than talk to anyone after Aunt Mary remarried. I still like to read. I just do more things now."

"Let's hope your new family will give you time to do both. I'm sad you won't be in my class next year. With all the older children getting their own schoolhouse, we'll be getting a piano. I'm sure with you bringing in your violin, we'd make beautiful music together."

She traced her fingers down my temple to my lips. Whatever her intent was, it only made me nervous. I stepped back just as Mom called me to the table where the cake was being displayed. I smiled a goodbye to Miss Du Lin and ran back to the party as quickly as I could go.

Gramma Morris and Cici were laughing as I got there.

"I see you aren't taking any chances on missing out on cake this time," Gramma Morris said teasingly.

When Aunt Mary made cakes, they were purely dreadful, so when I moved down here, I promised my first slice of one of Cici's cakes to Jason. After I tasted a bite, I realized what a mistake I made. She still chuckled about that. I didn't tell her the real reason I ran so fast. I was afraid she would think I was being silly.

Since I was the guest of honor, I got to cut the goodbye cake. It was a shame to dismember it, though. It was beautiful, with frosting flowers of red roses and big letters saying *Goodbye Amy*. I admired it for too long, apparently because Gramma Morris nudged me none too gently to get on with it. After I was done, making sure the servings were all nice and big, Gramma Morris took the knife from me with a dark glance and cut all the pieces in half.

"It's better if everyone gets a piece," she muttered to me under her breath.

It was a chocolate cake with apple butter frosting. I was shocked that a cake (or anything) could taste so good. It was truly a sugary delight. I was sitting with Elizabeth and Merry and they were also highly impressed.

"It must be nice to own a restaurant and be able to eat like this all the time," Merry said.

"I wish we ate like this all the time," I giggled, "But cakes are only for special events at my house."

"Same here," she replied, "We never get desserts, unless blackberries are in season."

"I want to taste them," I replied, "We never get them in New York."

"And you're leaving just before they're in season," Merry said sadly.

"Amy!"

I looked over and Cici was waving her hands at me, standing next to Mother Greenough and a few other women. I said goodbye to my friends and scurried over to say 'hi.' I reminded myself not to mention that I knew about her mother.

"Amy," Cici said with a big smile, "I hear you met my sister here, Noxolo. And this is my oldest sister, Luzira, sometimes called Mama Louviere."

We exchanged pleasantries. She was a large woman, with African features and much darker skin than her two sisters, and her back was hunched over a bit with age. Her scarlet and blue tignon was wrapped tightly around her head and stood almost like a tower over her brow. Black and white bead chains swayed whenever she moved. Her matching blouse also had beads sewn into it. She was as elegant as any woman could be. Mama Louviere didn't really smile at me. She inspected me before she read my palms.

"You go on a journey into the unknown, young miss," she said after a while, "You will come out wiser. You will understand what is important may not be perfect. But you don't want perfect. You just think you do."

"Oh," I said, confused.

"Listen to her," Mother Greenough said to me, "She is a First Matron of the *Hai-tak-koo* arts."

"What's that?"

"The *Hai-tak-koo*?"

"No, First Matron."

"Think of an archbishop of the church. She's the high priestess."

"One of them," Mama Louviere corrected, "The Marsh Matron is also very powerful. Remember, she killed two men before she ever even heard of our religion. A woman like that should never have been initiated into our circle."

"Spring Waters killed two men?" I was shocked. How could Grandpa Terrance leave a detail like that out of his story?

Mama Louviere stared at me, as if in shock.

"You know her real name? Spring Waters De Pilord Landacre Le Perat? Did you meet her in the swamp?"

"No, I didn't. My grandpa told me about her."

"She killed more than two men," Mother Greenough said, "She shot her husband and his cousin, the man who married them. Pretty bad marriage when it's not good enough just to kill one's husband but also the pastor who officiated the wedding. Then there were others. Some she killed with magic. Some she had others kill for her."

"That's all nonsense." Cici stomped a foot down. "The devil will take her soul when her time comes, I'm sure," she said sadly, "But it don't make sense that he lets bad people have that kind of power."

"It does, Cici," Mama Louviere said gently, "We all have the same God as yours. We just recognize the angels and saints who can help us. You don't."

"They're not angels."

"They are, sister. But we need to know what we're doing when we call on them for help."

Michelle was on her way over to extract me from their debate, so I politely smiled.

"It was good of you to come to the party, Mother Louviere."

"Mama Louviere," she corrected me harshly, "Mama indicates how familiar I am to the spirits. Mother Louviere means knowledgeable, but not familiar. Very important difference."

Michelle graciously extracted me from the spiritual lesson. Cici was a good, church-going Christian woman and Mom liked the fact that I spent time with her. But her sisters made Mom nervous and she didn't want anyone in the family to go to hell by listening to their bad advice.

"Mom wants you to meet everyone here, even the Harmons. She says that since they were good enough to come, you should be good enough to thank them. He's an elder at the Methodist church," Michelle explained to me, "We used to go there until Dad married Mom. Then they had some kind of issue and we started going to the Baptist church. Mom's hoping that after they meet you the issue can be resolved."

Of course, we knew what the issue was—me. Dad married a fallen woman and the church thought Mom would destroy it from within through wanton behavior and outright sin. They were standing between the table and fountain. Mrs. Harmon glanced at me and continued talking when we got there.

"Well in the long run, it's better for her to be raised by someone else. She already has the traits that will give her a bad life. I mean, fighting in school and running away and poisoning people at the restaurant are bad enough. Then to lie about where she was going with her friends. That alligator was retribution from the Lord, the way I see it."

"Hey now," Dad whispered, while scowling at her, "I don't think you're at the right place. This is a sad party because Amy's leaving here and she didn't poison anyone."

"I know," the woman continued, oblivious to all Dad's warning signals, "But it doesn't change things. A young lady needs a good Christian home."

"Excuse me," Dad said, getting closer while she backed away. Her husband, who was over a foot shorter than Dad dithered his way in front of her, but Dad ignored him. "She lives in a good Christian home."

"With a bank robber and a loosely made woman? I'm not impressed."

"I'm not impressed with you," Dad replied, looking straight at her, "And people everywhere have sinned and have been forgiven by God and brought into his church. Not your church. If you people could forgive in that building, we wouldn't have left. And I'll have you know, I was baptized in His name eleven years ago, right after the war."

"Well, I was baptized thirty years ago, I'll have you know, and my behavior and my children's actions have never shamed my church."

"So, you were baptized thirty years ago?"

"I certainly was," she huffed at him.

"Well, that's your problem. It wore off. You need another one."

With that, he picked her up and dumped her sideways in the fountain. She screamed and sputtered as she got to her feet. Mr. Harmon ran up to Dad and slapped at him with his puny-looking fist. Dad stared at him for a second.

"You know, Harmon," he said, almost grinning, "I admire a brave man when I see one, but if you ever hit me and I find out about it, you're in trouble."

With that, Mr. Harmon joined his wife in the water. Pastor Josephson was rushing to intervene, along with Father Cassidy.

"PAUL!" I never heard that kind of volume come out of Mom before. She was more than just angry. She was embarrassed and mortified.

Looking a little sheepish, he said, "Just trying to help."

Mom glared at him as some of our neighbors ran to fish the drenched Harmons out of the fountain. Dad seemed to melt a bit under Mom's harsh stare and he looked around for allies. Michelle and Anna Marie completely vanished. Holly just watched the Harmons in disbelief. I stepped back. My cheeks were redder than any apple, I don't think I was ever more embarrassed in my life. All I wanted to do was hide and pretend I didn't know those people. I had no idea what I should say or do. But I did know the party was over.

Dad did not. He found himself an unwitting ally in Father Cassidy. He and Sister Barbara were hovering around the Harmons now that they were dripping wet but at least back on dry land.

"Father," Dad said in a booming voice while clutching the priest's shoulder in an iron grip, "You know what I like about the Catholic faith? The idea of forgiveness. The ability of a priest to hear a confession and absolve the sinner of his fault. That's what I want right now."

"Confession?" Father Cassidy said blankly, "You're not even Catholic. And besides, you have to be penitent for your sins. And it's a private thing. And—"

"And I want it to be a public confession so the whole town knows how pent-it-al or whatever that word was that I am. If it means I'm sorry for my sins, then that's the word."

"I don't know what you want, but this farce—"

I could see Dad's muscles flex as he squeezed Father Cassidy's shoulder harder. A second later, a look of pain crossed the priest's face.

"Okay, okay," he said in defeat.

"Well, okay," Dad said back, unsure of what to do now.

"Bless me, Father, for I have sinned," I heard Sister Barbara coach him.

"Bless me, Father, for I have sinned," he repeated, "And tonight it was a doozy." His voice was loud enough for everyone to hear. "I embarrassed my whole family and ruined Amy's going away party. I really made a fool of myself and I heartily apologize, especially to my wife."

Mom still looked angry, but maybe not as angry.

"I also embarrassed my pastor and my whole church because I couldn't control my temper. I ask for absolutely-shun."

"Absolution."

"That too."

"Anything else?" Father Cassidy asked, obviously exasperated.

Dad shrugged. "Just your everyday run-of-the-mill sins. I don't think about them much so I can't say I remember them."

"What about throwing the Harmons into the fountain?" Father Cassidy raised his voice more than a little.

"Oh, that," Dad said slowly, "I have to admit, I don't feel sorry about that at all. In fact, I wouldn't mind dunking them again a few times." He looked around when he heard a few people laugh. "And I'm sorry I feel that way, too."

"So am I," Father Cassidy replied, rolling his eyes, "Paul, don't you think you'd do better talking about this with your pastor? Privately?"

"What's the point of confession that way?"

"Very well," Father Cassidy sighed, "Are you sorry for your sinful behavior?"

"I am."

"Do you even have a rosary?"

"No, but I have a couple rose bushes out back."

By now everyone was laughing or snickering except Dad and Father Cassidy.

"Okay," the priest said sternly while finally freeing himself from Dad's grip, "We'll do it this way. The first step of your penance is to apologize to these good people for your churlish behavior."

Dad glared at the priest for a bit then, without facing his victims, called out, "Elder and Mrs. Harmon, I sincerely apologize for my churlish behavior."

I failed to detect any sincerity in his tone, nor did I think he knew what 'churlish' meant, but it was a start.

"Next, I want you to apologize to everyone else."

"And the same to you all," Dad called out, like this was an apology.

"And on the way home, I want you to explain to your children why this is unacceptable behavior."

Does he even know this is unacceptable behavior?

"Yes, sir," Dad said.

"And next—"

"Apologize for ripping out your throat before you give me anything else?"

"No," Father Cassidy was unintimidated, "Come with me every Monday to Baton Rouge. We have a soup kitchen there to help feed the poor and unemployed."

"Every Monday?" Dad growled.

"For the next six weeks," Father Cassidy amended.

"It's a deal," Dad shouted, "Now, you see, if God can forgive me, the rest of you damn well can too."

There was a splattering applause for his sheer audacity, but people were leaving. The evening was ruined.

Dad tried to save the day by shouting out that there was still food, but he made too many people nervous with his temper. We just didn't know what he would do from day to day. We did have a few people continue to eat but most just left. It was time to go home.

Angus and Brigitte Nye were helping to get the leftovers on the wagon.

"Faucette just won't be the same without you," Brigitte said with a hug.

"Yeah," said Angus, "We'll be losing our one and only mermaid."

I froze for a second, then I remembered. When he found me on the creek, he called me a little mermaid.

"I'll miss you too," I said, "But you still have all your other nieces and nephews."

"And we just lost one and tomorrow we'll lose another," Brigitte sighed.

Mom and we children all hugged them goodbye while Dad stared into the night, waiting for the long farewell to end.

"Paul," Mom called, "Would you please come back and say goodbye properly to your brother-in-law?"

"I'm already in the wagon."

Angus walked over to him.

"You know, Faucette's a small place. It's bad for family to ignore each other. You yourself said you weren't mad about Edgewater anymore."

"It's not Edgewater."

"Well, won't you tell us what it is then?" Brigitte asked.

We were all around them now. Everybody wanted this to be resolved.

"It's the singing and dancing."

Singing and dancing?

"Oh, come on," Angus spit out, "Are you still going on about that?"

"Well, will you tell the rest of us what you're even talking about?" Mom said.

"It's the war," Dad said after he pulled himself out of the wagon, "Durrell and I were in the infantry. Angus here was in artillery. The Jerrys kept coming at us. The bodies kept piling high. Then they surrounded Angus' unit. We had to go bail them out."

"We only needed help because we ran out of ammo killing them folks," Angus added.

"That and the fact you didn't pull back when you had the chance."

"Talk to the Captain about that."

"Can't. He died. Anyway, try to understand what was

there. It was June. The bodies were stacked four feet high. They'd been there for days. The skin was turning green and black. The guts were bloating. I looked down on one, the face looked like it was melting, so many maggots crawling around. Rats were running around inside the uniforms eating…whatever. And the stench. Ruined my nose for years. I tripped over somebody's half-liquid leg and a whole cloud of flies shot up and flew around a few seconds before settling down.

"And we were exhausted. And we lost some mighty fine young boys. And Angus here steps out of the trench to join us. And he starts to sing and dance in harmony."

Dad planted his peg leg firmly in the ground and kicked his foot a bit in a dance imitation while singing and waving his hands in circles over his head, like he was twirling an imaginary cane.

"Oh, when the saints," he sang in a low bass voice.

"Oh-oh, when the say-aints," he switched to falsetto.

"Go marching in," bass.

"Go-oh marching i-in," falsetto.

"Oh, when—"

"Okay, we get it," Angus interrupted, "I had a 'war-moment.' I was tired, stressed, numb, excited. That's how I handled it. You never had a 'war-moment?' In all that time?"

"No."

"Well, that explains a lot of things."

"Like what?" Dad lowered his head a bit. We knew this to be another warning sign.

"Why you lose your temper and do dumb things. Why you throw people in fountains. Punch people. Fight so much. I figure my 'war-moment' got the war gone for me. You're still fighting it. Maybe you should take a midnight trip to the graveyard and dance with the dead for a moment. Can't hurt you none and might do some good."

"Everyone in," Dad said, rolling his eyes, "There will be no dancing with the dead."

That conversation was over. After we were in our places, the wagon jolted forward towards home. Brigitte and Angus were whispering comforting words to each other and we waved as we pulled on past them.

At the far table, sitting quietly, was Mr. Jarviston. He was finishing his cake. I nodded to him. Something big in my life just changed. Something much more than moving away. I was seeing the flaws in people now. I was growing up. He mock saluted me as we rode home in silence.

"By the way, kids," Dad said as the wagon clicked down the road, "As part of my confession, I want you to know that throwing people in fountains is bad."

"You were supposed to tell them why it's bad," Mom said through clenched teeth.

"Oh, right. It's bad because…Oh, who cares why it's bad? It just is."

Mom glared at him for a moment, then said, "It's brutish and uncivilized, hateful, mean-spirited, vicious, embarrassing, humiliating, just plain awful behavior. And they could have hit their heads on the concrete. And it's a reflection of everyone in the family. And the whole town is going to think we're ignorant and–"

Dad pulled her close to him and kissed her for a long time.

"I don't care if the town thinks I'm brutish and uncivilized. I only care that you know I love you."

She adjusted herself to snuggle up to him and the rest of the trip was quiet.

The next morning, we met Mr. Jarviston at the train

station. I had my frayed little carpet bag with me in one hand, filled with clothes and a few sheets of music. The other hand clutched my violin. It was my most treasured possession. It was a gift from the Countess and I loved playing it.

Mom, Dad and my sisters were there, as was Jason. My uncle Vincent and Aunt Sharon drove us in their truck. Aunt Sharon was five months pregnant. I told her she was having a girl before she knew she was expecting. I don't know how I knew, but I knew.

"I hope they let you come down to visit," she said while hugging me and swaying gently from side to side.

"Maybe it'll all be a mistake," Uncle Vincent said hopefully, "Maybe you can come back, just not as a daughter. You can be a second cousin or something."

Aunt Sharon poked him while Mom and Dad rolled their eyes. Mr. Jarviston seemed a little confused.

"Just trying to lighten the mood," he said innocently.

"We *like* a heavy mood," Aunt Sharon hissed.

I appreciated the effort anyway. I was just now getting used to Uncle Vincent's sense of humor. I hugged him because he was always there for us.

"As far as visiting goes," Mr. Jarviston said, "My opinion carries very little weight, but if Amy wants to visit next summer, I will recommend it. It would be a shame to have two families and lose one."

Which already happened with my New York family. When I still thought Aunt Mary was my real mother, I considered her and her daughter Julia and son Patrick to be my family. After she sent me to Faucette, I found out she was my aunt and my siblings from New York were cousins. It was a shock. I wrote to them all, but they never answered me. When Aunt Mary called the house, Mom never let me talk to her. The circumstances that led to my coming to Faucette caused a serious rift between them.

The goodbyes were said a dozen times. Saying it to Holly hurt the most. She looked at me with tear filled eyes but didn't say a word. I knew she didn't want to cry anymore. Neither did I.

Mr. Jarviston and I got on the train and I waved to everyone from the window. Gramma De Montfort arrived, but it was too late to get out to hug her goodbye. We all waved and waved until the train pulled out and they faded from view. Faucette was replaced by water and swamp. Since today was Sunday, my family was heading off to church to pray for my safety as we rode to Atlanta.

"Kind of sad to leave home?" he asked.

I nodded.

"Your Dad is quite the man," he went on, "Colorful. It doesn't seem to take long before people know he's there. Really dominates a party."

"It's humiliating. All my friends were there to see me off and everybody hightailed it before it started."

"Hightailed it?"

"Left."

"I know. I haven't heard that expression since the war. When we get home, you may want to forget the rustic phrases. Your family likes to impress people with their sophistication and proper use of language. Such informal talk would certainly be noticed in a not good way.

"Things will be different. Remember, your mother loves you. She gave birth to you. She wants to meet you and she wants you to love her back. She also wants what's best for you. When you start getting gentleman callers, she doesn't want them to lose interest because you sound… uneducated."

"I just skipped a grade, you know," I said, offended.

"And that's good. Just remember that slang is not allowed in your new home. Just follow the lead of your sisters. They speak marvelously, though I doubt they're as smart as you. None of them ever skipped a grade, anyway. Just remember: It's not how smart you are, it's how smart you sound."

I had nothing to say about that. I remembered something I heard sometime before. It is better to be silent and have people think you are smart than to speak and prove them wrong.

I stared out the window as we passed through Hammond. It was a small town, maybe the size of Faucette although its main street had more two-story buildings. Most of the stores were similar. People need the same supplies no matter where they live.

"Mr. Jarviston, aren't we taking a long sort of route?" I asked after Hammond was gone and swamp returned, with tall cypress trees rising out of the murky water.

"Call me Willie now, please," he replied, "You're Wentworth family. I'm a servant. The rules get reversed now. You are Miss Amy to me and I'm Willie to you. And yes, we're going the eastern route home in case the rivers flood. Also, your mother didn't want you going through New York City in case Gio tries to get you back the wrong way. I think you've had enough drama in your life."

It turned out to be a needless effort. About eight hours earlier, Gio the Giraffe and Antonio Dragucci were at their club, sitting in a corner booth and flirting with their girlfriends. Two men came up to their table and peppered them with bullets, while their bodyguards watched from the bar. Gio the Giraffe was no longer a factor in my life.

Chapter Seventeen

The Train Ride

It took two days to get to Pennyton. We got to sleep in
the Pullman car, which was not an experience I would want
to have again. The car was cramped, overpopulated and had
a bad smell. It seemed that not everyone made a point to
bathe before traveling.

Aside from his snobbish advice, Willie was a wonderful
travelling companion. We talked about life in New York
and my adventures in Faucette with my family and friends.
He almost seemed like a sophisticated replacement father.

"You don't know how much I'll miss them all," I told
him, "But Dad's behavior last night was embarrassing and
we had to call off the party. I won't miss things like that."

"Did you really have to call off the party? That woman
seemed to want to cause trouble. Was it necessary for her
to go there when she felt that way? Did she have to make a
scene? Did she have to pronounce judgement like she was
an agent of God? I think your dad was trying to save the
party. He just didn't know how to go about it the right way
and things went wrong.

"He can only make the decisions with the tools life gave
him. His tools seem to be intimidation, strength, and two
large fists. He is quite unique. A real handful for his wife.

But I clearly saw, from the moment we got here, that they both love you very much."

I nodded while looking out the window. I still wished Dad hadn't ruined the party.

"They'll be a phone call or a letter away. They didn't throw you out, you know. They wanted to keep you there. You have to look at things the right way. You aren't losing your family. You're gaining another family. You'll have a mother and six adorable sisters who'll be so happy to see you. The whole town of Pennyton knows you're coming and wants to meet you."

The forests broke in places here and there to display abandoned houses and fields growing weeds at breakneck speed. Rivers and creeks broke up the landscape with occasional small cities for our train to load and unload passengers. Louisiana became Mississippi, then Alabama. The red clay of Georgia guided us into Atlanta and we changed trains and direction.

The northern route was still green, but a different kind of green. The trees were different. Cotton and peanut farms surrounded us on both sides. Cars replaced horses and horses replaced cars as we went from rural areas to cities.

The cities became bigger and dirtier the further north we travelled. From Baltimore on north the air was darker and the scenery less green. Ugly brownstone buildings popped up everywhere. Unhappy looking people lounged on porch stoops, looking at the train as we went by.

"The crash hurt the folks here in the cities the most," Willie commented, "Factories all closed. People don't have money. They don't buy anything. No need to make anything. No need to employ anyone. When it isn't worth it for the farmers to plant crops, watch the cities go berserk.

Then it'll get fixed. Till then, folks are in for some rough times.

"And you'll want to be careful. A lot of the unfortunates blame the families with money for their situation. But that's not how it works. The economy is like breathing. You inhale, you exhale. Money floods the economy, then it becomes tight. Things will be normal again."

He was right, of course, but it took a long time for normalcy to return.

On Tuesday afternoon, we entered the Boston area. I changed into my Sunday dress since I wanted to make a good impression on my new family.

"You look lovely," Willie said, but his face said I looked quite a bit less than 'lovely.' The rest of the trip continued without incident.

Chapter Eighteen

Jerry Talkington

Boston was obviously much smaller than New York. It only had one skyscraper; the Custom House Tower, which stood tall over the nearby buildings. The city was larger than Baton Rouge, but I found the Louisiana Capital much more friendly. People packed the train station, milling about waiting for people to greet or locomotives to catch. Nobody smiled at us or said, 'Hi.' The station itself was functional but dirty. It didn't command awe like Grand Central Station or ooze charm like Baton Rouge.

"Repent!" A voice cried out, "Oh, you sinners, repent. The stock crash is only the beginning. The destruction of the world is at hand. You've languished in luxury and fallen away from God's Glory. Your rich and evil lifestyle may seem grand today, but everything will be taken from you and the only thing left for you will be the God you turned away from. Oh, sinners! Repent!"

The voice belonged to a middle-aged man with long oily hair and a cleric's collar. He was standing on a crate of some kind while he preached fire and brimstone. His audience did an amazing job of not noticing him.

"That's Reverend Sean McClelland," Willie said, "He used to run the Lutheran church down the ways. Then one day, he decided he didn't want to preach to people who already knew the Bible. He wanted the whole world to be his flock. These people ignore him just as much as his congregation did."

The air was hazy and the buildings all seemed to have a layer of soot. Most of the windows were dirty. Old newspapers littered the gutters and sidewalks. A couple of men slept in the alleyways, just off the main streets. Unkempt boys were running in circles, playing a baseball-like game in the street. Some girls played hopscotch on the sidewalks. They all scowled at me as we strolled past them. Being overdressed was not a good thing in this neighborhood. Luckily, we walked past them without incident.

"You will lose what you have until you *appreciate* what you have," the reverend continued, "Sorrow and poverty will be your future. The world is being swept away. Who knows what you will have left."

"Boston," Willie said as the voice faded, "Where streets are narrow and minds are narrower. At least Pennyton has a little style and character."

"It's very lovely," I lied, then added more truthfully, "I think I prefer Faucette."

"Don't judge a city by its bad side. Boston has a lot to offer. Ocean. Forest. Shopping. You are a girl after all. What girl doesn't like to shop?"

This one.

"The best fish in the world," he went on.

"Catfish?"

He paused as though I said something in Swahili. "Even better. Cod."

"I thought they made capes out of cod," I smiled.

"I don't believe that. Sounds too fishy."

My eyes lit up from the challenge.

"Are you going to be my of-fish-cial competitor?"

"*Cod* be. But they should be Atlantic fish puns. I have *Pacific* tastes."

He must have practiced that one. Now I had to think.

"I'm a big fin of puns, you know."

"Me too," he replied, "But they have to be *reel* puns. Nothing arti-fish-al."

"I surrender," I laughed.

He laughed too, "When we tell puns, people won't be able to count them. They'll have to weigh them on scales. That'll get the humorless folks all nettled. That'll be quite the tail. We would be at the top of the punster's guild."

"Guild?"

"Fish breathe through their gills."

"I got that part," I lied, "I don't know what a guild is."

"Oh. Like a union, only legal. Nothing fishy about them."

I was in the company of a true master of the pun.

The street was cobblestone, which I considered to be an improvement over the hard packed dirt we had down south. Horses and wagons begrudgingly shared the road with cars and trucks. Cars parallel parked on the sides, using every available space. Little (and not so little) piles of horse droppings dotted the red bricks. Some boys were inspecting them and picking up the drier ones. They walked with the load hidden behind their backs while trying to look innocent.

How disgusting.

Further down the road, I spotted their target. He was a well-dressed man sauntering down the street. A fancy walking stick twirled casually in his hand while he browsed by the store windows. The bushwhackers positioned themselves behind his back as he looked intently at a well-dressed mannequin.

He deftly jumped aside, allowing the first clump to fly by him and slam into the window. He batted another lump with his cane and the stool exploded with pieces flying everywhere, but mostly on his tormentors. He dodged a few more projectiles until he grabbed his nearest antagonist by the neck, using him as a shield as he steadily marched towards the other hooligans, who all dropped their ammunition and vanished from the street.

He proceeded to carry his nearly-choking prisoner to the nearest pile of excrement where he dropped him to the ground.

"Eat it," he said.

He stood straight after he dropped his captive, exposing what was once a face. I knew that some veterans of the Great War received terrible head wounds that left them disfigured. I knew they wore specially made masks, called facial prosthetics, designed to cover their scars and make their appearance less shocking. But this man's mask defied the purpose. It was dyed a bright crimson. His left eye socket held an obviously wooden eye with a painted green iris over a white background. If that wasn't horrifying enough, he pasted green and silver glitter to his artificial orb. His face was nothing short of nightmarish.

"Jerry," called out Willie, "Jerry Talkington. Over here." He waved and started over to talk.

The one-eyed man turned his head searching until he found my escort. His good eye (which was brown, not green) was caustic with rage but he calmed down when he saw who was approaching him. The boy tried to get up and run away, but the cane beat down on his lower back and he sprawled back to the ground, crying with fear and pain.

"Eat it," he whispered loudly to the sobbing waif.

"Just the man I wanted to talk to," Willie said smoothly, as though nothing was going on, "I wanted you to meet the newest addition to the Wentworth family."

He searched for me but saw that I wasn't following him. A man with the face of a monster who used a cane to beat children with until they ate manure was not a man I wanted to get too close to for some unknown reason.

He waved me over, obviously irritated, so I hurried to them and curtsied to Mr. Talkington. I couldn't help but stare at his wooden eye.

"This is Amy Wentworth."

Wentworth?

"Hi," I squeaked out in fear, not bothering to correct the last name.

"Another Wentworth, eh?" he sneered, "The others seem to be a bit taller."

"She only came out ten years ago. She's younger."

"The evil little monster came out ten years ago," Talkington stated flatly.

"They were switched at birth."

"So, you're the new evil little monster," he said while sizing me up, "You don't look very monstrous to me."

How do you respond to something like that? Especially coming from him.

"I'm reformed."

The boy was crawling away slowing, trying not to be noticed, but the cane came down hard on his rear end. He cried out again.

"You know, Jerry," Willie said, "I've heard it said, 'To err is human, to forgive divine.' Why don't you let him go?"

"He hasn't apologized."

"I'm sorry. I'm sorry," the boy cried.

"He didn't say 'sir' when he apologized."

"I'm sorry, sir. I won't do it again."

"You should be ashamed, attacking a war veteran like that," Talkington sneered at his victim, "Not just any veteran, but a wounded one, hobbled up and crippled forever because he fought to keep you and your thug friends safe."

"I'm ashamed and sorry, sir. Please let me go."

Talkington stepped back.

"Choose your enemies better next time."

The boy scurried off, damaged and humiliated, but at least he didn't have to eat horse manure.

"Catching the bus to Pennyton?" Willie asked, "We're going that way. Just looking for Chester. Care to join us?"

"I'd think about it, Willie," Talkington said laconically, "But your reformed little monster objects. I noticed she doesn't seem to like my face." He bent over to me with his hands on his knees and stared at me with a loathsome grin. "I can take my mask off for you if you want, Little Miss, but I don't think you'd like me any better."

Why did Willie invite him to ride with us?

"It's not your face, it's your—" I stopped. I felt that each word I said was making him angrier.

"My what?"

"Temperament."

"Temperament?" he repeated softly.

"Like you're mad at the world."

"I *am* mad at the world. I can't even walk down the street without those filthy beggars attacking me. And here I am, a wounded, disabled, veteran barely able to walk. Hardly capable of making a living. Two steps away from starvation and one step above poverty. Almost completely helpless in the city. I shouldn't have to deal with any of this garbage."

Of course, he didn't say garbage. If I spoke like him, my mouth would be introduced to a generous serving of lye soap. However, I thought it wise to not mention that fact to him. I also chose not to mention that he didn't look hungry and dressed rather well for someone who was impoverished.

"No, you shouldn't, Mr. Talkington," I simply agreed. I had doubts about the helpless part as well but decided not to voice them. "My dad in Louisiana lost a leg in the war and nobody treats him badly."

He'd kill them if they did.

"Does your dad have a face?"

"Well, yes."

"I'll give him my leg for his face."

"I think it's too small for him." My effort to maintain this very strange conversation was failing.

"Just as well. I think his brain might be too small for me, the more I talk to you. Just remember, Little Miss Wentworth, the world's different. The days of the rich families lording it over the rest of us are coming to an end. Soon you'll be running on the streets, like those little demons. You don't always get to pick your friends but choose your enemies wisely. You don't want me to be one of them."

"Absolutely," Willie added cheerfully, "Now, if you're done making an ass of yourself, we do have to go. And don't you mistake youthful stupidity for evil malice. They'd have gone for anybody. In fact, it wouldn't surprise me at all if I had been their target if you weren't here first. Now, how about that ride?"

Please say no.

"I still have some things to do down here, but maybe

next time. Why didn't you just take the train all the way there?"

"It won't be coming for another half hour. But as you wish," Willie smiled, "Come along, Miss Amy."

"My pleasure to meet you, Miss Amy," Talkington said, trying (unsuccessfully) to sound pleasant.

"And you, Mr. Talkington," I replied, hoping my nose wouldn't grow because of such a lie.

After he left, I asked Willie how he came to know Mr. Talkington.

"I grew up not far from Jerry. I played games with his father, Gideon, years ago. Their family ran the town's only pharmacy. The Talkingtons were above my station in life, of course. Pennyton was small then. I was the son of a tailor and had no desire to follow the family business. That was for my older brother. My father only had love in his heart for one child. Sadly, he had four. My brother is the only tailor in Pennyton. That's why I buy clothes in Boston.

"Regardless, there weren't many boys our age, so class distinctions were ignored for quite some time. Gideon asked me to join the army with him when the Spanish-American War started. I went in as a Private but came out as a Sergeant with my effort and his help. When the war was over, I drifted about for a bit. No job, no prospects. I ran into him one day and he secured my position here. I've been with Mrs. Tillie for twenty-five years now.

"Gideon is no longer with us, but I kept tabs on his children. Jerry went to college, graduated and enlisted as an officer. Left behind his wife and two sons to go. He asked me to re-enlist and serve under him as a Sergeant when the war started. Jerry was a Lieutenant for only two days. He got a flamethrower in the face and was sent home. He lives in town, not far from us.

"His brother owns the pharmacy in Pennyton and runs the Republican Party up here. Jerry inherited a nice house from his mother along with some funds that give him an income. Add that to his disability, he survives quite nicely as far as money goes. But you saw his…temperament. His wife took the children and ran away one night when he got in a rage, so he lives alone with his anger. I always try to talk to him when I can to let him know he can still reconnect to people. But I fear he will always throw away his future because he can't accept his past."

"Can't the army help him?"

"He got the mask. And a pension. And a silver star. Everything else is up to him."

"What about the rest of Gideon's family? Don't they try to help him?"

"Well, his wife remarried and lives in Ellsworth—"

"Ellsworth?"

"It's in Maine. She figures it's close enough if he wants to reconcile with his sons but far enough away that his rage would peter out before he got there. He never hurt anybody, but he can scream so loud you'd think hell opened its doors."

"How sad."

"And he has three brothers who work in the family drugstore. And two sisters who live in the Midwest. He also has five nephews and nieces, but he never met any of them. He figures he'd scare them with his looks."

"Not his behavior?"

He gave me a fake look of confusion. "Behavior? What's wrong with his behavior?"

We laughed as we walked on down the road. The air was cooler up here and a light breeze blew off the ocean to keep the mosquitos away. There was some grass, bushes, ivy, and the like but the good people of Boston didn't seem to like trees. What they had were shrubby and small.

"There's Chester, now," he said, pointing to a Packard waiting down the street.

The chauffeur wore a gray uniform, neatly pressed. He was a tall man, with slicked back hair and a permanent scowl. He waved to us in an insolent way and we hurried over.

"Chester Connery," Willie said pleasantly, "Meet Miss Amy Wentworth."

He tipped his hat with a frown.

"Miss Amy," he said politely and opened the door for us.

"Thank you, sir," I smiled at him.

"Please don't call me 'sir'. Just Chester will do," he responded formally.

"None of the servants are to be called sir or ma'am," Willie told me, "Just their first name or last name. It's part of the privilege of being a Wentworth."

"Thank you," I said, "It's almost the opposite of home. Why do you keep introducing me as Amy Wentworth? My name is Collins."

"That will be remedied," he replied, "The fact that Mr. Wentworth pulled this switch was truly awful, but your name should always have been Wentworth. And my instructions are to introduce you as Amy Wentworth. And you'll love your new name. You'll have six sisters who are adorable most of the time. It would be awkward for you to have a different name, don't you think?"

"No, not really."

"Well, the rest of your family thinks it would. By the way, they're all looking forward to meeting you tonight at dinner."

"All at once?"

"Oh yes, Miss Leticia and Miss Melanie will be there, along with their husbands. Melanie has a little boy named Sammy. He takes dinner in the kitchen because of his age. The rest of the family takes dinner together, all at once." He smiled.

I smiled back. At least when I moved to Louisiana, I got to keep my name. I wanted to scream.

CHAPTER NINETEEN

INTRODUCTIONS

The ride to Wentworth Founding was uneventful. We drove through Pennyton down Main Street. The post office, combined with a gas station and general store, stood on the corner of Elm Street, the first crossroad. A small office complex across from it showed nothing interesting to me. Talkington's Drugstore was across the way. A tiny bank completed the corner. Beyond those businesses lay posh multi-story homes with perfect yards and pretty flowers.

The next intersection was Godfrey Way. A Presbyterian Church dominated one corner. The City Hall sat across the street. A library was to our left and across from it was a small building that sheltered the police and fire departments. Private residences intermingled with a few more businesses but most of them just had the name of the owner, not what kind of service it provided. Just past Godfrey, a little train station faced a small but beautiful park with flowering dogwoods and tall oaks. Wrought iron benches dotted a cement walkway. It was lovely. Just past it and set quite a way back from the road stood a tall ugly brownstone factory labeled Langston Canning.

Further down Main Street, we turned into a driveway and approached two iron gates, not entirely flush with each other. It would be no problem for me to squeeze through it, if ever I wanted to, but I could see no reason why I would ever even dream of leaving this little paradise. The gates were automatic and opened for us, slowly sliding sideways along a track down the inside wall.

The house loomed over us as we approached. I had never seen a four-story home before and I was awestruck. Even though the paint was faded and peeling, it exuded grandeur and elegance, yet it made me uneasy. Something ominous lurked out of sight, I could just feel it. The premonition vanished when I saw the staff formally lined up outside to greet me, which I found embarrassing.

"This is Miss Amy," Willie informed them after he gave me their names, "And you will love her. She's certainly a wonderful traveling companion."

There was the cook, who we called Cookie, a pleasant middle-aged woman with a permanent smile. Two maids, Zelda and Kathleen, were introduced next. Zelda smiled at me, but Kathleen stayed neutral. They were followed by two relatively young men named Tom and Bob who I found out were footmen, though footmen were no longer really needed. Their jobs were mainly to help with the yardwork and do the heavy labor around the house. Bob seemed nice enough, but he looked at the ground the whole time. He only said 'hi' and that he 'helped around.' I don't think he even saw my face, but I was sure he became an expert on my shoes since his eyes never seemed to leave them. Tom was very self-assured, in an unpleasant way. He looked at me with a mixture of superiority and disrespect. Zachariah, who preferred to be called Zach, was the middle-aged and grizzled gardener. He obviously spent a lot of his life outside where the sun, wind, rain, and ice took their toll on his skin. He spoke with a New England accent that was a bit hard for me to understand. Other servants were lurking about in the house, too busy to come down. There were also a lot of unintroduced mosquitos that seemed to like my taste. I was feeling a bit overwhelmed. And itchy.

Willie dismissed them all and they went their separate ways, though Cookie lingered back for a moment.

"You come into the kitchen for a snack whenever you want to, sweetie," she told me with a smile, "There'll always be something for you. We do need to fatten you up a bit. It's not healthy to be so thin."

At least she didn't talk about my being short.

Willie retrieved my violin and carpetbag and we headed towards the front door. Four of my older sisters were on the porch studying me. They mostly all looked alike. Three had my color hair, not quite blonde, not quite brown, but they wore theirs tied up in fancy styles. The other girl had a rich, chestnut color and wore it loose, like a lion's mane. We just had to all be sisters, since there was such a family resemblance. The one with dark hair had brown eyes, the rest, blue. I had the only green eyes in this family. All of us had slightly upturned noses. Even though we looked alike, my sisters were all prettier than me since they were well-groomed and cared for all their lives. They dressed in taffeta, gossamer, and silk. I could see why Willie almost sneered when I told him I wanted to wear my Sunday dress from home. I looked and felt like a country bumpkin.

"Hi," I said, wondering if there was some kind of etiquette I was supposed to use when meeting such upper-class girls.

"Hi," came the responses, though the oldest said, "Well, hello."

"Well, come on up so we can see you," said another.

"Yes, do," said the smallest, who was at least three inches taller than me, "We've been dying to meet you. We heard so much about you."

All I heard about them was that there were six and I only found out today that two were married and I had a nephew.

"I hope you heard good things."

I would think everything they knew about me was good, but I did have a past.

"You mean there's some *interesting* things, too?" said the one with dark hair, "Do tell."

"Now girls," Willie reminded them, "She doesn't even know which of you is which."

"Or if there is a witch," I added, enjoying a bad and confusing pun.

"A which?" said one confused sister.

Willie laughed, "As in which witch is which? None of us have been to Wichita, but we'll all have a sandwich."

"Only if we've seen Dunwich." They all laughed back at him. This must be some kind of family routine.

"Introduce yourselves first," Willie told them.

"I'm Charity," said the tallest one, who wore a pastel taffeta dress with lace sleeves, "I'm the oldest one still at home. I play the piano a bit. I hear you're good with a violin. We'll play together." Not a command, but certainly not a suggestion.

"I'd love to."

"Good, Mother expects it, you know," she added.

No, I don't know what she expects. I just got here.

"My name's Lisa," said the next, "I take voice lessons

but I'm not really very good. I'm fifteen and why is your hair so short?"

Her hair was the longest of the four. It reached down to her waist and was pinned back with a bone clip, but still had lovely curls. Her bangs covered half her forehead. She was one of the loveliest girls I ever saw. We may have been sisters, but our shared features looked much better on her than me.

"We had to cut it off when the girl behind me in school put gum in it."

"That was mean. Why didn't you just put some castor oil in it? That'd gotten it out."

I shrugged, "We didn't know."

"That's okay," Lisa said, trying to recover, "It still looks pretty. It's just a little out of date, like your dress. I hear you like adventures. So do I. We can do things out of the house together. Very un-prim and un-proper. You know, fun."

"We like fun too," came the next, the one who made a point of saying they knew nothing interesting about me, "I'm Clarice, but just call me Claire, at least when Mother's not around. She's kind of formal." She lowered her in imitation, "If I wanted you to be called Claire, I wouldn't have named you Clarice." Her voice sped up and went up half an octave at the end.

The other girls laughed.

"I think your hair looks fine for an orphan girl. You look like a little wood sprite. And there's nothing wrong with wearing an old-fashioned dress. I was kind of expecting something out of style with you coming from the south and all. I'm just happy you have all your teeth and they're not all black and rotting."

"Oh. Well, we brush our teeth down south, too," I said politely. I didn't think I was going to like Claire very much.

"I'm sure they do. The toothbrush was invented in the south, you know. Anywhere else and they'd have called it a teeth-brush."

There was a bit of an awkward silence for a second.

"I'm Millicent," said the last girl with a voice that both drawled and whined, "I'm twelve. I like adventures, too, but I would prefer them without guns and alligators."

So would I.

"I'm sure you understand," she went on apologetically.

"Oh, I do," I replied, "I hope you don't think I went looking for robbers and gators. They just kind of found me."

"Yes, well," Willie said bluntly, "Let's go meet your mother, shall we?"

I nodded. He took my hand and we left the others. He opened the front door.

"They aren't coming along?"

"They already met their mother."

"Oh," I could think of no better response to that.

We all said goodbyes and I left with Willie.

"It was just a joke," I heard Claire defend herself, "I thought it was funny."

The responses from the others were unintelligible as they all spoke over one another. At least I wasn't the only one who thought she sounded nasty.

The front door opened into a great hall with marble floors and Persian carpets. Portraits of people long dead adorned the walls, along with shelves of mementos and a large grandfather clock ticking in the corner. Ahead of us were double doors that led into the ballroom. To the left, a long table and chair stood quietly in the corner, next to an enormous stairway. Another staircase was to my right. They curved gracefully to reach the mezzanine of the second floor. The wood rails and posts gleamed from polish and there wasn't a spot of dust anywhere. It was especially nice because I wasn't the one cleaning it.

The stairs were surprisingly steep. It was great exercise to get to the second floor. I was almost out of breath when we reached the top and looked down at the foyer. Hollywood movies could not have made a more beautiful house. We continued down the left side through a spacious hall with several doors, all closed.

"Kathleen?" I heard a voice call out from one of them.

"No, it's only us," Willie replied.

The door opened and small woman stared out at us with crooked, unseeing eyes.

"Us?" she asked with a smile, "You have my new cousin with you?"

Willie glanced at me with a world-weary expression.

"Veronica Pierpont," he said with a forced cheerfulness, "This is Amy Wentworth."

She looked to his left, not knowing I was to his right.

"Actually, my name is Amy Collins," I said, while taking her hand and squeezing it. I didn't know what else to do. The only other blind person I met was Mr. Benson, and I wasn't entirely sure if he was really blind or not. There was no doubt with Veronica.

Her head turned to me when I touched her and she smiled. She was obviously well taken care of by the family. Her dark hair had gorgeous long curls, pinned back with sparkling combs. A gold chain necklace adorned her throat and two pretty lobster-shaped earrings danced under her lobes. She carried a winsome attractiveness, at least to my eyes.

"It won't be Collins for long," Willie said, sounding annoyed.

"I was planning on just calling you Amy anyway," Veronica smiled, "I am so happy you're here and not a boy. The last one had character flaws. You see my room here? I want you to visit me. It's hard for me to get out, you know."

"It's hard for me to get up the stairs," I agreed, "They're so steep. You don't go downstairs?"

"Oh sometimes. Kathleen takes me to the park on occasion. She's one of the maids but also my companion. We use the back staircase. The steps are smaller but it's curvy. If I get out of the house, she goes with me so I can find my way back. I fear my family finds me quite embarrassing in public, so I'm only allowed outside with her. My glasses make me quite visible, you know."

"You wear glasses?" I was confused. She was blind.

Willie interjected, "Dark glasses to protect her eyes. Keeps dust and things out. But fascinating though this conversation is, I do think it's time for Amy to meet Mrs. Wentworth."

"Of course," Veronica said with a smile, "Aunt Tilly is so wonderful. You'll love her, I'm sure. I know you'll be busy today but do come and see me. I know I can't play games or music, but I still like to see people."

Odd choice of words.

"I would love to," I said and squeezed her hand again as Willie looked on impatiently.

"Veronica gets a little lonely sometimes," he said to me as we moved on down the hall, "When she was five her parents died in a ballroom dancing accident."

"A ballroom dancing accident?"

"Yes, they were upstairs doing a waltz on an open veranda and just kind of...danced off."

I stopped and glanced at him with my best are-you-kidding look.

kidding look.

"They have since put up a balustrade so it wouldn't happen again," he went on and we continued down the hall, "Poor thing had just lost her sight, too. Measles. Her mother was Tillie's…I mean Mrs. Wentworth's sister. Mr. Wentworth wanted nothing to do with her. He couldn't dangle her in front of some aristocratic family in search of a good match to add to the Wentworth empire."

The hall was shaped like a half-moon. As we walked past Veronica's room, I glanced out an open bay window at the yard. It was lovely and well-manicured. Zach was obviously a very good gardener. We angled down a bit more, passing closed doors with elegant glass knobs.

"Your sisters' rooms," Willie informed me as we passed them.

We continued to an alcove at the end of the hall and turned to a closed double door of polished oak. He knocked on it three times.

"Come in, Willie," I heard a musical voice call out.

Willie took my hand as we entered.

She was sitting up in bed wearing a sensible nightgown. A tray with an empty cup and plate was to her side and the blankets were kicked down to her ankles. She carried an elegance about her I had never seen before. She was a true lady, and I was in awe.

Willie stepped forward but I was momentarily unable to move my legs due to nervousness. He shot me an annoyed glance and pulled me forward and I followed his lead. It was ten steps to get to the bed and I made a perfect curtsy.

"Mrs. Matilda Langston Wentworth," Willie said ultra-formally, "May I present your daughter, Miss Amy Nancy Collins Wentworth."

She slowly sat up and got out of bed. She seemed a bit shaky but still had her arms out and I went to her for a big hug.

"Welcome home, Amy, dear. It's so good to know you're alive and my daughter and family and here and…*I'm so happy.*"

Of course, she was crying by the time she finished. Nothing says happy more than crying, I suppose.

"It's good to meet you, Ma'am," I said, at a loss for words.

Chapter Twenty

Zelda

Willie hurried me out of the room so she could 'recompose herself.' After all, I was new to her. Dinner would be served in less than an hour and I was expected to be refreshed and dressed in suitable attire.

"You'll be fine," Willie assured me, "We prepared for you, you know. We have some fine dresses that were made for you in your closet."

We walked down the hall the way we came, going by Veronica's room where I heard music being played on a record player. She was talking to another girl who I assumed was Kathleen.

"This will not be a formal dinner, tonight," he went on, "Just family. But Mrs. Wentworth wants you properly dressed. We have to see about your table behavior, you know."

"Table behavior?"

"Well, yes. We'll find out how much instruction you need before we can take you to public events. You wouldn't want to be embarrassed by using a salad fork to eat your main course in front of everybody. How mortifying."

"I see," I said.

"You'll do well."

He opened the door to a room across the hall from Veronica. I liked that. Veronica seemed nice. I knew she would be a wonderful neighbor. My room was huge. An old-fashioned dresser with a gigantic oval mirror faced the doorway, so we could see our reflections as we entered. There was a double bed with a canopy between two windows on one wall. Two chifforobes sandwiched a bookcase on the other wall. A music stand with sheet music stood in the corner, next to my violin and bag, resting on a small bedside table.

Zelda was fluffing the pillows. She was young but her uniform gave her a grown-up air. She glanced up at us and smiled.

"Well, hello, Little Miss," she said with a *very* Irish brogue, "I hope I set your room up to your liking?"

I looked at Willie, then I looked at her. "This is all mine?"

"All of it," Willie responded, "And you remember Zelda? She does some light housekeeping upstairs and supervises your room. She will keep it clean. You'll be too busy to dust and sweep and things. And Zelda is responsible for you. She'll draw your bath and provide clean towels. If you need another blanket, you'll call her."

He pointed to a blue strap right above the bed. "You pull on that and she'll be here in a flash. That rings a bell to the kitchen. Now obviously, you have to be reasonable. Can't ask her for a unicorn."

He smiled for a moment, but then it was gone.

"Zelda," he ordered, "Dinner in an hour. You will have her bathed and dressed and in the dining room." He turned to me. "Amy, Zelda helps you dress, fixes your hair, puts on your jewelry, and she will escort you to the dining room, where you will join the family. You probably didn't have people soaping you down and drying you off. Just remember, it's her job and she doesn't want to lose it. She will also give you tips on how to be ladylike. Don't make it difficult for her. Hmm?"

"I won't."

"Good," and he left, closing the door behind him while she very visibly relaxed.

I, however, was quite nervous about all this. She guided me to the closet where I chose a green chiffon dress and sensible black shoes to wear. Oddly enough, they both fit perfectly, like they already knew my size. Then we walked across the hall to the bathroom. She started the water and I picked the temperature after the heat set in. I had seen things like this in the movies but not in real life. Baths were quite arduous things where I came from.

Zelda had a bottle of calamine lotion and a cotton swab out for when I undressed. I was quite embarrassed and shy, but she whispered to me, "It's okay, Miss Amy. I won't look. But you must be clean tonight. Also, you seem to enjoy feeding the mosquitos.

"Tonight is the first impression for both of us. With you, it's a lesson on how Wentworth ladies act. With me, it's my job."

From butchering chickens and cleaning fish to having assistance taking a bath. Life is strange.

Chapter Twenty-One

My First Dinner

It turned out that Zelda was a wonderful help to me. I felt quite glamorous when I was introduced for dinner, wearing my gown and a simple gold necklace. My ears weren't pierced yet, so they were unadorned. Just as well. Having my ears punctured like that sounded like it would hurt and I try to avoid pain. Zelda stood off to the side as I made my entrance. Unfortunately, no one told me where I was supposed to sit. I started for the end of the table by my new sisters, but they were pointing to the seat next to Mother. I saw Zelda blush as I hurried to my spot.

"I want you to sit here in the guest of honor spot so the others can see you," Mother said, glaring at Zelda for a moment.

"Others?"

"All family, Sweetie," she replied.

So far, it was just us. My sisters were opposite me and down to the far end of the table. The servants all were standing in front of a China hutch. Veronica wasn't there. She never ate with the family I was told. She refused to be fed and spills were not tolerated.

Soon, Willie came into the room and announced, "Mr. and Mrs. Felix Hooker, along with Bonnie and Dianna."

"Shirley is my older sister and Felix is of the Bedford Hookers, of course."

What does that mean?

"Oh, like the Civil War general?"

"No, dear. From the family of Thomas Hooker, the man who founded Connecticut."

Uncle Felix looked old enough to have helped found Connecticut. Aunt Shirley wasn't far behind. It turns out they were slightly younger than Gramma Morris, but time was not so kind to them. They both had leathery skin and thin white hair. She obviously wore dentures. I could tell because they were crooked. His teeth looked real, but they seemed sharp enough to belong in a lion's mouth.

Bonnie and Dianna entered with them.

"We introduce them as *their* daughters, but in fact, they're *his* daughters. That relationship is obvious when they bear their fangs when they attempt to smile," Mother confided in me, "Your Aunt Shirley allowed him to adopt them and give them his name, but it was not an act of forgiveness or generosity. She controls the purse strings now. And more importantly, a scandal was avoided. Of course, they won't inherit anything. Felix and Shirley have their own children."

I nodded. The girls were about Charity's age and sat opposite of Claire and Millie, so I didn't really talk to them. I did have to stand up and hug Uncle Felix and Aunt Shirley before they sat down.

Soon a woman of about thirty slipped in and quietly sat at the very end of the table. My sisters all whispered a formal greeting and she nodded back with a kindly, if fake smile.

"Amy, that is Nadia, your governess. You may stay seated. You two will talk tomorrow."

"Yes, Mother," I said politely, nodding to Nadia.

"Mr. Henry Langston," Willie announced formally.

"Henry is my dear brother," Mother told me as he made his way towards us, "He was a stage playactor in his younger days. Then he made movies. You remember the *Captain Pope* serials?"

I shook my head.

"Captain Pope was the heroic ship master, always chasing his archenemy, the evil pirate Captain Learned. Henry was Captain Learned. He walked around on stage and in the movies with a big green parrot on his shoulder. It even had a name. Quincy." She giggled a bit. "Quincy the parrot. Henry played that role for almost thirty years. Then the studio got a little careless and a cat ate Quincy. He still talks to that bird like it's on his shoulder. It can be a little discomforting, but just smile and act like it's normal. He's been a little eccentric ever since his wife passed on."

Gray and stoop shouldered, I guessed Uncle Henry to be about sixty, but an old sixty. He walked slowly, like he was afraid of falling. He wore an old-fashioned suit, the kind with tails. Most of his hair abandoned ship, so to speak, but he kept what was left trimmed. My sisters all said demure greetings to him. Millie also greeted Quincy with an impish smile.

Uncle Henry ignored them as he kissed mother's cheek and gave her a one-armed hug. After they whispered their greetings, he came over to me and clicked his heels in as formal an introduction as I ever received.

"Mr. Henry Langston at your service," he said, "And this is Quincy, my beloved friend and companion. The parrot who stuck with me through thick and thin. You can't see him, I'm sure. He died a tragic death years ago, but his spirit keeps me company."

I stood up and curtsied to him. "I hope you and Quincy will always be friends to me," I said formally, though I felt a little ridiculous.

Charity and Lisa were looking down at their plates while Claire and Millie were whispering and giggling a bit. Mother had a sincere smile for me, though.

"Oh," he said with a delighted expression, "We will be. We will always be friends. Here now, would you like to pet Quincy? He won't bite, you know. And he especially likes to have his chest stroked. Nice and smooth."

He guided my hand up to his shoulder and leaned down to my height. I rubbed my curved fingers up and down on empty air with a confused smile, while Mother beamed with happiness. Soon, he mimed letting Quincy stand on my forearm and he petted the bird.

"Why, Henry," Mother said, "I am so surprised. You haven't let anyone touch Quincy in years. Not even me nor any of the girls."

"I know I'm jealous," Claire whispered with a dry sarcasm. The others giggled.

"He's afraid you'll eat him," Lisa giggled.

"No, thank you," Claire responded wickedly, "But maybe Millie will know how to cook him properly."

Uncle Henry gave them a murderous glance and Nadia leaned forward and whispered something to the offending parties.

"Amy's special. She can appreciate things," he said indignantly.

But I prefer real things.

"Maybe you should go back to your perch," I said to Quincy.

"Good idea," Uncle Henry responded, "I think Claire and Lisa are jealous that Amy's getting all your attention."

More giggling. Uncle Henry straightened up and sat back in his chair, occasionally whispering something to his invisible little friend. He faced his sister Shirley across the table but neither of them spoke to each other.

Next to arrive were my two oldest sisters and their husbands. Melanie and Larry Lee sat next to Uncle Henry. Larry nodded to me without speaking. Melanie gave me a fake hug. The kind where she put a hand on my shoulder and almost touched her cheek to mine.

"I'm afraid there will be too many people tonight for us to talk at all," she said, "But I'll make a point to get together with you soon. I promise."

"Sammy is in the kitchen?" Mother asked her.

"Yes, Cookie is giving him his dinner."

"Sammy is your nephew," Mother told me, "He just turned one a month ago. He'll show up after dinner. You know how babies can make a meal an ordeal."

I didn't. My only experience with babies I could remember was when I lived with Aunt Mary in New York. She adored feeding Patrick when he arrived. He got more love in a meal than I got in the ten years I lived with her. It was messy but hardly a problem. I thought changing diapers would be the real ordeal.

My other sister was Leticia, the eldest. She and Marvin Adams, her husband, did not have children. Or personalities. They sat next to Aunt Shirley and Uncle Felix with sour expressions. They greeted Mother, of course, but only acknowledged me with a nod after we were introduced.

The last person to arrive was Aunt Gladys Parker, my father's aunt. She was a frumpy older lady who looked like she never smiled in her life but spent years practicing how to scowl. I curtsied to her, expecting her to growl at me but she was very pleasant. I could not have been more wrong. She complimented me on my grace and balance and said I was adorably pretty. She later invited me to visit her in her house that overlooked the ocean.

Mother said a line or two of grace and dinner began. The servants walked around the table with platters of deboned chicken, mashed potatoes, and sweet corn for the family to partake. Millie and I had ours already on our plates. We had to be thirteen to help ourselves. As the evening progressed, I learned that there were other rules. Lots of rules.

One rule was that in formal gatherings the children always sit at a table in another room. There will be names on the napkins so we will know our places. If it is a party, the children will eat beforehand and be upstairs and out of sight, though we can watch through the banister rails if we must.

Another rule was that there would be no admittance to the third floor. Ever. Father's office was up there and it held important papers. The ballroom, where the formal business parties were held, would most likely never be used again. All the other rooms were unoccupied. Even so, it was still off limits.

Willie cleared his throat.

"Oh yes," Mother went on, "That applies to the fourth floor as well. That is where the women servants sleep. The men's quarters are next to the garage. And those rooms are *expressly* forbidden."

My part of the dinner conversation went well, I thought. Aunt Shirley was quiet and only spoke in one syllable sentences. Uncle Felix was not open for conversation at all.

"I wish you two would fight at home and leave it there," Mother said sadly.

"We're not fighting with each other; we're fighting with traitorous relatives," Aunt Shirley huffed while folding her arms. Conversation over.

"That would be us," Uncle Henry leaned over and said to me in a whisper.

"Us?" I asked, confused.

"Not us. *Us.* Quincy and me," he answered, "Their oldest daughter Iris married a man they disapprove of. So they disowned her. I let them live with me. She's going to have a baby, you know."

"I didn't," I replied, highly interested, "Why are they being so mean?"

"She married a jazz clarinetist."

"So?" I blinked.

"Jazz is black music."

"She married a black man?"

"No, a white man who plays black music. On a black instrument. At night, when it gets dark," he whispered in a menacing voice as though he was reading from a horror story.

"Isn't a clarinet black in the daytime too?"

"It plays Beethoven in the daytime. White music. But he plays it at night. Not Beethoven. Jazz."

"So?"

"They think jazz brings shame on the family."

"It does," Uncle Felix said, who was obviously annoyed at being talked about as though he wasn't there.

We needed to work on the volume of our whispering.

"See?" Uncle Henry said triumphantly.

"Felix and Henry," Mother said warningly, "Please stop with the jazz talk."

"Quite right," Uncle Felix said, "No jazz talk. A competent musician would play in the symphony orchestra.

Mozart and Beethoven. Iris married a loser who is always begging for money. She made that decision. She lives with that decision."

"He never asked for money," Uncle Henry said calmly, "Just a place to stay. Right now, he plays in a colorful little club in Boston with other *white* musicians until he hits it big."

"Hits it big? Playing Jazz? Please."

"So, we took them in," he told me while petting his bird, "Gets lonely in the house, just us, eh, Quincy?"

He devoted his attention to me now, "The Von Bright family is very old, and they disowned him when he stated his career was to be a jazz player. They would have nothing to do with a son who denigrates the family name."

He sipped his drink for a second.

"His father forbade them to see each other until he came to his senses," Uncle Felix said, "We wouldn't allow *her* to have anything to do with that miscreant. So, she ran off with him and eloped. That's so typical of her. Now they're disowned by both families. They can take care of themselves."

"And that's a good thing," Mother said firmly, closing the conversation, "If they're old enough to marry, they're old enough to take care of themselves. Now Amy, I hear you are good at reading."

"Yes ma'am," I replied, "I read to my family at home."

"This is home, we're your family, and don't call me ma'am, please."

"Sorry. I read *The Wizard of Oz* books to my former family in Louisiana."

"I loved those books," Uncle Henry said, "And they apply in life, too. Like Tip became Ozma, JP the fourth became Amy the first." He laughed and whispered to his bird.

"You see?" he said while ducking his head back, "Quincy likes it. He likes you too, Amy the first. See how he spreads his wings? He does that when he laughs."

"Oh."

"Like Tip became Ozma, JP the fourth became Amy the first," he repeated. Then he straightened up while calming the imaginary bird down by stroking its back. The adults were all shaking their heads sadly as he played with his invisible friend. "What's that? Good idea."

He turned to me with a lucid glance.

"You can read to Veronica. I'm sure she would love the company. She gets lonely, you know. Her mother was such a sweet thing. Our sister, you know. The first of us to…not survive."

Not survive?

"And even though Tilly is such a wonderful person, she won't let her so much as have meals with the family."

"That is so unfair, Henry," Aunt Shirley took up for Mother, "It wouldn't be right for her to eat at the table. She won't tolerate Kathleen feeding her and she'd get embarrassed when she spills. How can we expect her to use utensils when she can't even see them?"

"Doesn't that seem rather cruel?" I asked Mother.

"It does to me," said Aunt Gladys from her spot, "But I never say anything since it was Josiah's rule. Maybe Tilly can change it in the future. Just because Veronica's blind doesn't mean she wants to be in permanent exile. And besides, what harm is there in a little spill? We can always change a tablecloth."

"I never thought of that," Mother mused, "But that is right. I own this house now, and I will start setting the rules from now on. Veronica will have dinner when it's just family. She is one of us, you know. We can give it a try. I wouldn't want any of my daughters thinking I'm cruel."

She gave me a quick little hostile glare that melted into a smile.

"Not with soup or anything like that, though."

"Sandwiches?" I asked.

"Sweetcakes," Claire practically shouted and got her knuckles rapped by Nadia, "I could share them with her."

I don't think she knew how heartless she sounded. She later said she thought she was being funny. Nobody else did, though.

It didn't matter. Dessert was presented. Boston Crème pie, of course. It was wonderful. If I ever got to go back to Faucette, I would have to tell Cici about it. Our restaurant would be filled with dessert eating customers.

All in all, it was a successful evening. I favorably impressed all the adults that night. I found a new dessert. And Veronica was now allowed to eat with us.

"See you soon," Melanie whispered to me before she left.

"That went well," Charity told me on the way upstairs, "Mother forgot about our playing the duet that we didn't practice."

I nodded. If I was going to play with someone, I'd rather we play well together. And that meant practice.

"Best of all, Uncle Edgar and Aunt Vera didn't show up," said Millie.

There was unanimous agreement. They were Father's sister and her husband.

Lisa told me, "And if you think Mother is prim and proper, you should meet them. They don't believe in fun of any kind. Young ladies don't run, jump or play."

"We don't burp, belch or fart," added Claire.

"Or talk, whisper or mumble," added Lisa.

"We just sit quietly until we explode," Millie finished while the others giggled.

I was glad I missed Uncle Edgar and Aunt Vera.

Chapter Twenty-Two

Veronica

Bedtime was regimented in my new home. Zelda made sure my teeth were brushed and hair combed. She liked my hair short since it made her job easier.

"Not my choice," I replied, explaining about how we cut it after the evil Laura Sauveterre put gum in it.

"Well, nothing like that happens here. Such behavior would be the talk of the town and the family of the girl would hang their heads in shame. You'll be happier here."

Perhaps, but I missed my sisters. Even Anna Marie, though not as much. We slept in the same bed back home with Holly and we'd talk till we fell asleep. Holly brought all the joy in being the big sister. I had no little sister here. It wasn't much fun.

Even after the light went out, it was not so dark. The moon was full and there was a light under the door. After Zelda's footsteps faded down the stairs, I could hear music. I got up and opened the door and saw that Veronica's door was cracked open. I went over and knocked.

She turned towards the noise. "Kathleen?"

I replied, "It's just me. Amy. I heard music."

She walked over to the record player and expertly picked up the needle and put it on its holder.

"I'm sorry. I thought it was low enough that you wouldn't hear it."

"I like it." I really didn't. It was too different, with instruments competing instead of harmonizing. It was jazz, she told me. It certainly wasn't jazz as I knew it in Louisiana.

"Cousin Bixby plays music like this in a club, but I never get to hear him. He married Iris, my cousin. Our cousin now. I can't go to see him play. No one knows what to do with a blind girl. I'm not thrown to the wolves or anything, but there's so much life I'm missing because they're afraid I'll get hurt if I'm allowed to live."

"I understand. But you know, every time I made my own decisions, they turned out bad. I got lost in the swamp. I got shot. An alligator attacked me."

"Those are called adventures. The other girls are hoping you'll be taking them on a couple before you're all grown up."

"I'm not sure they'd want the sort of 'adventures' I've had."

"True, getting shot might be unpleasant, and the attack by the ferocious beast might be a bit much, but still…how fun."

Is she serious?

"I hope you'll take me on an adventure, too."

She is most definitely serious.

"Whenever I have the spare time, I'll take you out of the house and we'll walk in the park or something. Maybe I can read to you."

Just getting out of the house will be an adventure for her.

"Really? I would so enjoy that. Kathleen takes me out for walks occasionally, but we stay on the grounds. I embarrassed Uncle Joe. That's why I'm all alone here and everyone else is on the other side of the house."

"I'm across the hall."

"Yes, I know. I would have thought they'd have put you over with the other girls. In either Melanie's or Leticia's old room. But it's nicer like this. We can pretend you're the little sister I never had."

She laid down in the bed and patted the side next to her.

"Come lay down here and we can talk to each other, just like sisters do."

It never came up that I didn't like being the younger sister and her request made me a bit uncomfortable, but I did as I was told. We talked for a bit. I told her about how she could have dinner with us from now on and she was excited, if apprehensive.

"I wouldn't worry about it," I said, "I don't think I ever had a meal where there wasn't a spill of some kind."

I told her about my life in New York and Louisiana, my adventures, my fights. How the trial surprised us all. It was quite a shock to leave home and come here. She was greatly sympathetic.

Then she told me about the books that Kathleen read to her. She pointed to a shelf that had a few novels stacked and I began reading a mystery to her. It made me long for my home in Faucette where I read aloud to the family almost every night. I remembered that Annette also loved mysteries. I missed her. I would probably never see her or Guy again. California was a long way away.

After an hour, I went back to my room.

She called out softly behind me, "Come back anytime, it'll be good to have someone to talk to."

"I will," I promised.

Chapter Twenty-Three

Nadia

Zelda woke me up early for breakfast. Waffles with fresh strawberries and whipped cream. This was as good as anything we served in our restaurant and at the end of the meal, I asked Zelda to thank Cookie for her effort. She looked surprised but nodded.

I was eating with my sisters while Nadia looked on, giving me advice on how to hold my fork at the exact angle so it looked more ladylike. She also taught me the proper way to cut food with a knife. The fork in left hand with index finger on the crown. The knife is for the right hand and it gently saws down to the plate, cutting everything free before lifting it. Afterwards, we younger girls got dressed and waited in the drawing room. Since Charity was close to her societal debut, Nadia worked with her privately for an hour. The others were already reading their books. I had a copy of *The House of Seven Gables* waiting for me.

"You'll love it," Lisa whispered, "That house is haunted, just like ours."

Millie nodded excitedly, "We only see them sometimes. But they really are there. Especially upstairs in the private ballroom. They appear in the mirrors. They fade away after you look at them, but you can actually see them."

"Of course, you can't speak to them." Lisa continued authoritatively, "It's not like ghosts can talk, you know."

"Oh," I responded dryly, "Maybe it depends on the ghost."

"Oh? So that ghost in the swamp of yours was true?" Claire challenged.

They waited for me to respond with growing excitement, but Willie came in with tall glasses of iced tea.

"Ghosts again?" he said with his eyes rolling, "I never saw one around here and never will. And if any of you do, it will be a matter of grave concern."

"That joke shows great spirit," I laughed back.

"Yes, well, do your reading. Nadia heard you talking and asked me to remind you that good little ladies don't talk when they're supposed to be reading. Good little ladies do what they're supposed to. You know she prefers it quiet as a tomb, or there will be grave consequences."

And so, like the good little ladies we were, we stayed quiet and read our assigned books. Millie showed me a paper she wrote on *The Scarlett Letter*. I proofread it for her and made my only criticism.

"You say she has blond hair. When it's a girl, she has blonde hair, with an 'e' at the end. Boys have blond hair without the 'e.'"

"What kind of a dumb rule is that?"

"It's French," came Nadia's voice from behind me, "So it's a French rule."

"My first father said it's because the French can't speak or spell," I added helpfully.

"Your first father was an ignorant man. French has its own grammatical rules. That's because it's a different language. It allows for our gentle feminine nature by giving us an extra letter as an acknowledgement of our extra intelligence. Time for your routines now, girls."

The others were sent out to practice their horseback riding while Nadia and I got to know each other. I would have preferred to have a conversation with her while riding, but that wasn't an option.

"Horses and inexperienced riders are a bad combination. Horses and distracted, inexperienced riders can be a complete disaster, no?"

I nodded, thinking of the Countess and poor Fiona.

She looked a bit down her nose at me. She was a pretty lady, I thought, not beautiful or anything, but nice to look at, with dark blonde hair and liquid brown eyes. She took a pill of some kind and swallowed it with water from an ice filled glass.

I'm sure she was right but riding around with my new sisters seemed preferable to lessons.

"Life would be so much fun if ten-year-olds ran the world," I thought out loud.

"Perhaps, but they don't," she smiled, "Just remember, there's a ten-year-old in every adult. We all wish we could go back to being ten and make better choices. That's why I'm here. To help you make good choices *now*. And a good first decision for you to make is to not hit people."

I sighed. Yes, I hit my evil stepsister and got sent away to Louisiana. But she broke my violin. Yes, I hit Billy Kaker, the school bully, and split his lip. But he pushed me first. Why were adults so unfair? I think she sensed my resentment and changed the subject.

"You did bring your violin, yes?"

I nodded.

"Good. Let me hear you play."

I retrieved my instrument from the room and played the few pieces I knew.

"They are very elementary pieces, no?" she said to me, "You waste your talent on peasant music. I shall see to it that we get a tutor for you. You should be playing Beethoven and Mozart. Music that befits your class, yes?"

I guess I like peasant music.

"And please don't go thinking you like peasant music. You'll be like your cousin's husband. He plays jazz clarinet. Pure noise. And he won't stop and play real music, or even just get a regular job. His whole family disowned him. Won't give him a cent. He plays at some rat-infested club in South Boston for pennies and he has an expecting wife."

"I hear jazz in Louisiana all the time," I replied, a little annoyed at the snobbery, "And I like it."

She smiled, "And you are a musical blasphemer. Generations of your family on both sides hang their heads in shame. At least there are no such things as jazz violinists."

"Tell that to Joe Venuti."

"Who?"

"Never mind."

She sighed. "You should be more appreciative of your home and family. Otherwise, you'd be living in that swamp, eating snakes and drinking moonshine all day wondering why people say the world is round when it's flat as far as you can see."

I was speechless as she paused for a sip of water. Then she changed the subject.

"I come from Raconavia, Slovenia. My family name is Mitzack, hardly a royal name. We had a small dairy farm and my father worked hard to deliver milk and cheese to his clients. We were upper class peasants, you might say.

My father decided we were better than the other farmers who only grew crops to sell and trade. His children would marry aristocrats. He made sure we all went to school and became as educated as possible.

"While in school, I was infatuated with a young man named Andre Rashishi. Sadly, he did not love me. I was to be married to Aleko Pope, the second son of the Count of Janish. Quite the catch. Aleko was dashing and handsome. My father was quite proud of this match.

"There was a problem. Not that there was a lack of love. Aleko loved my father's money, and my father loved Aleko's aristocratic position. But Alina Dorsheck, my best friend, was the one who loved Aleko. Sadly, she was to be married to Andre. The Dorshecks were peasants like us, but much more well-to-do. I don't think Aleko or Andre ever even spoke to either of us until we were formally introduced by our parents. The boys were separated from the girls quite a bit in those days. We could only admire them from afar.

"Andre was in love with Danica Sobolov, the mayor's daughter. She was promised to Dmitry Szanbo, a general's son. There was a blood feud that was winding down between the Szanbo family and the Sobolov family. Their marriage would end it, everyone hoped. Our feelings were not a factor in any of these decisions. After all, we were just children.

"We didn't complain. Our parents knew what was best for us. At least everyone thought they did. They figured we were young and the love would grow. We hoped our parents would change their minds. After all, the world was changing. Maybe something would happen as we entered our teenage years. As you can see, our situation had all the makings of a great Shakespearian tragedy.

"Things changed, all right. Austria declared war on Serbia on my birthday, July 28, 1914. I was thirteen. Slovenia was part of Austria-Hungary at the time, but we were our own people and longed to live our lives free of the Hapsburgs."

"Hapsburgs?"

"The royal family that ruled Austria-Hungary. The young men dutifully signed up to fight and the war was disastrous. By the time I was seventeen, the Italians invaded, time and time again. We defeated them, of course, but the cost was tremendous. Cities were wasted. Our village was destroyed. Almost everyone was dead or gone. People lost their homes and farms. So much was destroyed. So much wasted life."

She was slurring her words just a little bit by now. I thought whatever her pill was must be making her drowsy.

"At first the war didn't affect us, but by 1917, all the young men were soldiers or dead. Andre and Aleko enlisted right after they turned sixteen. Aleko went in as a cadet second lieutenant. He looked so handsome in that uniform, with the epaulets. Andre was such a heart-stealer as well, though he was merely an enlisted man. They both had such futures ahead of them."

She sighed, blinking back tears.

"We women could only stay home and pray that nothing bad would happen to our friends, our future. My father was too old to fight, but he did everything he could to help the village as long as it didn't cost money. Food, milk, cheese, he gladly gave to anyone who needed it. But his cash and gold he buried in the barn. He showed it to me in case anything ever happened to him. I was to take care of my younger brother. My older brothers both were dead.

My brother-in-law was killed in battle. My older sister fled to Vienna.

"My younger brother ran off and joined the army in January of 1918 when he was only fifteen. Those disgusting pigs let him enlist. He was killed in battle before spring was over. Our house was destroyed by cannon fire. My father and I were sleeping in the barn, above the cows, what few we had left. My friend, Alina, volunteered as a nurse's assistant and was killed by a stray rocket blast.

"When it all was over, only Aleko came back. Andre, the love of my life, was shot for desertion. The war lasted longer than his bravery.

"Aleko had changed. War etched a lifetime of sadness on his face. I met him as he was wandering toward what was left of our village. I almost missed him; the fog was so thick. He was a full lieutenant by then. But it didn't seem to matter much to him. His uniform was dirty and ripped. His face was covered in grime. He wore a military backpack carelessly slung behind him and he carried what looked like a large hatbox.

"'Nadia,' he said when he saw me, 'You are here. I am glad you survived. Everyone else is gone. It's just the two of us, just like it was arranged. First on Earth, then in Heaven. We are here. Poor Andre died. They shot him. Our side. I don't think I'll ever forgive those Italians. They were supposed to be our allies, but they invaded us. Twelve times they invaded. Twelve times we beat them back. They were merciless. They killed Alina, you know.'

"'I know,' I said quietly. I could tell he was damaged by then.

"'How could I have not known Alina loved me? How blind. I fell in love with her, even though we knew it could not be. At least not here. We were going to live in America when the war ended. So, we set up the hospital again and we stayed together until I was called back to duty. I heard the next week the hospital was destroyed. Even though I could be killed for desertion I hurried back for my dear Alina. But when I came back, Alina was dead.'

"He was crying so I moved closer to comfort him. But I was repulsed by his odor. The smell of death. It was all around him. Nauseating. Unclean. I drew back, but he caught me around my waist and kissed me. The scent was everywhere. My mouth was filled with it. My nose rebelled. My stomach was retching. It was like kissing a corpse. A long dead corpse.

"I pulled back as far as I could and broke away. He tried to hold me close, but the box was jarred loose and fell to the ground. I saw Alina's head roll out. Oh, my Lord, I will never forget it. Rotted flesh. Maggots moving all through it. The dead eyes staring at me.

"'You see?' he told me. I looked up to face him, fear and dread overtaking me. I was afraid to run. I didn't know how he'd react. 'My Alina. She loved me. She followed me to war. She was the one. They were going to bury her in a mass grave. They wouldn't let me claim her body. So, when they weren't looking, I took her head with me so we could give at least part of her a resting place of her own.'

"He seemed to forget me as he tenderly picked up the head and picked out a few maggots and flicked them away. He held it towards him and stared into those lifeless, decomposing eyes. And then he kissed it. And that was enough for me. I turned away and ran into the fog. I ran home."

Her eyes filled with tears and she wasn't even looking at me. When she stopped talking, I thought the story was over but didn't move, in case I'd break something fragile in her.

"My father told me I still needed to marry him. His family had connections everywhere and I was still guaranteed a good life with him.

"But he's *crazy,* I said to him.

"'Women have been marrying crazy men ever since they invented marriage. Crazy men have money. See how you feel after he buries the head and comes to terms with her death.'"

"Come to terms? I came to terms the second her head rolled out of that box. I was afraid of him. His total fearlessness of that dead woman wasn't natural. I knew he must have been touched by a vampire. No fear of the dead, that shambling walk. Those dead eyes did something terrible to him."

"I thought vampires only come out at night," I replied, "No, wait a minute. I didn't think they were even real. They're just fairy tales."

"They are more than fairy tales. They are quite real, just not the way you think of them. They only have their powers at night. That's when their teeth grow long and they get their extra strength. And real vampires are dead, filled with rot, decay, and disease. And people with no fear of the dead will be cursed to walk with them."

She took another sip of water and stared at me intensely.

"I dug up the money my father buried and took half of it. I ran off to Koper and boarded a ship to Barcelona. From there, I went to London. In London, I met Mr. Wentworth and he offered me this job. I threw away my chance to become a wealthy aristocrat to become a servant. But I am happy here. We never need money to be content in life. We only think we do."

She shook her head like she was coming out of a trance.

"And such as it is, that is my story. I am sure there will

not be a war in your life to throw you into chaos. There's no need for any more wars."

Her ability to tell the future was about as good as mine. In less than ten years, the world would be at war again.

"Now you are in good circumstance, yes?" she continued, "We must show you how to make the most of it."

Doing schoolwork was a relief after hearing that story.

Chapter Twenty-Four

Time for a Party

After my new sisters returned, we met in the backyard. It was nice, with a paved path heading east that divided the lawn in half. Croquet had been set up in one half, near a large, well-trimmed hedge that could have passed for a fence marking the northern and western boundaries of our property. The Palmers lived to our north, they explained. The Palmer children squeezed through the hedges years ago when they were young and played with Laticia and Melanie. They all grew up, left for college and no longer played croquet.

"That's because the older you get, the less fun you can have," Claire said.

"Well," Charity argued, "I think as you get older, you learn to have different kinds of fun."

"You mean like with boys?" Milly made a face, "Hugging and kissing and holding hands? After he wiped his nose with his knuckles? No thanks."

"Older boys know better," she laughed, "At least the ones that count."

"And then they want to get married and boss you around all day," Millie continued, getting herself worked up a bit, "And then they do that thing of theirs and pee all over you to get you to have a baby. I wish we were Catholic so I could be a nun!"

"That's what happens?" I asked, mortified. When Mom and I had *the talk*, none of *that* stuff was ever mentioned.

"Absolutely not," Charity said, taking charge, "Millie, it's time you spoke to Nadia. You know just enough to be dangerous. Now, since Amy here has never played croquet, it's time we teach her. No more of that dirty talk."

They were kind and generous and decided I should go first, since I was the youngest and newest.

"Isn't the youngest always the newest?" I asked.

"Well, yes," Charity replied, "But the newest isn't always the youngest. Aunt Gladys was the last to arrive last night which made her the newest guest, but she was the oldest at the table. Sammy is the youngest, but he never even made it to the dining room."

"And he's so cute," Lisa added, "Unlike the last little boy we had in this place."

"Let's just play," Charity said firmly, glaring at Lisa for a moment, "Amy, let me show you how to use the mallet."

So, I played my first game of croquet. I found out rather quickly that my going first was not a kind and generous gesture after all. I also learned that they played not to win, but to annihilate their opponents, especially the youngest. It seemed that any time I got near the playing field, someone's ball clicked mine, usually Claire's. I was smacked miles away from the game. I soon developed a serious hatred for croquet.

When we finally finished, we plopped down on some outdoor chairs by a table and one of the maids set out a pitcher of lemonade for us.

"Did you really talk to a ghost?" Claire asked while the other girls leaned in to listen.

"Well, yes, but it's not much of a story," I replied and told them how I wandered into the swamp near home thinking it was a meadow and met Sarah, a little girl who showed me the way out. She knew my name and told me not to leave before my time. I explained the legend that anyone who saw Sarah had a friend or acquaintance die within a month. Then there was a robbery at our family cafe and one of the robbers, who I barely knew, was shot to death while I was slightly wounded.

"We read that in some old newspapers Willie showed us," Claire said, "But I didn't read the ghost part."

"Maybe the reporter was a ghostwriter," I quipped to blank stares, "Or not. He probably thought no one would take the story seriously with that in it."

"Makes a good spooky story," Millie said, "Is it really true?"

I nodded.

"We have ghosts here," Lisa said.

"I know," I replied, "In the mirrors in the upstairs ballroom."

"That's right," Lisa said, "I've seen them myself."

"How do you even get in there?" Charity asked, "It's always locked."

Lisa shrugged, "Not always."

"Sometimes I can hear them. They walk around the hall and occasionally, when I'm reading, a shadow walks between me and the light," Millie added.

"Sometimes I put my brush down on the right side of my dresser before going to bed, but it's in the center when I wake up," Claire said.

"That happens to me," Charity nodded, "I just thought it was one of you sneaking into my room because you think my brush is better than yours."

"Why?" Claire asked, "A brush is a brush. They're all the same."

"Not quite," Lisa said, "Ours are all flat, but hers is curved."

"What difference does that make?" I asked.

"It puts a bit of a curl in your hair," Lisa replied.

"You're sneaking into my room and brushing your hair at night?"

"No," Lisa said innocently, "I sleep at night. I saw you brushing your hair last week before I went to bed. I noticed it then. You left your door open."

"I never leave my door open. Besides, I wasn't even here last week. I was visiting Uncle Thad and Aunt Beulah in Vermont, remember? Ruby had her coming out party and they invited me. I wasn't even home. Nice try."

"You were here," Lisa insisted, "You were humming something and brushing your hair. You were wearing a gray dress."

"You know I don't have a gray dress."

"You're not scaring me," I said, though to be honest, the conversation was getting a little creepy, "I already spent a night here. I didn't see or hear anything."

"You're in the west wing. You'll be saying this house has haunts in it before the week is out," Charity pronounced with great confidence.

"That's why we are all on the east side," Millie confirmed, "Fourthy, that's what we called our brother, was on that side of the house. He absolutely tormented Veronica until he was put on the fourth floor with the servants. He said he saw her all the time. Dressed like a maid and walking down the hall until she disappeared."

"There's also the green ghost by the pond house," Claire stated.

"There's a house on a pond? Like a houseboat?"

"No, silly, there's a pond, and we have a guest house right next to it. But whenever people stay there, they complain that a woman is crying and screaming in the middle of the night, right around midnight. 'No, no, no!' she screams. Then they hear a gigantic crash, as though the glass from the French doors broke all at once, like something, or someone was thrown through them. Then there's a big splash, but when they look out, the water is calm. The doors are untouched."

Lisa added, "Father has the house kept up, but the servants only clean during the day. Whenever we have guests, they stay over here. Lord knows we have the room."

"Not all of them," Charity said, "He always had Mother's family stay there."

"Did they see and hear all that?" I asked.

"I don't know," Charity said while the others shrugged, "I don't think anyone asked. They'd be a might perturbed if they thought Mother and Father put them in a haunted house, you know. Anyone would."

"What's it like?" I asked, curious. I had never been in a haunted house. My one supernatural experience was outside in the open air. And it wasn't scary. At least not until it was over.

"What's what like?" Charity asked.

"The house. Is it big and lopsided, with bats in the attic and creaky doors and rattling shutters and—"

"Amy," Millie interrupted, "You'll give me nightmares. We've never been inside that house. Father would throw a fit."

Callous though it may sound, what 'Father' wanted didn't matter much to me. This was a man who threw me away like a sack of garbage because he wanted a son.

"Well, how about Mother?"

"Mother?" Lisa said blankly while the others looked at me, confused.

"Would Mother let us take a peek and just see what it looks like inside if we don't make a mess or anything?"

"That's a great idea, Amy," Millie squealed with delight, "We can spend the night there."

"We can have a sisters party," Lisa added.

"It'll be so much *fun*," Claire chimed in.

"You're the greatest," Charity nodded excitedly, "You just got here and already we'll have an adventure." She raised her arm up dramatically, as though she were pointing at a marquee sign. "Is the guest house haunted? Find out with those intrepid Wentworth sisters on their first exciting adventure."

"I never said 'spend the night there,' I just thought we could take a peek inside."

"You're being shy," Charity encouraged, "Being the new girl and all. Spending the night will be so much better. Cookie can make popcorn with sugar and we'll have the electric refrigerator stocked with soda pop."

"And we'll turn the lights down low and tell ghost stories with each other," Lisa added.

"Real ghosts?" I asked.

"Well of course, silly," Lisa replied, "We'll fill you in on all the legends and stories of Wentworth's Founding. There are enough spooks here to fill a graveyard."

"Sounds like fun," I said with no enthusiasm.

"It will be fun," Charity said, hugging me, "It'll be so much better than being alone in our rooms until we fall asleep from sheer boredom."

"I wasn't bored. I spent some time with Veronica, listening to music." I lit up with a fantastic idea. "I know, we can take her with us."

"Veronica?" Lisa asked with no enthusiasm, "She can't see. How will she be fun if we're looking for ghosts?"

"I was thinking more along the lines of helping eat the popcorn and telling ghost stories. Kathleen reads mysteries to her. Maybe she tells her ghost stories we haven't heard yet. Besides, she's terribly lonely. How often do you or anyone else visit her? She's blind, you know."

"That's a great idea," Claire said, "She can be the adult. You know how Mother will ask about grown-up supervision. She can be our official adult. And since she can't see, we'll be able to do whatever we want, so long as it doesn't leave a mess."

"I was thinking we would include her, not use her," I said, highly annoyed.

"Yeah, Claire," Lisa defended, "I think when you run your own home, you'll have your maids cram a broomstick up there rear-ends so they can sweep the floor while they dust."

We all broke out laughing, though I was uncomfortable with the joke and the fact I thought it was funny.

Chapter Twenty-Five

Getting Prepared

"Why do you want to spend the night together in the guest house?" Mother asked us, "Amy, don't you like your room? I know it's on the other side of the house, but I really like having Melanie's and Leticia's rooms stay the way they were when they lived here. I suppose I could move you over to one of theirs."

"I like my room, ma'am," I replied, "And I like talking to Veronica and everything—"

"Stop," she lifted her hand imperiously, like the Countess would do when I made a mistake playing my violin. Then she continued, "You are my daughter, not my maidservant. No more 'ma'ams.' Call me Mother like the other girls do."

"Yes, Mother," I said respectfully.

"Why do you girls want to spend any time in the guest house? Not one of you showed any interest in it before."

"That's because Father thumped our ears if we mentioned it," Claire said.

"Oh," Mother said thoughtfully, "That *would* be discouraging."

"We just want a little party," Charity said, "We can go over there and enjoy each other's company and talk and get to know our new little sister." She patted me on the head as though that was affectionate instead of annoying. "You know she's so far away from us. If we all spend the night at the guest house, we can just stay together until ten o'clock and go to sleep then."

"With no adult supervision? You'll be up till three, calling the servants every five minutes to make you tea and cakes. That is, unless the house settles a bit and then you'll come running back, waking everyone in the house because you'll think you were attacked by a ghost. And it'll throw off everyone's day."

"No, we won't," Claire said. I had already learned that her voice always had a defiant, almost resentful tone to it, especially now. She was not going to be helpful at all to our cause.

"We'll have an adult to supervise us," I said gently, "Veronica will be there."

"Veronica," she said flatly, in a voice that carried no confidence in our selection. Not even a little bit.

"She's a great choice," Millie said exhibiting as much enthusiasm as her whiny little voice could carry, "She's an adult. She's twenty-five."

"A quarter of a century," Lisa added.

"That's right," Claire agreed, "How adult can you be before you get too tired and worn out to have fun? Soon all she's going to want to do is sleep in the sun and tell old stories while drinking strained prune juice. And she's closer to thirty than she is to any of us."

I closed my eyes with disappointment. Obviously, my sisters were not well versed in the art of negotiation.

"Clarice," Mother said slowly, "Why is it that out of two million sperm, *you* had to be first?"

"Veronica can take care of us. She'll have the cord to

call the servants in case something happens. And she can shut the whole party down if we get to be too much for her," I said, "And it would do her good to be with us. She gets lonely, you know. And we'll all be there. What could possibly scare us?"

"A mouse, a spider, an owl in the tree, rain on the window—"

"Mother," said Charity through clenched teeth, "If we see a spider, we'll kill it. We'll feed the mouse to the owl. It's not going to rain and I don't recall any of us being scared by rain anyway."

"Thunder and lightning, I meant."

"We won't get scared," Charity said firmly and we all agreed.

"Could we have the chance, please?" I asked, trying to look fetching and innocent.

"Yes, please," they all said at once, realizing that 'please' had so far been left out of the request.

"Veronica as the adult?" Mother asked again doubtfully.

"Well, yes," I said, "I'm sure she likes to have fun, too."

"What about Kathleen?"

"Kathleen can come too," Lisa said agreeably, "Maybe she knows some good ghost stories from Ireland."

Lisa could be very unhelpful at times.

"So, you'll be running home at midnight because you've just scared yourselves silly. Wake up the household and crowd me out of my bed because you've seen shadows in the night."

"Well," I said, seeing that this really wasn't working out well for us children, "Maybe I could play my violin for you before we go."

"You play the violin?"

I looked at Charity. She shrugged a bit, obviously just as confused as I was.

"She does, Mother," Charity said gently, "You wanted us to play a duet last night. Remember?"

"No," she said with a yawn, "But that sounds nice. Have Willie set up the guest house for you. Now, I'm tired and ready for my nap."

Nap? She never got out of bed in the first place. I looked at her clock. It was three in the afternoon.

"Oh and do get some sleep. Don't forget that you leave for the Grable party tomorrow. You'll be gone till the weekend. I'm sorry, Amy, but you won't be going. It's a catered affair and it's too late to get you an invitation."

"She can have mine," came four helpful voices. Somehow, it didn't bother me that I was missing the Grable party.

"Nadia will be escorting them," Mother continued after sneering at them all, "Maybe you and I can find something to do together."

Conversation over.

We tumbled out of her bedroom to prepare for the outing, clamoring to the kitchen for the required snacks and drinks. They only wanted King's Crown Cola and popcorn, which sounded good to me. Afterall, who ever wants healthy snacks? My job was to tell Veronica she was invited, wanted, and expected.

At first, I had no doubts she would want to join us, but as I got closer to her room, the more it occurred to me that maybe it would have been better to ask her first. Especially since the whole thing now depended on her being there as the required adult. I didn't want her to feel like we only invited her because we needed her. I wanted her to feel wanted. Included. I knew what it was like to be left out. I didn't like it.

"I don't understand why you want me to go," she said, "What can I do? Someone has to guide me there. And up the stairs. Around the room. To the bathroom, if needed. I think you would all get tired of me after a while."

"I wouldn't," I said truthfully, "Besides, it seems that it's my party, so I can invite whoever I want."

"But I'd be useless."

"No," I replied, trying not to set off verbal mines, "You'd be the adult in the group. Mother wants a leader to keep order. Someone with sense. And who's more sensible than you?"

"Do I look like a piece of toast?"

"I'm sorry?"

"You're buttering me up like toast in tomorrow's breakfast."

"Not my intention," I said not entirely truthfully, "But Mother thought it'd be better with an intelligent adult with us. And you're intelligent. And an adult. And if you're there, it'll be more fun. What could possibly go wrong?"

"Well, I better go, then," she laughed, "Any more butter and I'll drown."

CHAPTER TWENTY-SIX

DINNER WITH MELANIE

Melanie joined us for dinner that night. Again, she left Sammy with the staff. He was more comfortable in the kitchen anyway. Melanie didn't exactly exude warmth and affection. She certainly didn't strike me as the type of woman who dealt with diapers or spittle with stoic grace.

"I am so glad we can talk a bit tonight," she said while towering over me when we greeted each other with a hug. She displayed an odd necklace of what looked like small quartz crystals.

"I wanted to spend some time with you last night, but it was so hectic. My friend, Ursula Chzerick, and I read up on your adventures. You're almost famous. And your name isn't even Wentworth yet. Ursula is coming over for tea tomorrow after your lessons. You'll love her."

"She tells fortunes," Lisa said dryly from her spot next to Millie.

"She reads palms," Claire added from the other side.

"Well, she does have the gift," Melanie said smoothly, "And she is one of Boston's most gifted psychic readers. Anyway, you'll just love her."

I noticed Millie rolling her eyes.

Dinner went well again. Veronica joined us but stayed

quiet and only ate bread. Since my food was already cut up, it was easier for me to not make any tragic mistakes.

Melanie wanted to join our outing at the guest house, but Mother firmly quashed the idea by loudly saying, "You need to raise your son, not pawn him off on the servants."

"Amy's playing her violin before we go," Millie told Melanie to soften the blow.

"Oh? I heard you played well," Melanie brightened, "I'd like to hear."

I wasn't sure I wanted to play anything after Nadia's criticism, but they started to applaud, so what choice did I have? I trotted upstairs to my room. When I opened the door, I thought I heard footsteps behind me. Light steps, like a small woman or child would make. I turned around but no one was there.

"Hello," I said, maybe a little loudly.

There was no answer, so I slowly got my violin, nervously looking all around. Satisfied it was just the house settling, I hurried back downstairs.

With Charity on the piano, we played a duet of *Nearer My God to Thee* while the others sang. Even though we never played together before, we sounded very good. We just played the music as it was written instead of personalizing it like some people do. It may have sounded a little stiff, but we played well together.

We received some applause when we were done and performed some other songs. Charity suggested some classical pieces, but I didn't know any of them. We stayed with things like *Oh Susanna* and *The Streets of New York*. The servants brought Sammy in for Melanie as he was tired and fussy. They quickly hugged everyone and left. It was just past seven. Time to go to the guest house.

Before I could get to the stairs, Mother called Charity and me back.

"You two play masterfully together. Now, Amy, Nadia told me she thinks you have potential with your instrument and I concur. I shall see to it that you continue your lessons. But I agree with Nadia that what you have learned so far is pleasant for a child, but I want you playing more mature pieces. Now, being that you are a girl, you have no future as a musician, but it might make you more attractive to a potential husband later in life. I will schedule you lessons from a real teacher who can have you playing proper music instead of these folk pieces."

I like folk pieces.

"Thank you, Mother," I said after counting to ten. I was sure she didn't mean for it to sound that way. Besides, why ruin a successful evening?

Kathleen escorted Veronica upstairs and I followed them to put away my violin and slip into a sweater. We all descended the steps together. Kathleen had a firm grip on Veronica and spoke to her in a very heavy Irish brogue. The only reason I could make out a word is because she spoke slowly so we could understand her.

She was saying that her husband died in the Easter Rebellion and she escaped to America after it was over. Jobs were scarce at the time, so she came to work here when she was fifteen. She was twenty-nine now, with thick reddish blonde hair and severe features that sat firmly on a big boned frame. If she could smile, she would remind me of Michelle. She could be pretty with a smile.

"Kathleen volunteered to stay with us in the guest house to keep the corn popped and water hot. At least until eleven," Veronica told me, "Aunt Tillie told her it's not required and there will be no extra pay, but she wants to go anyway."

"I've never seen the ghost house," Kathleen explained.

I thought about correcting her but decided it would serve no purpose. I already knew she meant guest house, or so I thought.

CHAPTER TWENTY-SEVEN

THE PARTY

Armed with a large flashlight and toothbrushes, we marched over to the guest house. Kathleen was leading the way for us. We followed the path on the east side of the lawn. After a long, lazy curve, we saw the house.

The windows greeted us with the glow of electric lights as we approached from the side. A wrap-around porch welcomed us with several chairs and lounges along with a cushioned swing that hung from the overhang.

Maybe ten feet of lawn separated the house from the pond. A steep downward slope warned us of the murky green water. Small waves gently lapped against its grassy edges. The rippling waves reflected the rising moon. I imagined that I walked into a painting, except for the movement of circular ripples where insects landed on the surface. A small canoe was tied up to a post on the other side of the house. I shuddered a bit. No canoes for me.

Zelda and another servant girl I hadn't met yet were leaving as we arrived.

"Fresh sheets on five beds," Zelda smiled at me. She frowned at Kathleen.

"We didn't know it would be six," she added with a touch of hostility.

"She'll only be here until eleven, I believe," Veronica said.

"I hope you all have lots of fun," Zelda said insincerely and they left.

"Did I miss something?" I asked Claire, who was closest to me and furthest away from Kathleen.

"Servant politics," she whispered back, "Where we don't care which servant we get because they're all the same, they like to think that we know that they're actually individual persons."

"Well, they are," I said, a bit miffed at her attitude.

"In a way," she agreed, "But does it really matter to us who pops the corn?"

I resolved that when I had my own house full of servants that they would not need to be reassured that they were real and individual people.

We were in the house by now. The door opened into a foyer that led to the main room. A couch and several stuffed chairs circled around an unlit fireplace with a couple of strategically placed end tables. It was a bit formal for a party room. We went upstairs and found the master bedroom which was perfect for us. An extremely large bed ('biggest I've ever seen,' Millie observed) pressed against the wall with a backless couch at its foot and two reading chairs on either side. Two collapsed folding chairs hid in the closet. French doors led to a veranda that overlooked the pond, which was still now that dusk was falling. Party-crashing mosquitos filled the air outside so we quickly closed the doors.

Kathleen was already whipping up some popcorn and iced tea. We girls all changed to our nightgowns and gathered on the bed. Since I saw a ghost in Louisiana, I began the 'Storytime.' I told them about my adventure and how the 'Marsh girl' named Sarah led me to safety. It was a rather gloomy sort of ghost story.

"All ghost stories are gloomy," Millie said with all the wisdom of a twelve-year-old, "How sad to be dead but not to be able to go where you belong."

"How sad being dead," Lisa added.

"Yeah," Claire said, "And when you're dead, you don't breathe. Hold your breath for a couple of minutes. Very uncomfortable."

"I don't think you're supposed to breathe after you're dead," Lisa mused, "That's part of it."

"I don't want any part of it," Claire said, determined.

"It's just the way of life," Charity said.

"Well, yeah," Claire replied, "When it's over."

Kathleen brightened the room with the snacks and drinks in the nick of time.

"So, you want to live forever?" Veronica asked.

"Well, of course, who doesn't?"

"I don't," Kathleen said quietly.

"Oh?" Veronica asked, "Why not?"

"Well," she replied, "I'd either be lonely or married. If I was married, things would happen and I'd have another baby."

"I didn't know you had the first baby," Claire interrupted.

"Hush," Veronica corrected, "Let her finish."

"Well, when a woman has a baby, she gets sick all the time. They call it morning sickness but it's really all day. Then the belly swells up to make room for the baby. Then it moves around. Think about swallowing a two-foot codfish and having it squirm around all day inside you for months at a time. Then it comes out, causing as much pain as it possibly can. And you'll be sore as can be down there and tired all day but still have to keep the little brat clean and fed. You already know how we'll feed it. Then when you get a wee bit of strength back, your husband will notice you. Then things will happen and the whole thing starts again. Year after year after year. And you'll be living forever. It'll never stop.

"Or you can avoid all that and live alone. Maybe in a swamp or on a high mountain. Nobody to love and talk to. Maybe you can get a cat for company. Then people will bother you because they think you're a witch. They'll want love potions, disease cures, or even worse things. Then they'll hate you because nothing you give them works because there's no such thing. That isn't anything I'd want to do either.

"So, it'll just be you and the cat. And all you'll get for your birthday is disgusting hairballs. None of it appeals to me."

"Well, *that* doesn't seem like much of a choice," Claire said dejectedly.

"Look at the bright side," Veronica said, "It isn't a choice. But what is an option is that we can enjoy being with each other tonight. Who has another ghost story?"

There was silence. No adventures. No stories. My sisters were rich in some things but poor in life experiences.

"What happened to 'there's more haunts here than in a graveyard?'" I asked.

Millie had to get up and go to the bathroom.

"That's another thing that's unfair," Claire went on, "Why do we have to drink water?"

Charity and Lisa looked at each other and sighed. I think they heard this complaint before. Millie didn't look back.

"I mean all it does is swoosh around inside for a bit then it comes out and we flush it away with more water. It would be so nice if we didn't have to drink anything."

"No lemonade? No tea?" I asked.

"I would gladly give up everything to not have to go to the bathroom."

"Even food?" Veronica asked with a smile.

"Especially food. It turns into even more disgusting stuff."

"You know, Miss Clarice," Kathleen said dryly, "I know of a great many people who have solved those problems. They don't eat or drink or go to the bathroom. They don't worry about any of those things."

"Really?" Claire was so happy at that moment, "Can I meet them?"

"I can say with all assurances you will eventually meet them. They're dead."

Kathleen had a slight smirk on her lips as we all howled in laughter. Except Claire. She wore an unhappy scowl.

"What'd I miss?" Millie asked as she came back and got on the bed.

"Nothing," Charity said, "Sometimes, you have to catch the moment."

"Well, if you won't be needing me," Kathleen started.

"But we do," said Charity, "We need you to tell us a ghost story."

"Yes, do," Veronica enthused, "Tell us one from Ireland. They're all so sad."

The maid rolled her eyes with impatience but went ahead with her story.

"Near Lough Nevik in County Monaghan is an old mansion. Three stories and twenty bedrooms it is with a fountain out front. For over eighty years, visitors can hear the voice of Lord Geoffrey O'Dell, a heartless English earl, crying out for forgiveness. For you see, in a fit of temper he banished his girls from home.

"It was during the potato famine when the story happened. People literally starved to death while the English lords exported shiploads of food overseas. There was no telling how many people could have survived during those hard times if Irish food was given to Irish people. But the English never cared about human life. Only the English pound. Oh, and Lord O'Dell also loved his nasty English gin.

"Well now, the five girls were English. Cold, mean-spirited, and unfeeling, just like their father. One day early in March, the Irish spring seemed to come early, with gentle breezes and warm sunshine bathing the land in contentment. The lasses decided to have a picnic on a ridge near the lake's edge. They had the servants wrap sandwiches in paper and fill a bottle with cool tea. Then they walked to a hill that gave them a stunning view of the green hills and blue waters of Lough Nevik."

"If I may," Veronica interrupted, to Kathleen's obvious displeasure, "Lough is the Irish word for lake."

"It is indeed," Kathleen agreed, no anger in her voice at all, but I could still see it in her eyes. "They had a wonderful time, enjoying the crisp Irish air and giggling about silly things, when an old woman chanced by and saw them and their basket.

"'Well, good morrow young ladies,' the woman said to them, 'Such a nice Irish day it is and I've been walking far to get to Derry. Would you fine lasses have a few leftover scraps to be sharing now?'

"'Of course,' said the oldest, and the girls all reached into the basket. They unwrapped the food and presented to her the paper with mean laughter.

"Now this old woman was not one to be trifled with,

they soon found out. She looked at the worthless paper and shook her head.

"'Ah now,' said she, 'It's paper you give to the hungry even when there's those who are starving and dying just out of your sight. And you have more than an abundance of food for yourselves. Such children. Well, if it's paper you give, it's paper you eat.'

"And off she walked away from them, unable to conceal her distaste for the uncaring little brats. They laughed at her as she walked onwards and reached in to get their sandwiches. When they put the food in their mouths, it turned into paper and they could only spit it out.

"'I guess the joke's on us,' said the oldest to the rest, 'Perhaps we should go home now and say our prayers, for we have vexed a powerful spirit.'

"They said their prayers faithfully and when dinnertime came, they sat at the table with their father. The servants served a wonderful meal of carved ham with cabbage sweetened in molasses and bread. Sadly, the lasses' prayers did not lift the curse, and all the food they tried to eat turned into paper. Dry foul-tasting paper that defied chewing and had to be spit out.

"'What devilish mischief is this?' cried out the earl, 'I give you food that cost me money and you spit out paper?'

"And the chastised little girls confessed their misdeed to the man. He flew into a rage. 'I will find this witch and bring her back to lift this curse, then we will burn her at the stake. Ireland is part of England now, and there is no room for these pagan spells and enchantresses anymore.'

"With that, he rose from the table and stormed out of the house and into the night to search for the witch, leaving the daughters to go to bed hungry. He was gone the whole night. The next day, the girls woke up hungry. The younger three were crying, but the older two were determined, and so they all went back to the lough to find the witch.

"Well, March is a bit tricky. There can be a perfect spring day followed by pummeling storms the next. It was cold and there was nothing but gray clouds in the sky, but they were hungry and determined. So, they went back and called for the old woman to return to them.

"They begged and they pleaded for her to come back, but only got silence for an answer. Just as they were giving up and about to go home, they heard a laugh. 'Giving paper for food not as funny as you thought, was it now?' They turned but could not make out where the voice came from.

"'We're oh so sorry, please lift the curse. Sharing everything we have forever more, we will. Please forgive us.'

"'I forgive you,' the voice said, 'But I haven't the power to lift the curse. Only you have that kind of power.'

"'But how?' they all asked at once.

"'Prove to the people in town that you are generous, not parsimonious. There are enough uncaring people in the world. Does it need five girls growing up to be miserly and stingy? Or does it need kind young girls growing up to be generous and loving. Show the people who you are. Who you really are.'

"And so, they went home. They told the servants to load all the meats, potatoes, breads, and vegetables in a cart and they wheeled it into town, a good three miles from their mansion, and shared everything with the starving villagers. There was a feast for all. They held a festival with dancing and music. And the girls were able to eat food again. When it was over, they were invited inside a hut by one grateful family. There was no table, just a flat stone on the floor. A hollowed-out log was the couch. Dirty straw served as the beds. They went back home and came back with all the estate's furniture. Except they wisely left the father's room be. Again, there was merriment and gratitude.

"But when the girls came home, their father had returned. And he was furious. No food for him, just porridge. All the sofas and chairs given away. No thief could have done more damage. And in his fiery rage, he disowned them all and sent them away. Never again would they steal what was his. So, they walked out the front door and headed back to the village, in hopes of finding shelter.

"Well, never in the history of the island was there a blizzard so terrible as the one that struck that night. They trudged into a freezing wind. Then, one by one they laid down in defeat and exhaustion and went to sleep and never again woke up.

"Lord O'Dell awakened the next day and demanded to see his children, but they couldn't be found. Somehow, he thought they would sleep in the barn. It never occurred to him that they would believe they were to trudge into town in such a storm. So, he organized a search party. And one by one, the lifeless bodies were found.

"Lord O'Dell went into a rage, then a grief. And for the rest of his life, he drank Irish whiskey until he was stinking drunk and started screaming for the girls to forgive him. Every night until he died. It's said that he opened the front door and walked to Lough Nevik where he drowned himself. But the tale also is told that he left footprints in the snowy grass. At first, when the servants tracked them, they were just his. They led to the ridge where the lasses had the picnic that started it all, five more sets of prints from smaller feet joined his own. And they all led to the water, not far from where his body was found. 'Tis said his ghost still haunts the house looking not for his daughters anymore, just forgiveness."

There were some definite shivers coming from Millie's direction as Kathleen finished her tale. I rather found the story more mysterious than scary.

"So did the girls lure their father to his death?" I asked, "Or did he take a midnight walk and get accosted by bandits with small feet?"

The others laughed.

"I suppose you really have to watch out for those small-footed bandits," Claire said caustically.

"I think the father's story is like the girls," Milly said with some adult sounding insight in her whiny voice.

"Oh?" Kathleen asked while Veronica turned her head to face Milly's voice.

"Yes," she went on, "The girls had the power to break their curse. They probably came back to let him know they forgave him and that he had to forgive himself. But he couldn't do it. His heart was too filled with hate. That's why he always calls out for their forgiveness."

"Oh," Kathleen replied, "I rather thought they lured him to the lake, like mermaids call out to lonely sailors, and when he reached out to them, they pushed him into the icy waters and drowned him for their revenge."

Mermaids. Mermaids always scare me. Even though I know they aren't real.

After a few pleasantries, Kathleen went back to the main house. We girls were all alone. We attacked the popcorn and tea, then we went to the kitchen. There was a bottle of cola for each of us. Afterwards, it was water since the servants only brought enough tea to make one pitcher.

None of the other ghost stories were as interesting as Kathleen's. Lisa told a tale of two star crossed lovers who eloped. They died while crossing s frozen lake that wasn't quite frozen enough. To this day, their ghosts can be seen trying to escape the frigid water.

Charity enlightened us with one about a beautiful heiress whose father disapproved of her lover, so they ran off, chased by the angry father. They died when their carriage crashed and their spirits have haunted that site ever since.

Claire's was eerily similar, about a rich young girl who ran off with her young lover. They sheltered in an old, abandoned house to escape from her father. When they were caught, the father burned the house to the ground, thinking they would run out, but the flames blocked their escape. The phantom lovers can still be seen at night in the ruins, along with ghostly fire.

"Where did you find these stories?" I asked.

"Father told them to us when we were little," Lisa replied.

"I guess he didn't want you to elope," I deduced.

Millie had a similar yarn, but she described her haunted house in great detail, including the furniture and wallpaper. How the window grime affected the light. The squeaking of the staircase.

"Is the ghost ever going to arrive or did it forget it was part of your tale?" Lisa exclaimed.

"Now I know why when someone dies, they're called the 'late' so-and-so," Claire commented, "They're so darn late getting into the story."

Veronica recited an old Bram Stoker short story I already read. I guess since I read so many horror stories to Grandpa Terrance, I may have had higher expectations than were realistic. Especially since my sisters led such sheltered lives.

I was beginning to feel sorry for the other girls. This was obviously the biggest night of their life. Even Veronica was thrilled and acted like she was our age. But then, how would she know what a full-grown woman would behave like? Her whole life revolved around her books and music. This was the first time in years she even got to eat with family since she was always served in her room to avoid embarrassment. How sad.

Claire got up and closed the closet door, making sure it latched tightly.

"I hate looking at dark shapes inside a closet. You just don't know if they're clothes or something else."

"Something monstrous?" Charity smiled.

"Zombies wearing our good clothes?" Lisa started laughing, followed by the others.

"Something that moves," Claire said defiantly, "The clothes seemed to be swaying. I don't know why and I don't want to find out."

"Probably just a draft," Charity said, "They seemed pretty still to me."

Soon the conversation changed from unknown things in closets and ghosts to my sisters' friends and relatives. They gossiped, laughed, ridiculed, and praised people I hadn't met yet. First, I was bored, then I was asleep.

Chapter Twenty-Eight

Midnight

I don't remember all my dreams that night, but none of them were pleasant. The drone of my sisters' voices combined with the chirps of the crickets and cries of the nightbirds sounded disturbing. Evil, dark voices spoke a language I didn't understand. The bed shifted a bit as my sisters moved about. Then I heard my name.

"Amy, come out to see me." It sounded like Melanie's voice.

I went to the window and stepped out onto the veranda. A young woman was in the pond, swimming happily.

"Come join me, Amy. We have much to talk about."

My blood ran cold as I watched her swim. No legs, just a silver tail propelling her to and fro in the water. I turned around to run but she was behind me now, shaking my arms, her piranha-like teeth threatening my throat.

"Amy, wake up."

It was Charity shaking me. I was on the bed, trembling from my dream. The door was open and Millie and Lisa were just inside the threshold, tears staining their faces. Veronica was on the chair facing my direction.

Thank goodness for sisters to wake me from that nightmare.

"Did you hear it?" Charity asked.

"The mermaid?"

"No, the screams. A woman was screaming next door, in Millie and Lisa's room. That sent them flying back over here. Then we heard the glass break from their doors and a big splash in the pond, just like the stories all said."

"Mother's going to kill us for breaking the window," Millie said.

"Where's Claire?" I asked.

As if on cue, a scream came from down the hall. Concerned, Veronica leapt to her feet, while Mille and Lisa jumped over to her side for comfort and Charity sprang behind her.

Wonderful. The only bravery here is from the blind one.

Claire burst into the room in tears.

"What?" I asked, wide awake by now. My eyes glanced at the clock by the door—12:05.

"There's a man in the house," she cried.

"Where?" Veronica asked.

"Right by my room. He looked at me when I came out of the bathroom and I thought he was going to grab me. That's when I screamed."

"Oh, goodness," Veronica said, as Claire scurried over to her for comfort, even though the line was long by now. "Maybe we should go back home. This wasn't a good idea at all."

The other girls all agreed through their crying and tremors.

"Wait a minute," I said, "I don't get it. Weren't we all together?"

"No," Veronica explained, "You fell asleep so early we decided to slip out next door to continue the party for a while, and then we all went to our rooms."

"You left me alone in here?" I asked, vaguely

remembering someone shifting their weight next to me while I slept.

"Well, yes," Veronica said, "When they told me you were asleep, I had us all go next door to Millie and Lisa's room so we wouldn't wake you up. Then when Millie said she was tired we broke it up and went to our rooms."

I hurried to the window and looked out. The pond was reflecting the moon, still as can be. No traces of glass reflecting in the light. No evidence that anything ever happened. Was this all an elaborate joke?

One look back to see the terrified looks on my sisters' faces told me it was not a joke. Besides, they wouldn't have the acting, planning, or directing skills to pull off such an elaborate hoax.

"Come on Charity," I said, "Let's go see what broke next door."

Her eyes widened, "You mean by ourselves?"

Well, yes, everyone else will be useless.

"I'm sure Mother will want to know what broke. We'll have to tell her something now, won't we?"

"Can't we have one of the servants come back in the morning?"

"No."

"But shouldn't we stay together? Here in this room? It's safe. Nothing happened here, yet."

"Don't be so sure," I said dryly, thinking of the voices I may have heard in my sleep, and the idea that something was in bed with me was horrifying.

"Veronica?" I asked.

"Yes, let's go see," she replied firmly, unaware of her almost comical choice of words.

The other girls started pulling on her while yelling, "No, no, no," and other cries of dismay. Clearly, they considered her their best chance of protection from whatever creature lurked in the house. Though it did occur to me afterwards that they may only have wanted her around so that if a monster really did show up, they could push her into its mouth to increase their odds of escape.

"Charity?" Veronica called out after a moment, indicating that she was bowing to public demand.

Charity rolled her eyes, but determinedly went to the fireplace and grabbed the poker and followed me into the hall.

"Wait a minute," I said, right as we got to the other room, "Why am I in front when you have the poker?"

And so I gained a weapon and lost respect for a sister in an instant. With a deep breath, I turned the handle and opened the door. The lights were still on but there wasn't anything unusual to see. No broken glass anywhere. The mirror on the dresser wasn't even cracked. The French doors were closed. The room was completely still and empty. I lowered my poker and we went in.

"There's nothing here," I called out to the others, and they quickly filled the room, also looking for supernatural evidence.

No sooner said when Lisa screamed. We all looked over at her, with Claire and Millie running up to her.

"What happened?" they asked in unison.

"I saw the green lady," Lisa said, "She was in the mirror, looking at us."

The rest of us apparently were getting braver and we all examined the mirror at every angle while Lisa clung to Veronica. Nobody saw anything.

"What did she look like, Lisa?" Veronica asked.

"She was wearing an emerald green dress, very old fashioned, and a velvet hat with ostrich feathers and an ermine capelet. She was very pretty but seemed sad."

"Lisa," I was exasperated at her abundance of detail, "How long did you look at her? What even is that? Ermine?"

"It's fur. White with black spots," Charity said, becoming calmer by the moment.

"Oh. Was she frightening, this lady?" Millie asked Lisa.

"Not really," she replied.

"Then why did you scream?" Millie persisted.

"She just…wasn't supposed to be there," Lisa stammered.

"Okay, then," I said, "Let's go back to the other room and keep each other company."

"I want to go home," Millie whined. Her voice could really irritate me.

"Let's just go to my room again," I said firmly, "And keep together."

The others meekly followed me and we arranged ourselves on the bed and furniture as before.

"It's probably the servants playing a trick on us," I said.

They nodded at first. Then I noticed the closet door. Claire had shut it tightly but now it was slightly ajar.

"But what about that man I saw?" Claire asked.

"And the woman in the mirror?" Lisa added.

"I tell you what," I responded after a moment, making sure I didn't keep looking at the closet door for fear of a stampede, "Let's compromise. We can grab some blankets and sleep on the furniture on the porch. That way we won't be in the house anymore, but we won't go home where everyone will laugh at us."

Veronica laughed, "Amy Collins Wentworth, I am so happy you're home."

All the others agreed. Unfortunately, just before we

opened the door, we heard footsteps quickly walking down the hall, past our room, then down the stairs. Millie, Lisa and Claire were terrified and wanted to go home to their own rooms.

"We'll be fine on the porch, Millie. We just can't go home now," I said firmly, thinking of the predictions Mother made that afternoon.

"Why not?" Millie asked, still trembling a bit.

"Because they'd all think we're scared."

Chapter Twenty-Nine

A Day in the Park

The warm sun in my face woke me up in time to hear whispering and giggling nearby. When I went to see who was there, Veronica and Zelda were talking with one of the maids I hadn't met yet.

"Doesn't sound like they'll be wanting to stay here again for a while," Zelda was laughing.

"Never, in fact," I said, interrupting them, "I might have slept through everything if they didn't all wake me. But I didn't see anything."

But I certainly felt something.

"Neither did I," Veronica said.

I looked into her unseeing eyes to see if she was serious. Her lips twitched a bit as she suppressed a smile.

"Well," Zelda said, "You're the last of them. Your sisters were all up and home before six. I don't know if any of you had fun or not, but I think I can safely say that none of you will win any medals for bravery. So much for 'Those intrepid Wentworth sisters on their first exciting adventure.'"

She pointed to the imaginary marquee like Charity did yesterday. They laughed and I scowled.

"How did you know about that?" I asked, highly annoyed.

"I was there when she said it."

"I don't remember seeing you there."

"Thank you. A good servant should never be seen, you know."

"Well now, Sleeping Beauty," Veronica said, "Now that you have awoken, let's get breakfast. You can guide me to the house." She offered her elbow to me and I led the way.

The other girls were in their rooms, grooming for the party. I could hear Nadia going from room to room to inspect them and change minor things to make them presentable. This must be some party they were going to.

Veronica went to her room after breakfast and Kathleen was dusting. Zelda was still in the guest house. Mother had just taken her medicine and was asleep again. The other servants had orders to start a deep clean of the house while the others were away.

Nadia came to my room with my assignments, looking a bit unsteady. Maybe she took another one of those pills. I was lucky that my schoolwork was mostly reading, although she gave me a few starter problems in algebra. There were also some history and geography work sheets. Apparently, learning about the Carpathian Mountains was quite important to my education.

"This is quite an affair we go to. Your cousin's eighteenth birthday. She plans to announce her engagement, as well. We will be gone for four days, until Monday. I think it is not too much to expect this to all be done. You can rest a bit by playing your violin to your mother. She loves music."

She looked at me staring at the mountain of work she left.

"Any questions?" she challenged.

"Yes," I nodded, "If a boy pees on a girl, does that get her pregnant?"

She glared at me for a minute.

"We'll talk about it when I get back. You need to learn enough to not ask questions like that. Young girls shouldn't have interest in sex. It can cause problems."

Mom and Annette would agree to that, I was sure.

After they all left, I decided to take a walk. I loved my new room, but today it had a heavy atmosphere to it. The light from the window was not as bright as yesterday and it seemed cold, dark and gloomy. I just didn't want to be there. So, I put on some old things I packed from home and quietly snuck down the stairs. Nobody paid any attention to me and I escaped.

It was good to be forgotten for a moment. Occasionally, a soul just wants some time alone. The front door opened easily enough and I went down the long driveway to the gate. Just as I thought, I was small enough to squeeze through the space between the iron fences. It was time to explore the town for a bit.

After a look both ways, I headed towards Pennyton. I remembered the small park near the train station. It would be nice to hear some city noises again and enjoy the fresh air without someone hovering over me, reminding me of some rule.

It was not a long walk to town. I sat on a wrought iron bench and instantly regretted not bringing some leftover popcorn for the pigeons. They were walking all around, their little heads sharply turning here and there as they looked for food.

The sky was blue, the sun was warm. A couple of seagulls were flying about and the sea air perfumed it all. It was nice to be outside and alive in the little bit of nature that was allowed to survive. Some women were strolling their infants and a few old men were talking politics. Herbert Hoover wasn't very popular up here. Of course, he was absolutely hated in the south.

Opposite of me, a small group of men were talking angrily. One loud and disagreeable voice overpowered the rest. It belonged to a small man, maybe thirty, with thin hair determined to retreat into oblivion. He could speak though. The other men were nodding their heads in agreement as he made his points. The more they encouraged him, the louder he got. Soon, men were gathering around him and occasionally I could hear a thunder of agreement.

"The time has come," he started screaming, "The workers have been kicked to the ground and forced to crawl for too long. It's time to rise up and demand what is rightfully ours. Wentworth Produce and Langston Canning have got to come to terms. OUR TERMS! We can beat these robber-barons and make American free again. The unions will make us free."

More cheering. Fists were raised in the air. They started moving past me towards an exit that led to the big building I saw earlier, *Langston Canning Co.* I turned to watch them as they shouted about their union. I was aware of unions, since I came from New York, but didn't know why anyone could get so worked up over them. In fact, there weren't any at all in Faucette.

The police met the mob at the park entrance, moving in quickly to disperse the crowd. There was a lot of shouting, swearing, and insults going both ways.

"We were on your side last time," one man screamed out as he was brusquely turned around and pushed forward.

"Go back to work," I heard an officer shout back.

"I don't *have* work."

"You were going to strike a business you don't even work for?"

Within minutes, they were all gone. No strike today. The factory was unharmed. And I had the park to myself, or rather almost to myself. There was a man approaching me, walking his adorable little cocker spaniel.

I want a dog.

They walked by with the dog sniffing at my feet. I petted him while the owner smiled.

"He's so cute," I practically gushed, "I just love dogs. They're so loving and fun and they play and keep people company. I've always wanted a dog, but my Mom won't allow it. Dogs eat eggs and that's bad for the chicken business."

"I wasn't aware we had chicken hatcheries around here," he smiled.

"At my home in Louisiana we sold chickens and eggs. But no dogs are allowed there. Dogs will be dogs and dogs eat eggs."

"That might make a good song. Dogs will be dogs and dogs eat eggs," he laughed, "All we need now is melody and more lyrics. Then we have a song."

"I suppose. You can write a song about dogs eating eggs?"

"I can. It's all about the melody and lyrics. People like anything if it makes them laugh. If we meet again, maybe we can write a song about dogs looking for eggs. That might be fun. It might even get played on the radio if it's good enough."

"I think that would be wonderful," I said.

"I'll carry some blank music sheets with me from now on. You bring your imagination." This was more of a command than a sentence.

"I will," I said, "But I don't know when I'll be able to come back."

"I understand. You have to be a Wentworth, otherwise you'd be in school. I hardly ever see any of you out alone. I walk Sniffy every day, though, we'll look for you. You may want to bring a guardian with you next time, though."

"That's right," I replied, "I'm Amy Collins. I'm not a Wentworth yet."

"You will be. I'm not surprised you're by yourself. I've heard all about you and your adventures. You won't stay a Collins for long if I know your family."

We exchanged some more pleasantries and he and Sniffy walked away. I forgot to ask him his name.

The sun was high now. I was getting a little hungry and decided it was time to go back home. Although I didn't think anyone would notice that I was gone for the morning, if I missed lunch, they would come looking for me. I turned around when my arm was grabbed from behind and I was wrenched back.

"Hey," I yelled while whirling to face my attacker.

It was the union man. His eyes glittered with hatred for me and his hand squeezed tighter on my wrist, hurting me.

"So, what do we have here? It's a Wentworth brat come out to spy on us poor people."

He pushed me backwards where I banged into a tree and he caught my other hand, twisting my arm around.

"For generations, you people have worked us to the bone for nothing while you got the fancy houses and yards. You wouldn't have anything if we didn't work to make you rich. And what do we get? Nothing.

"But that's going to change right now, deary. I'm taking you to my neighborhood and I'm not letting you go. I want you to see how us poor folk live while you Wentworths bask in luxury. Now you're going to give us everything we deserve. It's time you learn a real lesson. The only thing that separates us is who we had as mothers. That's all. Now you people are going to give us what's rightfully ours."

I was screaming to the top of my lungs for help. There were a dozen policemen here fifteen minutes ago, where did they all go? I was trying to kick him, but his grip prevented me from doing anything and he increased the pressure on my arm when I tried. He was pushing me out of the park, towards a beat-up looking Dodge coupe, when I heard a sharp whap and he released me.

"Darnell Miller," I heard a familiar voice calmly call out, "I see you still like to find opponents who don't stand much of a chance."

It was Jerry Talkington, still wearing his devilish mask and twirling his cane in front of him while looking down at my attacker, who was on the ground gasping for breath.

"How about instead of a little girl, you take on a poor, one-eyed veteran who can barely take care of himself because of his war injuries? Let's see how you do."

He kicked the other man in his side hard enough for me to hear the thud of his shoe as it hit below the ribs. Miller rolled on his side, trying to protect himself. Talkington slammed his cane on his upper arm, making the man wince with pain.

Miller rolled away quickly and was on his feet while Talkington kept his eye on him.

"This isn't your business," he whined.

He was clutching his arm and close to tears. Then he charged at my rescuer, pounding his head into Talkington's chest as they rolled on the ground. Miller was on top and had Talkington's face held down with one hand and hit a glancing blow with the other. As he raised his fist up to land another blow, Talkington found his cane and slammed it hard into Miller's chin. That stunned him and Talkington seized the advantage to break loose and stand back up. I thought he was going to hit Miller again. Instead, he just stared at his defeated opponent as he slowly got up, completely dazed.

"Such a man," Talkington said with contempt, "Can't even beat a poor crippled man, totally helpless in the world. Now, get in your car and go, unless you still want to fight."

Miller was exhausted from his effort, and much the worse for the wear, with bruises forming on his face around his jaw. I thought he might attack again, but he just walked towards his car.

"Later," he panted out, and hurried on his way.

Talkington turned to me. He had a small cut on his cheek and his good eye was starting to darken. The fight took a lot out of him, too.

Before I could thank him, my protector grabbed me none too gently by the back of my neck and pushed forward, guiding me out of the park.

"Hey," I groused at him, but it had no effect.

"What were they thinking? Letting you roam the streets out here with no escort? The amount of people who hate Wentworths in this town are in the millions. And only ten thousand people live here! Who's supposed to be with you? Jarviston'll boil them in oil. Bet you're surprised, huh? Didn't know the whole world doesn't bow down to you. Don't like you lording your name and wealth all over town."

I was trying to break his vise like grip on my neck with no success.

"I didn't think anyone bowed down to me. Everyone

was busy and I wanted to see the town. And nobody has to look out for me. I could go anywhere I wanted back home."

"Well, this is your home now. One big rule for you to remember is you have money and other people want it."

We were on the road now headed for Wentworth Founding.

"Are you going to keep dragging me all the way home?"

"You would be behind me if I was dragging you," he replied, "I am propelling you."

Some answer.

I tried to squirm out of his grasp, but his hand just closed tighter, like a steel vise.

"Ow," I yelped, "Would you let go? I can walk, you know."

"I know," he replied, "I just want to make sure you walk to the right place."

"Hmmf," I muttered back.

"And it will be worse if I catch you out without an adult escort again. Always have an adult with you. You don't know what you'll meet around here."

"Yeah, I know what you mean," I muttered.

It was a long walk and nothing short of humiliating. I felt as though hundreds of people were watching my forced march. The masked man with the glittery wooden eye and the little girl. Nobody offered me any help, though. This scene would have played out very differently in Faucette, I was sure.

We got to the gate and he had me ring the bell. Within moments, Chester was there with the key and let us in. Talkington never said a word, just marched me up to the door while Chester just stared at us in shock. I made a mental note to never rely on him if I needed protection.

Talkington finally released me after Willie opened the front door.

"I believe this is yours."

"Yes, she is," Willie said, utterly confused, "I thought you were in your room, doing your assignments."

"I thought I'd get some air," I replied, rubbing my neck.

"There's plenty of air here," Talkington said, "You didn't need to go to the park." He turned to Willie, "She ran into Darnell Miller. I don't know what he was planning to do, but he's an angry man."

I looked at him. He obviously knew all about being an angry man.

"Ah," Willie said, "That man's going to go too far one day. If you want to dedicate your life to hating people, rich people aren't the best choice."

"Especially the ones with teeth."

Willie nodded, "All rich people have teeth. And they know how to bite."

"Don't all people have teeth?" I asked.

Talkington turned his eye to me, "Most people have teeth to chew with. Some people have fangs to bite with. If you bite off your enemy's fingers, he can't pick your pocket. And your father's pockets were untouched."

"Oh," I said politely. I thought I understood the gist of what he said but I really wondered why he had to say it in such an obscure way. "I should get to my reading now."

"Yes, you should, young lady," Willie agreed, his tone less than pleasant.

I always hated being called 'young lady,' because it always meant I was in some kind of trouble. I skipped away and ran up the stairs to my room before anything else could be said.

Chapter Thirty

The Bedroom

I started my school assignments, but I just didn't want to do them in my room. It was still cold and gloomy. Although the window was open, the sun wasn't coming in. I could hear wind blowing through the trees, making soft rustling sounds, like two people whispering loud enough to hear but too soft to understand. I kept seeing movement just barely in my line of vision, but it was gone when I looked up. I thought I heard a sigh or two near me. I was familiar enough with old houses to know they occasionally creak as they settle, however, these sounds were disconcerting. I took my books over to Veronica's room.

She was nowhere in sight. Her room was warm and I thought about doing my work there. I needed a desk, however, and her dresser barely had enough room for her record player. I didn't want to move anything, so I turned to leave and found Kathleen looking at me curiously.

"Lost?" she asked, with an eyebrow lifted.

"I was looking for Veronica."

"She's on the back porch sunning herself while I change the sheets and tend her room."

She stared at me for a few seconds.

"You should be in your room studying. Instead, you

were at the park. Now you are here instead. Your room makes you nervous?”

“Not exactly nervous…”

That's exactly it. Nervous.

“…Just empty. No one there.”

“That room is never empty. Bad things happened there in the great long ago. The man who built this place wanted to show off his wealth and power. It was not really for his family. His wife and children were only needed to complete his image of himself. They were neglected and grew to become adults without a father to love them. They were here only to keep up appearances. And marry well. He figured with six children properly married to the right families his fortune would increase six-fold. They were little more than gold coins to him.

“Sadly, his oldest daughter fell madly in love with a young Irish immigrant. Well, of course, that would never do. A Wentworth lady marries a scion of the rich and powerful.

“But she was young and headstrong and decided to elope. They got as far as Flowerton when the father's men caught them. The young man was hanged from the nearest tree for kidnapping. The daughter was locked up in your room. No one was allowed to speak to her.”

“At first, she was quiet, but then she started to talk. To herself or her dead lover? Someone…something else? It doesn't matter. One night, she stopped talking. They found her the next morning. She hanged herself with a bed sheet. To this day, people say they can hear her sighing and talking.”

She abruptly changed subjects.

“That boy wasn't normal from the start. But when they put him in there, that's when he became evil. Really evil. I think he tried talking to her. It is never a good thing to have a conversation with a ghost. Nothing good can come of it. People shouldn't talk to dead things."

Chapter Thirty-One

Tea with Ursula and Melanie

At four o'clock, Zelda tapped on my door. I hurried over and opened it for her. She was smiling at first, but she yelped a moment later, glancing behind me. I turned to where she had been looking. All I saw was my mirror with our reflections in it.

"I thought I saw something," she said, "Anyway, your sister, Melanie, and her friend, Miss Ursula Chzerick (she pronounced it ZARE-rick) are in the drawing room for you."

"Oh, that's right, she said they would be here for tea."

Zelda fluffed my dress a bit and ran a brush through my hair a couple of times and led me downstairs. She opened both doors to the drawing room and announced me, "Miss Amy Wentworth," and backed out, closing the doors quietly behind her.

Melanie was dressed in a casual lilac chiffon dress with a gossamer wrap, while her friend wore a silk skirt and white blouse. Both looked elegant. Ursula was a striking woman of maybe fifty, with a youthful figure and gray hair peeking out of a small hat with ostrich feather trim. Neither woman wore make-up, nor did they have to. They were beautiful the way nature made them.

Ursula studied me for a second or two through stylish glasses. She had gold earrings shaped like small mermaids and a gold necklace that looked like rope. Her left wrist was covered in bracelets of different colors. She was as fashionable as a woman could be in 1930.

They both rose to greet me, which I felt was a little odd. Melanie gave me a slight hug and fake kiss on my cheek. Ursula's greeting was a strong hug, then she pulled away leaving her hands on my shoulders.

"Oh my," she said to Melanie with a heavy accent, almost like Nadia's, "She looks just like Yvonne."

"Yvonne?" Melanie asked, confused.

"My sister. She died when she was nine, when we lived in Romania. They said she died of fever, but I always knew she was kissed by a vampire."

"Vampire?" I asked skeptically, "Did you live in Transylvania?"

"We did." She was serious.

"There's such a place?" I hoped not. There was something about reading Dracula to Mr. Benson this past winter that just made vampires the worst of the fictional monsters.

"It's part of Romania. The largest part. The most important region in the country. Where the world's greatest mystics live."

"That's where you come from," I said.

"It is. How did you know?"

"Lucky guess."

They both laughed.

"Perhaps I was a bit obvious," she conceded.

"So, what happened to your sister?" Melanie asked.

"There was a priest. Odious man. He was evil and doing God's work. Not doing God's work, to be truthful. He was in love with my aunt, if such a demonic soul can feel love. But my aunt was engaged to the Baron's youngest son. He had family, money, connections, and she was the daughter of a banker. And they were in love, so they told me, and I have no reason to doubt it. I was young and completely oblivious.

"Well, Constantine the priest, he did the unthinkable. He went to The Solitary Caves, where an ancient king was buried. Confined is a better word. He was a vampire."

"Like Dracula?" I was getting quite skeptical, more from hope than certainty.

"No, child," she responded, "If a being existed like Dracula, we would all be undead. We couldn't hope to beat such a thing. No, this was a true vampire. Dead in the daylight. Alive at night. But human. Almost. No turning into bats. The mirror does reflect him.

"He ruled his land at night. He killed and drank the blood of those who displeased him, or who were there when he needed sustenance. The people lived in fear for a decade. According to legend, they drove a stake through his heart, but he rose again. They sealed his tomb with a large stone and a warning notice to never enter. Constantine broke the seal and freed him. He cast some wicked spell and commanded the demon to kill my aunt's fiancé.

"And it did. But it was diseased and brought the fever to our city. The old and young were most susceptible. Many died, including my aunt. I was sick for a week and when I recovered, my darling sister was gone. I was too sick to attend the funeral. I also was delirious when the men of the town tied up Constantine and threw him into the cave with that demonic thing and sealed it shut again.

"Life went on, but there would always be an emptiness in our hearts for the children. Gone before their time."

I am going to have nightmares.

The visit did not improve after that. I was the image of Yvonne. Perhaps my soul was her soul, born again in another time. Brought back from beyond. Sisters forever. It was an uncomfortable conversation. My soul was my own and I didn't want another sister. Especially her.

"Melanie, you must bring Amy with you next time you visit me on my yacht," then to me, "It's called the *Sirena*. We can sail to the ocean for a while and just enjoy the blue sky as it meets the water. We can toast marshmallows on the open deck."

"That would be wonderful," Melanie replied, "You can read her tarot."

"My what?" I asked.

"Tarot cards, Yvonne. I mean, Amy. It's a way of telling the future. The cards know all, but one must know how to read them. I will read yours for you."

We stayed and talked for a while. Small talk, now. Ursula told me stories of Romania and I told her stories from Louisiana. I think I might have liked her a little more if she had stopped calling me Yvonne.

When the clock struck five, they prepared to leave. Ursula hugged me again, quite tightly. I didn't like it.

"You have the gift," she said, "Not in a great way, but still. Trust your instincts. Then you'll know."

"Know what?" I was totally confused.

"What is safe."

After they were gone, I went back up to my room. I can't say I disliked Ursula, but she certainly made me nervous. And I did not like being called Yvonne.

"Your mother is ill tonight," Zelda informed me a little later, "It'll be just you two in the dining room. You can sit at the head of the table and pretend you're the grand dame of the house and talk to Miss Veronica. Won't that be fun?"

"Yes," I replied, "But why in the dining room? Isn't it a bit of work to have us sit there? Wouldn't the kitchen be more practical?"

"No. The family certainly doesn't eat with the help. Not here. The lady would toss us all in the street if she even heard the idea."

"Seems like a lot of work for just the two of us."

"Do you want me to sit with you and watch you eat?" she asked, not unkindly.

"Can you join us?" I asked hopefully.

"No. Servants eat with servants. Mr. Willie would have me peeling potatoes for a year if I even mentioned it."

It was a wonderful dinner, despite my reservations. Both plates had the food cut up for us and Veronica had perfect table sense and ate just as well as I did. It's so sad that they isolated her for so long. Willie soon joined us to see how well she was doing. He smiled his approval to me.

"Hello, Willie," Veronica said after a second.

"How'd you know it was him?" I asked.

"I recognized his footstep."

We talked for a bit. Willie seemed quite happy with us eating together and, more importantly, didn't seem angry about my walk this afternoon.

"So, with the exception of Mr. Miller, what did you think of our park?" he asked.

"You went to the park without me?" Veronica seemed hurt.

"I didn't know you wanted to go. I'll ask next time."

"So, how was it?" she asked, unaware of Willie's disapproving glare.

"Nice at first. I met a man who was walking his dog. Its name is Sniffy and it was so adorable. We could never have a dog at home. Mom and Dad don't like to compete for eggs."

"We used to have one here, but Fourthy killed it doing some kind of medical experiment," Veronica said sadly.

"Well, can we get another one?" I asked excitedly, "I can take care of it."

"Yes," she said, "Now that Fourthy isn't here it should be safe enough."

Willie agreed to talk to Mother about it.

With that, we continued to talk. I told her about my encounter with the evil Darnell Miller and his fight with Mr. Talkington. Then we started to talk about her music. She listened to classical on occasion but really preferred jazz.

"Our cousin Iris married a jazz musician. He plays clarinet in a band. His name is Bixby Von Hellbright. He's very nice and his family is quite well off, but they disowned him. They think it's a great shame to have a son who plays jazz. It's not white music, you know."

"I noticed in Louisiana that pretty much all the jazz bands were black. I guess that's how it is, but I don't think it matters if the musician is black or white."

"It matters to some people," she replied, "Even if it's family."

CHAPTER THIRTY-TWO

VERONICA'S MUSIC

After my evening bath, I was in my nightgown. Zelda said good night and turned out the light. My room felt clammy and the air was heavy again. I soon heard music in Veronica's room, so I got up and knocked on her door.

"Hi, Amy," she said sweetly, "Can't sleep?"

"Not really," I replied, "How did you know it was me?"

"Who else is home? Besides, I recognized your footsteps. You don't walk lightly like the other girls. You kind of stomp."

"Stomp?"

"You walk heavier. Remember, I hear you walk. I don't see you. Now, why are you here? Lonely?"

"I wouldn't say lonely. But my room is kind of…I don't know, creepy."

She shrugged. "I never go in there. I don't know where the furniture is and barking my knees against things can be quite painful."

"I know," I said, and attempting to be humorous added, "And pain hurts."

She blinked, unamused.

"I'm so glad you told me that. I wouldn't have known."

She stepped aside for me to come into her neat and

orderly room. The record player was on a bedside table and her records stood sideways on a shelf above. Little paper clips were on the sides of the album sleeves. The highest ones were on the left and they descended as they moved right. She explained that she felt for the clips to know what the record was.

"Pretty clever," I remarked.

"Organization is survival," she replied, "Here. This is a record by Bixby Von Hellbright, Iris' husband."

His music was good. It was lively and pleasant to listen to. I could see he had a future in jazz. It was such a shame that his family disowned him for doing what he wanted to do.

"He's made several recordings, but he never quite caught on enough to be mainstream. He was on the radio here in Boston, but New York is where success lives. The stations there don't seem to be impressed with him yet."

"That's too bad," I said, "Maybe he can change his venue. Lots of jazz in St. Louis."

I could already tell from the soft, easy thrust of his music that Louisiana would offer him no success. He would stand no chance competing with Louis Armstrong and Sidney Bechet.

"I don't think they're thinking about St. Louis. Iris has been thinking about Los Angeles. A lot of those Hollywood people go to clubs. Maybe he can catch on there. Do movie soundtracks. Anything's possible with talking pictures."

"I have a sister who lives in Hollywood. Maybe they can show them around," I said brightly.

"A sister?"

"From my old family," I said, stumbling on the words.

The idea seemed kind of silly now. My old family wasn't really family anymore. My eyes were heavy and I was too sleepy to care about whatever made me uncomfortable in my room. It was time for bed.

235

CHAPTER THIRTY-THREE

THE THIRD FLOOR BEDROOM

In those days before clocks had illuminated hands, before streetlights conquered the night, and before nightlights were provided for children, nights were confusing. The moon hadn't risen yet and it was pitch black. Something woke me up, but I was unable to see anything, not even the white pillowcase I was sleeping on. I had no idea what time it was. But I could hear whispering. The words were unintelligible. But the sound was there. I shrank down to as small a ball as I could turn my body into.

"Now is perfect," a man's voice whispered angrily.

"Then what?" a woman with an accent answered, "We must follow the plan. Everything must be thought out. We know the important part now."

I think I may have whimpered a bit.

"You're alright," the woman said, "Go back to sleep."

I woke up with warm sunlight streaming through the windows. A cool breeze was blowing fresh sea air into the room.

"You know," Veronica said to me at breakfast, "Caitlin, the upstairs maid, left here a week after Uncle Joe died. If your room makes you nervous, maybe you should ask your mother if you can move upstairs to her old room. Not only would you get her room, you'd get the whole floor."

"I thought that's where the servants slept," I replied, "Wouldn't they resent me being there? They might think I'm there to spy on them."

"They sleep on the fourth floor. The third floor has the small ballroom. Uncle Joe had business dinners there. Sometimes, he had parties with married couples and they danced. Uncle Joe's home office is on the other side, and there are six bedrooms we don't use unless we have a lot of guests. They're mainly for Uncle Joe's business friends when they spent the night. One of those bedrooms was Caitlin's. She was in charge of setting up the ballroom decorations and making sure the guest rooms were ready."

"That was her job? What happened when there were no guests?"

"Uncle Joe would find something for her to do, I'm sure. He spent a lot of time up there in his office."

"They were alone together?"

"Well, Miss Suspicious, I'm sure nothing *adulterous* happened."

"Oh, I didn't mean anything," I apologized, "I'm sure it was all professional."

From a very old profession.

"You should inquire about the room."

I was convinced. After last night, anything sounded better. I went to Mother's room to talk to her about it and she cheerfully called me in after I knocked. She was obviously having a better day. The blankets were on the floor and a tray of leftover breakfast littered her bedside table. She was working on a crossword puzzle from a magazine using her fine point fountain pen.

"Crossword puzzles in ink?" I was impressed.

"Easier to see that way," she answered, obviously happy at my reaction.

"You must be good. I think I'd ruin the puzzle."

"Then *you* shouldn't do them in ink. I am confident in my ability to do things right. By the time you're done with finishing school, I hope you will be too."

I asked about moving upstairs to one of the unused bedrooms like Veronica suggested.

"Absolutely not," was the firm answer, "There are important papers in the office up there that can't be touched. The lawyers will throw a fit if they are. You can go up and see the floor if you must, but not the office. It's locked up anyway. I know that if I forbid you to at least see the floor, the taste of forbidden fruit will prove too much. Take Zelda with you."

"Thank you, Ma'am," I said, but quickly corrected it, "I mean, Mother. But you know, since it does get so dark, couldn't I get a little companion dog? I saw a cocker spaniel in the park being walked by a man—"

"What were you doing in the park?"

"I just went to see the town."

"By yourself?"

"Well, yes."

It was obviously not a good thing to tell her.

"Never do that again. You are a Wentworth now, although you may not know it yet. Your behavior is a reflection of me and your sisters and you will not embarrass us. You need to be escorted everywhere from now on."

"Yes, Ma'am," I said, reflexively using the wrong word again.

"And don't call me ma'am."

"Yes, Mother."

"You know," she said looking off into space, "We used

to have a dog. A friendly, happy little springer spaniel. She died though. That woman's son killed it in a 'medical experiment.'"

I knew right then that Mom and Mother would never be friends.

"Well now that you mention it," I said, "I was hoping to call Mom and let her know I arrived safe. She's probably wondering about me by now."

I completely forgot about calling her. Truth was, I almost forgot her. In less than a week, I hardly ever thought of my old family. My new one took up so much of my time. I was just too busy. I started to feel guilty.

"No," she said, "I don't think that would be a good idea. They are not family to you anymore, just strangers. You will certainly not call her Mom again. You may send a post card to let them know you're here if you must."

She seemed to be thinking about something else.

"The more I think about it, the more I think it might be nice to have another little puppy around. All you have to do is feed them, and they give you boundless love in return. I'll talk to Willie about it. Everybody loves dogs."

That afternoon, I told Veronica about Mother's decision.

"We're really getting a dog?" Veronica asked with a delighted smile.

"We are," I said, but my enthusiasm was limited by the fact that my old family was now consigned to being strangers. They were good to me even if they did occasionally embarrass me. They were still family and now that I remembered them, I missed them.

I was guiding Veronica down the stairs, although she could descend them unassisted. But as she explained, if she was too independent, then maybe there wouldn't be a need for Kathleen anymore. She didn't want that. Kathleen was not just a servant. She was her friend.

Lunch was wonderful. Cookie called it 'a simple affair.' It was shrimp in a garlic and butter sauce on toast with melted cheese on top. I wished all my lunches were 'simple affairs.'

Zelda sat behind us to see if we needed help with anything. We didn't. I almost went to the kitchen to get another glass of water, but she stopped me. That was her job. It felt a little stifling.

"Thank you," I groused when she returned.

"I'm sorry, Miss Amy," she said, "It's what I'm supposed to do."

I think I hurt her feelings.

"No, I'm sorry," I apologized, "It's just that I wanted to call home and talk to my old family for a bit, but Mother won't let me. She says they're strangers. I have to write to them."

"I'll stock your room with stationary."

"What's that?"

"Writing paper with matching envelopes. It looks nice. Refined, as they say here."

"I'm surprised that Aunt Tilly would say it like that. She's usually so diplomatic. So smart with people."

"She is smart," I replied, "I mean, she does crossword puzzles in ink. What confidence."

Zelda replied, "It's easy to be confident when the answers are in the back of the book."

After lunch, we three went upstairs to the third floor. The stairs ended in a perpendicular hall. To the left, an open archway led to the ballroom. Frosted mirrors reflected the hardwood dance floor, making it seem bigger than it really was. Two switches guarded the wall for the lights. The first turned on a set of soft pink lights. The other activated regular lights but they must have been on some kind of timer to flash on and off every five seconds.

"Creepy. They dance in that?"

Small bedrooms dotted the hall. Beds and nightstands stood lonely with only little table lamps to keep them company. Two bathrooms offered relief on each side of the dancehall. The office wasn't locked but looked undisturbed. The mahogany desk was clear and dusted. We could find no papers, important or otherwise, anywhere.

I presumed the last bedroom next to the office was Caitlin's. It was substantially bigger than the others with a nice sized round bed with silk pillowcases and sheets tucked under a crimson comforter with gray fringe. A square table with a lamp shaped like the Eiffel Tower sat next to it. Two switches were next to the door, embedded in old wallpaper. One was for the table lamp. The other activated the ceiling light, but it also blinked on and off in a slow rhythm. The closet door was to the immediate right. It was huge. It ran the length of the bedroom.

Zelda turned on a light switch and a bare bulb shone faintly. We walked all the way to the end. A small viewing door was carved in the wall just out of my reach. We were able to open it and I jumped up to see a perfect view of the bed. I heard a crunch when I landed and looked down at the floor to see a camera's crushed flash bulb.

"Are you sure?" Veronica asked when I told her.

"She is," Zelda confirmed, "I thought there was something off about Caitlin. So, she entertains men in bed," she clicked her tongue with disapproval, "And while the ceiling lights are flashing, Mr. Wentworth or somebody took pictures."

"Blackmail," Veronica said firmly.

Chapter Thirty-Four

Back to the Park

After we finished exploring, I returned to my room to do my assignments. I was able to read a few chapters of *House of Seven Gables*, but the air grew heavy again as I started geography and I began to get sleepy. After all, I was learning about the canals and waterways of the great lakes. It was like a sleeping potion in book form. I soon gave up and went to visit Veronica while she hummed along to her music.

"It's so nice out," she said to me, "Let's sit on the front porch."

I guided her down the stairs with ease and we sat enjoying the late afternoon sun and cool ocean breeze.

"You know," she said when we were barely settled, "I'd like to walk about for a bit. Exercise my legs for a while. I'm tired of always being cooped up in my room. Let's go to the park."

"I don't know, Veronica," I said, "Mr. Talkington made it very clear he did not want me in the park alone without an adult. And Willie agreed with him. And Mother was upset about it. And that man who attacked me might be back."

"I'm twenty-five, you know," she replied, "And I was

the adult at your party. Just because I'm blind doesn't mean I'm a child. And as for that man, I can scream pretty darn loud if I need to."

That's definitely an adult.

Just to be safe, I looked around inside for Zelda to give us permission to leave, as she seemed to be a soft touch. Unfortunately, I only saw Willie. No permission there. So, I grabbed some bread for the birds, collected Veronica, and we headed outside. We boldly marched through the open gate and escaped Wentworth Founding without incident. After all, what's so great about being safe? Lightning can't strike the same place twice. Or at least, not exactly.

Only a few birds greeted us at the park so we had it to ourselves. I broke the bread into bird-friendly pieces and fed the pigeons while Veronica sat at her end of the bench with her eyes hidden behind dark glasses, soaking up the sun as she napped. We were there for all of ten minutes when I felt someone grab my wrist in a vise-like hand.

My newfound feathered friends scattered in the air like the cowards they were. I grabbed the bench back and stood up defiantly to my attacker. It was Jerry Talkington, wearing his ridiculous mask.

"Didn't I tell you to always have an adult with you when you go outside?" he hissed angrily.

"I brought an adult," I replied smugly, pointing at my cousin with my chin.

Veronica was awake by now but obviously confused about the commotion.

"She's blind."

"Amy!" Veronica's voice had a new quality to it. She sounded downright imperious, "Who is this man?"

"Jerry Talkington," I said.

He released me and stared at her.

"Is he always so rude as to talk about someone right in front of her as though she doesn't exist?"

Jerry looked at the ground for a second.

"A thousand pardons," he said to her, "Never did I mean to hurt your feelings or be disrespectful. Please forgive me."

Her voice softened. "Of course," she said, "Mr. Talkington, Amy's knight in shining armor. You are from the pharmaceutical Talkingtons?"

"My father and two brothers run the Pennyton Pharmacy, yes."

"Do you participate in the family business?"

"No, I do not," he hesitated, "But you see…no you don't see." More hesitation. "I was injured in the war. I lost half my face—"

"More like only a third," I interrupted, trying to be helpful.

The cuff to the ear I got from Veronica and the angry glare from Mr. Talkington drove home the point that my assistance was not appreciated.

"How does that keep you away from your family business?" she asked. She was leaning on an elbow, looking almost right at him. If I didn't know better, I would say she was watching his every movement.

He sighed, like he had lost his spirit. "I'm a hideous monster. People take one look at me and are repulsed. They hate me for being so ugly. They make fun of me and talk behind my back. Throw things at me. Just ask Amy. She was there one time."

"Horse manure," I said, nodding as if she could see me.

"Oh?" she stated, "That was an impolite way to disagree with a person."

"Not what he said. That's what they were throwing at him."

"Oh."

"Anyway, as long as we're here, maybe I should escort you two young ladies back to The Founding," he offered hopefully.

"Oh, you wish to take us home?"

"Yes, of course. We have another hour before the sun sets. You don't want to get burned, do you?" he replied while gazing at Veronica's dark glasses.

Actually, the sun was well on the way down, but I didn't say anything.

Veronica's lips were pulled back in a dazzling smile. She looked just thrilled.

"I can't think of anything more enchanting than to be escorted home by such a kind gentleman," she said to him, offering her elbow.

He entwined his own arm with hers and off they went. I was glad he was walking with her instead of propelling her forward by the neck. I kept back enough to not eavesdrop on their conversation, but close enough to hear them laugh and giggle occasionally.

Maybe I should become a professional matchmaker.

CHAPTER THIRTY-FIVE

A FUN DAY

Chester must have closed the gate while we were gone but I squeezed through the little opening and zoomed over to press the key for the others.

"So that's how you got out yesterday," Mr. Talkington said as I closed it back, "Very clever. I suppose if they fixed it, you would find another way out. I bet you're an expert at breaking rules."

"Not really," I replied, offended, "No one told me not to go to town. And then you said I should have an adult with me." I pointed to Veronica with my open hand like a magician indicating his assistant.

"I think he meant someone not blind and more useful than me," Veronica said sadly.

"Nonsense," Mr. Talkington said, "Who could be more useful than a beautiful young lady who can enchant the leaves off the trees with just a smile? I daresay even Jesse James would sit at your feet promising to never again even think about robbing a bank for just one kind word."

She giggled and blushed redder than an apple, while I tried not to throw up.

The front door was locked so we had to knock to be let in. Kathleen stared out at us, looking none too happy, especially with me. Veronica wanted to entertain her caller with lemonade on the front porch, so a pitcher and two glasses were set up on an outside table. I was none too gently nudged back into the house.

"Your mother is feeling better and will join you for dinner," Zelda told me when I got upstairs. "I told her you and Miss Veronica enjoyed dinner together last night and she is looking forward to you all eating together. This will be her first dinner with Miss Veronica since I started working here two years ago."

"Two years?"

"Mr. Wentworth was always yelling at her to get better at eating. So, she started taking her meals in her room to get away from it all. Nobody wants to be yelled at during dinner."

I can imagine.

Mr. Talkington left soon after his glass of lemonade and it was time for dinner.

That night, Mother was a little unsteady at first, but seemed to get better as she ate. We had chicken stew, which surprised me a little bit, as we normally had more elaborate meals. But this reminded me of home and it was the best meal I had in Pennyton so far. Tonight, the chicken was cut into tiny pieces and mixed with small cut potatoes and carrots so that everything would easily fit into a spoon. Cookie told me later that she made it this way especially for Veronica.

Willie and Kathleen hovered in the background while we ate; Willie to wait on us, Kathleen to silently help Veronica.

"Well, Amy," Mother started the conversation, "I have a puppy coming tomorrow. It'll be a Cocker Spaniel. With papers of course. I'll keep them in my safe."

"You're going to paper train the dog in your safe?"

Veronica avoided a smile by frowning. Willie looked down for a moment until he recovered. Kathleen was impassive.

"*Newspapers* will be in the kitchen," Mother told me, "These papers are to show the dog's lineage and history. We can't have just any dog in the house, you know. The neighbors would complain."

"They only like Cocker Spaniels?"

"They only like purebreds," Mother said, "No one would want just anything running around. We will have no mongrels in our neighborhood."

Having been called a *thing* to my face in Louisiana, that stung me a little bit, but as usual, I didn't say anything. It would serve no purpose. Besides, she didn't mean anything by it.

"You will be here when we get it, so you can name it. But remember, it won't be exclusively your dog. The other girls will want to play with it too, I'm sure. And sometimes these creatures just decide they belong to someone else entirely. Maybe even a servant. Watch out for Willie," she smiled, "He can steal a dog's heart in a second. I imagine a young woman's as well. He can charm the spots off a cheetah."

"Really?" I tried for some levity, "I have these freckles I'd like to get rid of."

They all laughed, even Kathleen.

"Now, tomorrow we will go calling on our neighbors. You are such a lovely young thing."

I don't like being called a thing!'

"I want to show you off. I was worried at first when I saw you in that hillbilly dress, but now I'm sure you're a young lady who will make us proud."

I liked that dress.

"So, Chester will have the car ready at nine and we'll visit all the neighbors and people in town in our social circles. Maybe stop and get an ice cream. Would you like that?"

Her fake enthusiasm made me believe she thought I was four. But I could tolerate a lot for ice cream, so I nodded happily.

"We'll visit the Palmers first. They live next door. The hedge serves as kind of a property line, but their children always squeezed through to play with the girls in days gone by. The hedge was smaller then, so were the children.

"And we'll go see everyone down the street and then we'll go to the coastal part of the city to see old Mr. Gorman. He lives in the most…unusual house I've ever seen. You'll love it."

"Is that the doll house?" Veronica asked.

"It is," Mother replied, "And it's not a doll house. It's an expressive way to communicate the need for companionship."

"It's creepy."

"It is not, and how would you know, dear? You've never seen it."

"I felt it."

"Oh please," Mother sighed, "It's not like I asked you to go with us. You are most welcome to, of course, but I really wanted to have some time with Amy."

"I see," Veronica did love to use that ironic term, "Then I think you two should go and have fun. I'll look through my old records and see what I can find."

She said it with a straight face. She would be good at poker if her eyes worked. Mother gave her a confused sideways glance and then turned to me.

"It will be nice for us to have some time together. I've been under the weather for a while now, you know."

I nodded, "Well, it's understandable, what with losing a daughter, a son and your husband all so soon."

She stared at me for almost a minute, until I shrank down in my chair.

"Rosemary was a loss of course, but she wasn't entirely right. God just realized He made a mistake and took her back. Losing my husband and that monster they told me was my son was a complete blessing. You will never know how lucky you are to have never met them."

Veronica and Kathleen were both nodding in agreement.

"Regardless, I am so happy. That boy is gone and I have another daughter, rescued from the gates of hell and back home, where she truly belongs."

"I'm happy, too," I said, feeling guilty about saying that as I wondered what my Louisiana family would think of me.

"We'll have fun tomorrow."

CHAPTER THIRTY-SIX

VISITING

'Tomorrow' was cloudy and almost cool. One look outside told me we'd have rain before the day was over.

"That's okay," Zelda assured me, "That's what umbrellas are for. Now the mistress wants you in this orange taffeta dress today. It'll be cool and won't be too formal for visiting. Plus, you'll look adorable in it."

"Oh, dear," Mother said when she saw me, "I thought you'd look adorable in that dress but it's all wrong for you. It brings out those awful freckles. You look exactly like Leticia when she was your age. She was cursed with those freckles, too. So deforming."

Deforming? What am I? Some kind of freak?

"But not to worry. That's what dermatologists are for. When you're older, we'll get that fixed. A few acid baths and you'll be fine. No more spots."

Acid baths? I'd rather have freckles.

"But not to worry," she continued, "We'll wait a few years for that. Leticia had a horrible time with pimples, too. If we wait, we can cure both items. And then you'll be pretty. It's a sad commentary on life. Men love beautiful women. You can walk around with a meat cleaver dripping blood and a couple of half gnawed fingers in your mouth and still have prospects if you're pretty enough. Always remember: It's better to be a pretty demon than an ugly saint. You'll be even happier when we can make you a *pretty* saint."

She squeezed my shoulder a motherly way and Chester held the car door open for us. I always knew I wasn't the prettiest girl in the room, but this was the first time an adult so bluntly confirmed it. What made me sad was that she wasn't trying to be cruel. She was just stating the truth.

We visited the Palmers first. Although we shared a hedge with them, it was a long drive to their property. We headed roughly a half mile before we turned right on Winfred Way. We drove to the end and turned right, driving another half mile, until we turned down a long tree lined lane that led to their three-story mansion.

The butler let us in and we waited for a few minutes until our hosts came to greet us. I could tell they were Catholic since several small figurines of St. Mary glared at us from shelves and tables. Martin and Maureen Palmer were elderly people with droopy cheeks and smiling faces. They both walked like they needed new feet, but they were very gracious. Mother and Mrs. Palmer did that fake hug thing adults do while I curtsied.

Most of the conversation was about me and how I wound up in Pennyton. What did I think of my new family? How great is the culture shock? Are my sisters nice? I really like easy questions like that. They gave us lemonade and sherbet for a refreshment. I enjoyed visiting them so far.

They showed some actual interest in me and my former family. I told them about my sisters and brother. How Annette and Guy got married and moved to Los Angeles. I left out the part about the shotgun. I somehow thought

Mother might not consider such a thing to be proper. She already had a low opinion of my southern family.

Mr. Palmer said, "You know, I used to be an actor out in Hollywood, several years ago."

I didn't know that, of course, but why say anything?

"I was never a star, just a bit player. I'd be in one or two scenes at most. It was fun, but after a few years, it was just time to go home. But I still have some friends. Have your brother-in-law—"

"Martin," Mrs. Palmer growled.

"Or however you refer to him," he continued smoothly, ignoring her, "Here's a name and number. It's for Max Barrow. He's the director of security for American Entertainment Studios. He's always looking for good men. The pay is good too. Just make sure he doesn't try to get in front of a camera. Max only hires professionals. Not wanna be actors."

He wrote down the name and number and I promised to send it right away. Then the subject changed to how empty the house was now that their youngest son had moved away. Mother reminisced about how he would squeeze through the hedge and play croquet with my sisters. He was sweet on Charity for a while and maybe after she completed finishing school they could renew their acquaintanceship. Maybe have it grow into something more.

Mr. Palmer saw I was growing bored. He took me by my hand and led me to their backyard. There was a marvelous little house built on a platform slightly above the ground with something rustling around inside.

"It's a Guinea pig," he told me while opening the cage.

He reached in and handed me a plump little puff of fur with eyes. It was so adorable. It walked up my arm to my elbow and tried to jump over to Mr. Palmer, who took him back.

"My youngest son, Freddy, bought him six years ago. He moved out last year to attend Dartmouth. This little guy's name is Chubby. He used to *be* quite chubby when your sisters snuck through the hedge and fed him popcorn. But they stopped visiting as they got older. He's thinned down since then."

I petted and cooed to him until Mother called us back. It was time to go. I thanked the Palmers before I left. They were nice people. I could tell they were lonely now that their children had all left.

We drove up to the next house and paid our respects to a family named Warren. They were kind, but a bit more reserved than the Palmers. They had a son and daughter about half my age who they introduced to us.

The boy was Rabbit and the daughter was Bunny.

"Rabbit Warren and Bunny Warren?" I asked.

Mother elbowed me none too gently.

"Well, yes," Mrs. Warren said with a smile, "You have to admit that the names go well together."

"Well, yes," I said, "Since bunny rabbits live in warrens. But still," I gave up. It was done and it wasn't my business anyway. "Well, I guess it's good your last name isn't Penn."

Then their names would be Pig and Hog.

They all laughed since they didn't know what I was thinking. Mother tried to start conversations with them, but her responses were all one syllable. She later explained to me that she had been so ill over the last few years she stopped her weekly visits. As a result, our neighbors had lost touch and were little more than strangers. They never called on her because they didn't want to be around my late father. He obviously was not a popular man in Pennyton.

Years later, I found out that Mr. Warren was one of many men in Pennyton who my father was blackmailing. We called on other neighbors, but those visits were very short as well. I don't think Mother knew how much the good people of Pennyton hated my father.

Our last visit was to a house set high above the town, near the ocean. We stopped a few hundred yards away so I could get out of the car and look over the steep cliff at the churning water, hundreds of feet below. The waves viciously attacked some boulders, slowly turning them into sand. About a mile away, an outcrop of larger rocks towered over the waves searching to find any careless boats that it might sink. The ocean seemed to be a very dangerous place.

It was enchanting, though. Every wave was different, but somehow the same. It had a hypnotizing effect. The salt air was healthy and pleasant. The crash of the water on the rocks was musical to me. I loved the ocean.

But not the house. I had never seen a more frightening place in my life. It stood three stories tall, with a sharply gabled top floor that held a widow's walk. The foundation had settled over the years, giving it a slightly tilted appearance. Two large windows glared out at us while other smaller windows echoed the deep hostility. Three rickety stairs led up to a dilapidated porch. Huge pine trees towered behind it, leaning over at impossible angles, dangerously close to toppling on us.

That was the least of it. This was the building Veronica called the Doll House. There were literally hundreds of them everywhere. They covered the pine trees all the way to their tops. Most of the images were simple, cheap, homemade, wooden dolls with painted faces, faded from the weather. Under the eaves of the windows were stuffed rag poppets with button eyes that all fixed their stares at me. Porcelain dolls claimed the windowsills with glass eyes and baleful expressions that exuded hate.

Mr. Steed Gorman, its owner, helped Mother out of the car so we could admire his ghastly little palace. He was a thin, balding man of maybe fifty or so who looked like the type of man who just blended into the background to be forgotten. He had colorless blue eyes that hid behind wire glasses but seemed to study everything around him.

"Why, Tilly," he said trying to sound jovial without succeeding, "It's been ages. And this pretty little girl must be Amy, the long-lost daughter come home."

Pretty little girl? I liked him already.

"She is indeed," Mother replied, "She's pretty today, but wait a few years. She'll be gorgeous. I already see movie star beauty in her."

That's not what she said earlier today when we were talking about freckles.

"Indubitably," he replied, "She'll put Clara Bow to shame."

"I was hoping for more of a Mary Pickford kind of genteel."

"How do you know how genteel she is? She's an actress. She may only be acting genteel."

"Clara Bow doesn't even know how to do that."

"Who's Clara Bow?" I asked.

And so I found out the most famous movie star of the century (so far) did not make movies I had any desire to see. Mr. Gorman was quite an expert on movies and actors. He produced a few movies in his younger days. He decided to leave Hollywood because he thought the studios made a big mistake by transitioning to talking pictures.

He was currently an exporter who bought goods and

merchandise from the factories and sent them overseas to customers. It was a lucrative business.

"Why don't the factories just sell things directly to the buyers?" I asked.

He laughed. "Because each country has its own tariffs, languages, customs, regulations, and other systems. It's my job to know how to get the merchandise to the customers. A lot of the countries I deal with just became independent after the war. Their laws aren't beneficial to normal business practices right now."

"That's a very polite way of saying he's a smuggler," Mother smiled.

"Sometimes that's the only way to give the people what they want," he replied smoothly, "Your late husband knew all about getting what he wanted."

If Mother was offended by that remark, she never let it show. She seemed oblivious.

He invited us into his house and Mother surprised me by accepting. I was less than enthusiastic about going into his yard, much less his home. Those dolls just stared at us. And there were so many of them. And they shouldn't have been hanging on the trees and eaves and sitting in the bushes. They should be locked away somewhere. They may not have scared me, but they *did* make me a little nervous.

"They won't hurt you," Mr. Gorman told me as we walked past them, "You see, my house is haunted. Legend has it that two tribes of natives fought each other here over a thousand years ago. Their spirits still roam the land, looking for release. They wander around the property, so I put the dolls out for them. They think they're returning to their bodies and get trapped inside. Eventually, they realize it's time to go to where they belong."

"You mean the dolls are possessed?"

"Occupied, I think is a better word. Like so many places in the world where the citizens are ruled over by foreigners. But soon they will be free."

He turned on an electric fan to move the air around.

"The countries or the dolls?" Mother asked.

"Both."

More dolls stared at me when we entered the parlor. Mostly porcelain dolls with glass eyes that looked real, but there was one other. It was beyond scary. Whatever it was made of it looked like a demon from hell. It was maybe a foot long with rough dried skin covering a small base. The eyes were brown and weren't made of glass but still sparkled with something like life. Evil life. A hole replaced the nose and sharp, deadly looking teeth that were at least six inches protruded from its dried lips.

"I see you like my Brazilian Rezidon Doll," Mr. Gorman said, "I'll bet you'll never guess where I got it."

"Brazil?"

"Good guess. She is exceedingly bright, Tilly."

"I have been finding out daily," Mother replied happily.

I smiled at them, pretending to be proud when I was only confused and annoyed.

"It does indeed come from Brazil. The Maycock tribe in the upper Amazon made them. Rezidon is the Maycock word for revenge. These dolls have all the properties one would expect from such a hellish instrument of revenge. They're made from death itself. It's a still born baby. The brains and organs are sucked out and the skin is soaked in a tea made from some South American herbs to preserve it. It especially has a wonderful effect on the eyes, don't you think?"

I nodded politely, making a note to try and ignore anything else I saw in his house.

"Then they stapled piranha teeth in its mouth, usually coated with Curare, a toxin that paralyzes its victim in small doses, though it can be fatal in large quantities. The medicine men would attach a lock of hair or fingernail clippings of some enemy in a small bag around the neck. Then they chanted an incantation to their gods. On the third night of its existence, the doll would go find its victim and maul him to death.

"Of course, we don't know all the ins and outs of creating this wonderful little masterpiece, and we don't have the spells they used, obviously, since the Maycock tribe all died out."

"For some reason," Mother said dryly, "I doubt I'll ever feel real remorse for their passing."

"Me, too," I agreed.

He laughed and promptly covered the hideous thing with a towel. Soon his manservant Edmund, a tall man of maybe thirty years with leathery skin, served us the tartest lemonade ever made. This would never escape Cici's kitchen. A curvy young woman with a sultry demeanor wearing a maid's dress that was three sizes too small for her served us some slightly overdone divinity. I guess I was a bit critical, since I worked in a restaurant, but I was polite enough to say it was good.

The servants left and the two adults talked about grown up things like the economy. I was bored and Mr. Gorman's soothing voice almost put me to sleep. The dolls still stared but seemed less hostile. The fan's gentle drone soon filled my ears and the conversation seemed to stop. Soon my eyes were closed.

I still saw dolls. Dolls, dolls everywhere. Running away from me, coming at me. They walked by me, saying things too garbled for me to understand. Too many voices, too much activity. Then everything was still.

"Will you stay with us forever?"

Mother's hand was on my shoulder, gently shaking me awake. It was time to go and I was obviously tired. This was not a good house to have dreams in. However, our host was very pleasant as he walked us to our car.

"Come again soon," he said, "I have other unique dolls to show you."

Mother smiled tightly.

"Thank you for your hospitality," she said.

I thanked him too. I had no desire to be shown other dolls of any kind, especially 'unique.'

"It was a dreadful thing to have at all," Mother said to me on the way back home, "Much less in a room where he entertains his guests. And that woman pretending to be a maid. If she did any work in that dress, all the buttons would burst. If my dear departed mother even thought I was taking you to see such a thing, she'd come back to haunt me."

"I hope not," I said without energy, "There's too many ghosts around here anyway."

But if I shared a room with a ghost, she was gone for the day. A gently cool breeze swept into my room while I studied the books Nadia left me. I fell asleep again with no visions of dolls or mermaids. Just the ocean rocks I saw from the hilltop and the waves sweeping over them. I'd only been here a few days, but I already fell in love with the sea.

Chapter Thirty-Seven

Mother

Zelda was all smiles when she woke me for dinner. I changed into a gingham dress and white sandals and Zelda primped my hair a bit. I studied myself in the mirror. Green eyes, fair skin with dark freckles. Possibly brown or dark blonde hair. Upturned nose. Slightly crooked teeth, but a nice shade of white. Completely average. Not pretty, but not ugly.

"Mother says my freckles make me deformed," I told Zelda.

"Your mother doesn't say things right all the time. I'm sure that's not what she meant. It's all that medicine. Anyway, Melanie and her friend are going to have dinner with you tonight."

"And Veronica?"

"She has a gentleman caller. They'll be out until past dark."

A Cocker Spaniel puppy was waiting for me in Willie's arms. It was an adorable little fluff ball. In fact, I named it Fluffy. After it made itself comfortable in my arms and everyone was finished petting and fussing over it, we sat down. Willie removed the dog at that point and I had to wash up again.

"I would love to have a dog of my own," Ursula was saying to Mother when I came back, "But I live on a small yacht that I keep moored in Flowerton. Oh, here's Yvonne now."

"Amy, please," I said not hiding my annoyance.

"Oh, that's right, Amy," she corrected, "You should visit me next time with Melanie. You'll just love the *Sirena*."

"I think that would be wonderful, Amy," Mother said, "I'm so happy you're making friends up here. Especially educated ones. I was really worried about how well you'd adjust after living with those people down there."

Those people down there were my family.

Dinner was pleasant. We had beef stroganoff with new potatoes and carrots. I preferred my potatoes mashed, but I didn't want to seem ungrateful, so, as usual, I said nothing. Mother and Ursula had a long conversation about spiritualism and occult practices. It was clear that Melanie thought Ursula was a highly accomplished medium. It was just as clear that Mother was a sceptic.

It was not an unpleasant conversation, there was no rancor, but there were no shared beliefs. It seems there were several times that Melanie asked about having Ursula perform a séance in one of the upstairs rooms but first J.P. then Mother forbade it. It was bad for appearances and not Christian.

After they left, Mother and I went to the drawing room. A servant I never met before brought Mother a martini and a cold root beer for me.

"Thank you, Barbara. You know Amy, I think the whole medium profession is total tommyrot," she said, "But I hear the *Sirena* is a beautiful yacht. And you'll get to travel the ocean for a bit, at least the cape."

"I'd really rather not," I replied, "Ursula makes me

uncomfortable. She always looks at me funny and calls me Yvonne after her dead sister. It's not right."

"Show some grace. See how well you do at names at her age."

"Mother, doesn't it strike you as creepy that she keeps calling me her dead sister's name?"

"Well, you remind her of her little sister."

"That doesn't mean I want to know about it."

"I think you're being silly."

She drained her martini and rang the bell for Barbara to bring her another.

"I don't approve of Ursula all that much," she continued after another swallow, "But Melanie was always fascinated with ghosts and seances and things like that. Leticia said it was because they saw ghosts in the house. So? All the children saw ghosts. My husband saw them when he was young. So did his brothers and sisters. But they forgot. We all lose our childhood sooner or later."

She paused as Barbara brought in another drink. It went down in a couple of gulps. I wondered if those Martinis had alcohol in them.

"When I was nineteen, my parents called me into our drawing room. They found a husband for me. Not just any husband. Josiah Pierce Wentworth the Third, of the Wentworth Department Stores. It would be quite a match. We were from two of the biggest corporate empires in the country. The Wentworths had stores, clothing lines, leather, and a few factories here and there. The Langstons had shipping, fishing, canning, farming, textiles, steal, railroads, just about everything. But we had no cash, just assets. The Wentworths had cash by the barrelful. And we were beautiful young people. Our combined assets would make us among the wealthiest people in the nation. And

Wentworth cash was needed to update the canning business.

"Well, I agreed to meet their choice for my husband, but not to marry him. The Wentworth fortune was only matched by the Wentworth reputation. And that was not good. My father-in-law was a brute. He never met a pretty woman he didn't put his hands on. And he could get any husband, brother, or father fired anywhere in the country if she fussed about it, even if he didn't work for the Wentworths. And a lot of women wound up in trouble because of him. A great many of his employees were said to be part of his mongrel brood. Women of culture avoided him and his whole family.

"But Joe was so kind to me and quite handsome," she continued, "And he just swept me off my feet. I fell in love instantly and before I knew it, we were married, with a child on the way. Within a few years, he turned what we had into one of the biggest fortunes in America. I wanted for nothing."

She paused, "Except love. Companionship. Friendship. He was always working or…otherwise occupied. He never had time for me or the children. Now, he's gone and not a single tear at his funeral. But everyone was so complimentary regarding him. His eulogy had the kindest words money could buy. I would have bought sincerity, too, if it was available.

"But Joe did provide money, wealth, prestige, and status. It was all my father thought I needed. I really didn't have as much choice in the matter, as I thought I had, you see. In those days, a daughter was a valuable asset. I was allowed to make my own choice when it came to marriage, but my parents didn't allow me to meet very many boys. So, my options were limited. Joe was my first love only because I met so few other young men. And he made me comfortable. I felt guilty about wanting anything more."

When it was bedtime, Willie escorted me to my room. He did a quick double take when he opened my door, then shook his head.

"You girls and your ghosts," he shook his head, "I just thought I saw one."

Zelda arrived and helped me with my clothes and I was soon asleep. Although I wanted Fluffy to be in my room, she was confined to the kitchen. Dogs and messes go together. Messes on the bed were unacceptable. I understood.

But it would have been nice to have her next to me. I had an unnerving dream that night about being chased by that horrible doll that Mr. Gorman covered up. Fluffy wouldn't be any help, but she would be comforting and cuddly when I woke up.

Chapter Thirty-Eight

A Dream?

Something woke me up in the middle of the night. The moonlight was streaming through the window. Everything was still and cold. I heard a slight click and saw my doorknob start to turn. I just knew that dreadful little doll was coming for me, but I didn't cry out. I pulled the covers over myself and watched as the door slowly opened. The doll must have grown. It was the size of a full-grown man slinking into my room. I held my breath as I hid in my bed.

"YA," it cried out as if getting ready to pounce and I screamed back. The thing retreated into the hall, slamming the door behind it. I heard the pounding steps as it ran away. Fluffy was barking an alarm from the kitchen.

I jumped out of bed, opened the door and ran to Veronica's room. Her door was already open and she came out, her crooked, unseeing eyes darting about in the dark. I ran to her and hugged her closely while she turned to listen to the noises down the hall.

The window at the end of the hall blew shut with a hollow thump but didn't latch. Then it opened a few inches and shut again with another thump. Lights turned on throughout the house and we heard footsteps running up and down the stairs. Seconds later, Kathleen, Zelda, and

Willie were with us. Kathleen went to the window and secured it.

"Such a fuss over a window," she tisked at me.

"There was someone in my room," I said, "I thought it was a dream, but it wasn't. He came in and yelled out. Then he ran away."

"I heard it too," Veronica defended me, "The little scream. Amy's loud scream. Then he ran out the window."

"Well, I didn't see anyone running away. Maybe it was your ghost."

"Hmmf, I never saw a ghost. At least here," I replied.

"That's not what you were saying when you had your little party."

"That's not true. I was the only one who didn't see anything."

"I didn't either," Veronica agreed.

Kathleen rolled her eyes. "Well, the window's locked now. We can all go back to bed," she said as she stomped back upstairs.

Zelda gave me a shoulder squeeze. "Sometimes dreams can seem so real."

"They can indeed," said Willie as they turned to go back to bed.

"It happened," Veronica said to me, "I think you had a visitor of some kind. You know, when people go into your room, they sometimes say they see a ghost in your mirror. Maybe that's why he ran away."

We said goodnight and went back to our rooms. Even with all the excitement, I was soon asleep.

CHAPTER THIRTY-NINE

THE MISUNDERSTANDING

Mother had a sick headache the next day, so it was just Veronica and me for our breakfast of waffles and maple syrup. She suggested that whatever happened last night was just a dream and I woke up just as the house was settling. My visit to the dollhouse was enough to give anyone nightmares. I was scared to disagree with her because I was afraid she wouldn't like me.

"I suppose you're right," I said, "But I think maybe there is something in my room. Other people seem to see things there."

"I never saw anything."

Obviously.

"Oh. Are we going to the park today?" I asked.

"I'd love to, but Jerry is coming by and we're going to walk barefoot on the beach."

"He called you on the phone? How nice. You two make such a sweet couple," I lied. I was a little afraid of him. His temper was quite intimidating.

"I hardly think we're a 'couple.' But that would be a nice thing. He's such a kind and gentle man, you know."

When he's not kicking someone's teeth in.

"I suppose. I only just met him, you know."

And I didn't like the way he 'propelled' me home.

"Yes. He told me about how he rescued you from that ruffian the other day. How chivalrous. Like your own knight in shining armor. He told me he regrets treating you a bit harshly on the way back home."

So do I.

"Well, I guess all that matters is I got home," I replied graciously.

"I'm glad to hear you say that. He's uncertain how to treat young girls when he's protecting them. Still, he was afraid he may have handled you the way the army handles a young recruit."

More like a prisoner of war.

"It's all right," I sighed, "You're the one he's visiting."

"Oh, I forgot," she said, concerned, "The other girls are all gone. Would you like to come with us? I'm sure Jerry would love to have you come too."

"Oh no. I have Fluffy to keep me company."

And so Kathleen helped her upstairs to get ready for her date while I went to the kitchen to find my little four-legged friend. She practically jumped into my arms and Cookie ushered us outdoors.

"You misnamed her," she said sternly, "You should have called her 'Underfoot.'"

She ran all over the yard, finding little twigs to chew and she rolled over and over in the soft grass. She also left a couple of messes for me to clean up.

"When you have dogs, you have messes," Cookie laughed as she watched me clean up after her. Messes didn't bother me. The total love and demand for attention more than made up for a little work.

After maybe an hour of playing with Fluffy, I heard the

doorbell. Jerry Talkington had come for Veronica. His mask matched his skin tone and he had a glass eye in his socket. If I squinted a bit, I could almost think of him as handsome.

I took Fluffy back out to the yard to play. She limited herself to digging and sniffing at the hedges. I tried throwing a twig for her to chase but all she did was chew it for a while then went back to digging.

There was a commotion in the kitchen and I heard my sisters' voices. They all ran out to the yard to see Fluffy, while Nadia took a quick nap.

"Oh, how cute," Lisa called out when they made their way to the backyard. Soon the other girls were out admiring her.

"So how did it go? Where did you go?" I asked them as they cuddled with the puppy.

"Philadelphia. Aunt Audra lives there with our cousins. She's our father's sister. Our cousin London had her birthday party," Claire replied while waiting for her turn to play with Fluffy, "That's why you weren't invited. The plans were made a long time ago. No one knew you even existed then."

"London?"

"Yeah, they named her that because she was born in London."

"Oh," I responded, "Good thing she wasn't born in Schenectady."

Claire glared at me for a second then threw an old ball she found for Fluffy to chase. After a few tosses, it got close to the hedge so of course she lost interest in it and scurried under its thick branches.

"Oh no," we all yelled.

Millie and I started to struggle through the hedge but

Fluffy came back with a dirty body, something that looked familiar.

"Is that Chubby?" Claire cried out, "Oh heavens! Fluffy murdered Chubby the Guinea pig."

"But how?" I asked, "Chubby was in a hutch and Fluffy had to get on her hind legs to nudge open the lock with her muzzle, scoot to the side and pull the door open with her teeth. Seems kind of beyond a puppy the size of Fluffy."

"What are we going to do?" Claire asked, getting upset.

Charity surprised me by stepping forward and retrieving Chubby from Fluffy's mouth.

"I suggest we clean it up as much as possible and sneak it back in its cage. Chubby's pretty old by Guinea pig standards. Maybe they'll think he just died. No one will blame Fluffy if they don't know about it."

Lisa and Claire washed it up while making faces about touching some dead thing. Millie and I found some rags in the garage to dry him off while Lisa distracted Fluffy with the ball. Millie and I then sneaked through the hedge with the evidence, getting pretty scratched up and tearing our clothes in the process.

No one was there so we put the body back in the hutch and snuck back out, getting more scratches. We all washed up, quite proud of our success and changed clothes. We had just started playing croquet when we heard voices from the Palmer home.

"Jesus, Mary, and Joseph! Everyone, come here!" their butler called out.

We all looked at each other. Now we would find out if our scheme worked.

"What is it, Masters?" I could hear Mr. Palmer's voice as he rushed out to his backyard.

We girls all gathered as close to the hedge as we could.

"It's Chubby. He's come back."

"What? Oh, my god," Mr. Palmer sounded confused.

Mrs. Palmer's voice was there now. "What's going on? Oh my God. We have a demon in the backyard. I can't believe I'm seeing this."

"Calm down, I'm sure there's an explanation for this. Masters, what do you think? Have you checked the grave, yet?"

Grave? We all looked at each other. What grave?

"It's there, sir. It looks like maybe something dug him out. It doesn't look like he dug himself out."

"Well, of course not. Whoever heard of a zombie Guinea pig? He was dead and bleeding from the mouth when we buried him. Who would have dug him out and put him back in his hutch?"

"A demon," Mrs. Palmer cried out, "We have to get the priest and have the house and yard blessed. What else would have done such a thing?"

"Now hush," Mr. Palmer sounded quite annoyed, "There has to be a reasonable explanation for this."

"A demon," Mrs. Palmer said firmly, "Now we have to call Father McHale and have the house and yard cleansed and blessed. Poor Chubby, he looks so peaceful. And clean. Did you two wrap him in something when you buried him?"

"Of course, we didn't," Mr. Palmer said, "Why be wasteful?"

I looked over at Millie, but she was suppressing giggles. Lisa and Claire were both staggering back to the house so that the Palmers wouldn't hear their laughter. Although it was funny, it wasn't that funny and Charity didn't seem at all amused. She gently pushed our shoulders back and led us to the porch. The other girls were going into the kitchen and we could hear their loud braying laughter. We soon joined them and Charity began giggling as well.

"A demon named Fluffy," she said between laughing fits as she looked down at our confused puppy and started petting her. "We should have named you Demon."

"Well, at least she's not a pig murderer, after all," Lisa sputtered.

"Yeah," I responded, "She was just trying to bring home the bacon."

I didn't think it was that funny, but they were all howling.

"She wants us to live high on the hog," Lisa said after they calmed down.

They appreciated that one too.

"Then we can have parties with cheese and swine. They won't be boar-ring, and if they are, sow what?" I added.

"Oh my," Claire said after they calmed down again, "Amy, you sure do like to ham it up."

That brought on another burst of laughter.

CHAPTER FORTY

A DAY AT THE MUSEUM

Nadia came down to shut us up because Mother was sick.

"So, give her a pill. God knows she takes enough of them," Claire said rudely but Nadia wrenched her arm viciously.

"No, your mother is sick. So sick that any disrespectful jokes you make will haunt you for the rest of your worthless, unappreciative life," she growled.

"What's wrong with her?" Charity asked.

We were all serious now.

"We don't know but the doctor thinks she has a cancer."

Cancer was untreatable back in those days. Millie and Claire were crying immediately. Lisa and Charity were asking questions so fast and talking over themselves that it was hard to understand anything they said.

"She has a lump below her breastbone. It's inoperable. We can only make her comfortable and happy. She may be here a year or ten years. Only God knows the future. Now go to your rooms and think about it."

As we went upstairs, Fluffy barked a bit because she wanted to join us, but her paper training was suspect, so

Cookie kept her in the kitchen. My sisters trudged down their side of the hall as quietly as possible. I went alone to my room. A box of flowery paper with matching envelopes was on my dressing table. I started to write a letter to my other family, but my room was too cold. The warm sun wasn't even trying to get in.

So, I grabbed a few sheets of paper and a pen and walked to Veronica's room and sat down to write home. Or former home. I told them a bit of my adventures so far. How everyone saw a ghost at the party except me and Veronica, who's blind. I gave the phone number of the studio to Mom for Guy to see if it would be helpful. I also wrote a separate letter to Holly telling her I missed her and hoped I would see her soon.

After I put the letters in an envelope, I walked to the end of the hall to the window. It was unlocked. I opened it and looked down at the ivy growing on the trellises. I didn't see anything that looked like someone had climbed up recently, but I realized I wouldn't know what to look for anyway. I closed the window and locked it.

I turned around and almost ran into Nadia and Millie. I yipped in surprise or fear. They both started back.

"Nervous, are we?" Nadia asked.

"Well, no. I just didn't hear you…sneak up on me like that."

"Sneak up?"

"Walk so quietly," I explained, not entirely accurately.

"Oh," she said, somewhat unsure, "But anyway, we are here for a reason. Independence is something important for young girls to have. So, I have decided that you and Millie need to take the bus. Go anywhere you want but be back by six in time for dinner. I want to feel comfortable that you two can get somewhere by yourselves. That is a skill every young lady should have."

"Whatever happened to not being alone outside?" I asked.

"Some people say, 'think before you speak.' In this case, I say, count before you speak. You won't be alone. There's two of you and you should be safe enough. When you get married or go to Finishing School or even college, you may need to figure out how public transportation works. Nothing annoys me more than a grown woman who can't do simple things. And America is full of them."

Go to Faucette and say that. I just dare you.

She pulled out a dollar for each of us.

"Just remember: if you go a dollar's worth of distance, a dollar's worth of walking back won't feel good on your feet. You will also miss dinner because you won't get back in time."

We hurried out the door and ran through the gate and down the road. She led me to the bus stop where we sat down for a bit to catch our breath. I found a mailbox and dropped off my letters. Then we raced to the next stop.

"Where are we going?" I asked.

"To catch the bus, silly," she replied, happily.

"We're here." In fact, we almost passed it.

"Well, we have to see which bus to catch."

"Someone going to throw us one?"

"One what?"

"Bus. Can't catch one if someone doesn't throw one," she looked at me blankly, "Humor. Ha-ha, ho-ho."

"Oh," she said, unsmiling, "Anyway, is there somewhere you want to go?"

"Is Flowerton close?"

"Flowerton? It's about four miles. Aren't we supposed to stay in town?"

"I didn't hear that."

"What's in Flowerton, anyway?"

"I think there's a museum of Edward Dupree works. He was a famous sculptor from home."

"The Dupree Museum? I've been there. It's just statues of naked women. Big deal."

I told her Mother Greenough's story of Gisette Gagneux and Edward Dupree and how her statue was supposed to have the remains of a gold charm in her clenched fist. Her tears were supposed to look as real as could be. It was his last work before his murder.

"I remember that one. You go through a long hall of statues. Maybe twenty or so. And that one is special. It really does look like a woman. Only made of rock. He even sculpted her hair down there." She discreetly waved a hand down the front of her dress.

"Oh," I replied. I didn't know how to respond to that.

"Well, let's go see it if you want," she said after a second, "There's nothing better to do, I suppose."

And we were off. The bus ride was maybe ten minutes. The scenery was just a few buildings, some trees, then some more buildings. Our stop was on Main Street. Flowerton looked like Pennyton. Maybe a little less kept up, but still a nice little town. A couple of seagulls flew overhead, screeching out bird talk. The sidewalks were cracked and the curb chipped. Piles of dog leftovers polluted the ground. Too much for all the flies to eat, but they were certainly well fed.

"This way," Millie said and we turned left and walked a bit down Main Street.

If we were less oblivious, we might have noticed a brown Chevy that stopped right behind the bus. Two men were inside, making a show of looking at a map, but in reality, they were watching us.

A block further down was a black Cadillac. If we paid any attention to it, we would have noticed that it also followed us from Pennyton. It was too far away for us to see the occupants. We were too busy enjoying our free day to even worry about such things, anyway.

The museum closed at four o'clock and we arrived at a quarter until four. The glass door opened with a swoosh as the rubber seal scraped across the floor. A man and woman were in the back room laughing. They didn't hear us enter. Since students didn't have to pay admission and we didn't want to disturb them, we just went inside. The main hall displayed all the life-sized works while two rooms were on each side showing off Dupree's table sized pieces.

"Now keep your hands to yourself," we heard the woman say using a tone of voice that sounded as though she liked those hands where they were.

Millie shook her head in disgust. I froze for a second until she took my elbow and we went into one of the side rooms.

"Why don't we close up a little early?" the man asked, "I'm sure none of the residents will complain."

I started to giggle but Millie elbowed me and put her finger over her lips in the "be quiet" motion.

"I have a plan," she whispered.

"You need new material," the woman replied, "I've heard that one too many times."

"*That's* why you're so stone faced."

She laughed again, while I looked down, swallowing my own giggles.

"You and those bad jokes," the woman said.

"Like a rock," he replied.

We heard the lock of the front door and their footsteps

going down the main hall, fading with their voices. The lights all turned off and another door in the back closed. We were alone in a locked museum.

"Why did we do that?" I asked Millie, "How are we going to get out?"

"First question: because you want to look at the statue's hand and you'll have to climb onto the pedestal. They won't let you do that. Second question: the back door they left through has one of those new-fangled locks. You can turn it from the inside and it opens. Then you push a button and turn it and it locks behind you. No key needed."

I had seen those before but most doors I encountered required a key to both lock and unlock.

"Let's go," Millie said.

We hurried down the main hall to look at the life-sized works. There were sixteen statues, eight on each side, forming a walkway to the center of the room where Edward Dupree's last work was exhibited. We went down the aisle to examine it.

It was centered on an enormous pedestal. She was beautiful, lifelike and naked. Well endowed, as Mom would say. And Millie was right. Her pubic hair was sculpted as well, with some thin, needle-like strands sticking out. She was on her knees with her head pointed skyward, an anguished look on her marble face. The tears Mother Greenough told me about were barely visible. One arm hung limp by her side. The other was clenched in a fist angled away from her torso.

We hurried onto the platform to examine her fist, looking for a trace of the magical gold chain that supposedly brought her to life so long ago. The bottom part of the fist was absolutely solid. I had to wiggle between the torso and hand to search for the chain. Just as I was about to get a good view, Millie distracted me.

"Um, Amy?" she said, her voice losing all the confidence I had heard in her before.

"Hmm?" I responded while running my fingers on the top part of her fist.

"The statues."

"What about them?"

"They don't like us. They're moving."

"What?" I turned to look at her, then the statues. They were all where they should be. "Don't try to scare me, I've been scared by experts." I heard something like that in a movie and it sounded good.

There was a small hole in the fist, right by the curled index finger. I didn't see anything that looked like a gold chain, though.

"Moving statues aren't experts?"

"What?" I looked up at her, just in time to see movement in the mirror from the corner of my eye. I turned to glance, but the mirror just reflected the statues, all where they were the last time I looked at them.

"Let's just go," she hissed, "Before they attack."

"Fine," I said, I couldn't find anything that looked gold anyway, "Let's go."

I started to walk down the aisle back to the front door, but Millie grabbed my arm.

"What?" I hissed, getting irritated.

I could see all the way to the street, where the front end of the black car was parked near the door. Across the street was the brown sedan, parked quietly, with its two occupants staring at the entrance.

"They want us to leave by the back door."

"What? Who?" she wasn't making sense to me.

"The statues. Every time you look away, they point that

way," she nodded her head to the rear exit.

I looked back, aware of a small movement just barely within my vision. I jerked my head towards it, but everything was the way it was supposed to be.

"I don't see anything," I said hesitantly.

"Well, I do. We need to leave by the back door."

"Fine, let's just go," I said, "Nothing much more to see here, anyway."

So we went into the back room, which was just a little storge room with a small table and coffee pot. The door opened easily and Millie secured the lock as it closed behind us. We were on a street called Mulberry Lane. Another bus stop was a straight ahead of us, just on the other side of the road. After a short wait, we were home.

Chapter Forty-One

Back Home

"You are late," Nadia told us when we got home.

"No, we're not," Millie replied defiantly, "It's five forty-five. We're fifteen minutes early."

"Well, get ready for dinner. Your mother is having guests."

We went to our rooms. I thought it was odd that Nadia didn't ask us where we went or what we saw on our excursion. I was also annoyed that she accused us of being late when we were early. My clothes were rather sweaty from the sun and humidity, but Zelda took them to the laundry while I sponged down a bit. A few brushstrokes to the hair and a change of dress were all I needed to be ready.

I can't say I remember what we had to eat, because Mother made an announcement that simply shocked everyone.

"Now, I don't want to scare any of you," she started.

I figured she was going to announce her cancer, but she didn't.

"When the *Curious Virgin* went down, oh, I'm sorry Amy. That was the name of your father's yacht, *Curious Virgin*. Only your father would name a boat something so vulgar. Anyway, it seems the boat was sabotaged. Someone drilled holes in the bow, just above the waterline. Every wave that hit the boat filled it with more water. By the time they noticed it, they were too far from shore. They could only go down."

The room was abuzz with shocked chatter.

"Why would anyone want to kill Father?" Lisa asked with watery eyes.

"Well," Mother replied, "The Chinese have a saying. 'A good business deal benefits both parties.' As you may have guessed, your father was not Chinese. His business philosophy was, 'Crush them, squeeze their assets dry, drive them into bankruptcy, and buy out what's left.'

"Also, he lacked tact when it came to the workers. They knew that if they asked for a raise, they'd be fired on the spot and replaced. We've always had union agitators looking to cause problems, but Joe always took care of that sort of thing. Sometimes none too gently, from what I have been told recently.

"Regardless, the police will send an officer to interview all of us, except Amy, of course. His name is Detective Wyatt Trask. He will be here tomorrow morning so please, act like the perfect little ladies you are. Dress elegantly and use your best elocution."

"Even Veronica?" I asked. "I'm pretty sure she didn't see anything."

"I'm sure she didn't," Mother said dryly, "But what might she have heard? Anyway, I wanted to tell you that before our guests arrive. Your cousin Iris and her husband will be coming for dinner."

"Bixby!" they all were excited.

The murder investigation seemed to be forgotten. Bixby obviously was popular with my sisters, if not my mother.

"That is correct," Mother sighed, "I wanted them to

meet Amy. Also, because tonight is the best night for them, your Uncle Edgar and Aunt Vera Tyler will be coming, also to meet Amy. Now Amy, Vera is your father's sister. Edgar will be taking over Wentworth Enterprises and will be the Chairman of the board and the Chief Executive Officer, CEO, for short, just like your father. They are very important people. He's from the Tyler family of Newburg."

I didn't know what that was supposed to mean but I nodded politely.

"Mr. and Mrs. Bixby Von Hellbright," Willie announced from the door.

They were quite the couple. He was dashing and debonair with a pencil thin mustache and slicked back dark hair that matched his deep brown eyes. Full lips and an angular nose rounded off his smiling face. When I saw him, it was the first time in my life that I my whole brain just shouted out "WOW!" Fortunately, my mouth stayed quiet.

Iris, on the other hand, seemed rather plain and mousy, though she was friendly enough. She was seven months along and had a belly the size of Delaware. All my sisters forgot etiquette and ran up to hug them both. Obviously, they were close. I stayed in my chair, uncertain of what my response should be.

"Well, go up and offer them your hand," Nadia whispered from across the table while my sisters' volume could muffle the words.

So, I went up and waited for the others to calm down and take their seats then curtsied and held out my hand, palm down. He laughed, a pleasant, ringing laugh that made my heart skip a beat.

Kissing the back of my hand he said, oh so formally, "How wonderful to have such a polite young cousin joining us."

I blushed and turned to Iris, but my mind went blank.

"I'm sorry," I said, "I don't know how to greet you."

She laughed in a friendly way with her brown eyes almost dancing. I liked her immediately.

"Well, I don't kiss hands, but I think a hug will be very nice."

We hugged and she whispered in my ear, "Welcome to the family."

We were back in our places when Willie announced Uncle Edgar and Aunt Vera. For a second, I thought two nineteenth century monarchs strode into the room. He had a thick head of gray hair and an equally dense handlebar mustache. His double-breasted suit fit perfectly without a wrinkle and his shoes gleamed a reddish brown. Just his presence alone made me think he belonged in a general's uniform.

She was just as grandiose in a pink and gray chiffon dress with diamond buttons and a fox (complete with eyes) shawl. Her elegantly styled gray hair matched her dress perfectly but she had a thin, wispy mustache which almost ruined her appearance. She hid behind a gigantic diamond necklace with matching earrings. Clearly, she couldn't offer youth and beauty but was content conveying age and money. They both knew how to exude superiority.

I would have thought the rich and pretentious uncle and aunt would make scathing remarks to the poor disowned couple, but they all seemed to enjoy each other's company, in an odd extremely formal sort of way. All my sisters stayed quiet when Uncle Edgar and Aunt Vera arrived. They curtsied and sat down in their chairs straight and proper. Not a whisper. Nadia had a contented smile on her face.

Things went well until Bixby leaned over and asked me

how I liked my new home.

"Well," I started while holding my fork.

"Amy," Aunt Vera said quietly, "A young lady never starts a sentence with 'well.' Also, she puts down her fork next to her plate, places her hands in her lap and leans forward to make eye contact with the adult."

I was stunned. I never heard of these rules. I looked at Mother for guidance and she nodded so I did as I was told.

"It's nice," I corrected, picking my fork back up.

"I hear you play the violin."

Fork down. "I'm not very good at it but I have been playing for a few years now," I said, trying to be modest while gripping my fork.

"I am sure you're excellent at it," Aunt Vera said, "Otherwise your mother would find something more ladylike as a hobby. I'd like to hear you after dinner."

"Yes, Ma'am."

"Ma'am?" she repeated, "I like that. It's a vulgarization of 'madam' which is the English version of Madame. It's a title of nobility. I think that is a wonderful piece of southern charm. Ladies," she addressed my sisters, "From now on, instead of saying yes, Aunt Vera, I think yes, ma'am will do. Understood?"

"Yes, ma'am," came a chorus of resentful voices.

They all glared at me. I didn't want to be alone with any of them for a while. My life might be in danger.

Aunt Vera made several suggestions on my appearance and table manners, all of them negative. Soon the ordeal was over and we were waiting for dessert.

"Miss Bonnie Hooker," Willie announced.

Everyone seemed surprised. In the south, it wasn't unusual for a girl to visit her aunt without advanced planning, but it did seem to be disconcerting to Mother.

She whispered to the maid to begin serving.

As it happened, Bonnie wanted to talk to Uncle Edgar about getting someone a job at the canning company. Uncle Edgar seemed amused, though both Mother and Aunt Vera were obviously *very* annoyed.

"Amy," Mother commanded, "Please go upstairs and get your violin."

I traipsed up the stairs and found my instrument and tuned it before returning. As I walked down the hallway, I peeked over the rail. Bonnie and Uncle Edgar were chatting. She was leaning into him and he had an arm casually around her waist while his other hand squeezed her breast. I was shocked and disgusted. I turned and walked back a few feet and traced my steps forward, this time banging my case against the wall once or twice. When I looked down, they were at a respectable distance.

Good.

After Bonnie left, we enjoyed a silent dinner before moving to the drawing room where I played a few songs. I played well enough that Mother asked Nadia when I would begin my lessons. Two days was the reply.

Bixby took out his clarinet and suggested we play a duet. I was to play the melody of *When the Saints Go Marching In*, while he played a few jazz riffs to go along. We sounded good together. He played a lively version. Soon Charity was on the piano and we played and sang the rest of the night. There was a light knock on the door and when Willie answered it, Veronica and Jerry Talkington entered.

"Oh my, Veronica," Mother exclaimed, "Have you been out all this time?"

"My fault," Jerry said chivalrously, "I had such a good time I forgot to get her back."

"Oh, my lord," Aunt Vera said, turning red with anger,

"Proper young ladies never consent to being alone with a man without a chaperone. I am so surprised you would risk your self-respect and our reputation by such behavior."

"We were in full sight of a great many people until we reached this house," Jerry said in a low voice.

"That is completely outside the point," Aunt Vera went on, "What is important is a young lady is never alone with a man. They have chaperones."

The party was over. We were ushered up the steps by Nadia, who watched until each one of us was in our room. We could hear disappointment and anger in Aunt Vera's voice as she repeated several times that young ladies always have chaperones, each louder than the last. Then we heard the phrase that ended the whole conversation.

"Vera," Veronica said firmly and loudly, "I don't care."

I heard her running up the stairs without help and she walked to her room. She fumbled around a bit until she found the doorknob. There was some quiet talking downstairs, then I heard the front door close. There was some more talking as Bixby and Iris left. Some more angry words and then Aunt Vera and Uncle Edgar also departed. Then one by one the lights turned off.

CHAPTER FORTY-TWO

INTERVIEWS

Zelda woke me up a little later than normal. The other girls were already off to their dance lessons, so she let me sleep a bit later. The detective was scheduled to arrive in less than an hour, so Veronica and I were to have breakfast and stay in our rooms.

After breakfast and personal grooming by Zelda, I looked at another small mountain of schoolwork that was left for me by Nadia. Algebra seemed useless, but at least I understood it. For geography, I got to read about the Ural Mountains, which by and large bored me, although I did find the ancient stone monuments there intriguing. My new book was *Oliver Twist*.

It's too bad we're rich. If we were poor, I could feed this book to the fire to keep us warm.

After a couple of pages, I heard a tap on my door. It was Veronica.

"Come to my room and I'll show you a secret," she was being mysterious. She was good at it.

"The house has central heat from the furnace in the cellar," she explained, "What I found out years ago is that this vent lets me hear everything in the ballroom upstairs, which just happens to be where that Detective Trask will be conducting the interviews."

A small stool stood underneath the open vent. She must have used it to climb up high enough to reach it. I wondered how she knew how to do such a thing without eyesight. I didn't ask though.

Since she was the matriarch and owned the house, Mother was the first subject.

"Tell me what you remember about those last few days," I heard a deep voice. I pictured a tall, heavy-set man with dark hair and biceps of steel.

"Well," Mother began.

"How come she can start a sentence with well and I can't?" I asked.

I got a cuff in the lips as Veronica clamped her hand over my mouth and whispered, "If we can hear them, they can hear us."

I nodded and she released me. Mother was still talking.

"I can't really say as I know too much. I was taking some medicine to help me cope with Rosemary's death, you know."

"That must have hurt both of you very much," I think he was trying to be sympathetic, but he sounded more sarcastic.

"It hurt me. I don't know about Joe. I don't think he cared about his family. Certainly not me. Our marriage was over years ago. I was under heavy medication ever since Millicent was born. Something inside got pulled or twisted. I hurt every day ever since."

"But you still had Amy and Rosemary."

"I love them, but I didn't want either of them until after they were born. They weren't my choice."

"So, he forced you?"

"Yes, he would take advantage of me while I was sleeping. Then he denied that he was the father of Fourthy and Rosemary. But to avoid the scandal, we kept quiet. But he did say Fourthy would be a boy. And he was, even though she wasn't."

Interesting way to phrase it.

"Why didn't he do the same thing with Rosemary? By the time she was born, Fourthy was showing signs of being…difficult."

"I'm sure I don't know. But Fourthy and Amy were born in New York. If he tried something like that here in Boston, enough local people would know about it and maybe want a little extra cash to keep quiet."

"Did any of the servants talk to you about Mr. Wentworth? Maybe one of them might hold a grudge."

"No. I think he had an unusual relationship with most of the women servants. There seems to be something odd in the way he speaks to them. Like they're hired help but more. That's why I rarely talk to them. Why give them the satisfaction if they're sleeping with him?"

"Why keep them if that's the way you feel?"

"I could be wrong."

After a half hour of questions that seemed pointless to me, Trask called Willie upstairs.

"Let's start with the easy ones," Trask started, "What is your name?"

"William Peter Jarviston."

"How old are you?"

"Fifty-two."

"Do you have any theories on who the murderer might be?"

"No, but I think we can eliminate anyone who didn't know him."

"So, he was not so popular?" Trask asked.

"No. He's well hated in town. Not much liked at home.

But he didn't care."

"Was he sleeping with the girls?"

"His daughters? Certainly not."

"I meant the servant girls. They all seem to be quite attractive."

"Certainly not. Barbara, Kathleen, Zelda, they're all his children from different mothers, or at least, they might be. Tom and Bob, too. Not all of them know it and there is no proof of it. They're not allowed to discuss it with him if they want to keep their positions.

"Now, Darnell Miller knew he was the master's son and that Mr. Wentworth wanted a son. Made sense to talk to him about it. He was fired instantly, but he latched on with the union and stayed in town to be a thorn in the family's side."

"The mill isn't union," Trask replied.

"Not yet. But Miller's job is to agitate and make the men feel there should be a union. Mr. Wentworth allowed it because Miller wasn't successful. Have you ever met Darnell Miller? If it requires personality and likability, he will never be successful."

"Couldn't he have gone public and cause a scandal?"

"What proof? A little resemblance? The Wentworth lawyers would make mincemeat out of him. Some factory workers might think they'd get a bonus if they roughed him up a bit. And they might have. Mr. Wentworth wanted him to be the face of the union because he figured he would fail at organizing."

"Did Mr. Wentworth have a lot of girlfriends?" Trask changed subjects.

"I wouldn't call them girlfriends. Most were married women whose husbands worked for Mr. Wentworth. Men who had great ambitions but mediocre talents. He offered these men a deal. They get a big promotion and an opportunity to prove they can handle a high pay position somewhere in Wentworth Enterprises. They had a year to prove they could handle the responsibilities. In return, Mr. Wentworth slept with his wife. That is how a lot of his managers got their starts. And if a baby came along sometime near the nine-month mark, he made sure the man stayed employed to provide for his possible child. He did transfer them out of state to avoid any issues, though.

"He did what he thought was the right thing. It's just that he was so reprehensible that he didn't *know* the right thing."

"I see, and there were a lot of…problems?"

"Not many were problems. Very few knew about his arrangements."

"So, tell me about these arrangements."

"I'm sure you've heard the rumors. Sometimes the wife was quite willing to go to bed with Mr. Wentworth to help her husband's prospects. The majority were not. In fact, most of these men never even broached the subject with their wives. In those cases, the prospect and his wife were invited for a business dinner. Afterwards, while having a sip of champaign or a cup of tea, the husband would slip something into the wife's drink and well, you know the rest.

"Sometimes he just found a pretty servant girl. If she had the problem without a husband to hide behind, he employed the mother in some menial position. When the child was of working age, they got an employment offer. That's why we have Kathleen, Barbara and Zelda here."

"And Mrs. Wentworth was a part of all this?"

"No. She was given morphine as well and helped to her room. After a while, she just started taking the pills on her own. She did ever since she gave birth to Millicent. She'll take them forever now. I think those pills may explain why young Amy is so small."

"So, these men just stayed put while their wives were drugged and raped?"

"Oh no. Wentworth had an upstairs maid named Caitlin. She entertained the men in her room. Sometimes business clients as well. They always left a bit of evidence with her by the morning. Helped keep them quiet about the whole thing. Helped in other business ventures as well."

"Evidence?"

"Pictures of them in…compromising positions."

"I can imagine. Is this Caitlin available?" Trask continued.

"Oh no, sir. She left right away after the deaths. No more need for her kind of skills."

"I see. And you saw nothing wrong with any of this?"

"I thought it was terrible," Willie said, "But what was I supposed to do? If I came to you with this story, what would you think? Resentful butler trying to get back at his employer. Mrs. Wentworth wouldn't believe it. She wouldn't want to. I would lose my position and never get another one. Servants with big mouths are forever unemployed. But if I thought someone would believe me, I would have."

"And the other servants?"

"Well, Kathleen's mother told her that Mr. Wentworth was her father. Of course, when he hired her, he told her if she said anything she'd be fired immediately. She's from Ireland, you know. Being in a foreign country and unemployed would be daunting for a young woman. And she needed the money. Her husband was killed by the English and she had to leave her son behind with her mother. He would be about thirteen now. She sends her salary home to them."

"Any other little surprise children employed?"

"Everywhere. Cookie is his half-sister. Her mother and JP the second. My father thought I was his half-brother, which is why we never got along well."

"Like perverse and disgusting father, like perverse and disgusting son."

"The Wentworths were known to be ruthless in all aspects of life."

"I heard the Langstons were at least their match. A lot of problem people just disappeared or turned up dead in the old days. Two families of wolves, so to speak."

"I don't think Zachariah the gardener has blood ties to the Wentworths. Hard to say, between all the uncles and fathers and cousins and things. Men love pretty women. Women love rich and powerful men. Men like the Wentworths know how to take advantage of that."

"What do you know about Jerry Talkington?"

"He is the son of a friend."

"Could he be a Wentworth?"

"I've only been with the family for twenty-five years. He's thirty-six. So, I wouldn't know."

"He seems to have a nice standard of living for a man with no job."

"He gets a pension. He inherited a house."

"Does he hire out as a handyman?"

"Not that I know of."

"You have never seen him working with tools?"

"Maybe a hammer. But no, I have never seen him working with tools."

"Does he sail?"

"I would doubt it. He only has one eye."

"Does he go boating with friends? Maybe meet them at

the marina and go boating and drinking?"

"I doubt he has friends and drinking is not entirely legal, you know."

"The oldest daughter, Leticia. What can you tell me about her?"

Veronica nudged me, "What time is it?" she whispered.

"Ten-thirty," I replied after looking at the clock.

"Close the vent."

I stepped on the stool and closed the vent. It must have been well oiled because it made no squeaky noise at all.

"What? It's just getting good."

"We have to go to the park," she explained.

"We do?"

"We do. I'm meeting Jerry there and we're spending the day together."

"We are? Isn't he a suspect?"

"We are," she nodded, "And everybody is a suspect except you. You're escorting me to the park to keep Aunt Vera happy. Jerry is taking me to Boston to see the sights."

"Oh," I said, "What sights are you going to see?"

"I don't know, but Jerry says we'll have fun."

"Fun? With Jerry?"

"Yes," she said, a bit miffed, "Fun with Jerry. If you don't want to take me, I'll go by myself."

"I would love to take you there," I backtracked, "I simply can't picture Jerry being fun. He's so angry."

"He has a lot to be angry about. Now help me with my hair."

I had her nicely brushed while she hummed a bit.

"I wonder what all those questions were about. Jerry and sailing. Jerry and tools. I wonder if Uncle Joe ever took him on *The Curious Virgin*."

CHAPTER FORTY-THREE

BACK TO THE PARK

A few minutes later, we slunk out of the house like escaping prisoners. We were brilliant. We were quiet. We were stealthy. We were caught.

"And just where do you think you're going, you two?" Willie asked from behind us. Obviously, he was done with his interrogation.

"I was just taking Veronica to the park for some fresh air," I replied, trying to look innocent.

Willie glared at me. My innocent look needed improving.

"I am meeting Jerry today. We're going to Boston," Veronica replied icily.

"After that big scene with your aunt and uncle?"

"I don't live with them."

"You live here. Mrs. Wentworth expressly told you to never see him again."

"I will obviously never see him in the first place. However, I will spend some time with him. Aunt Tillie forbids it because of those people. And those people aren't related to me. Not by blood. Ask Aunt Tillie yourself, now that they're gone."

"She's asleep."

"Ask her when she wakes up."

"Now, Veronica," Willie said with a slight growl, "You know the rules."

"Yes, I do," she replied coolly, "Sit in your room until you die and then we'll wall you up. I worry you might wall me up before I die. Until Amy got here," she reached for me but awkwardly grabbed my head near my face before she found my shoulder and pulled me close, "The only person who would talk to me was Kathleen. And she has to be paid."

"Now, Miss Veronica," Willie started.

"No," she didn't sound the least bit angry, but I could feel rage inside her, "Now I found someone who enjoys my company, and I want to be with him for a while. We're not running off to get married. We're just going to Boston."

"Oh," Willie said thoughtfully, "The bird show."

"Is that it?"

"I would think. You might not be able to see them, but you certainly can hear them sing."

"Then you won't make a fuss?"

"No," he said, "But Amy can't take you. What if she meets up with Darnell Miller again?"

"She won't," Veronica said with certainty, "He's in Arkham with Kathleen. He's been seeing her, you know."

"No, I didn't," Willie mused, "Her taste in men is worse than yours." Then before she could respond, "Okay, Amy, you may escort your lovely cousin to the park. But be home quickly. I noticed you didn't touch your schoolwork."

I froze for a second. I forgot about it. But it was summer and I shouldn't have to do schoolwork anyway. So, I nodded and we left.

"Well, if my father might be both Darnell Miller's and

Kathleen's parent, shouldn't they stop seeing each other?" I asked as we strolled to the park to meet Jerry.

"He might not be," she replied.

"Shouldn't we tell them?"

"You can. Don't expect them to believe you."

I nodded. It was a pleasant enough walk, though I was certainly feeding a few hungry mosquitos. Veronica was quite pleased with herself for standing up to Willie and getting him to back down. I wondered how well she was going to fare with Mother, especially if Aunt Vera was around.

Jerry was waiting for us on a bench. A saxophone was playing jazz music a bit further in. It had a nice sound to it. Slow and quiet. Almost bluesy.

"Well, if it isn't the two most beautiful young ladies the state has to offer," he said when he saw us.

Veronica blushed while I scowled. He could take insincerity to whole new worlds. The music even stopped.

"Yes, Amy, that means you, too."

"Well of course it does, Amy," Veronica agreed, "How could you even not think you're pretty?"

Just then I felt a cold wet dog nose on my calf. I jumped a bit and looked down.

"Sniffy," I exclaimed and bent down to pet him for a bit. He jumped back and came forward to sniff my hand, "Well, I see how you got your name."

"He always remembers a friend," came a voice behind us.

I turned. It was Sniffy's owner. He had a leash wrapped around his arm and was carrying the saxophone.

"Oh, hi," I said and did a failed curtsy, "Was that you playing the music?"

"It was indeed," he replied, "I had to stop by and see if

you still wanted to write that song."

"Well of course she does," Veronica gushed, "She plays the violin. She'd be a great musician if she wasn't a girl."

She was unaware of my glare.

"Girls can be great musicians," the man gently corrected, "Ever hear of Jenny Lind?"

"No," we all said at once.

"Well, she was a great musician," he replied, unflustered.

"What did she play?" I asked.

"She sang," he replied.

"Everyone can sing," Jerry said.

"Not everyone can sing *well*. Some people sound like tortured cats when they go caroling."

"How true," Veronica said soothingly, "So how do you know Amy?"

"I don't. I spoke to her a bit the other day. All about dogs that eat eggs. We were going to write a song about it."

"You must have had quite the discussion if you know she plays violin."

"We didn't and I don't. Well, I guess I do now. So, let's sit down and compose a jazz classic. Do you like jazz?"

"I *adore* jazz," Veronica practically gushed, "So we're invited too?"

"Certainly," the man said, "And so we can address each other properly, allow me to introduce myself. I am Steven Robert Sleath. And you are?"

"Veronica Langston, and my friend Jerry Talkington, and my wonderful cousin, Amy Wentworth."

"Amy Collins," I corrected.

"Not for long," Veronica re-corrected, "I so love music. I have a cousin who plays jazz clarinet down in Boston. Sadly, his family disapproves and disinherited him. But I know he'll be famous one day."

"Disapproval gives a musician incentive. Being disinherited gives him motivation. He has to play well, because if he fails, he starves. And starving makes you hungry."

I glanced at him for a second as everyone laughed. Nobody laughed when I used that kind of humor.

"So, tell me about your cousin. Is he good?"

"He's the best," I said, "I played with him last night. He can make old songs sound brand new."

"It may sound immodest since I'm related to him, but he is very good. So is she." Veronica gripped my neck to present my head to him.

"I don't think Mr. Sleath wants to hear about child violinists," I protested.

"Please now, Amy," he said, "I am not so formal. Call me Steven."

"I think maybe we should let the composers write their song now," Jerry said quietly to Veronica.

"Can't we stay and watch them? We can go to the aviary tomorrow, can't we? Please?"

"How did you know I was taking you to the aviary?"

"A little bird told me," she said to his bemusement.

First, Steven got out some blank sheet music and told me to think of rhymes we might use. Then we put them together while we fed the mosquitos.

Oh Hannah Hen was so proud of her nest
She said, Come see my new home
I think it's the best
But old Lucy Leghorn shook her head with a frown
She said, You built it so low
That it sits on the ground
And your eggs will be gone when that dog comes around

But Hannah was young and she thought she knew best
That dog is our friend
He won't bother my nest
He chases the fox, the snake and the pests
And Lucy said, Hannah you're breaking my heart,
You understand much but you're missing one part
As sure a dog begs a dog eats eggs
Because a dog is a dog and dogs eat eggs
Yes, dogs are just dogs and dogs eat eggs
And Hannah said, Lucy, I do understand
I'll move to the treetop
High over the land
My eggs will be safe and my eggs will be sound
And out of the reach of that hungry old dog
I'll give him no reason to ever come round
There'll be nothing here for that old worthless hound
Because
As sure a dog begs a dog eats eggs
Because a dog is a dog and dogs eat eggs
Yes, dogs are just dogs and dogs eat eggs

It was safe to conclude that Cole Porter would never consider us worthy competition, but I liked it. The music he composed was catchy and lively. Veronica was highly impressed with our effort. Jerry had nothing bad to say about it, but I thought he might be jealous.

"So, your cousin Bixby plays music like this?" he asked.

"He does," Veronica replied, "Maybe the two of you can get together and play. His band plays at The Bluesy Blue Blues Club in Boston."

"I can't say I ever heard of it," Steven mused, stroking his chin.

"It's on Rosier Heights and Tenth," she explained.

"Rosier and Tenth? Does he drive a tank to get there?" Jerry smiled.

"A tank?" Veronica and I never saw a tank and obviously missed a joke.

"It's a rough neighborhood."

"It is," Steven said, "But I'll take the chance. I just signed a contract with Elliot Brothers Studios. They make cartoons and they're hiring jazz players like mad. Those slapstick little shorts just cry out for jazz accompaniment. They can't hire enough and a lot of musicians aren't reliable. You know, get in trouble a lot. If he's stable, I can get him in. I'll give a listen when I can."

Chapter Forty-Four

Back Home

The visit was over. Jerry and Veronica still had time to stroll around the city and talk, though their trip to Boston had to be postponed. Steven took Sniffy home after saying goodbye. I had schoolwork. I did manage to get a lot done until Zelda came in and told me Melanie and Ursula were waiting for me in the drawing room.

Just before we got to the doors, I could hear Melanie say, "Remember now, her name is Amy. I think you scare her when you call her Yvonne."

I would have loved to just stay there and listen to them talk but Zelda announced me before I could stop her.

Eavesdropping is very difficult in this house.

There were the usual hugs and those fake kisses that I don't really like but tolerate and then we sat down for tea. I watched Melanie pour the proper way. Nobody up here just filled up a cup. It had to be done perfectly and ladylike and I didn't quite possess the right amount of femininity to handle such an important assignment. Besides, I wasn't the hostess. I actually was, I found out later on. Since Melanie was also visiting me, I should have poured.

"I knew I had the gift when I was your age," Ursula was saying over her tea, loaded with four lumps of sugar, cream and lemon, "At first there were just premonitions and intuition. Then I met an old herbalist who recognized my abilities. She taught me all about palmistry, tarot, charms, and even how to conduct a séance. But we have to be careful because bad things can happen when you talk to the dead. They're not all friendly, you know."

"I suppose not," I replied.

"But after a while you learn how to handle them. Some just want to inhabit a body long enough to say something to a loved one. That's where you, as a medium, will come into the picture."

"What?" I was stunned, "No. Besides, I'm not a medium. I'm a small."

There were probably better ways to say it.

"I agree," Melanie said, giving me a sideways glance, "I told you I thought she was too young. Besides, what does she even know about the Spiritual Arts?"

"Nothing, I suppose," Ursula sighed, "And with all the bad literature designed to scare people, she probably has no desire to learn. But here, I tell you what." She reached into her purse and pulled out a deck of cards. "I brought along a tarot deck. We'll do a reading."

"Wow, Amy," Melanie said, "She charges five dollars for a reading."

"I do indeed," Ursula agreed while shuffling the deck, "It is a rare gift I was given. Nature smiled on me. I smile on you. Now, touch the deck. Press down on the top card so that your spiritual essence influences the reading."

I suppressed an eye roll and did as she asked.

She started humming with a smile. She was really in her element. The first card we turned over was the mermaid.

"The drowned girl lives on," she said, "The innocent princess who embarks on life. You have friends who are attracted to you. Not all are true friends. Beware of who you trust. Some people you trust will betray you. Of course, that's a predication we can make for everybody. You are kind and will stay kind. Think of the people in your life as the sea. It can change in an instant from calm to stormy. From tranquil to dangerous."

I pictured my stepfather throwing the Harmons in the fountain.

The next card was the joker.

"Fate plays games with you. Wherever you may go. Whoever you may be with. All can be changed. Things never go as planned. But you will marry well and be happy for as long as it lasts. You will always have friends. Some treat you well, others do not. It is the same with your enemies."

Then came the death card.

"You will have a long and happy life. But because of that, you will watch the ones you love die before you. You must accept it. Some deaths will be expected. Some will be a surprise. One will be soon."

"Cheery thought," I said dryly.

"We are born, we live, we die," she shrugged, "But we rejoin the ones we love when it is our turn. I will teach you more on Saturday."

"Saturday?"

"Didn't Mother tell you?" Melanie asked, "Ursula invited you and me to spend the day on her yacht on Saturday. She already said you can go."

"I am so looking forward to you visiting me," Ursula said, her eyes sparkling in a wolfish sort of way, "I'm sure Saturday will come sooner than we think."

"So, Amy," Melanie said with a happy smile, "Won't that be fun?"

No.

"I'm sure it will be," I lied.

Chapter Forty-Five

A Phone Call

The next day, I was itching from mosquito bites on my shoulders and back. I tried rubbing the welts on the doorframe, but my dress was too thick to be successful. I went looking for Zelda to see if maybe I could get my bath early. Warm water and a good rubbing might be helpful. I didn't really know where she would be or what she was doing this time of day so I thought the most logical choice would be the kitchen.

Fluffy jumped into my arms and squirmed around to lick me. It took a moment for her to settle down before I could ask anything.

"No, I haven't seen her," Cookie said. She was cooking Lobster Newburg and was making the sauce. I watched as the cream and egg yolks bubbled. It smelled good and after seeing my longing expression, Cookie gave me a taste.

"Nifty," I exclaimed, "I used to think that Cici, our cook in Faucette, was the best cook in the whole world, but you're just as good. Better even. I don't think Cici ever made anything like this."

"What does she make?"

"Shrimp etouffee, gumbo, red beans and rice, jambalaya, things like that."

"I don't know the first thing about any of that. I'm sure she'd beat me hands down," she thought for a moment, "Especially the beans and rice. I don't cook beans. Beans give people gas and gas is embarrassing to have in public."

"I know," I said, thinking of the beans I gave to Laura Sauveterre and her family.

"Besides, beans are a sign of being poor. The Wentworths would never allow them in the house. They worry about what the neighbors think."

"I like beans," I said, "And I don't worry about what the neighbors think."

She smiled, "Wait until more of the Wentworth family priorities dig in."

She pulled out a couple of wrapped codfish to put on the cutting board.

"Do you want me to help you clean the fish? I know how to do it. We had a restaurant in Louisiana, you know."

She stopped and gave me her full attention.

"A Wentworth lady does not clean fish, scale fish, cook fish, filet fish, or catch fish. All you do is eat fish. A Wentworth lady never works. They are only decorations. If Willie even saw you so much as look at a raw fish, he'd have me gutted and filleted. Now if you're not hungry, go do something ladylike and stop getting me in trouble."

"I didn't mean to get you in trouble. I was just trying to help."

She looked at me for a second and then grabbed me up in a ferocious bear hug. I thought for a second that maybe she knew she was my aunt. Or half-aunt. Or not. The relationships in this house were hard to figure out.

"I love tiny little girls who aren't prissy and useless. I'll be sad when you turn into the others."

"I won't," I said, "I have too much not-Wentworth in my upbringing."

I was trying to think of a better way to phrase it when the phone rang.

Cookie answered it, "Hello?" After a pause she glanced at me with a frown, "She's right here."

It was the very first phone call I ever got. It was Mom from Faucette.

"Well, hi, little stranger," she said, "Nobody's heard from you, so we wanted to make sure you're all right."

"I'm fine," I replied, "I love it here. Everyone's so nice to me. I have four sisters that live with me and we have lots of fun together. They love that fact that I had adventures back home and want some here."

"This is your home," Cookie hissed at me.

"I meant former home," I was flustered, "But it was still home. I mean, I don't think I threw a family away, I gained one." I thought for a moment. "I mean, I said it wrong. I loved it there. I love it here though."

She laughed, "I'm sure you do. Tell me about your new life."

I told her about my sisters and how we always had fun when they were home. I was studying for sixth grade throughout the summer to get a jump on it. I was learning to ride a horse, taking dance lessons and continuing with my violin. I left out the part about only knowing 'peasant' music.' We spent the night in a haunted house, but I didn't see or hear anything. We had hot and cold running water and I took a bath each night with my maid to help.

"You have a maid to help you take a bath?" I could hear the frown in her voice.

"Well, yes, I like that part. She puts calamine lotion on

my bug bites and makes sure I have clean clothes ready. It's really nice."

"She can just stay up there if she thinks she's getting maid service like that down here," I heard Gramma Morris' voice in the background.

"I never said I wanted a maid," I was a little angry, "And don't ask me questions if you're just going to get mad at the answers."

"Now, Amy," she said with dramatic patience, "No one's mad. Your Gramma Morris is just thinking you'll come back for a visit and expect something like that. I don't know how she would get that idea. You were a perfect daughter to us."

There was a pause as I heard her drinking something.

"Most of the time, anyway. At least there aren't any alligators up there, so we don't have to worry about you. And we do want you to visit us. I don't care what some Yankee judge up in Boston thinks. You are my daughter. As sure as I gave birth to you. And I'm sure I did."

I was mollified a bit and we talked for almost half an hour. They got my letter and Guy had a job interview next week. Annette was so happy when she called to tell everyone about it. All was forgiven. Anna Marie was having trouble with her grades again and absolutely despised Miss Du Lin. Michelle was thinking of becoming a nurse. And then came the two big pieces of news.

"So, your Dad has been talking to us about changing churches," she said, "You remember your going away party? How he promised Father Cassidy how he'd go Baton Rouge with him to help with the food bank?"

"As part of his penance. I know."

"Well, he feels more accepted around the Catholic men than the men of our church. Or his previous church. Just think how nice they were to you. Our church was less kind when you moved here."

"I can't argue with that."

"And that was just wrong. If I made a mistake, which I did, they can be unforgiving to me, but they should leave my children out of it. And speaking of children," she continued, "Your Aunt Mary may be moving back down here after her baby is born. With Julia and Patrick."

"What about Sophie and Isabella?" I asked, the distaste building.

"Not them. They're going to Italy with their aunt. The plans aren't final yet, of course, it's just the talking stage. That Isadora woman wants custody of the baby. She doesn't think Mary is a fit mother. Imagine that.

"We'll have Louis look into it if she pursues it."

There was a pause and I thought for a moment we were done talking.

"Now Amy," she said, her voice turning solemn. Whatever was coming next was going to be bad. "I want you to know that sometimes when we lose someone we love, it's not a loss. It was a blessing to have known them in the first place."

"Who died?" I asked. It was obviously someone important to me.

"The Countess had a cerebral hemorrhage."

"A what?"

"Her brain started bleeding and she passed on."

"The Countess?"

Some deaths will be expected. Some will be a surprise. One will be soon.

"I know it's sad. What's really bad is that her children are all coming only for the inheritance. They all disowned her years before for some reason. Now that there's money to be got, they're all over her corpse like flies. Only the flies are more respectable."

Yes, they would be. It was sad. The Countess was such a wonderful person. I knew her family was angry and disowned her, maybe because she married Killy, or possibly they found out about Cici. Even though the Countess gave birth to them and raised them through reconstruction, they turned their backs on her. I may have thought better of them if they didn't want her money. But they weren't angry at the money.

I didn't have much to say after that. I needed to be alone with my memories. All that was important to me was that I would never see my friend again. She was so very kind to me. Not everyone in Faucette was nice to me when I arrived.

She looked so frail and confused the last time I saw her. I knew something was wrong and I knew it was serious. I wanted to cry but I had no tears.

"That doesn't mean you didn't care about her," Zelda said later while brushing my hair, "Eighty-seven years is a long time. It wasn't the tragedy of early death. She moved on to the next level of existence. She was probably happy to go. It may sound sad and it may sound scary, but we all go to that destination sooner or later. And our reunion with our friends on the other side will be oh, so happy. Just the same, I would rather grieve over the loss than go to that reunion just yet."

Can't argue with that.

Dinner was quiet for me. My sisters were all happy and energetic, but I didn't feel much like talking or playing around. Uncle Edgar and Aunt Vera were over again. At least I was at the end of the table with the other children and not on display. I think Zelda told Barbara I was out of sorts, so she made sure I had small portions of the veal and mashed potatoes. I ate enough to satisfy the adults and made my excuse of needing time to finish my schoolwork.

"Why didn't you do that this morning with all your free time?" Aunt Vera asked.

"Well—"

"No 'wells.' A lady answers a question firmly and with confidence.'

"My free time wasn't so free, Ma'am."

"Oh, well, I see," she replied.

I didn't bother to ask her why she could say 'well,' but I couldn't. Besides, it was obvious that she really didn't care to 'see.' It wasn't like she asked me what I did during my free time.

"And by the way," she went on, "A young lady doesn't clean fish. We hire people for that. If you get too familiar with the help, you wind up being no better than the help."

"Yes, ma'am."

Cookie ratted me out.

"Imagine my surprise when I went into the kitchen and heard you offering to do such a thing. You could smell like fish for hours."

Cookie didn't rat me out.

Mother interrupted, asking Aunt Vera, "Why were you in our kitchen in the first place?"

"Because the doctor said you should be eating lots of fish and green vegetables. I wanted to make sure that bit of information was passed down. I care about you, you know."

"Oh," Mother was almost confused, "Well, thank you."

If I said 'well,' I'd be groused at.

"If something happened to you, I'd be stuck with all these children," Aunt Vera continued.

Well, I guess there's caring and REALLY caring.

I escaped to my room to start my homework.

Although Zelda was my maid, she had other duties to attend to, especially during dinnertime, so I trudged upstairs alone. I was rather happy to be isolated with my own thoughts. I opened the door to my room and gave myself a critical inspection. My hair was growing back now and was at least covering all my ears and reached down to the collar in the back. Zelda always parted it just right of center and had the locks separate so they covered my forehead. From the distance, my freckles weren't visible and my skin was smooth enough. My hazel eyes were nothing less than gorgeous. I was certainly cute enough to not have people tell me what I needed to do to become pretty. I was pretty.

I went to my schoolwork pile on the dresser and picked up *The Red Badge of Courage*, my assigned reading for the week. It was better than *Oliver Twist* but not by much. I only had about thirty pages more to read so I opened it. I wasn't really reading it, only looking at words. I wasn't going to complete anything that required thought, so I dug through the pile until I found my algebra. All I had to do was follow the formulas and write the answers. Sadly, I ran out of problems before I ran out of daylight.

My room was warm and stuffy, so I went over to the window and opened it to let in the breeze. Unfortunately, there was no breeze, but Massachusetts made up for it by sending me mosquitos. Although the rooms on the first floor all had screens, the bedrooms on the second floor did not. I quickly slid it shut since they made such rude and greedy guests. It seemed like there was a black cloud of them that I just barely escaped. As I latched it shut, I noticed a movement by the hedges. They swallowed up a large shape and after a little shuddering they were still. I watched for it to return but the bushes stayed unmoving.

I resolved that I was just going to be slightly uncomfortable tonight. And I was restless and bored. And to make matters worse, I didn't feel like doing anything to not be bored. I flopped on my bed and stared at the ceiling, thinking of Faucette. I missed the Countess. I remembered her kindness to me. How sad I felt the last time I saw her.

I thought about my home down south. Did I really want to go back and visit next summer? The Countess was gone. Mom would be busy with the baby. Dad just embarrassed me so much at the party. And I knew it would happen again. I didn't want to sleep three to a bed now that I had one all to myself. I enjoyed electricity and a private bath without having to heat the water and fill the tub. I never wanted to use an outhouse ever again.

The negative thoughts were soon replaced by pleasant memories. I had some friends down there. I met nobody my age up here. Only my sisters. Probably because everyone was too afraid to go out.

I set up my music stand and started playing *Shenandoah*. This was only the second time I played it, so I didn't play it well, I thought, but I enjoyed it. I played it again, a bit slower and more evenly. It sounded so mournful, like the way I felt. I reached down to find something else to play when I heard footsteps coming up the stairs. I found a copy of *Loch Lomond* and sat it on the stand when I heard something like a cross between a gasp and a scream.

Lisa was at the door staring in the mirror. My movement must have startled her or something and she turned to face me. She seemed downright afraid.

"Are you alright?" I asked.

"Well, yes," she stammered back, "I just saw—" she

pointed at the mirror.

I glanced over but it was just a mirror showing our reflections.

"You saw how pretty you are?" I wasn't sure what to say and that sounded disarming.

"No, I already know that," she replied, "I saw a woman. She was in the mirror looking at you play."

I shivered a bit. The room was getting colder.

I looked again. It was just a mirror. I started putting my instrument away.

"Well, anyway," she said calmly, "Mother wants you to play your violin downstairs. Everybody loves what you're playing. Millie's talking about getting lessons now. I'm serious."

I picked it back up and gathered the music.

"That song should be famous," she said as we made our way down the hall.

"It kind of is."

"Oh, well, I never heard of it."

"Lisa? Why is it that you can say 'well' and I can't?"

"Because Aunt Vera can't hear me."

"Yes, I can," Aunt Vera's voice invaded our conversation from downstairs, "You're not getting away with anything."

We looked at each other and suppressed our giggles.

The conversation started with a long, mandatory explanation of how vulgar and unladylike the term 'well' was, and how it sent a verbal clue that the woman (as opposed to 'lady') who said such a word was plain and uneducated. Certainly not wife-material for a true gentleman. And as young Wentworth ladies, we wouldn't want to wind up married to some common *Nouveau Riche*.

Imagine if that poor woman ever met any of the men in Faucette.

We thanked her for the lesson in etiquette and for warning us of the possible fates worse than death that awaited the poor ignorant damsels who ever used the word 'well' for any meaning other than a hole in the ground used to pump water. The lesson in vernacular would stay with us always. We never actually followed the lesson, but we laughed about it a lot as we got older.

I played *Shenandoah* again. Twice, as Uncle Edgar seemed to really enjoy it. Nadia looked on with disapproving eyes. Then I switched to the Beethoven pieces I was learning. Charity soon was drafted to play along on the piano and eventually it became a sing along. Veronica came in, helped by Kathleen and they joined us. Veronica enjoyed the time together while Kathleen obviously felt awkward. Even Fluffy joined us, running around in circles, but not singing.

Zelda brushed my hair before bedtime. I tried to look out the window, but the light only allowed us to see ourselves. There was no moon and clouds hid the stars.

"Do you want me to open the window tonight?" Zelda asked.

"No. The mosquitos will carry me away for dinner."

She laughed, "Those must be big mosquitos. I can open it just a crack."

"No, thank you. Let them eat someone else."

She nodded absently and we completed my bedtime routine. I was almost asleep on my side when the buzzing drone of an attacking insect tickled my ear. I felt the little bloodsucker trying to crawl up my lobe and into my brain. I swiped at it, but it came back with an amused buzz. It attacked again and I kept swatting at it unsuccessfully until I pulled my sheet over my head to keep it away.

Maybe an hour of battle went by before I heard two

men shouting in the yard. I put on my robe and went out to the hall. Veronica was there and we were joined by all my other sisters. Soon Kathleen, Zelda, Nadia, and Willie were there. Willie was in a robe like Veronica and me, while the maids took the time to throw on their dresses. Fluffy was running around and barking until Lisa picked her up.

"What was it?" Claire asked me.

I shrugged, while Millie was hugging Charity for safety. I wondered why she chose Charity. Her performance at the guest house didn't quite make me think of her as a tower of strength.

"Sounded like someone shouting," Veronica said, "But it's after midnight. Who'd be out shouting at this time of night?"

"Someone who shouldn't be here," Charity said, displaying a firm grasp of the obvious.

Lisa must have agreed with my thought. She glanced at her and shook her head.

Willie disappeared down the stairs and came back with a nasty looking poker, covered in soot. I wouldn't want to be hit with it.

"Be careful with that," Kathleen hissed impatiently, "We could spend hours cleaning clothes if that soot gets on one of the ladies."

"Or the floor," Zelda added, though mopping the floor didn't strike me as that much of a chore. I used to help Mom in Faucette do housework. Getting soot off of clothes was a forever project, but mopping up the floor by the fireplace was hardly a major chore.

There was some more rustling at the window and then a tall shadow climbed off the vines onto the landing and opened the door. It was Chester, dressed in black, almost invisible in the night.

He looked surprised that we were all there and gave us a sheepish grin as he closed the door behind him.

Kathleen rolled her eyes impatiently. Willie lowered the poker and we girls all relaxed.

"What are you thinking making all that noise?" Kathleen practically yelled at him, "You woke everyone in the house up. Including the dog." She pointed at Fluffy, who obviously enjoyed being in Lisa's grip.

"Hush now, Kathleen," Willie said, "Miss Tilly is still asleep."

He turned to Chester with a cross between a smile and a sneer on his face. After a deep breath, he set the poker down. Zelda quickly grabbed it up with a little mutter of "my floor."

"So now Chester," Willie said in a quiet voice, though I detected a slight growl, "Would you like to explain to us what you were doing just now?"

"Yes, sir," he said, giving a quick look to Kathleen, "Well, sir, it was strange. I couldn't sleep so I got dressed and went out for a walk to see if that would help."

"At one in the morning?" Zelda asked skeptically.

"Yes, at one in the morning," he replied haughtily.

"I was sleeping fine until you came stomping in."

"Zelda, please," Willie said, "And so you climbed up the vines to the second floor to help you sleep?"

"No, sir," he was quite flustered now, "I was walking along and there was this guy on the property and he was climbing the vines and I started yelling at him and he shouted something at me. So, I charged over here but he jumped down and ran off."

"So why were you climbing up the vines?" Willie asked.

"Well, sir," he said, "I wanted to see if the vines could actually hold the weight of a grown man. You know, see if someone could get in here. He can, sir. And you saw the door was left unlocked. He could have gotten all the china in the house if I didn't stop him."

"Good show, Chester," Willie said, "And here I thought you were just trying to get to the girls' apartments upstairs. Now we know we should cut all the vegetation off the wall. I'll have Zack get it done tomorrow. We'll have to be more vigilant too. We could have lost something far more valuable than china," he said looking at me and my sisters.

"But I love those vines," Zelda said, "They're what gives the house its charm and makes it so pretty."

"Well, we'll be living in a charmless and ugly house for a while," Willie said in a conversation-over voice, "Now let's lock the door and get back in bed and go to sleep."

I went back to bed, but that little mosquito kept buzzing my ear, so I didn't really get any sleep.

Chapter Forty-Six

More Interviews

The next day brought Detective Trask back for more interviews. I found out at breakfast that Veronica was scheduled to be first so I hurried through my Eggs Benedict so I could listen in. Sadly, when I got back upstairs, Kathleen was already there, cleaning and dusting.

"As if it isn't bad enough we can't sleep at night anymore," she told me, "Now she wants me to clean her room early today while she's upstairs. Throws off my whole routine."

"Maybe she thought it would be easier for you to clean without worrying about where she is," I replied.

Maybe she didn't want me to hear her interview is more like it.

I got out my geography. Nadia was having me study the watershed of Siberia. It was worse than the Ural Mountains. No interesting stone carvings. Just a frozen swamp. Might as well study grass growing.

After that was science. I was studying the human body and its systems. Today was the heart and blood. Arteries and veins. White and red cells. Yesterday, Nadia gave Millie and me a more detailed talk on boys and sex and reproduction and things. We also got a little speech on not talking about such things ever again.

After I finished science, I tried to finish *The Red Badge of Courage*. I heard Kathleen escort Veronica to her room. I waited a minute or two for Kathleen to walk downstairs to do maid-stuff, then I knocked on the door.

"What took you so long?" came the response.

I flounced in and we talked for just a bit.

"You were up there a long time and Kathleen was cleaning your room forever," I said.

"I was," she replied, "It was a strange talk. He asked me a lot about the night my parents died. Then a few questions about Uncle Joe and Fourthy. I can't say I liked Uncle Joe. He treated me like I was an idiot instead of being blind. Fourthy was evil. He was always trying to sneak in here to see me when I was undressing. I always caught him and whapped him one."

"How did you know you *always* caught him?'

"He *always* had to breathe."

We soon had the vent open and were laying quietly on the bed, listening to forbidden things. At first there was nothing, then a knock on the upstairs door broke the silence.

"Come in," Trask called.

There was some rustling of clothes and the click of shoes.

"It's a girl," Veronica told me, "That swoosh is a dress and men don't wear shoes that make that much noise."

"Can you tell me your whole name?"

"Kathleen McGuinn."

"How old are you?"

"Twenty-nine."

Her story was surprising. When Mother and Father married, he assumed control of *Langston Fabrics*. That company did quite a lot of business in Ireland. When Father went there on business trips, he met Kathleen's mother and they had an affair but it ended.

"My mother was broken hearted," she said, "Everything was in the pipe. They even had a wedding day picked and a church. Then he told her he had to break it off. He was already married. She was already pregnant.

"He abandoned us without a penny or a word, but we survived as best we could. He came back on another business trip maybe ten years ago. That's when I was hired. But no one could know our relationship. If I said a word, back to Ireland.

"He made it clear to both of us that he was not entirely sure if he was my father or not. My mother was quite offended, but he didn't care. I refused to consider going with him, after he insulted her on top of everything else. But she insisted. Even a servant girl here in America is better than anything Ireland could offer. So, I came back to America with him. That was the simple choice. Take a job and have a nice life in America or live in dirt poor poverty in Ireland. I could at least send some money home to my mother to support my son."

"Son?"

"You want to say it? Like mother, like daughter? Only he married me. Then he started ranting about Irish independence and he was shot."

"My condolences. So, you were an extremely young widow with no resources. It seems you were lucky Mr. Wentworth came back when he did. But are you not happy with the circumstances Mr. Wentworth offered?"

"Of course not," she practically screamed, "Would you be? I am obviously the daughter of himself. I look more like himself than any of those girls. Me, Clarice and that little monster look just like *him*. We were obviously blood. But he wouldn't have it. He wouldn't see it. That woman wouldn't tolerate scandal in the family."

"Well, you can hardly blame Mrs. Wentworth for not wanting it to come out that her husband is…less than faithful."

"His wife? Ha!" Kathleen was excited, "It never occurred to her he goes around hopping in every bed without a lock. She's too busy taking pills. It's his sister. Mrs. Vera Tyler. She runs this family more than either Wentworth ever did. Himself? He would have set me up in a lady's shop, selling clothes and perfumes. But Vera Tyler wouldn't have it. Too good for a bastard child. She was afraid it might come out himself was my father. So, I had to be kept in the house like his others. Not to be seen. People would talk. People would laugh."

Her energy level was slowing down now.

"So here I am, serving the family when I should be waited on like them. Clean up, serve food, watch after that blind little moron downstairs. At least the others are part sisters. Miss Veronica is nothing. A blind drain of resources. She'd be out on the streets begging for pennies back home. That's all she's good for."

How cruel!

The interview went on for a while longer. Where was she the day before they sailed? Who was she with? Any ideas who could have done it?

I held Veronica's head on my chest while she quietly wept. Kathleen was her companion for so long.

I closed the vent while she freshened up in the bathroom. I wondered if we were done with the eavesdropping now that she received such a shock. But she came in and expertly made her way back to the bed.

"That's exactly why they say to never listen in on other people's conversations," she said with a fake but determined smile, "You'll never know what you'll hear about yourself."

"Well," I said, "I don't think she knows you at all."

"Don't let Aunt Vera hear you say 'well.'"

We laughed.

"Why does she call him 'himself'?"

"It's the Irish way of saying 'the big shot man,'" she replied, "Anyway, it's okay. Jerry likes me. He won't have me sitting on a corner begging for pennies."

"Well, good. I mean, just good. Maybe Jerry's not as bad as I—. Well, no. What I mean is maybe I misjudged him."

I didn't think I misjudged him at all. He was mean. But I could overlook that since he was so good for Veronica.

"Maybe you did. He brought you home, after all. He may have been a little rough about it, but he wanted you safe."

A little rough?

We discussed the difference between being a little rough and child abuse for a minute or two and then it was time to open the vent for the next interview. I recognized the swoosh sound as a dress, but the shoes barely registered in my ears.

"It's Zelda," Veronica whispered, "I think she wears dance shoes, they're so quiet."

"Can you tell me your whole name?" Trask's harsh voice sounded.

"Zelda Fiorella Blake."

"How old are you?"

"Twenty."

After the usual questions about where she was when the boat was sabotaged, he started inquiring about how well she interacted with everyone else.

"Well, they all treat me real well for being just a maid. Coming here was the berries."

"The berries?"

"It's great. I enjoy working with the family. I am just thrilled I got out of Dublin and didn't even have to look for a job. Yes, it's a little sad that I can't tell everyone that I might be part of the family. But you know, I don't look anything like my father. It might cause troubles if I said anything, especially now with him gone."

"What did you think of his son, your half-brother?"

"He was a monster. I glad he's gone."

"Well," Trask said, somewhat surprised, "That's harsh."

"The little demon tried to reach under my dress when I was bent over making his bed."

"Bad technique. Good taste."

"What does that mean?"

"There are some things men do that women hate that men understand."

She snorted, "And we know why you understand."

Trask ignored the taunt.

"What about the rest of the family?"

"What about them?" she asked.

"Who do you think would have motive to kill your father and brother?"

"I wouldn't know. I know several people who think he was their father and are unhappy he only gave them jobs but not any money. But you know, I think a person should do for themselves, like I do. Just getting out of Dublin was blessing enough for me."

"Some of the servants resent not being full members of the family?"

"Some. And some people about town too."

"Oh?"

"And there's some who don't know, like that Jerry Talkington fellow."

"Jerry Talkington is Wentworth's son?"

"So they say, but he may be his half-brother. Or cousin. I can't keep it all straight. Neither can anyone else. Good thing Miss Veronica is a Langston, or they'd have a brother-sister-romance. Not a good thing, that."

Veronica stiffened.

"They don't know, of course, but the older ones say he looked just like Himself before the war. Don't know how they can tell with that mask."

"I see. So, you had no resentments against Mr. Wentworth?"

"Well, of course not. He took me out of poverty and misery and gave me all this."

I can only imagine what the Detective thought about that. There was certainly a pause in the questioning.

"What can you tell me about the rest of the family?"

"They're good to me. Especially Melanie. She took me to meet her dear friend a few months ago."

"Her dear friend?"

"Ursula Chzerick. She gave me a few palm readings and she's looking for an assistant. I've been thinking about going to work for her. In fact, on my off evenings after I put Miss Amy to bed, I go visit her and do some odd jobs, cleaning and stuff. Just to prove my worth, you know. And it's easy work. She mostly asks about Miss Amy. Her favorite foods, what she likes to read. Things like that."

"I see. What can you tell me about Kathleen?"

"She's nice enough but she always seems angry just underneath it all. I was hoping her new boyfriend would be a calming influence on her, but that's not to be. He's just as angry as she is."

"Who's her new boyfriend?"

"Darnell Miller."

"She's seeing Darnell Miller?" Trask asked.

"Yes, sir."

"She shouldn't be."

"No, she shouldn't be," Veronica said after we closed the vent, "I wonder if Uncle Joe knew that going to bed with every girl in town and then importing his progenies home might cause that to happen. Especially when he won't let them talk about it. Someone should warn Kathleen."

"Someone like you?"

"No," she replied with a bitter voice, "Someone who cares."

Bob the footman was next. I hoped the detective would be kind to him. He obviously wasn't right. His looking down at the ground when he introduced himself made me feel sorry for him.

He would have no useful information, of course. I was sure he never looked up long enough to see what was going on around him. But they still had an interesting conversation.

"What is your full name?"

"Bob Hartford."

"The Bob is short for Robert?"

"Yes, sir, it is short for Robert."

Veronica and I looked at each other for a second.

"Does the family treat you okay?"

"Yes, sir, the family treats me okay."

"No problems?"

"No, sir. No problems."

"Who do you like the best?"

"I don't know, sir."

"Is that because they all treat you badly."

There was a pause.

"No, sir."

"Does everyone treat you well?"

"Yes, sir."

"In the family, that is?"

"Yes, sir."

"And your fellow employees?"

"Yes, sir."

"They are mean to you." That was a statement, not a question.

"Not always, sir."

"Not always," Trask repeated, "Who are the ones who are mean to you?"

"Tom. Kathleen."

"Tom and Kathleen are mean to you? How so?"

"Tom hits me. He says I don't work fast enough. He has to do my work."

"Does he?

"No, sir. I do my own work. Every bit of it. Even Zach says so. But Tom, he still hits me."

"I see. And Kathleen?"

"She hits me with a belt."

"A belt? Was this before or after the boat sank?"

"Before."

"What happened?"

"We were cleaning the guest house. Getting it ready for summer."

"They use it for guests?"

"Sometimes. Mr. Wentworth had people there. They stay a week or two and leave. We clean up. Nasty. Nasty people leave nasty things everywhere for us to clean."

"Oh? I didn't know it was rented out."

They paused. Maybe Bob was nodding his head or shrugging. Whatever it was, we didn't see it.

"So, you were cleaning up after the party? Getting it ready for another?"

"I was outside, wiping down the furniture. The birds perch there and leave messes. I was working. Tom and Kathleen were inside, by the couch. They were kissing. Really kissing. Like he was helping her with her dress. Getting it off. And she saw me out the window and screamed and they ran out. Accused me of looking. Tom started hitting me. Then Kathleen, she pulled his belt off."

"It was loose already."

"Yes sir," Bob said.

"Then she started swinging it at me. Called me names. Said I was spying. She was swinging at me, so the buckle was hitting my face. Then she missed and hit Tom. Then he grabbed her and I ran away."

Trask thanked him for his time and said he could go back to work. I started to get up to close the vent when someone else knocked on the door upstairs.

"Come in, Tom."

"Well, they told me it was my turn for this big waste of time."

"Trying to find a murderer is a waste of time?"

"It is for this one. Nobody cares who killed them and most people would give the killer a medal."

"Oh? Why is that?"

"He was a disgusting pig. So was his son."

"Not your favorite people?"

"Not at all. Every time I asked for a raise or just a day off, he just said, 'no.' No reason, no nothing. But he kept piling on the work. And I was the one who cleaned up after him when he had those parties in the guest house."

"I heard they left an occasional mess."

"They destroyed the place. Him and his 'business clients' and all the girls from out of town. Drunk and throwing up on the walls and floors. Writing things in the vomit."

"Like what?"

"Hi, Tom," he spit out.

"So, you took a hand drill and screwed holes in his boat?"

"What?" Tom screamed.

"Sit down," Trask said calmly, "Or you'll spend the next few nights in jail for threatening a police officer in the line of duty. That may cost you your job. Jobs are hard to come by these days, you know. And your dad won't get you another one."

"My dad? He never did a thing for me to get this one."

"What is your full name?"

"Thomas Moran."

"And Mr. Moran, your father never did much fatherly things for you?"

"What is this? You can't ask me questions like that. They have nothing to do with nothing."

"You enjoy hitting Bob? He doesn't fight back, does he? Makes you feel good to hurt him? Makes you feel like a father? How far a jump is it from beating up some little deficient like that to killing a man?"

"Hey, now," Tom was getting nervous. We could hear it in his voice.

"And then you have your girlfriend hit him with a belt. Class act."

"Now wait a minute there, sir," Tom was learning

respect, it seemed, "We had an easy job of it that day. And Kathleen and me had better things to do than go back to the house and do drudge work. Normally, Bob's just sweeping up nothing until I tell him we're done. But that day, he wasn't looking at the ground. He was looking right at us."

"So instead of chasing him off or giving him something else to do you just start beating him?"

"Well, Kathleen and I were doing something private. She was something special to me then. I didn't want him watching, getting ideas, you know. What we had may have faded away for her, but not for me. And I don't want her to be with other men. Especially that little pea brain."

"Or J. P. Wentworth?"

"I had nothing to do with that."

"But did you think of him as a rival? She's young enough to have been his daughter. Young girls and older men with money have a way of pairing off."

"I wouldn't put it past him to try."

"Even at his age? Old enough to be her father?"

"That don't mean nothing."

"How about the fact that he was her father?"

"What?"

"All the servants in this house are his children from the…wrong women."

"My mother was married to my father."

"Your father was in jail at the wrong time. You don't think I do research?"

"All of us? You mean Kathleen and I…"

"Have a slightly incestuous relationship? Yes, you do. And just think about how the two of you treat your brother."

"That's not true. Willie and Cookie are too old to be his

children. Willie was only three years younger than him and I don't know how old Cookie even is, but she's fifty if a day."

"It seems that J. P. Wentworth the second set the family example."

"Willie and Cookie are my aunt and uncle?"

"So it seems. Maybe you should be nicer to your family. And a little less nice to your sister."

"Wow, Veronica," I said after I closed the vent, "We're related to everybody in the house."

"Not 'we.' You. Uncle Joe is my uncle by marriage. Thank God. By the way, you may be related to a whole lot more people than you realize. Uncle Joe took a lot of business trips and hired a lot of men with nice looking wives. So I'm told."

That was certainly something to think about.

"When I'm old enough to date, I'll ask Mother to send me to Switzerland."

"The little country girl certainly seems to know her big city options," she laughed, "You sound like everyone else in the house now."

That made me realize I had some serious thinking to do about myself. I opened the vent.

"Zachariah Leach."

"How old are you, Mr. Leach?"

"I'll be sixty next week."

"Sixty. Kind of past the prime to be a full-time gardener, don't you think?"

"They give me help."

His English was good, although he had an accent I couldn't quite place.

"The help would be Tom and Bob?"

"Yes, sir. Bob does well enough if he knows what he's

supposed to do. Tom could be a master gardener in his own right if he wanted to work. As it is, I spend more time making sure he's doing the work than it would take for me to do it myself."

"That doesn't surprise me. How long have you worked here?"

"Since I was eight. I started by helping my father. He was the gardener before me. I just grew into the position, so to speak."

"That's quite a while. You must have seen some really interesting things here."

"You could say that, sir."

"Anything interesting right before the boat accident?"

"Nothing out of the ordinary."

"In your job, do you have a lot of tools?"

"Everything you can think of."

"A hand drill?"

"Five. Different sizes."

"I see. Do you keep track of them all?"

"Not really. They're in the shed. Anyone can get anything, if needed."

"Anyone?"

"Yes, sir. Well now, I don't reckon any of the girls ever come down to get one, of course."

"But they could if they were of a mind to?"

"Well, I suppose."

"The maids?"

"The door is always open. The grounds are all fenced in, you know. Don't worry about outsiders getting in."

"How about insiders getting out?"

"I'm not following you, sir."

"You know anything about murder?"

If Trask thought he was springing a trap, it failed, but

he was about to get quite a bit of information he may not have wanted.

"I do indeed, sir," Zach said, like he was relieved he was finally getting to tell a great story, "In the spring of seventy-six, it was."

"A murder?"

"A couple of murders, I was told."

"Who told you?"

"My father. He was doing some special work for Mr. Wentworth."

"Wentworth the second?"

"Yes, sir. Now he was a mean man. Just loved to make people hurt. Make them suffer. The women mostly, but their husbands if they had the gall to stand up to him. He imported all kinds of poor ignorant Irish girls as maids. Made them do what he wanted if you get my drift. If they said no, he'd make them say yes. Locked them in the cellar."

"Beneath the kitchen?"

"Oh no, not here, sir," Zach corrected, "In the guest house. Mr. Wentworth's father was remodeling this house at the time to make it bigger. He moved the family back here when it was done. So, the next Mr. Wentworth—"

"The second?"

"Yes, sir, he just hired women all the time. Like I said, treated them bad. If they got with child, he sent them away, though he always found some lowly position for the children. The last Mr. Wentworth was like that."

"I know."

Trask was very patient, I thought. This new information was surprising to me. I was sure it was a bombshell to him. But his voice did not portray any excitement.

"Well, right before he went to Heaven, my father says to me, 'Zach, I helped to do a bad thing. That devil-man, he got real mean with this Irish girl. Killed her.' He and my father got her body from the old house and buried her here while the house was still being remodeled. Said he cried as he watched her gray dress disappear under the earth. Covered the grave in old crates and things. No one knew anything about it. So sad for her. Rescued from poverty and obscurity only to be beaten and murdered and forgotten.

"Well, now, that was bad enough for my father. He went to the church to talk to the pastor about what he should do. But the pastor was visiting his family in New York. His wife was home and she listened to his story. She decided to go to the police and confront the man, but my father asked her not to. He had no other job and a servant who talks about family will never get hired again, you know.

"She understood so she wrote down his statement and told him to keep it safe, in case the devil-man decides to get rid of him. Kind of like an insurance policy.

"But then her conscience got the better of her and she went to the house to confront him. Such a bad idea. He hit her hard and she started screaming like a devil was after her. My father heard her and came running. When he turned the corner, he saw her screaming body falling into the pond. She was wearing a heavy green dress and all the latest styles, so when her clothes got wet, she sank to the bottom fast. They fished the body out and buried her next to the servant girl."

"In this house?"

"In this house, yes, sir."

"My father thought he was fired for sure, but the devil-man didn't say anything. His look said it all. My father never said a word ever again. And nothing ever happened to him or me."

That ended the interview. Within an hour, there were all

kinds of activities in the house. People came with picks and shovels. Reporters were kept at a distance, but they were everywhere. We were completely forbidden to go off the property.

Two bodies were found, buried side by side. A recovered necklace was enough to identify the parson's wife. The other body remained a mystery.

The story did manage to get into the national press, but locally, it was just an interesting little unsolved crime. Nobody even offered to speculate that a Wentworth might have been involved. And that made sense, since Wentworth industries and their subsidiaries kept the papers profitable with their advertising.

Chapter Forty-Seven

The Sirena

Although the police activity went on for days, other things happened as well. On Saturday, Mom called to see if I was alright. What kind of house do I live in? Now what do I think of my new family? Do I want to come back home where I'm safe instead of some murder-house? Yes. Fine. Fine. No, I belong here now. Besides, it wasn't like there was any kind of choice.

Guy was working at the movie studio as a security guard. His job was to keep aggressive fans away from the stars. They had a small apartment of their own now, but still helped his aunt whenever possible.

The police investigation just captured my old family's attention, though. The conversation always came back to the bodies.

"Wasn't it creepy to be sleeping on top of corpses like that?" Anna Marie asked.

"Well, they were in the basement and my room is on the second floor. It's not like I was in bed with them," I replied, "In fact, I never saw them."

"Eww, I would hope not. Do you think there are any more?"

"Hush, now," Gramma Morris called out from the

background, then she took the phone, "You've been there less than six weeks and already you cause all kinds of upheaval. It's like you live in the eye of a hurricane. Bodies in the basement, now they're investigating a murder. Things keep going like this, in another ten years, you'll have us all in another Great War."

"Not my fault," I replied defensively, "Those bodies were only found because of the investigation. And Himself was killed in a boat, and it was all before I even got here."

"Himself?"

"My father. They call the master of the house here 'Himself.'"

"Paul's your father."

"So were Michael Collins, Gio Corelli, and Hugo Landacre."

One little victory for me. Holly spoke to me for a minute before they took the phone with a reminder of how much this call was costing. She missed me and wanted me back. I could tell she was fighting back tears and it broke my heart.

"At least you're safe from alligators while I'm here," I joked.

"I'm safe from alligators anyway," she replied, "They only like you."

"Everyone likes you," I heard the whole family say.

We all laughed and said our goodbyes and Holly cried out, "Come home soon." And the call was over.

I loved them all so much. Well, maybe I only kind of liked Anna Marie, come to think about it. Even so, I didn't want to go back. I had a life of fun and adventure and things to do here. Over there it was bare existence where every day required hard work. The choice seemed obvious.

I was done with *The Red Badge of Courage* and my new

assignment was *As You Like It* by William Shakespeare. It was enjoyable after Nadia told me what I read. It was incomprehensible nonsense until then. Respiratory system for science. Breathing is kind of complicated, it seems. India was the topic for geography. They certainly like long names in that part of the world. I thought it was nice that the English shortened all the names when they took it over.

I soon started getting ready for my lunch date with Melanie and Ursula. Mother had just ordered me a beige dress that fell just below my knees with double breasted buttons that provided decoration from the hem to the collar. It was closed by one of those new zippers in the back.

"It's a brilliant invention, this zipper," Zelda told me, "I imagine no one will ever use buttons again, but it's such a shame they put in them in the back. How do they expect you to zip it up by yourself?"

Some questions have no answer.

I inspected my new appearance with my dress, matching gloves and sun hat. I wore white stockings that pulled up to my knees, so I was protected from the sun and leering eyes. I thought I looked adorable. I went searching for compliments.

"Do you like my new dress?" I asked Charity.

"It's okay. I prefer a little color."

"I don't like those kinds of buttons," Lisa said.

"They're clothes. You wear them," Claire was no help.

"It's a great dress," Millie said, "You can stand up against the wall at the train station and blend in so well that no one will see you."

These were not the sort of answers I was looking for. I went up to Mother's room to show off, hoping she would also call it 'adorable.'

"Oh dear," she said, "Beige just isn't your color. I should have gotten green to match your eyes. And it just highlights how bland your hair color is. Oh well, it'll have to do."

"I like it," I defended, "I think it makes me look elegant."

"When I get better," she replied, "I am going to take you to the best stores in Boston and you'll really be dressed. In the meantime, I think you should look up 'elegant' and see what it means."

I know what it means.

Melanie was there by eleven o'clock to take me to *The Sirena* for lunch. She didn't notice my outfit and I chose not to get her opinion. We drove to the edge of town in her limousine. She didn't introduce me to the driver and he didn't look at me. We drove past the road that led to The Dollhouse and turned north. The high cliffs were soon behind us as we drove towards the ocean.

"That's Tarrelsett Beach," she told me as we watched a few scavengers search for lost treasures, "It's an Indian name. It means 'The Still Waters.' That big rock formation blocks the wind and monstrous storm waves so water is calmer than other parts of the shoreline."

Tarrelsett Beach. The name seemed familiar, somehow. I heard it before, but I didn't remember where or when. I shuddered as we drove by. The ominous monolith seemed to glare at me.

The marina had a gated entrance guarded by a young man who looked quite smart in his blue uniform. He waved us through. We parked next to a brown Chevrolet and walked to the end of a concrete boat ramp. A small motorboat was waiting and we soon were splashing through the water to Ursula's yacht, which was waiting for us a mile or so in the cape.

We climbed up a ladder onto the boat where the captain greeted us.

"Francisco Garba, at your service," he said flamboyantly taking off his hat and bowing so low that one leg was off the ground.

He straightened up to kiss Melanie's hand, then mine after I remembered to offer it. I was not fond of men slobbering over my hands, so I was glad Mother had me to put on gloves.

He offered Melanie his elbow and she walked with him to the cabin, where he held the door for us. A small staircase of five steps and sturdy rails led down to a dark and incense filled square room. Ursula wasn't there yet. A round table was bolted to the floor and some chairs were attached to the wall with metal and wood slants. Garba slid two off and set them up for us. Then he set three more on the opposite sides.

"Will you be joining us, Captain?" I asked.

"No, dear," he said, "I will be sailing the ship."

A door opened on the far side and another man entered.

"Andy," Garba said with false joviality, "Here are the guests. Make them feel at home. I'll start the engines."

With that, he was gone and Andy silently threw a checkered cloth and dishes on the table, followed by napkins, silver and glasses.

"Dinner will be breaded codfish, with sweet peas and French bread," Andy announced.

"Sounds delightful," Melanie replied.

I agreed, although peas, sweet or sour, were hardly a favorite of mine.

The door to the deck opened again and Captain Garba and another man entered. Our hostess followed, escorted in by another man. His face was blocked by the sun behind him. A younger woman followed them down.

"This is Bar, my first mate," Garba said in his falsely jovial voice as he indicated the first man, "We call him Bar because he comes from Hershey, Pennsylvania."

"And Hershey *bars* are made there," I completed.

"That's right, miss," Bar said with a smile, "Not everybody gets that so fast."

"After lunch, we'll be skimming the cape to show you the shoreline and maybe do some fishing," he smiled.

"How thoughtful," Melanie said, "But we're not dressed for it."

He nodded and tipped his cap to her while he and the captain left to do sailor things. Ursula gestured for us to all sit down.

"I am so happy you joined us," she told me as she leaned over to Melanie for a sideways hug, the kind I called a check touch. She reached over the table to me and squeezed my hand, "I want you to meet my youngest daughter, Fortuna. My other children are still in Transylvania. It's hard to leave home. Everything you have is there. The land is etched into your soul."

Suddenly, I missed Faucette very much. My soul yearned for home, imperfect though my southern family was.

Fortuna was about Melanie's age with brown eyes and black hair. Her clear skin was dark and she held herself high. Almost arrogant. She nodded to us and sat down quickly.

"Now I want you to meet my dear friend and companion, Reverend Sean McClelland."

"That name sounds familiar," I said, remembering my arrival in Boston.

"Perhaps, but I don't think you ever met. He used to be the pastor of the Lutheran Church in South Boston, near the rail station."

"And now I go to that station to preach to those unfortunates who need spiritual guidance."

And scream at them.

"He also discovered that there are things in the world that aren't seen that are just as spiritual as anything any religion has to offer. The occult offers much in the line of spiritual guidance."

No, I don't think it does.

"Yes," the Reverend agreed, "People can get closer to God through the use of occult practices."

They can get closer to something.

"This is why I find Madame Ursula to be such an attractive and gifted woman. She has so much to offer the world. Both worlds. Here and beyond."

He reached over and squeezed her hand. Ursula actually blushed. I didn't think people as old as her could do that. Fortuna rolled her eyes. I liked her so far.

"Oh, Sean, you are just too kind."

And you two are just too old to be having this conversation.

One look at Fortuna and I realized we both had that same thought.

"And so, when we met," Sean went on, "I knew we were meant for each other. God isn't only in a church building. He is everywhere. His ancient priests, such as Moses, used all kinds of supernatural powers. He even turned his staff into a serpent. We can do that, too. All we need is to be at one with the power of God. Ursula and I can merge this world and Heaven together to do God's true bidding."

I'm not sure I want to be here with these people.

"That sounds like science fiction," Melanie said, "I'm not sure it's even healthy."

"It does seem dangerous. What if God doesn't want Heaven and Earth to merge?" I asked.

"Then He'll stop us. Little things can go wrong. Bigger things. Then we just look at it and say, 'Let's do something else,'" Sean replied smoothly.

"Speaking of something else," Ursula said.

Andy opened the door with lunch. This may have been the best lunch ever for me. The cod was as light as air with a coating heavy in garlic and oregano. The peas were really sweet. They had honey butter sauce on them. And the bread was still warm from the oven.

The conversation became more earthly and less unsettling. Reverend Sean McClelland left his church because of his new spiritual calling *and* because he abandoned his wife to spend his evenings with Ursula. He departed before he was removed, it seemed. Ursula phrased it a bit more diplomatically, explaining that they had big plans for their future. Being tied down to a church inhabited by people whose religion began and ended on Sunday mornings was little more than a distraction.

A fallen pastor and a medium. Mom would throw a fit if she knew I was having lunch with these people. Gramma Morris would attack them with a spoon.

Soon the talk turned to family. Sean had four sons and three daughters. They all disowned him for leaving their mother to run off with Ursula. Although Sean tried to paint himself as the misunderstood victim who was simply trying to live his life in the way God led him, he garnered no sympathy from anyone except Ursula. That was a large family to just throw away.

Ursula's husband had died maybe ten years earlier. Of

her four children, only Fortuna chose to emigrate to America.

"I was too young to have a say in the matter," she interrupted.

"Of all the wonderful decisions I made for you, that was the best. Romania will eventually be conquered or destroyed. Why be there when it happens? And it will happen. My spiritual guide told me so."

"Why is that?" I asked.

"Its borders have changed over the ages because of wars and other countries think that Romania belongs to them. A time of great upheaval will befall eastern Europe soon and survival will be the only thing that matters."

Sean encouraged her to go on about the future. She made some bizarre predictions involving wars, death, murders, and betrayal. Although she was never very clear because she avoided precise terms and firm dates, most of what she said did come true. Then she started to talk about the past. She pulled out an old photograph of her family from her childhood. I looked at it for a long time. The little girl in the front looked exactly like me, except bathed in sepia.

"Now you see why I call you Yvonne," Ursula said.

"I can see why you think she looks like Yvonne," Melanie said, "But really, Ursula, you make her nervous when you keep calling her Yvonne."

"She's right, Mother," Fortuna said, "She's not Yvonne. Yvonne would be almost forty if she lived. Sometimes, families endure tragedies. And I'm sure this child doesn't even speak Romanian."

"That can be remedied."

"Mother," Fortuna raised her voice quite a bit.

"Just kidding. Laugh a bit."

Sean and Ursula giggled, though I think the former pastor was only being polite. No one else at the table even smiled.

After lunch, we cruised around the cape. It was pleasant enough. The captain called me to the front of the boat and we watched a school of dolphins swim in the distance. We zoomed towards the big rock formation near the shoreline. It was larger than I expected it to be, and extremely rugged. I would never be tempted to swim out there and climb it.

Fortuna enjoyed the cruise with us. She made a point of showing me where the seals were swimming. When the sun was beginning to sink over the land, the captain told us it was time to go back. Fortuna sidled to me for a brief moment.

"My mother thinks you more than look like my Aunt Yvonne. She thinks you are her soul in another life. She has obsessed over you being her. She would never harm you, but I don't think her fixation is healthy. Always correct her when she doesn't call you Amy."

After the cruise, we exchanged pleasantries over cheesecake and the afternoon was over. It was an enjoyable if eerie visit. Melanie was glad that I had fun.

"Didn't you find their conversation about merging Heaven and Earth a little weird?" I asked, as we drove home.

"Downright disturbing. But Ursula knows how to read those situations and nothing bad will ever happen. When it comes to matters of the occult, you can always trust Ursula."

How about if I just avoid matters of the occult?

Chapter Forty-Eight

Settling In

June gave way to July. A few more reporters wrote articles about the bodies under the kitchen. Eventually, the story faded away and the excitement was over. A new routine was put in place for me. My violin teacher, who only taught classical music, came on Monday mornings. Horseback riding was on Tuesdays. Dance on Wednesdays. Schoolwork was every day, of course. Mother did not believe in summer vacations.

It was a good thing I had a house full of sisters. I had no time for frivolous things like friends, even if I could find other children in Pennyton. Although we attended church on Sundays, the other families never mingled with us. Father's business practices made him a great many enemies and absolutely no friends. It carried down to our generation. Whenever we had free time, my sisters and I walked around town together.

We had fewer meals with relatives, other than Melanie and Letisha. It took a while to warm up to Letty, as she preferred to be called. Her husband was Marvin Adams of the Springdale Adams family. As opposed to any other Adams family, I supposed. Marvin was a rising lawyer in the law firm of James, Booth, Rothstein, and Associates.

"A delightful name for a pack of lawyers," Uncle Henry said to me one day in front of Marvin, "The most famous criminals in America."

"Jesse James, John Wilkes Booth, and Arnold Rothstein," Millie whispered to me.

I thanked her but I already knew. I thought it was a better name than Mr. Tremble's firm of Robb, Swindle and Cheatham.

Marvin never appreciated the humor, though everyone else did. He was a rising star in his field and his clients were important men. His firm put him in charge of all banking issues. And with the depression going on, he was quite busy.

Since he was so serious, we were never invited to their home. Marvin didn't want a 'gaggle of giggling girls gawking' at his clients. These were famous and severe men. How famous a banker can be is debatable, but there was no doubt they were important. And that meant Marvin might be able to add his less derogatory sounding name to the firm's title.

Lettie was always under pressure to put on exquisite parties and dinners when Marvin's clients stopped by. A beautiful wife and spotless house along with fine dining was certain to assure his senior partnership. Quality of work didn't seem to be a factor. That was why there would be no children for them at the moment. Screaming brats could quickly ruin an important evening.

We did visit Uncle Henry, along with Iris and Bixby a couple of times. Uncle Henry's only son died in the Great War, but he still had two daughters who lived in California. They corresponded and had an occasional phone call but never visited. They didn't want to compete for their father's attention with a dead bird.

Iris and Bixby were good for him. They were people he could talk to and they took care of him when he and Quincy delved into his fantasies a little too deeply and had to return to reality. Uncle Henry had trouble remembering who they were sometimes. Once, he thought they were his dead son and one of his daughters and threw a fit when they were alone in the bedroom together. They quickly settled him down and everyone laughed it off.

We also visited Aunt Gladys in her house by the sea. The more I got to know her, the more I liked her. She reminded me of Gramma Morris. Crusty, but caring. Certainly not a woman who put up with nonsense.

Although they didn't live close to each other, her next door neighbor (if living a mile and a half away from your neighbor can qualify as 'next door') was Mr. Steed Gorman. Aunt Gladys did not like him at all.

"Any man who defaces his house with all those hideous dolls has to be a few cards short of a full deck," she pronounced.

I politely nodded but didn't add anything to that conversation, although Millie said they were evil and always stared at her.

"You get so dramatic," Charity said, unaware that she was a bit of a thespian herself.

"You don't think so? Why don't you walk up to the door and knock on it. What would you do if that Brazilian Rezidon Doll answered it?"

"Run. What do you think you'd do?"

"Die of fright."

We all laughed, even Aunt Gladys. Those did seem to be the only two options.

"You know," Aunt Gladys told us one day, "He could

just move those things inside. He has all kinds of room in that house. The cellar has a secret passageway that leads all the way down to Tarrelsett Beach. There's a cave down there where his family used to smuggle rum. They brought it in that way to avoid all the taxes the British were inflicting on them at the time. I have something similar here, but I don't use it. No telling what lives in that old cave today."

I, for one, didn't want to find out. The other girls all were begging Aunt Gladys to let them at least go down the stairs to see the cave, but their pleadings stood no chance against her will. No telling what kind of sea monster we avoided. Besides, the currents were strong on that part of the ocean because of that tall rock formation. It jutted up forty feet above the water. Flat on top with little peaks and plateaus on the sides.

"Some of the braver boys would swim out there and climb it to the top and scream like Tarzan," Aunt Gladys told us, "Not all of them made it back."

"Oh," said Lisa, "I don't think any of us heard that part."

"You should have. It's a rather important part," Aunt Gladys replied.

"The currents and undertows and vortexes are something fierce. You can wade in that part of the ocean, up to your knees if you must, but never swim any further out than that."

One day we heard that Bixby had an interview in New York for a regular job as a musician for cartoons. After several more auditions, he was hired. Uncle Henry was furious when they told him. Now he and Quincy would have to live alone. We sisters all promised to visit him every day.

"Even in the rain," I added before realizing that Chester

would drive us in bad weather.

But Uncle Henry wasn't calming down. He kept going on about how he could die all alone and only the stink of his bloated and rotting corpse would give anyone cause to think something even happened.

"One of us will come over here every day," Claire repeated, "And when the time comes, we'll make sure you're properly buried before you start bloating and rotting."

He simply glared at her.

"Yes," I added, trying to ameliorate the damage, "We all just love to see you and Quincy. And we can get you to a doctor if you feel sick."

That mollified him. He even mentioned that I was the only one who mentioned his parrot. As a reward, I had the privilege to stroke the empty air where Quincy was perched, much to the amusement of my sisters.

I remember that day well. It was when things started going wrong. By the time we all got home, Claire and Lisa were both complaining of a sore throat. Soon Charity was in her room sick as well. The doctor visited us and announced they had Scarlett Fever. Very contagious. Possibly deadly.

CHAPTER FORTY-NINE

QUARANTINE

The doctor prescribed castor oil for the patients. It's bad enough to be sick but the medicine only made it worse. The fluid smells worse than turpentine and it 'cleanses' the body more effectively than a bushel of prunes. We were very lucky we had more than one bathroom.

The house was now under quarantine. Nobody was to come in or leave. We were prisoners of the disease. What was worse, Millie and I didn't even have it. However, since we were with the other culprits, we were also confined to our rooms, although we quietly snuck in and out of each other's room when we could. It didn't matter that we weren't sick. It made everyone suspicious. It was just a question of time before we got it too. Zelda brought me trays of food for meals and placed them outside my door with a quiet knock before scurrying away. Going downstairs for snacks was out of the question.

Veronica also avoided the fever. Sadly, she suspected we might be carriers as well and kept to her room with the door closed. I went over one day to talk to her through the door just to say something.

"Don't contaminate my door with your fever."

I was a little hurt. Apparently, we were just as sick as the others. Just not taking castor oil. Yet.

"I don't see how it can hurt for them to take a few doses," I overheard Zelda say to Barbara one day.

Castor Oil not hurt? In Italy, Benito Mussolini used it to kill and torture people. His policemen would tie people to chairs and make them drink a pint of the nasty stuff. But since he made the trains run on time, people didn't care. Except for the ones tied to chairs.

Obviously, not all the servants were the friends I thought they were. But at least the others weren't talking about tying us to chairs. Yet. As it turned out, it may not have been a bad idea.

After about a week, Millie started thinking about liberty. We lived in a wonderful house, but it was becoming a prison. She had several plans for us to sneak out of the house and go have fun somewhere. We could avoid people outside just as well as inside. The one thing her schemes all had in common was that they assumed all the adults were either stupid or disinterested in what we did. One day, we boldly walked out the kitchen door, but Zach caught us and turned us over to Willie. He had us wait outside while he got out a handkerchief and dipped it in camphor before escorting us back to our rooms.

So, if we were caught again, we would get a serious punishment. Possibly arrested. Maybe even thrown in a dungeon, if Pennyton had one. Neither of us wanted to find out one way or the other.

Nadia gave me *The Island of Dr. Moreau* by H. G. Wells, so I started reading while Millie continued plotting. Now this was a book worth reading. I had no desire to put it down. And my room wasn't creepy anymore. This was a perfect time for reading.

Alas, Millie thought up a plausible escape for us. Mother

and Veronica were afraid of us and wouldn't even shout a pleasant word our way and there were no other adults to worry about on our floor. While we were eating our lunches, the servants were having theirs in the kitchen. That left the front door unguarded.

"But everyone knows us and they know we're quarantined," I said.

"We don't have to go anywhere where there're people," she replied.

What's the point?

"We can sneak past the guest house and slither through the hedge to the field and run down the hill while nobody's looking. We'll wait till all the traffic is gone, skitter across the street, slink through that little patch of forest and we'll be on Tarrelsett Beach. We can hide out there."

"If we can't be seen or talk to anyone, why don't we hide in our room and that way we don't have to worry about getting in trouble again?" I was proud of my logic.

"Amy," she said with a combination of amusement and exasperation, "It's not exciting that way. What happened to that adventurous Amy spirit?"

"An alligator ate it."

"You want to get out for a while. I just know it. I know you. We're just alike and we're going to *die* if we don't get out of this house."

"Well, maybe a little bit, I suppose."

"Well, come on then. Let's go."

We went with her plan. She put some real thought into this project. We both dressed in green gingham that matched the color of the hedges and slipped on soft soled tennis shoes. The dress didn't cover my knees so we could run faster if we needed to. We quietly made it out of the house and as soon as we reached the hedge we crawled through. We were rewarded with scratches and bug bites and freedom. Although I was the reluctant fugitive, I was warming up to this. I could almost imagine myself as a prisoner of war who had just escaped the military compound and was now behind enemy lines.

"Girls don't fight in wars and become POWs in the first place, you know," Millie said, "We stay behind and pray for victory."

"My grandmother was a nurse in The Great War, you know," I said, a little miffed. It dawned on me that the hard-edge life down south may be preferrable to the prissy uselessness Pennyton offered.

"She was?" Millie was confused.

"From my other family," I said, daring her to correct me.

"Oh," she said, "That's good. Maybe someday we women can have better things to do in life than look at clothes and things. Not cleaning fish, though."

That surprised me, coming from her. Of all my new sisters, she seemed the most devoid of ambition, even if she was the most prone to break rules. She was also the daintiest, as her reluctance to clean fish indicated.

We raced down the hill now. The outside air definitively felt good. So did the running. I enjoyed our house but not being cooped up in it.

"You know," I said while laughing, "It's so much easier running downhill than jogging up."

"That is a brilliant observation, my dear Holmes," she panted, "Maybe we should hire a tutor more in tune with your superior brain, like Albert Einstein."

"Ha-ha. I think you're missing the point about doing work. I think looking and wearing pretty clothes is fun," I told her, "Cleaning fish is useful. In case we lose all our money, we can get a job as fish cleaners."

"I only want to eat the fish. I'll get a job modeling clothes."

"Well, at least you know you can get a job," I said diplomatically. I was not sure how many modeling jobs there were for twelve-year-old girls.

We reached the bottom of the hill easily. We hid in some bushes until both sides of the road were empty and then ran across. The forest camouflaged us immediately. We may have heard an occasional car, but nobody could see us.

Millie traipsed through the sunnier part of the path while I took the shady spots. A lot of ferny undergrowth grew taller than either of us on my side. Pretty little red tipped leaves surrounded me, with buds that looked like upside-down ice cream cones. The wind allowed the leaves to attack my exposed skin on my legs and arms. Even though there was nothing sharp on the leaves, it stung where they touched me.

"Oh, no," Millie exclaimed, "You haven't been walking over there, have you?"

"Well, yes. You saw me," I said.

"That doesn't mean I was paying attention," she said back, "You've just been wallowing in Poison Ivy."

"What? Are you sure?"

"Well, pretty sure," she said inspecting all the vines from a safe distance (like a coward), "The leaves are in threes. You know what they say, 'leaves of three, let it be.' But that's not accurate all the time. They have a glossy shine to them, like these, but sometimes they're dull. They have red tint in the leaves, but not always. They have silver berries except for when they don't, like these."

I glared at her, "So either I have it or I don't."

"Yeah," she concluded, "One or the other."

"Wonderful," I growled. This idea was getting worse by the minute.

"The problem is that with everyone else having Scarlett Fever, if you get a red rash, you may get bed ridden like the others."

"The others are sick."

"With Scarlett fever. The Scarlett part is a rash like Poison Ivy. Let's worry about it later. Here's the beach."

It was mostly flat river rocks as big as my toes interspersed with patches of sand. Boulders were scattered just in the water and the waves swooshed over them. That familiar rock monolith seemed almost on top of us. It shaded a huge part of the blue water, giving it an ominous look. I couldn't believe that boys would swim out to it at all, much less climb it.

I had to admit that this was a fine idea, though. The salt air blew through my hair while the sea mist from the crashing waves just barely touched my skin, making it itch. Lucky for me Zelda wouldn't be washing my hair until after quarantine and the doctor already said we'd be locked up like convicts for another week. I enjoyed watching the seagulls fly overhead as we waded in the ocean, though the water was too cold to soak in it a long time. By now, I was getting thirsty and my throat was sore from lack of water.

This rocky beach soon narrowed to just enough room for us to walk side by side. The cliffs were rising high on our right. I thought I saw Aunt Gladys' house in the distance. The beach, such as it was, ended in a large cove. The cliffs shed rocks everywhere. A rather large flatboat was tied up to our left. As we were still carrying our shoes, we waded over just to see what was in it. No one was around so we were safe.

CHAPTER FIFTY

CAPTURED

Two coffins were inside the boat. They were unfinished pine caskets, not at all embellished or decorated. Six handles made of pot metal decorated the sides for the bearers to handle.

"Smugglers," Millie pronounced.

"Smugglers?" I asked, unsure how she could make that conclusion so quickly.

"Well, sure," she replied, "Why would you put people in coffins if you're going to bury them at sea? I bet these babies are filled with whiskey and beer and rum."

"How do you know they're not something else?" I giggled, "Bodies of gangsters from Boston? Or vampires. They'd be safe from the sun in there."

"You listen to Nadia too much. Vampires aren't real. Here, help me get the lid off and I'll prove it to you."

"You really don't need to prove it," I said, but it was too late.

She had already reached down and opened the lid, which was not nailed down, just snugly secured by tiny dowels. It took us no effort to pry them off, although I really felt we should just leave them be. Underneath some burlap packing a couple dozen rifles rested. Boxes of ammunition were secured at the head.

"Oh my," she said, "We better get out of here."

I certainly agreed. I wanted to get far away from there.

"At least you now know that there aren't any vampires in this world," Millie said to me as we secured the lid back on.

"Unless you count politicians," came a man's voice from behind us.

We whirled around. It was Edmund, Mr. Gorman's manservant. He was glaring at us. More importantly, he was pointing a revolver right at Millie.

"And you're both in a very bad place. You should never have come here. And you should leave things be."

"I see that," I said, "I think we'll just go home now and think about how wrong we were."

He impatiently jerked his gun towards the shore and we walked toward the base of the cliff. He pulled back some kind of bush and we entered a cave where he quickly retrieved a flashlight from a natural ledge and led us to a damp stone staircase. We started climbing.

After an exhausting ascent, we entered the kitchen. Mr. Gorman was sitting in one of the chairs with the maid on his lap and his arms around her in a compromising position. She jumped up and scurried over to the range and started straightening out her uniform.

"What are you doing?" Mr. Gorman almost shouted, "Row the boat out to the submarine and get it loaded. How hard was that?"

"Shut up, Steed," Edmund said as though he talked to Gorman like that all the time, "Can't you see what was waiting for me in the boat?"

Mr. Gorman looked at us.

"Did they see anything?"

"Just the two coffins you're smuggling the guns in," I answered.

"You let them see the rifles?"

"I didn't let them. They were there when I came back with the oars. We can't let them blab all over town about what we're doing."

"We won't blab anything," Millie said. She was already crying, "And please don't tell our mother we left the house without permission."

"We won't," Edmund said, while he was tying our wrists up in twine, "We'll kill you instead. Less messy that way."

"Well, if you were going to do that, why didn't you shoot them at the beach?" Gorman asked.

"Two millionaire girls shot on the beach? When their bodies are found the police in every town will be looking for us. We'll kill them here and bury them somewhere."

We were both crying now.

"Hush girls. I have a better idea," Gorman soothed, "We're sending the rifles to Egypt, right?"

Edmund nodded.

"And in Egypt, men have more than one wife and they can marry child brides. Even better, the sheik we're selling the guns to just might be interested in adding to his little harem. And we have two disobedient little girls. Pretty little girls." He stroked my cheek while I flinched and pulled away. "We can make more money with them than we ever could with arms. In fact, we could add another whole dimension to our business. There's lots of naughty little girls in this world that can just disappear. They can disappear for us."

Edmund smiled. We were marched upstairs, with a little pushing and slapping on our backsides to encourage us to move fast and be quiet. I was put in a bedroom loaded with dolls with the most evil expressions imaginable and tied to a bedpost. Edmund gave some good advice about being quiet so I wouldn't get my tongue cut out. Millie was put in another room. I didn't hear anything from her, so I assumed she wanted to keep her tongue as well.

After sunset, the maid came up with dinner and Gorman followed an hour later to untie me long enough to use the bathroom. After a while, I heard the toilet flush again. Millie was still alive.

I cried and I prayed for I don't know how long, then I fell asleep. My sore throat was worse now, and my hands and legs were bright red from the poison ivy. I had dreams that night. The dolls in my room were talking to me. I can't remember what they said, but oddly enough, they made me a little less afraid.

By the time morning came, I had a fever and felt lethargic. The running around, lack of water, poison ivy, fear, adrenalin surges, and being tied up certainly took their toll. Since children are not the most logical of creatures, it never occurred to me that I now had Scarlett Fever.

Chapter Fifty-One

Escape

"Why is she so red?" Edmund frowned at me the next morning.

We were down in the dining room with our legs tied to the table legs having a breakfast of runny eggs and burnt toast.

"Her 'loving' sister had her run around in a patch of poison ivy yesterday," Gorman replied, "It'll clear up. It won't affect the price. Salzar is going to give us ten thousand dollars each, subject to approval, so we have to be careful and get her cleared up."

"I didn't 'have' her go into the poison ivy," Millie said defensively, "I didn't notice it until it was too late."

Of all the things to worry about.

"Children should be seen and not heard," Edmund growled at her.

"He should know," Gorman laughed wickedly, "His father was your father. Edmund wanted to be part of the family. Ah, but the rules were to never bring up the family relationship. So out he went. I hired him here. Joe hired my possible son, Chester. Chester did the same thing to me. You might say we traded our problem children with each other.

"I got the better end of the bargain. Edmund makes a great partner in my less than entirely legal enterprises. After we get payment for you two, we plan to go about our separate ways for a while. The master lawbreaker knows when to lay low. After we get our ten thousand dollars, plus our money from the guns, Edmund will move out west. I'll stay here and be the eccentric country gentleman. We'll be rich until we need to arrange another deal. And you'll be safe in Cairo."

"Even better because you're Wentworths," Edmund added.

"Yes," Gorman smiled, "My partner here spent a little time with Caitlin and 'impressed' her with our business deals. Your father immediately demanded a piece of the action. Revenge is sweet, even if old J.P. is dead. What a perfect plan."

"That's good for you," Millie said defiantly, "But we don't like that plan at all."

"Not now," Gorman agreed, "But what happens when you grow up? You get married and have children. You'll be bored when you sort through all those dismal husband prospects. I'm saving you all that work. I mean, does it really matter to you if you share a husband with other women as long as you have the rich and wealthy lifestyle you have now?"

"I'd rather sort through the dismal prospects," Millie replied.

"Eat your breakfast," he changed subjects, "Edmund, the next delivery is the day after tomorrow. You need to make sure everything is in readiness."

Edmund glared at him for a moment and left without saying anything. When the front door closed, Gorman leered at us.

"I have an errand to attend to in the kitchen. It would be unpleasant for you if I hear any noises other than chewing. You've been good enough so far as to avoid being punished. I find that disappointing. I do so love punishing unwanted little guests." His lips curled up into a sadistic smile.

I rather thought that was sufficiently intimidating, but Millie was more determined to escape than I was. I wanted to sleep. The table moved up and down a bit and when I glanced over, Millie had lifted it high enough to slip her rope under the leg. Tying up prisoners was not Edmund's greatest skill. She quickly untied her feet and helped me get free.

We headed to the front door as quietly as possible, but it opened a moment before Millie reached for the handle. Edmund stood there, glaring at us. We were all shocked. But he recovered faster than us and grabbed Millie, wrapping an arm around her chest while covering her mouth with his hand. She kicked and tried biting him. But she was completely overpowered.

I wanted to help, but I knew I was tired and useless. I could try to run, but I was too sick to make it far. I kicked at him, but he swatted me away with one blow to the head. I landed in front of the couch beneath that hideous Brazilian Rezidon Doll. It still sat there, covered up in its towel.

I had no idea how helpful it would be, but I knew those piranha teeth were sharp and even if it had no effect, I'd go down helping my sister. I pulled the towel off and ran over to them while wedging open that toothsome mouth.

Edmund already stuffed a napkin in Mille's mouth, tied her hands behind her and was binding her ankles. I ran up as quietly as I could and with all my ten-year-old might, gored his right triceps from behind and then clamped down on the jaw so both sets of teeth stabbed him all the way down to his bone.

The effect was immediate. Edmund dropped to the floor without a sound and just lay there. His eyes were open and I thought he was aware of us, but he didn't move. There still must have been some curare on those teeth. I pulled the napkins out of Millie's mouth so she could breathe. I could untie her ankles, but her wrists were too tight for my little hands.

"I'll go in the kitchen and get a knife," I whispered. We didn't know where Gorman was and didn't really want to find him. I snuck off and as I peeked in the kitchen, I saw them together. Mr. Gorman and his maid in the absolute ultimate compromising position.

I ran back to Millie.

"Mr. Gorman's in the kitchen," I said, leaving out the part of what they were doing.

"Check his pants," she said, nodding to Edmund, "All men carry a pocketknife, you know."

I didn't know. I really didn't want to put my hand in his nasty pocket, but our options were rather limited at this time. He did have a small pocketknife. I unfolded it and cut her free. We were soon out the front door.

We ran down the driveway to the road. The dolls were swaying gently in the wind, malevolent grins plastered on their faces.

"Come back," I thought I heard them calling to me.

"Millie, did you hear them?" I asked.

"Who?" Millie panicked, "They're following us?"

"No, the dolls," I replied.

"Never mind the dolls," she hissed impatiently, "Just run."

So we ran down the road for a bit. It was starting to sprinkle. The cold water gave me a chill and I was shivering, even though it was almost August. Then Millie insisted we get off the road so we'd be out of sight when Gorman came looking for us. We were at the cliff's edge and I watched that great rock tower defy the ocean with its existence.

Someone was waving to me from the top. I blinked and looked again. It was a mermaid. I couldn't really see her features, but I saw the silver tail. Over the wind and rain and distance I heard her call to me in a sweet musical voice.

"Come down and visit, Amy," she sang, "We have much to talk about."

I stopped to look at her. She seemed so friendly and caring. I thought I might be able to jump the hundred or so feet into the water to talk to her, but Millie pulled me away.

"Come *on*," she groused, "They'll catch us."

I looked at her for a moment and turned back to the mermaid, but she was gone. I hurried and tried to keep up with my sister, but I was too tired, cold, feverish, and just plain sick. She dragged me gently along for what seemed a long distance.

CHAPTER FIFTY-TWO

SCARLETT FEVER

"There's a car coming," Millie told me excitedly, "Stay here. I'll flag them down."

I nodded and watched her leave. Then I laid down. I was cold, shivering and crying a bit. I was miserable and feeling sorry for myself. Soon, I was asleep.

Mom was in the kitchen washing the dishes. Michelle was playing (sort of) the piano in the other room with Jason at her side. There was a bassinette near her and I peered in to see a sleeping baby boy under a light blue cover. Aunt Sharon was sitting near Mom but not helping. Just enjoying her company. She was huge with her child. She must have gained at least one hundred pounds during her pregnancy. If she lost it all, it would take time. But I knew she would always be heavy from now on, not that it mattered. Uncle Vincent would always love her.

Mom looked up and I think she saw me. She gasped and whispered my name. I wanted to say 'I love you' but I couldn't speak. It was only a dream.

There was a rustle in the grass near me and the dream was gone. Nadia and Kathleen were there, with Chester not far behind. Chester picked me up like I weighed nothing and he ran with me back to the car. We were safe.

I was asleep with my head on Millie's shoulder while she

told them about what happened. Nadia gave me a pill with brandy to help my fever. The brandy really woke me up as my stomach revolted against the hard alcohol. The two combined made me feel a little better, enough to listen to the conversation.

"Why wouldn't they just put a ransom on their heads instead of selling them off," Chester asked casually from the front seat.

"It's obvious," Nadia answered, "They live here and the girls saw them. They have a lot to lose."

"Well, they saw us, now," he persisted.

"It's alright," Nadia answered smoothly, while taking a pill that was obviously not aspirin, "It just means a slight change in plans. We'll book steerage to England and go our separate ways. Two young heiresses. Two hundred thousand dollars. That's fifty grand each. We'll live better than royalty. I can live in the best part of Ljubljana."

"Slovenia?" Millie asked, "You're kidnapping us just so you can go live in some po-dunk nowhere place? We trusted you. We hired you. You were like family. We took you to Montreal, Burlington, everywhere."

"As hired help," she responded angrily, "And you didn't hire us. And we were nowhere near 'family.' And Kathleen wasn't even allowed to eat at the table with 'family.'"

"And in case you didn't know it," Kathleen said spitefully, "Your father and my mother made me. I'm your half-sister. I should have been treated like family, but I wasn't."

"What?" Millie was shocked, "No, I didn't know that. How would I?"

"I knew," I said, though my eyes were still closed.

"What?" Kathleen laughed, "How would you know? You haven't even been here three months."

I glared at her with all my strength, "I knew."

I should have kept my mouth shut. The last thing I wanted was to tell anybody that Veronica and I listened to the interviews.

"Don't listen to her," Nadia said harshly, "She's sick and delirious."

"You know," she continued to Millie, "You made it so hard for us. First, Amy there walks right into Darnell, but gets away. Then you had that party. It was a Godsend for us. No one to help you. Kathleen got so far as to get on the bed to tie Amy's hands and get her ready for Chester. We really wanted you, Millie, but you all left Amy completely alone. She was such low hanging fruit. Then all hell broke loose. Broken glass, screams, everything collapsed."

"I had to run hide in the closet," Kathleen added.

"That explains why the closet door was ajar," I murmured.

"Who chased Claire down the hall?" Millie asked.

Chester laughed, "He didn't chase anyone. He was headed for the hills when he saw you were all awake. Too many of you, too few of us. He was more scared than she was. He thought for sure we were caught."

"Who?" Millie persisted.

I already knew.

"Darnell Miller," Nadia said absently. The pill was relaxing her.

It made sense. Miller hated our family intensely since he was my father's disinherited son. Kathleen also hated us because she was just a servant instead of a daughter. And those two were dating each other. That gave them plenty of time to talk about their common enemy. Our family.

"We should have known," I told Millie, "He's been dating Kathleen. That's how he got involved in all of this."

"How did you know that?" Kathleen asked, not at all happy with me, "Are you spying on us?"

"I overheard it," I said, "You're both his children, at least probably. You both resent that you were left out of the family. He only gave you jobs. You wanted the wealth and money and the Wentworth name."

She paled.

"You mean Darnell is a Wentworth son?"

Chester chortled out a mean laugh.

"How about that? Two Wentworth bastard children find each other. The resentful brother and shrewish sister. Made for each other, but not really, huh? Aren't there laws about this sort of thing? Don't you two ever talk to each other?"

"Well, obviously," she retorted, "We had other things to talk about."

"I can see that from your baby bump."

Kathleen screamed and started hitting Chester on the back of his head, making the car swerve. Nadia pulled her back so that Chester regained control of the car.

"Well, Chester," Nadia said slowly, almost content, even though we could have been in an accident, "Now you know why the chauffer never talks. So anyway," she continued as Kathleen simmered, "I gave you money to go on the bus and Chester and Darnell followed you. Why did you want to go to Flowerton? That was so confusing. They were going to pick you up there, but you snuck out the back door for some reason. I was so angry when you came back home."

"I remember," Millie said.

"So, we had Kathleen leave the balcony door unlocked for Chester to get up to Amy's room. Then he screamed at something and ran off."

"There was a woman in the room. Just staring at me."

"So, you yelled as loud as you could and ran off."

"I'm not sure you'd do any better."

"It's that mirror," Kathleen said, "I know that there's some kind of illusion that makes people see a woman there. Scares everybody. Maybe it's the ghost of that maid woman that was murdered."

"Yeah, well," Chester muttered, "It would have been nice to know that it's not a normal mirror."

"But the real coup de grace," Nadia continued, "Was the next time you tried. Again, you made all kinds of noise."

"Yeah," Chester interrupted, "Some guy was already climbing it when I got there."

"Good protective skills to chase him off like that," Nadia said, "But you started yelling at him, which woke everyone up again. Which would have been okay because you could try again. But for some reason you climbed up the trellis after you woke the whole household. By the time you got in the window, everybody was there waiting for you."

"I didn't know that. We were outside."

"So are birds but we still hear them," Kathleen said caustically.

"Then you convinced them to cut everything down," Nadia droned on, ignoring them, "Now the only way to kidnap one of them was by some kind of public abduction. Very risky. But here we are. They just walk right up to us with no witnesses. So, it all worked out for the best. The Wentworths get their precious little daughters back, and we get two hundred thousand dollars. Everybody's happy."

"I'm not," I heard Millie whine before I drifted off to sleep again.

CHAPTER FIFTY-THREE

KIDNAPPED

I had no idea how long I slept but the sun was down when I woke up. Our abductors bound my wrists tightly behind my back and secured one of my ankles to a ceiling support. I certainly wasn't going anywhere. I looked around and found Millie similarly tied to another support.

This place was dank and moldy smelling. Mildew ran up the walls like a disgusting yellow plant. Scraggly bushes hid the entrance from the outside. I could hear the ocean waves pounding the nearby shore. Miller was sitting at a table between two dimly lit storm lanterns, holding a large bottle. I could tell from the nasty smell that it was gin. It didn't improve the fecund odor of near-death, mold, and general unwholesomeness.

We were in a cave. The front entrance was so small that Miller must have crawled to get in. Behind him, the room faded into a thick and fearsome blackness, as though something unholy lurked back there, watching us.

The floor was damp from the ocean. The air smelled of it, when it wasn't overpowered by the rancid smells from within the rock cavity. An occasional seagull screamed out its mournful call.

What have you to cry about? You're flying in air, free. I'm tied up in a cave.

"Oh good, you're up," Nadia's voice echoed.

I turned towards the darkness. The other three kidnappers emerged. Nadia tottered over to me with a small glass of water and a pill. She was not at all steady on her feet.

"Here," she said, "It's aspirin. It'll reduce your fever and make you feel better."

I hesitated. I didn't trust her. I never would again.

"It will be easier if you take it by yourself, but Chester can force it down you if you prefer. We aren't going to hurt you, you know. You are worth sooo much money, but only if we keep you alive. We may need your voice on the telephone to confirm that little point. Nobody's going give us anything if you're dead."

"I'm so glad you're concerned," Millie muttered from her pole while I swallowed the pill.

"I have great concern for all of you," Nadia said over my head to her, with a slurred voice, "That's why you're still alive. Both of you. Kathleen wanted to kill you. But not me. You can't understand, I'm sure, but I genuinely love all you girls. I wanted you all to think of me as the best governess in the whole wide world. But then it occurred to me: I'd rather have cash."

"I hope you choke on it."

"Oh, Millie," she replied in an oh so sugary voice, "How many people said that to your father? Grandfather?"

She stood up to her full height and wobbled like she would fall before she caught her balance.

"Do you know why your father hired me? I was educated but unemployable. A foreign refugee living in London like so many others. A woman living in a world where all the men were killed in war.

"But I learned a skill in the war. I knew how to terminate unwanted pregnancies from foolish young girls. Yes, my title was governess. But my primary job was to make sure unwanted little Wentworths didn't find their way into the world. I don't think he cared if the woman was married or far away. But the unmarried ones always seemed to be coming for help. It was inconvenient and that's why I was hired.

"Certainly, I can teach. I can discipline. I can listen and give advice. I help you in all aspects of your life. But my primary job was to kill unborn children."

"How can you live with that?" Millie asked.

"The salary helps," she shrugged.

She clapped her hands and wobbled a bit.

"Now remember what I taught you. What we are doing is not evil. It is good. This is capitalism at its best. Your family gives us money for merchandise. You just happen to be the merchandise in this case."

"Capitalism?" Millie asked, "Our family did the work but you're taking the profits, even though you didn't do the work. Wouldn't that be socialism and wouldn't that make you a Stalinist?"

Miller laughed, "You taught them too well. So, we're socialists today because we're taking our fair share. But tomorrow we're going to be capitalists because we're going to *have* our fair share. From good guys to bad guys. White hats today and black hats tomorrow."

Nadia turned to the others with a scowl.

"Time for us to go back to the house. The ransom note should have been found by now. We have to be above suspicion. Can't have anyone wondering where we are."

"Kathleen?" Millie called out as they were leaving. Kathleen froze in place.

"Your story from the party. The five girls who died. Those were us, weren't they?"

"Five selfish little brats. Unconcerned about anything but themselves. What do you think?" Kathleen responded.

Soon they were gone, leaving Miller to guard us. I could hear Millie crying and whimpering and I started to cry as well.

"Oh, shut up your caterwauling," Miller sneered, "Nothing's going to happen to you if we get our money."

He took a giant swig of his foul-smelling gin and pulled out a deck of cards and started playing solitaire. By the end of maybe an hour, he drained the bottle and opened another. Our captor soon staggered out onto the beach to relieve himself several times. But he always came back and downed more gin. Finally, he laid his head down on the table and started snoring.

After a long while, he woke up. Dawn was coming. Our captor went over to a corner and pulled out a carton of water. He took a long swing of it and set it down.

"I want some," Millie whined.

"Me too," I said.

He grunted and staggered over to Millie and collapsed next to her in some kind of cross between sitting and squatting, holding the container to her lips for her to drink. When she was done, it was my turn. Then he untied Millie for her comfort break and resecured her bindings. Soon it was my turn. When he was done with us, he went back to the table and pulled out another bottle of gin.

How much of that stuff can he drink?

He had stale bread for breakfast, which he cut with a rusty looking knife. He shared it with us. It made us thirsty and we got more water. He got more gin. Millie struggled with her trusses and gave up. She asked for another comfort trip, which he gave her.

"Why are you doing this?" Millie asked.

"Because you have everything and I got nothing. Nothing at all. I want what's fair. All of us should have the same things."

"Oh, so you're getting two hundred thousand dollars for us and there's four of you. Your share is fifty thousand dollars. So, you're going to give the first fifty thousand people you meet a dollar until you run out? You'll all have the same thing."

"Not hardly," he sneered, "'The Lord helps him who helps himself.' And that's what we're doing. Helping ourselves to what you should be sharing."

"But you won't be sharing," she pointed out to him.

"I will be. I'll be eating at fancy restaurants and sleeping in the best hotels. All kinds of people will be helped by how I spend your money. My money," he corrected.

"Isn't that what Father did? Isn't that capitalism?"

"First socialism. Then capitalism," he slurred his words so much it was hard to understand him at all, "Is it so wrong to take just a little bit?"

"What happens if Mother doesn't pay?"

"You know what."

"That's not wrong?"

"Your family has so much and you don't even use it all," he slurred after taking another giant swig of booze, "Do you even know where you are?"

"In a filthy cave near the shore?"

He snorted, "We're in your Aunt Gladys' house. My Aunt Gladys, too, but she don't know it. They were smugglers a few generations ago. Unloaded and stored their stuff here. There's a stairway in the back," he tilted his head further back into the midnight black, "It leads right up to her kitchen. Of course, she never comes down here. All this space and she never even uses it."

I glanced around the space. No wonder she never used it. Mold. Mildew. Fetid air. Dirt. Stale water on the floor. My clothes were ruined. I never would have even thought about my clothes back in Faucette. Quite a difference between being a city girl and a country girl, I realized.

"What would she use it for?" Millie asked, glancing around with distaste.

"You see? You rich people just don't see the world. To feed the homeless people looking for work. People are beginning to go hungry."

"You'd set up a soup kitchen down here? Isn't that a little far from everything?"

"No," he was exasperated now, "But it would make a fit place to have people stay, out of the weather. In fact, why does she need that big house? She only needs a bedroom. The rest of it can be put to good use. In a perfect world, everyone has the exact same living space, clothes, food. Everything the same. That's the only way to be fair and just."

He downed almost half the bottle of gin.

"What if someone wants something different?"

"Then they have to be educated in justice and equality."

"And if that doesn't work?" Millie persisted. She was doing a good job of keeping him talking, which I later found out was what she was trying to do.

"There is no place in a perfect world for imperfect people."

"So, you'd exile them somewhere?"

He shrugged, "No place for them to go. They can't stay

in this world. Not anywhere."

"You'd kill them?"

He nodded, but his face was starting to turn a bit green. He stared a bit at the wall before slowly getting up and crawling outside. Within minutes we heard him throwing up. Millie pulled her hands forward, the twine falling to the floor while she untied the knot on her ankle.

"He didn't tie me up very well the last time," she smiled knowingly. I was freed in a couple of minutes. I stood up but things went dark and I almost fell. Millie caught me and helped me back to the table where she grabbed one of the kerosene lamps and we marched deep into the dark recess of the cave. It seemed like we walked for miles before we came to the stairs. Millie estimated we travelled only thirty feet. But then, she wasn't sick.

The putrid air almost made me gag as we started up the mossy stairs.

"Watch out for rats," Millie warned me. Luckily, we didn't see any.

The stairs were uneven, so I leaned on her as we climbed the steps since there wasn't a guardrail. Millie maintained a firm grasp on me with one hand, held the lamp in the other, and up we went.

It was a dangerous climb but we soon arrived in front of a rotted wooden door that was waiting for us. We tried, but we couldn't push it open. She swung the light up and down looking for a lock or latch and I noticed a small lever. With our combined strength, we managed to pull it down, and the door clicked. We pushed it open enough to squeeze through.

We were in the cellar now. We leaned back on the passage door until we heard it click shut. We were safe at last. The lamp was running low on kerosene, but we made it up the stairs and into the kitchen. Millie ran through the house calling Aunt Gladys. I walked into the living room and collapsed on the couch.

CHAPTER FIFTY-FOUR

ANOTHER DREAM

I saw the dolls as soon as I closed my eyes. They stared at me from the shadows. Not angry. Not hostile. Why was I ever so afraid of them? Those lonely little beings only wanted to be loved and keep me company. They were talking to each other with high pitched and distorted voices, like they just inhaled helium. I could hear Millie and Aunt Gladys also talking to me, but I couldn't understand them. The dolls were too loud.

It didn't matter. I was too weak to move, much less reply. The voices were changing into something else. The high-pitched squeals rose and fell like ocean waves as they hit the shore. The water was rushing in and receding, in perfect harmony and rhythm. I was on the beach. That gigantic rock formation was in front of me. Aunt Gladys' voice was fading away until I could no longer hear her. I couldn't see her either. Or Millie. They were gone.

"Amy," I could hear that. All the other voices were gone.

Her call came from the ocean. I looked over at the violent waves. The water was angry and topped with foam. Whitecaps whipped and smashed against the shoreline. Then it was calm. My perspective changed. I was looking down into the water from the top of the monolith. The shore was much farther away. I had no illusion that I could ever swim back to the beach.

"Amy," she said again.

A mermaid laid on her side behind me, smiling. She was petting a small seal, who obviously enjoyed her attention. It was like the mermaid from the Tarot card had come to life. Dark, disheveled hair framed her beautiful face and oversized sea blue eyes stared at me. She smiled with white piranha teeth. Colorful, beautiful scales ran from her forked tail to just above her breasts, like an expensive and alluring (to men at least) evening gown though the tail did somewhat ruin that effect. She appeared to be filled with curiosity and cunning.

"We have much to talk about."

"We do?"

"We do."

"Amy, wake up!" I could hear Millie. She sounded scared, desperate.

Everything seemed to sway back and forth, as though reality was a curtain being blown in the wind. I thought I heard Millie crying, but I couldn't see her.

"Your next journey is beginning. You will ride on a real mermaid. She will take you out to the ocean and then back. She will be destroyed. You will go back to where you belong. And you are truly blessed, because instead of one family, you have two, though not everyone will claim you."

"Back home?"

"Where's home?" she teased, "Is it in a house of ghosts? A farm in the country? An apartment in New York? Is it here with me?"

"I don't know," I was confused.

"Who was your mother? Your father? Your sisters and brothers?"

"My sisters are here."

"Some. Perhaps there are others."

"Others?"

"That's right. Listen to your heart and you will have a long life."

She was squirming closer to me. Her teeth getting nearer my throat. I wanted to push her back, but I was at the edge of the precipice. There was no place to go. Her eyes shrank into small slits. Her seal barked once and splashed off the rocks in a hurry.

"What does your heart say?"

"I have to go," I whispered.

"You have to jump to go back. Or you can stay with me. We'll swim the oceans together. Forever."

I turned and jumped quickly.

Like a feather, I drifted and fluttered slowly down an endless abyss, until I landed in ice cold water. My eyes opened up. I was in a bathtub filled with ice and water. I screamed in pain and shock. Then I was out. Zelda was putting on my nightgown. I saw faces through some kind of mist. Charity, Lisa, Clair, Millie, and Mother. But Mother looked different. Pale and gray. Thin and unhealthy.

They were gone. I was drifting and fluttering through space. Or was I being carried somewhere?

The mermaid was back, looking down at me from the stone formation that now looked like a castle tower from long ago. No matter how young and strong a castle is when it is built, it will always become forgotten ruins.

I hit the water and sank like a stone to the bottom and kicked my feet back to the top. She was still there looking at me.

"The drowned girl lives on," she called to me as I aimlessly swam away.

Chapter Fifty-Five

Waking Up

I woke up in my room. The sun was streaming in through the open window. I reached down to adjust the blanket and realized I had to use the restroom. I was washing my hands when I heard Zelda.

"Oh, dear," she called out, "Miss Amy?"

"Be right out," I called back.

After drying my hands, I walked back into the hall. Veronica was at her doorway with a big smile as she stumbled over to me. She had a surprisingly strong grip when she hugged me.

"Oh, we were all so worried," she said.

"We were indeed," Zelda added, "Now let's get you back to bed. Cookie's been making chicken broth every day for you. She'll be so happy she can finally get some in you. I'm afraid it'll be a few days before you get anything solid."

"That's fine, I'm not hungry anyway."

"That's what you say now."

She pulled up a chair for Veronica and tidied up a bit before announcing to everyone that I was awake. Veronica felt around the bed to make sure the blankets were snug. Of course, it was still summer and I really didn't need or want them. But I appreciated the concern.

"Well, Miss Amy," she said sternly, "You were gone for a week. Then you slept for a week. We got ransom notices and all kinds of instructions and threats. We didn't know if you were alive or dead. You two had everyone worried sick. And during a quarantine, too, when no one could leave the house to search for you. Those people from Louisiana called every day looking for news. Poor Willie didn't know what to say to them. We all thought you'd be safer up here than down there with those alligators and snakes everywhere.

"Then when you came back, we couldn't wake you at all. Your fever was through the roof. Zelda and Cookie had to dunk you in a tub of ice to break it. Then you screamed like the world was ending. Then went back to sleep. You certainly know how to have adventures."

"Now wait a minute," I laughed, "That was all Millie's idea. I was innocent."

"Oh, so during quarantine, Millie hit you over the head with a hammer and dragged you out of the house at just the right time when no one would be looking, almost as if it were planned. Pushed and pulled you through the woods to the ocean. Pried off coffin lids to see if they held vampires—"

"I thought it was rum."

"Pried off coffin lids to see if they held rum, although Millie said the whole point was to prove to you that there are no vampires. And this after you managed to get the worst case of Poison Ivy ever seen in the state at the same time there's a Scarlett Fever scare. Bad combination, Little Miss.

"Then you get kidnapped. Escape. Get kidnapped again. Escape again. Get rescued. Then, you come home with the fever you might have avoided if you stayed put. And you never willingly participated. It was all that big mean Millie who forced you to tag along."

"Well," I replied, after realizing the Millie-made-me-do-it defense was not going to be helpful, "There was no hammer. She didn't *exactly* drag me."

"Then how did she coerce you into breaking quarantine?"

"Well, she said something like 'let's go.'"

"What a twister of arms! I shall have a talk with her on the sheer physical brutality of that."

"Ha-ha," I said, unamused. And Veronica was my friend. If that was her response, what would Mother's be? I had a sense of impending doom.

"Well, anyway," she went on, oblivious to the high crime of starting a sentence with 'well,' "You made national news. You and Millie were all over the radio and Barbara read me the write-ups in the papers."

She held her arms out like she was reading a paper.

"Two spoiled rotten rich brats break the quarantine rules and run all over the country until they were kidnapped by their own servants. Held for two hundred thousand dollars in ransom money for over a week and then escape when their guard gets so drunk he can't stand up."

"Wait a minute," I interrupted, "They weren't the only kidnappers. What about Mr. Gorman? He was going to sell us to the Arabs as child brides."

"Egyptians," came a voice from the door.

Millie leaped onto my bed, just barely avoiding a catastrophic collision.

"It's about time you woke up," she said while cuddling a bit, "I was beginning to think you were going to pull a Rip-Van-Winkle on us. I mean, Aunt Gladys thought you were dead. She kept shaking you to wake you up, but you just laid there. She called an ambulance and the police and the sheriff."

"My goodness," Veronica added, "While you were asleep, they came in and arrested Chester, Nadia and Kathleen. They were so…wicked. Kathleen yelled and screamed all sorts of mean things to everyone. The other two went quietly. I heard Nadia say to someone, 'Well, we gambled and lost.' And here we thought they were part of the family. I guess I wasn't surprised that Kathleen hated us all so much. Especially me."

She sounded so sad, like she might start to cry. I felt like I might start to cry with her.

I told her, "They weren't part of the family. They may have shared a father with us, but they weren't certain if they were his or not. He did take a small interest in them. Made sure they had jobs. But what did they do to show appreciation? They just waited for their opportunity to strike. We weren't family at all to them, just a source of money. Thank God they failed."

"Was Nadia related to us too?" Veronica asked.

"No," Millie replied, "She was just some war refugee who caught Father's attention and he hired her to be our governess and handle other problems."

A nice way of saying it, I suppose.

Millie told me, "And Mr. Gorman said that both of us must have had the fever and hallucinated. The police searched his house and his beach for caves. They couldn't find anything. And Edmund was out of town doing some kind of business in New York. He got rid of all the evidence so nothing's going to happen to him. Oh, and he doesn't want us within fifty feet of his property ever again or he'll feed us to his dolls."

"The dolls won't hurt us," I replied, "They only wanted company."

"Oh," Millie said, somewhat at a loss, "Well I don't want to keep them company. I get the heebie-jeebies every time I go by that house. You know, I played with dolls until recently and I keep my favorites in my closet, but after all that I think I'll give them to charity."

"Why would Charity even want them?"

"I mean give them to the Salvation Army or something."

I thought for a moment.

"You seem awfully healthy. Didn't you get sick?"

"No. Did you want me to?"

"Of course not. But we were together for so long."

"Obviously not that long. Besides, I followed all the rules. I didn't break the quarantine."

"What?" Veronica and I asked together, disbelieving what we had just heard.

"I stayed away from everybody who was sick. Otherwise, I'd be sick. That's the whole purpose of a quarantine, you know."

"No, you didn't. Amy was sick. You should be sick. You were just lucky," Veronica hissed in disgust.

"Extremely lucky, if you ask the doctor," Millie agreed, "As sick as Amy was, he couldn't believe I avoided it like I did."

"You had an adventure without us," Lisa accused from the door, smiling as she ran to me and hopped on the bed opposite Millie. Claire and Charity were right behind her, though there was no room for them on the bed. They were all talking at once, asking me how I felt after sleeping for over a week.

"That all happened a week ago?"

"Oh, no, Amy," Claire said, "Last week, you slept. All the good stuff happened the week before."

"I've sleeping for that long?"

"Well, off and on," Charity said, "We'd come in with some broth and you were able to swallow it and Zelda and Barbara helped you to the bathroom and you were able to take care of all that. But all you talked about was mermaids and dolls and things."

"Well, yeah, I was surrounded by mermaids and dolls and things. I mean, it was the worst week I had here."

They all looked from me to Millie.

"Well," she said in my defense, "I *did* see the dolls."

Zelda came in with some broth and toast. It was so filling. After that little snack, I went back to sleep.

CHAPTER FIFTY-SIX

MOTHER

It was dark when I woke up again. But no matter how black the night was, I was not going back to sleep. I was fully awake and healthy. The sickness was past. I stumbled over to the wall and turned on the light and inspected myself in the mirror. I lost weight. If people thought I was thin when I got here, what would they be thinking now? That thought made me realize I was hungry.

I tip-toed down the stairs, making sure I didn't 'stomp' and wake anyone. The kitchen was dark, so I turned on the light. The clock showed three eighteen. I was on my own for any kind of an early breakfast. But that was okay. I still had some country girl left in me. I sliced up some bread to make toast. I had a frying pan on the stove and an egg on the counter ready to go while I searched for some lard or salt pork.

"Who's up?" came a voice right outside the door.

I gently pushed it open to see Mother there, standing in her robe and looking somewhat confused. Gray streaks and white strands of her hair blew everywhere. Her eyes were bloodshot and sunken, almost like her brain pulled them inward. She was gaunt, with loose folds of extra skin all over her neck. Her complexion was gray. A dark gray, like the Countess on the last day I saw her, when she didn't recognize me. Mother didn't seem to know me now.

Tears were already in my eyes as I hugged her.

"It's me, Amy," I said.

"Amy," she repeated, "The lost girl who came home. Then got lost again. I thought you were going to die. I saw you with the mermaid. 'The drowned girl lives on.'"

"I thought it was a dream," I said, disturbed a little. How would she know about that unnerving phrase from my dream?

"It was," she replied, "I dreamed about you a lot the last few days. I am afraid for you. Something bad is going to happen."

"It already did and it's over," I reminded her as I took her hand and led her to the kitchen table, "Are you hungry? I was going to make breakfast."

"Yes," she said as she pulled the cord to call Cookie to the kitchen, but not hard enough. I didn't hear the bell ring, "But I want Cookie to do it. Come to the living room with me. We have much to talk about."

Another phrase I hear in my dreams.

I shivered as we sat down on the settee.

"I want you to know," she said, "That I brought you here to be part of our family. I handled it all wrong. I should have known better too. I took you away from your other family. They called every day asking about you. And long-distance phone calls are so expensive. I reversed the charges every time. They were so concerned and worried. You know, Willie only wanted you to visit us for a while. Maybe every summer, but I wanted you here always. All my daughters are wonderful girls and I love you all. But you, I don't hardly know.

"And you fit in so well. We took a barefoot country girl into our house and made a little lady out of her."

I wore shoes.

"You also made me realize that I kept my other girls away from life. They want to live outside of my protection. I see that now. After all that you two went through, you know what the others all said? Even Melody, who should know a lot more than she does?"

I shook my head.

"They wished they were there with you. They thought you were having fun and left them behind."

"Fun?"

"And that's where I failed them. They don't know what fun is. Now I have to worry that they'll all want to go out and get kidnapped, just for the experience."

"I think we had fun when we were out and about without adults. The kidnapping part and getting sick wasn't a good time at all."

"And that's what I said. And you all have the shared experience of being sick, except poor Millie. She was left out of that opportunity."

Some opportunity.

"But anyway, you're my magical little girl. You can do so much and you've taken them on adventures, especially Millie. Makes sense since she's closer to your age. And you never grew up with the privilege they had. At least until you arrived, they were all content to stay inside and read or play together."

"Charity plays piano," I added.

"She does," Mother agreed, "And Lisa sings. Charity plays well, but somehow not...oh, what's the word? Interesting. But then, the piano's not interesting. You just press down on the keys. It's like that with all music, I suppose. Maybe I just don't like music anymore. I don't suppose it matters.

"But they were raised to be perfect ladies and desirable wives. On judgement day, I can say to the Lord, I did my duty. Charity will debut soon, you know. We'll have to send her to finishing school now. I don't want another governess. No more of those people in the house."

"*Those* people?"

"Your father was a dreadful man. I gave him everything he asked for and he still went off with other women. Never seemed to be a shortage of them. They're all his children, you know, except Cookie and Zack. And she's his sister. Half-sister, anyway. But it's not as though Joe cared about anything like that.

"Anyway, Nadia and Kathleen are being deported. We didn't file charges to avoid the scandal. The police went through their things looking for evidence of any other crimes. Kathleen and Chester were fine.

"Nadia had a box with an old rotten skull in it. She said it belonged to her fiancé, who died in the war. She kept it as a keepsake."

"She had the skull? I thought her fiancée kept it."

"How did you know about it?"

I explained the story Nadia told me when I first met her.

"I wish you had told me that sooner. I would have thrown her out of the house. Maybe none of this other stuff would have happened. She was the ringleader, you know. The police wanted to have her committed but I said no. Send her back home to Yugoslavia. Let that country handle her."

"You mean Slovenia?"

"It's Yugoslavia now, dear. Slovenia was never independent. She just wanted it to be. We just want her gone and no trial. Chester and that Darnell Miller were convinced to go join the French Foreign Legion so they wouldn't have to go to jail. So, they're all gone. Never to bother us again."

She paused and opened her pill box. She had no water, so we went back to the kitchen. I poured her a glass and buttered my toast. I put back the egg. I wasn't going to cook anything.

"You four, Lisa, Clarice, Millicent, and you, will be off to boarding school. Willie's making the arrangements. How sad I have to send you away. But you'll be with your sisters. And I expect you all to be home every Christmas and holidays."

Tears were filling my eyes. I didn't think she'd be here by Christmas.

"Is someone in my kitchen? Bob, are you sneaking around out here?" Cookie came in, wearing her nightclothes. It was the first time I saw her not in uniform. She reminded me of Gramma De Montfort. I wondered if I would ever see anyone from Faucette again now that I would be sent away.

"It's only us," I said.

"Did you make your own toast?" she asked, frowning.

"I did," I replied, "I was hungry and didn't want to wake you. I love it here with you, Cookie, but I can do for myself, at least sometimes."

She looked over at Mother, obviously unhappy, "Miss Tilly, are you all right with that?"

"Cookie," Mother said, "I am so blessed to have you in the house. You are not just a wonderful cook; you are a wonderful person."

"Why, thank you, ma'am," Cookie said, looking confused.

"I, on the other hand, have given my daughters too much, and by doing that I took away even more. I stole their independence. Their ability to thrive without me. Let Amy 'do for herself' a bit. I think the world is changing. Perhaps we'll be better off being less decorative and more independent. There may come a day when men want smart, capable women instead of pretty, dainty, little ornaments who have boring tea parties and heads full of straw."

She nodded her dismissal to me, "Go cook yourself something."

I went back to the stove. My toast was cold, but I buttered it anyway. Then I got out my egg again and found the oil and made a scramble. While I was eating, Cookie came back in and pulled the cord for Willie.

"The missus is almost asleep. She swallowed another one of those damn pills," she told me, "Now Willie's going to have to get her upstairs. She can't walk and I can't carry her. I wish she'd take them in her room."

She shook her head sadly while I scraped off my plate.

"Stop," she commanded and finished cleaning it, "I don't need some young whippersnapper trying to steal my job."

She gave my shoulder a squeeze.

"Now go sit with your mother. She needs you more than you need her."

She was sleeping when I got back. I held her hand until Willie came to carry her upstairs. When he had her back in bed, I sat next to her and stroked her hair. She didn't move. The sun came up a little later. Barbara slipped in and shooed me away. My mother was sick and needed her sleep.

Chapter Fifty-Seven

A Phone Call

I studied my books even though there was no one to monitor my progress. I just thought that was what a responsible 'young lady' would do. Until everyone else woke up, there really wasn't any better option.

My current reading assignment was *The Tempest*, another play by Shakespeare. I put it at the bottom of the pile. I wouldn't like or understand it without Nadia there to explain it. The next book was *Ivanhoe*, which I did like. I read until the others got up.

We played croquet and cards all day. It seemed I was the only one who even thought about continuing my studies with Nadia gone.

After the doctor looked at Mother, he examined me and pronounced me fit. We were free to go out and about again, though I was told to not overdo it. My sisters were all excited about going to visit people again. Millie wanted us to go see Aunt Gladys, who saved my life by calling for help.

I was still weak from the fever and was thinking a nap would be better for me. Veronica agreed. And since Veronica was the only adult in the house who was awake, they all went and had fun for the day. I listened to jazz in Veronica's room until I fell asleep on her bed.

I slept through lunch but was wide awake for dinner, though all that sleep gave me a nagging little headache. Mother also slept through the day and missed dinner. So, it was just us girls. The conversation was all about our daring adventures and sensational escapes.

"Daring and sensational aren't the words I would use," I replied dryly, "A week of being tied up in a cave with poison ivy and being sick was more like 'wretched' and 'miserable.' At least they fed us. I think."

"Peanut butter sandwiches and vegetable soup. Twice a day. Nadia made sure it was available," Millie replied, "Kathleen would have starved us. Chester sneaked us some chocolate bars a few times. That other man offered me some gin, but I said no."

"That's good, Missy," Barbara said as she was serving beef and lobster stew.

I didn't get any because I was still recovering and rich foods like that might upset my stomach. I got broth and bread.

"I don't remember any chocolate."

"You were too sick to know what it was and that man said you might throw up if you ate it. So, I made the supreme sacrifice and took your share to keep you from getting sick. There's so much I'm willing to do for you."

I opened my mouth to tell her what I thought of her 'supreme sacrifice,' but she went on talking.

"No need to thank me. I did it all for you. Even though it was your fault we got kidnapped," she was obviously kidding me, but I was annoyed.

"Now how do you think it was my fault? I didn't want to go in the first place."

Veronica found my wrist under the table and gave it a warning squeeze.

"Sure you did," Millie replied, oblivious to me, "Otherwise you would have stayed home. And I would have stayed home. Besides, if I went alone, I wouldn't have opened the coffins because I wouldn't have had to prove to you that there weren't any vampires in them and that's how we got caught in the first place."

The other girls started giggling.

"Well, Nadia told me there were such things. And so did Ursula."

"Great," Charity laughed, "A criminal and a lunatic. How can anyone argue with them?"

"I don't know," said Lisa, "Melanie is quite taken with Ursula. There might be something to her."

"We might have thought the same of Nadia, or Kathleen, or Chester," Claire added.

"And Kathleen thought she was family," Charity said, "Thought she was Father's little love child."

I said, "That's why she was hired."

"Now how do you know that?" Charity asked, suddenly attentive.

"I remember it being said in the cave."

"Well, we can certainly do without sisters like that," Charity concluded.

I noticed Veronica lowering her head a bit.

"It's okay," I told her, "It's better not to have friends like her. My sister, Anna Marie, had friends like that and they turned on her like nobody's business. Worse than snakes. At least you know you have us. We won't turn on you."

I snuggled up to her shoulder just a bit. I was surprised that all the other girls got up and gathered around her to rub her back and let her know that they were there for her. I was touched. She was too. She started crying. Not because she was sad but because she was so happy. I hoped that when I became a woman I would only cry when I was sad. It just seemed more logical.

It was a wonderful evening for us all. Charity and Lisa bought all the newspapers while we were gone and along with Claire put together a scrapbook of the kidnapping and a copy of the ransom note and more newspaper clippings and finally how we escaped.

"Oh, my goodness," I said, "I should call my mom back in Louisiana. She's probably worried to death about me by now."

"I wouldn't worry about it," Claire said, "They're not your real family like us. They're just…your hillbilly friends."

"They are family to me. I just happen to have two, and I don't want to lose one," I replied without hiding my annoyance.

"That makes sense to me," Lisa agreed and the others all concurred.

"So, call them tomorrow," Claire amended.

The evening was wonderful after that. It was like our party in the guest house without the ghosts and bad guys trying to get one of us. We were all together. No one cared that Veronica was blind or that I just got there. We played music and sang until Willie ordered us to bed.

I was under the covers when Zelda came in to see me. She was startled a bit when she opened the door.

"I do declare," she said, "Sometimes I just know I see a woman in that mirror staring at me."

"Chester would agree with that."

"I'm sure. Anyway, I know I'm late, and you're already in bed, but do you need anything?"

"I think I'm fine."

"We'll get the bath tomorrow, then. They're not replacing Kathleen, you know. So, I'll take care of you all now. It's a chore getting to you like I should."

"It's okay. I can pour my own baths. But maybe a little lotion for the bug bites would be nice."

"Of course."

Good. I like a little privacy.

We chatted for a little about my adventure. She agreed to wake me up early so I could call my other home to tell them I was all recovered. We didn't know if Mother would approve or not, but we decided it would be better to just make the call than disturb her.

The sky was turning gray and magenta when she woke me up. I quickly dressed and hurried to the kitchen. Fluffy woke up and ran around me, demanding attention and threatening to bark if she didn't get picked up. It was five o'clock, so I figured it would be a good time to call home. The hour change would make it six so I could speak to everyone.

On the seventh ring, Gramma Morris answered with a grouchy, "Hello?"

"Hi, Gramma Morris," I said, "It's Amy."

"Amy?" she said quietly, "Are you alright? You were supposed to be safe up there. Next thing we know, you and some girl get kidnapped and escape and you're sick and in bed. And you broke quarantine. Sometimes I wonder how you think. Now do you see why you don't break quarantine rules?"

"I do," I agreed, kind of regretting making this call, "And that 'some girl' is my sister. She's the one who got me out of there. Next time I'm on quarantine, I'm just going to read every book ever published. At least the ones in English."

"Good idea. Now, why are you calling at four o'clock in the morning? Everyone's asleep."

"Four? I thought it was six. It's five o'clock here."

"You're an hour ahead of us, not behind. That's not important. Just tell me all about your adventures."

And so I told her everything I remembered. How Chester tried to snatch me out of my room a couple of times and how they laid a trap for us at the museum, but we got away. How Melanie introduced me to her medium friend, Ursula and she introduced me to the tarot cards. I told her about the mermaid card that Ursula thought was so meaningful. 'The drowned girl lives on.'

"Oh, my," she said, "That's all doings of the devil. I hope you do a better job of staying away from those people. Nothing good can come from that but a whole of bad is hiding behind the curtain."

"That's not what makes me nervous about Ursula," I said, "She keeps calling me Yvonne. That's her dead sister from before the war. She thinks I'm her, come back to life. And she's one of the best mediums in Boston, so she should know. Melanie is like an apprentice to her. She wants to be a medium too."

"Then you should stay away from her too. People like that won't see their mistakes until they're at the gates of hell and Satan is pulling them in. And by then, it'll be too late. You mark my words."

"I know what you mean, but with Mother still sick, we have all these adults coming and going but no one is really there for us. We take care of each other. And Melanie is an adult, you know. She's twenty-two and has a baby."

"And you think that's all it takes to be an adult?"

"Well, I guess I don't."

"No, you don't. Takes some plain old brain power. Playing with demon cards and holding seances and all that shows me a total lack of common sense. Or any other kind of sense, except nonsense. What happens when you call up something that doesn't want to go back? What do you do then?"

Good question.

"How's everyone?" I asked.

She was getting loud and I didn't want her to wake up the baby.

"They're all fine. Your dad. Paul. Your real dad. The one who loves you. He misses you to no end. He still regrets not shooting up all them lawyers in court, but he knows it wouldn't have done any good, except to make him feel good for a few minutes."

"I thought his Christian principles made violence forbidden."

"As he says, 'Sometimes, you have to do what God wants you to do, not what God tells you to do.' Otherwise, the bad guys always win. I'm not sure that's biblically sound, myself.

"He was thinking of converting to the Catholic church, but it would just be him. The rest of us ain't praying to no statues. And where does that pope guy get off telling everybody he's always right and never wrong. We can read it in our own Bibles and have God guide us the way he wants, thank you."

"But you can't read."

"I want you to find the biggest wooden spoon in the house and whap yourself with it. Pastor Josephson reads it for me and the others in church.

"Anyway, Paul decided not to convert. They came back

from Baton Rouge and stopped at the church to talk about something and the phone rang. Father Callahan had to take it privately. So, Paul goes out to the pews and he finds some crackers and starts to eat them. So, when Father Callahan comes to get him, he gets all uppity and angry-like. Said he ate all of the Eucharist host, whatever that is. Really threw a fit about it. So, Paul dunked his head in the holy water font in the front of the church and left."

"How embarrassing," I exclaimed, "Mom must have been humiliated when she heard that."

"Not in the least," Gramma Morris snapped back, "Paul's a good man inside, he just has a low threshold for disrespect. And your Mom would never tell him to tolerate any such thing. He may not be perfect, but he's no embarrassment to family."

"You're right," I apologized, "It would have been awkward the next time he went to confession anyway."

"So, we just don't go to church anymore. It's a lot of trouble just to be treated the way we are. But I wished we did.

"Paul and Angus Nye, that heathen, for some reason went to the old cemetery a few nights back and sang hymns to the top of their lungs. If that wasn't bad enough, they started dancing between the mausoleums to relax Paul's soul. Talk about crazy ideas."

"He danced with the dead?"

"I don't think so. From what I hear, it was just them, thank God. Depjim had to drive them home. Angus was too drunk to open the car door. Paul wasn't much better. Who knows? If it makes him a little less prone to hit people, I'll keep quiet about it.

"Your Uncle Vincent offered to drive us to church but Sharon's getting ready to labor. Your baby brother is already here, you know. Your mom and Holly spend every minute with him. They named him Matthew, after Paul's brother. The one who raised him after their father died. I hope he doesn't grow up to be like him. He may have been good to Paul, but he was a mean man."

"I had a dream where I was back there, and the bassinette was in the kitchen with Mom and Aunt Sharon was there—"

"That wasn't a dream," she interrupted, "You were here. Cassie and Sharon both saw you. They said you looked pathetic and sick. Red all over. They didn't know what to think. And then you were gone."

"I had the fever. I kind of felt like I was drifting away. But Millie came back and they got me to the cave. Nadia, my governess, was one of the kidnappers and she gave me medicine to keep me alive. Kathleen would have let me die but Nadia said I was worth more alive than dead."

"How kind of her."

"I wish they'd let me come visit you. I miss you all."

"Well, we miss you more. There's more of us, you know."

I could hear Cookie clomping down the stairs.

"Well, everyone's awake now," I said, "I have to go. Tell everyone I love them and miss them."

"I will. They'll be disappointed they didn't get to talk to you," she replied.

After a couple more goodbyes, I hung up and left the kitchen, Fluffy following me every step of the way.

CHAPTER FIFTY-EIGHT

A DEATH IN THE FAMILY

Cookie ran by me without so much as a 'Good Morning.' She seemed frantic, so I followed her back to the kitchen to see if there was anything I could do to help. She was pulling on all the ropes for the servants and was on the phone demanding to talk to the doctor.

"It's the missus," she said into the mouthpiece, "I think she's dead."

I hurried out to run upstairs but Zelda caught me. I tried to get by her, but she had an iron grip on one wrist and clamped me in a bear hug. I was pinned until I stopped struggling.

"It's not good to look at a body for anyone," she said softly while I cried, "Especially for one so young. Just remember her as she was. The wonderful woman who loved you and rescued you from that awful life down south."

It wasn't an 'awful life.'

She guided me to my room and sat with me until Veronica got up. The three of us talked about Mother. Zelda said she was always so kind and loving to her, even if she did suspect she was her husband's child from another woman. She knew that wasn't Zelda's fault.

Too bad the women in Faucette didn't have that perspective.

Veronica felt like the rock of the household just washed away. Mother was her defender since my father was very harsh with her. Veronica was an annoying expense to him who would never marry into a wealthy family or provide any other kind of financial benefit to him.

I had little to say. I barely knew my mother. We visited the neighbors that day and I had a few conversations with her, but those were my only memories. I left out the negative parts where she said I wasn't pretty and would need acid baths.

The doorbell was ringing intermittently during this conversation. People were coming and going all over the house. Zelda was discreetly rounding up my sisters and sending them to my room. Tears were in every eye. We were all in bad shape, but Claire was just devastated.

"I just didn't know she was that sick," she cried.

"Well, she had cancer, then she got fever, then these two got kidnapped and she was worried sick," Charity comforted, although when Millie and I looked at each other, it was plain neither of us were impressed with her style of consolation.

"Those people should be charged with murder," Claire said before crying too hard to be able to speak.

Charity put her arm around her and swayed back and forth while she calmed down.

Soon Willie knocked on the door and entered. He glanced at the mirror, freezing for just a second as though he spotted my ghostly roommate before he turned to us.

"I'll need you all downstairs in the dining room. The coroner's men are here to pick up your mother. It's a sight I don't think you need to see."

"Can't we at least say goodbye?" Lisa asked.

"No. Say goodbye at the funeral," he was rather sharp with her.

So, we marched downstairs to the dining room and took our chairs at the end of the table. Uncle Edgar sat at the head with Aunt Vera on his right side. They looked positively grim. Neither had even a trace of moisture in their eyes.

"You poor little dears," Aunt Vera started with as much fake empathy as she could manufacture, "I want you to know that everything will be alright. Nothing much is going to change for you. Right, Edgar?"

"Absolutely. Your Aunt Vera will move in here with you until school starts next month, when you will be transferred to boarding school. I have to stay home with our daughters, of course."

"That was Matilda's plan, you know," Aunt Vera said, "She knew she was going to be too sick to raise you girls. Charity will go to finishing school at Fedworth's School for Ladies. The rest of you shall go to my alma mater, Bridehead's Academy for Girls, in New York. It will be especially good for Millie and Amy," she said looking straight at us as she called our names, "Since it has a ten-foot-high wall. It's to keep…distracted young boys from trying to talk to the young ladies. In your case, it will serve to keep you two from getting out and getting yourselves hurt. Or worse."

I'm not sure it would be all that difficult to get over a ten-foot wall, depending on how thick the vines are.

"And don't even think you'll be able to scale the wall. It's smooth brick and if they even remotely suspect you'll try it, you'll be in the kitchen peeling potatoes and other dirty work under constant supervision until lights out. And there are bed monitors that walk through the dormitories every hour. There will be no absconding away."

"Is it a school or a prison?" Lisa asked with a put-upon voice.

"Both. You can make it what you will. Edgar?"

"I just want you to know there have been some problems at the company that require big changes, though I don't want to bore you with the details. We were on a decline because of some strange decisions, mostly in hiring, that your father made. I plan to rectify that and get us back on an even keel. By the time I'm done, you girls won't believe the differences that will happen in your lives."

"But first," Aunt Vera continued, "We have a little uncertainty here."

We all looked at her while she sipped her tea. She had a definite flare for drama.

"I find it hard to believe that my late brother would practice the behavior that he has been accused of. To think that he would throw away his daughter and take in a son with no blood connection and make him his heir is just not something I ever believed. Now, Matilda was led astray by that butler and lawyer, as you know."

"So were Kathleen and Miller?" Lisa asked, "And Nadia and Chester?"

She frowned.

"She's right," Veronica said, "Uncle Joe hired a lot of people throughout the house and his companies based on his…amorous relationships."

"Those are just stories told by people trying to get attention."

"Like the hospital staff?" I asked.

"And if they told the truth, they switched babies for money. How do we know they didn't testify that way for money? A liar is a liar, you know. I just don't know what the motivation for all this was."

"Motivation? I didn't even know you existed until I got here."

"I'm sure you didn't. We didn't know about you either. But somebody wanted you to be part of the family. And we'll find out what the reason was for it. As of now, we want to know if Amy is actually related to us or not. There's a whole new procedure to help determine everything, one way or another."

We were all confused by this and I was a little nervous. No matter what she had in mind, I felt certain that she would see to it that my days as a Wentworth were numbered.

"Mother just died, Aunt Vera," Charity said, "She's not even in the ground yet and you're already doing something like this. Can't it at least wait until after the funeral?"

"Of course, dear," Uncle Edgar replied, "But no longer than that. Not just because of the scandal involved, but why should a stranger get a full share of the inheritance? That's only for family, you know. Rest assured, nothing will happen until all the paperwork gets done and everything is legal. Then we will settle our issues with Amy, if we even have issues."

Chapter Fifty-Nine

More Surprises

Our routines were all properly adjusted due to everything that happened. There were no more activities required until September, which was only days away. School started the third week, at least for my sisters. My fate was yet to be determined. At least I still had my riding, dance and violin lessons for the moment.

Veronica was back to eating in her room and I joined her. I was happier not being around Aunt Vera anyway. The other girls also wanted to eat upstairs, but Aunt Vera insisted on the family having meals together. Veronica and I just weren't quite family anymore.

The Monday after Mother's funeral, Willie took Aunt Vera and me to Boston to see a doctor to determine my status in the family. We rode in silence. Willie wasn't going to converse with me because Aunt Vera would get upset. She just stared straight ahead while I looked out the window at the passing scenery.

The office was in a small brownstone building with a glass door. I assumed we would be going to a medical doctor but when we got to the building I was confused.

"What's a hematologist?"

Aunt Vera just walked into the building as Willie held open the door. He rolled his eyes in disgust.

"It's a doctor who studies blood," he replied, "You see, after the Great War, the doctors discovered that there are four different types of blood. Your Mother was Type O. Your father was Type A. So, they'll take a sample of your blood. If you are Type A or O, then he could be your father. If you are AB or B, then he is definitely not your father. But it doesn't really prove that he is. Nothing can prove he is your father."

"He's absolutely right," Aunt Vera said coldly, "But it's a good first step."

We waited in the office for maybe ten minutes and the visit itself lasted twenty. He took some blood and explained the procedure. We left for home after that. We would get the results before school started.

Our days were regimented now. Aunt Vera was annoyed that she was staying with us. We were sympathetic to her on that point. We didn't want her here either. Eventually, she hired out a temporary governess, named Beatrice, to help maintain our ladylike behavior. Aunt Vera was too busy salvaging things from Mother's room.

Our going about town and visiting were over. If anyone wanted to see us, they could visit us at home. Beatrice disapproved of us walking about town, even if we did all stay together. Maybe she hoped we would die of loneliness.

One rainy day, Charity received a phone call from a boy she knew. She was talking for a while and we could hear excitement in her voice, though she was trying to suppress it.

"You won't believe it," she squealed when she hung up.

"What?" We all gathered around.

"That was Preston Hartnett. You know what he wanted?"

"A date?" Lisa asked.

"Yes," Charity was jumping up and down now, and the rest of us were caught up in the excitement, "We'll be going fox hunting this Saturday."

"Fox hunting?" I asked.

I stopped jumping. From what I knew, hunting was waiting in bushes getting bored and insect bit until some innocent animal wanders within range and BANG.

"It's not like that here," Charity laughed, "It's a big party on horseback. First, they release the fox from its cage and after they wait a while, they turn loose the dogs. Everybody brings their best hounds, usually around thirty. Then, about twenty of us follow them on horseback until they corner the fox."

"Then you put it back in its cage?"

"No, silly," she said with an exaggerated eye roll, "They kill the little beast."

"Why don't they just not release it from the cage?"

She glared at me for a moment, then went on.

"This will be my first hunt. I'm so excited."

"I thought Preston was interested in Martha Burnside," Lisa said quietly.

"They had a fight."

Surprisingly, Aunt Vera approved of the hunt and Charity was gone for the day. We were not allowed to be spectators, which was just as well. Although I was sure the fox would be well-hunted, I didn't think we would be well-entertained. Besides, the phone was always ringing. My sisters' dozens of relatives called to wish them well. They all offered to speak to me, but I thought that would be awkward because I never met them. What do you say to complete strangers?

"How do you think they'll ever not be complete strangers?" Lisa asked after another polite decline.

"I'm not sure," I said, "But I think I'd just rather meet people in person."

She rolled her eyes but didn't pursue it. The day ended without incident, which was nice. I was through with excitement.

I had just gone to bed when I heard the front door open and close later that night.

"How did the hunt go?" I heard Aunt Vera say and snuck to the railing to hear the conversation. They were in the foyer near the stairs, so I could hear them perfectly.

"It was kind of strange. Preston met me at the field and introduced me around. Martha Burnside was there as well. Although I was Preston's date, he spent all day with her and ignored me. I guess I was there to make her jealous."

"What a blackguard. I do hope you never speak to him again. How dare he treat a Wentworth like that?"

"It's all right," Charity replied, "I met another young man there."

"Oh?"

"His name is Gunther Von Heltor. He's a lieutenant in the German army and is assigned to the embassy. He asked if he could call sometime."

"Hmmf. A pipsqueak little junior officer? And from Germany? I'll let him call, but you are still going to finishing school. No. Matter. What."

I snuck back to my room before they saw me.

The next day, Millie called me over to her side. She had that dreaded telephone in her hand, so I pretended I didn't see her and hurried out of sight.

"They're your family too. How will you ever get to

know anyone if you don't talk to them?" Millie asked me after she hung up. All my sisters were waiting for my response.

"Some questions have no answer," I replied, embarrassed.

"She's shy," Zelda said firmly, "And there's nothing wrong with that. You'll see. When the boys come calling, you four will always get first choices, the handsomest. You just watch." Then she whispered to me, "But the best one to have will be the one who takes the time to talk to the quiet one. You'll see."

"When will the boys even start calling?" Lisa asked.

"When they find you," Zelda replied simply.

"Wonderful," she muttered, "How will they ever find us up here under lock and key?"

"Well, they do have to be determined. You are delightful young ladies who need to be wooed and won over. You're not some pretty little pinecones laying around in the forest for anyone to pick up."

"I couldn't have said it better," Aunt Vera's cold voice came from behind, "And even the ignorant servant girl, who starts a sentence with 'well,' understands the value a young lady has, even if the young lady doesn't."

"It's not about 'value,'" Lisa flared, "I don't think of myself as some canned good on a shelf to be bought."

"No," Aunt Vera retorted, "A canned good has natural value. A lady must learn hers. If you don't, you run the risk of marrying a man who loves your money, but not you. I am sorry you seem to prefer running around the streets like orphans instead of pursuing your God-given lady-like talents. But I will tolerate your anger today, knowing you will thank me tomorrow. Besides, Charity seems to have been found by that nice young officer."

I was surprised. I thought Aunt Vera disapproved of him.

"Amy," she practically yelled, even though we were in the same room, "Please meet me upstairs in the third-floor office. The rest of you. I have a pleasant surprise. Beatrice is going to give you lessons in the long-lost art of embroidery."

"We already know how to do needlepoint," Millie whined.

"Needlepoint is creating a decorative fabric. Embroidery is sewing wonderful decorations on to fabric. Beatrice will show you things to do and encourage your imagination and creativity. Come Amy."

Come Amy, indeed. Sounds like she's calling a dog.

And so we went upstairs. I would have preferred to stay downstairs since I didn't know how to do needlework or embroidery and they sounded kind of fun. That obviously wasn't an option.

Uncle Edgar was already in the office, seated behind the desk, whispering to another man whose back was turned to me. My uncle glared at me with eyes that frowned and lips that scowled. Aunt Vera sat next to him, looking almost demonic. The other man turned around to me. I knew him from Faucette.

"Hello, Amy," he said with a tight little smile, "Do you remember me?"

I nodded, "You're Mr. Newell Davis, the lawyer who brought me here."

He nodded and indicated to me to have a seat next to him in front of the desk.

"We're all a little confused here right now," he started.

"There's no confusion," Aunt Vera interrupted, "This child is a fraud and is certainly not a Wentworth. I knew my brother would never do anything so immoral as to switch babies and leave his own daughter to live with hillbillies and gangsters. That whole family belongs in jail for all the harm they caused us."

"What?" I was stunned.

"Hush, Vera," Uncle Edgar soothed, "Everything will be alright."

"Oh, the scandal of it all," she went on, "Poor Tilly so humiliated and now she won't even know what happened."

"What happened?" I asked, totally confused. Obviously, the blood test proved I wasn't a Wentworth. All they had to do was send me back.

"Amy," Mr. Davis soothed, "Although it is possible that Tilly Wentworth may be your mother, though probably not, J.P. Wentworth was not your father."

"Oh, so I should have stayed in Faucette?"

"Only if it has a jail," Aunt Vera growled at me.

"It has a jail," came a voice from the door.

I turned to see Willie walking in. He stood proud and tall. He was more than just a servant now. He was his own man, equal to everyone else in the room. His posture said that.

"What are you doing here?" Aunt Vera practically screamed at him, "Nobody called you."

"But I came. As soon as I heard you were all having a meeting, I knew I had to be here."

"No, you didn't," Aunt Vera practically spat at him, "This is about our family. And you are merely a servant. A soon to be unemployed one, at that. How dare you even think that you are one of our peers."

"Because I'm looking out for family. No one else here cares about little Amy. So, I'm here for her. And, yes, Faucette has a jail," Willie continued, "And Paul Villians spent quite some time there. Her real stepfather should have spent even more time there. You see, Tilly Wentworth is most assuredly Amy's mother. I kept track of the child every time something happened to her. When the time came for us to tell Mrs. Wentworth about Amy, she would want to know all about her.

"Mr. Wentworth had no interest, of course. They were having some troubles in their marriage, and he knew he wasn't the father. He would have remembered an evening with her. And there wasn't one.

"When he found out she was expecting, he was angry, originally. He even thought of leaving her, the ultimate scandal. But then he had an idea. The lady would have a son. He would have an heir. Amy was just a way to get a male heir."

"How do you know all this?" Uncle Edgar asked harshly.

Willie dragged a chair over to the table so he could sit with his peers.

"He told me. He had me help him make the arrangements," Willie went on, "He was a man used to getting what he wanted and he wanted a son. He got one.

"The lady's mistake was obvious. He figured she would want to atone for her guilt. So, he forgave her because he was going to have a son at last. By any means possible. Then he could hold it over her head that she committed adultery. Tilly would become a nonentity. Just a happy little housewife who knew her place and stayed there. Or be humiliated.

"But she was a Langston. The Langston family was every bit as cunning and cold-blooded as the Wentworths. And Mrs. Tilly was prepared to go to war. Mr. Wentworth underestimated her. He had many girlfriends who came and told the lady all about their…adventures with him. She listened and wrote down everything they said. She soon knew that almost all the employees in the house were his children. She knew that the factories and stores were loaded with his children and girlfriends. Men offered their own wives up to get good jobs.

"She knew that she did far less to him than he did to her. She stood up for herself. She reminded him that her family owns the controlling shares of Wentworth enterprises. If he left her, he would lose the family house, his title and position as well as his standing in the community. He only had a good reputation because he could buy off everyone he needed to. And without the Wentworth lawyers," he nodded to Mr. Davis, "There could indeed be charges brought against him. Misuse of company funds. Blackmail. He could go bankrupt just fighting them in court. Mrs. Wentworth could have a review of his business dealings. She could get the press involved."

"What are you talking about?" Aunt Vera said coldly, her eyes boring into Willie with a hatred he had to feel.

"I'm talking about business deals. Like the munitions he sent to Germany during the Great War. He and Steed Gorman sent rifles to Ireland. He bought and imported whiskey from Canada. He provided cement for bridges and buildings made with beach sand and bonemeal. I'm sure you know about the land deals in Florida where he bought swamp and sold it as farmland. And he made contributions to politicians to ensure that there would be no investigations.

"It can still all come out, you know. As I said before, it's all written down. Mr. Wentworth lost his control over his wife when he got his male heir."

"Well, Mr. Jarviston," the lawyer said quietly, "Those are certainly some interesting fantasies."

"All true events."

"Fantasies," Davis repeated quietly, "Unless you have proof. The written musings of a drug addict will hardly suffice as evidence. And if you know anything, you know she was taking laudanum long before she had cancer."

"It's all written down. Names, dates, everything. She gave it to me in case she died under unusual circumstances. I can give it to the Boston Herald to find the 'proof.' They'll have a field day."

"They certainly will," Uncle Edgar said softly.

"What?" Aunt Vera cried out, "You mean you knew all this?"

"I found out after I started reviewing the books. Your brother destroyed the business. It will be everything I can do to save any of it. He had quite a few managers who could barely read and write. Now we know why. He thought it was all perfectly acceptable. The right people approved of everything he did."

"For the right price," Willie added.

"Speaking of price," Uncle Edgar said with a hateful glare, "What's yours?"

"Several things," Willie replied, "First and foremost, the welfare of Amy. She seems to be a source of irritation to you people. I want what's best for her."

"Why?" Aunt Vera sneered like some kind of wolf, "What's she to you?"

"Oh, my God," Uncle Edgar whispered, looking at Davis, "He's her real father, isn't he? Joe knew he wasn't the father and Jarviston was the only one she had any contact with. And Tilly wouldn't let Joe fire him."

Davis looked at Willie.

"I am," the butler said quietly, "Tilly and I were together right after Millicent was born. After six daughters and no male heir, Mr. Wentworth left her bed forever. She invited me in, knowing that even though my station in life was below hers, I truly loved her. We had two children together. Amy and Rosemary."

"So, what do you want?" Davis asked gently. Since Aunt Vera wanted to avoid a public scandal, Willie controlled the situation. Both Willie and Davis knew this basic fact.

"Ten thousand shares of Wentworth stock, and total parental control of my daughter. However, no one is to know about that part. I want her to stay with the other girls. They're family now. No one has to know I'm her father. No need to have the neighbors talk."

"Under no circumstances," Aunt Vera said, rising to her feet, "You want ten thousand shares of Wentworth Enterprises and have us accept her as family? Absolutely not."

"You'll be sending them off to boarding school. Will it make a difference?"

"That's a lot of stock," Davis started to say.

"It's a deal," Uncle Edgar pronounced, "Davis will have the shares in your hand by the end of tomorrow. Amy, my 'niece,' will stay with the girls and together they will go to boarding school. Maybe you can arrange for her vacations and holidays to be spent with those hillbillies. I see no reason for my wife to be reminded of her brother's…vile behavior."

"I'd like that," I whispered, too afraid to make more noise than that.

"Probably not an issue," Willie smiled at me, "Now why don't you run downstairs and give them a call? Make sure they think it's a good idea. But tell no one anything about what you heard here."

I nodded and ran downstairs to make the phone call.

Chapter Sixty

The Curious Virgin

"Well of course we want you here for the holidays and summers," Mom squealed with delight, "Amy, you just don't know it, but you made today the happiest day since Matthew was born. For all of us. I just don't know what can be wrong with those people. I know the woman who thought she was your mother wanted you. Now these other people only will send you to boarding school, then down here. Not what I'd call a family at all."

There was some talk in the background and Dad got on the line.

"Now Amy," he said, "I want you to know you just made me the happiest man in the parish. I truly thought I would never see you again when that train left. My heart just broke, but we carried on. I can hardly wait for Thanksgiving now that we know you'll be here."

"Me too," I cried. Tears of happiness were rolling down my cheeks. And to think that I thought we should only cry when we're sad. I was understanding a lot more about myself and people in general as I got older.

Soon I spoke to everyone else. Michelle met a boy in Nueville who came calling a few times. Aunt Sharon was due in November, which was now less than two months away. Anna Marie was going to spend time helping her with the baby (cleaning the house being more accurate, I suspected). Holly was playing with friends, so I missed her. Jason only said 'hi' to me and repeated it a few times until Gramma Morris took the phone.

She shooed everyone else away then whispered to me, "Alright, now what is really going on up there?"

"Well—," I started.

"No 'well,'" she stopped me, "When you say 'well' you're thinking about only telling half the truth, and half the truth is a whole lie. Be straight with me."

You and Aunt Vera would get along quite well.

So, I told her about J.P. Wentworth the third and his children. How he treated his wife. How he made deals. I told her how his sister, Aunt Vera, wouldn't believe it, even though the kidnappers stated that their primary motivation was revenge for not being treated like the rest of the family. I failed the blood test. I was not a Wentworth. But I was a Langston. And Willie was my real father.

"Paul's your real father," she corrected.

"True," I said, "But Willie has legal custody now. Aunt Vera doesn't want me around because I'm not her blood relative."

"Sounds like a good thing," she observed.

"I think so," I said, "I'd rather be down there than anywhere near her."

Cookie came in and chased me off the phone.

"I don't like children in the kitchen when I'm cooking," she groused.

"Tell that woman she'll be cooking her whole life if she don't get to teaching the young ones how to use a stove," Gramma Morris harumphed.

"I will. Love you all. Bye."

The doorbell rang just after I hung up.

"I'll get it," I called, since I was the closest.

It was Jerry Talkington for Veronica. He looked nice enough. He wore an unpainted prosthetic and fedora that helped cover his glass eye. I had him sit in the foyer so Aunt Vera wouldn't see him and climbed up the stairs to get Veronica.

She was wearing a frumpy looking housedress and worn slippers while she stared out the window. One of her jazz records was softly playing.

"It's a shame your meeting was in the office," she said when I walked in, "I couldn't hear a thing."

"Not a whole lot was said," I lied, "I'll be going to boarding school like the other girls, but my vacations will be spent back home. Louisiana home. Aunt Vera would prefer to see me as seldom as possible since I'm not part of her family."

She laughed, "How sad for you. And for me. I'll hardly ever get to see you again. Let's go to the park while we still can."

"I'd love to, but Aunt Vera likes us to be home. You can go, though. I found you an escort," I lowered my voice in an effort to sound formal, "Mr. Jerry Talkington is downstairs for you, Miss Veronica Langston."

"What? Why? He didn't tell me he was calling. I'm a mess."

She was indeed. Her hair needed brushing and Zelda wasn't there to touch up her face. I helped her as well as I could, but she was rushing me and we had to stop several times to coordinate our efforts. First, a nice dress, then shoes. Finally, I pinned back her hair. Next, she went to the bathroom sink to clean her teeth.

She missed the doorway on the way out and banged her

shoulder on the wall. She stopped to get her bearings.

"He has called on you before, hasn't he?" I asked in exasperation, "I mean, I don't remember you being so…unsettled before."

"He's been talking about moving away. Selling everything and moving to Alaska. Start a fresh life for himself. Then he's going to send for me. Maybe he wants to go now. Take me with him. Get married in a quaint little church somewhere. Oh, Amy, that would be so wonderful."

"I suppose it would," I agreed reluctantly.

In a grown-up moment, I realized she probably wouldn't do much better. Jerry was in love with her. Most other men would have only loved her money.

I helped her down the stairs. Jerry took her arm gently and embraced her with a sincere passion. I realized that he was exactly the man she needed.

"I have a hired car out front," he said to her, "Come with me and we'll make a life together. You and me. Man and wife."

"Certainly," she replied, weeping with happiness, "Let me tell everyone and pack some things."

"No, sweetness," he responded firmly, "We have to go right away. Some…things have happened and if we're going to go, it has to be now."

"But…"

He tried to guide her, but she resisted. That may have cost him his life. They argued a bit more, then Jerry said firmly, "I have to go now. I'll write to you, send you money to meet me, but I *cannot* stay any longer."

He grabbed her in a ferocious bear hug, lifting her off her feet, then put her down. She squealed a bit, in delight. None of us heard the doorbell ring, or Zelda answering it.

"You want me to go like this?" she asked.

"Yes, nothing else."

"Let's go," she said, almost laughing, she turned in my direction, "Amy, you see? Now *I'm* going on an adventure."

"It'll be a short one," Detective Trask's voice said softly from behind us. He was not how I envisioned him. Here was a short, stocky man and he blocked the exit, with two other policemen beside him. His suitcoat was open and his pistol rested on his chest in its holster.

"What's going on?" Veronica asked meekly.

"Jerald Talkington," Detective Trask said very formally, "You are under arrest for the murders of J.P. Wentworth the Third and J.P. Wentworth the Forth."

Veronica screamed, "No! Please dear God, no!"

Jerry stepped beside her and drew out a small revolver while the household all ran to watch the drama. It was pandemonium. Everybody was yelling and screaming.

"Jerry, don't be a fool," I heard from Willie.

"I knew he was a bad character," Aunt Vera was on the stairs calling out triumphantly, her face a mask of satisfaction.

"Officers, do your duty," Uncle Edgar commanded from behind her in a voice filled with sadistic glee.

All my sisters were quietly taking this in. I was horrified, but didn't know what to do, so, like them, I just watched.

Trask had his hands extended in a peaceful way.

"Let's talk about this," he said quietly while the other officers slowly were reaching for their weapons, "It's all over. You were seen at the marina the night before they sailed on *The Curious Virgin*. You bought the hand drill earlier that day. No reason for you to need a hand drill. No reason for you being on the boat. What I don't understand is why. Why did you do it?"

He shrugged and in a quick movement raised the pistol up to take a shot. I didn't know how many shots were fired. Later on, I was told it was five. One of Detective Trask's men was slightly wounded. Jerry Talkington was dead. Veronica was screaming and Zelda and Charity were comforting her. The other policemen herded us children back into the kitchen where we just sat at the table, in complete shock.

"I don't ever want to have an adventure again," Millie said blankly.

The others all silently nodded. I tried to tell them. Adventures aren't always fun.

It wasn't until years later that I understood it all. I inherited Willie's diary and letters that told the whole sordid story. It was Rosemary's death that started it all when Fourthy visited her and she died.

Rosemary demanded almost all of Mother's attention, since she was a sickly infant. Fourthy was left alone and in his diseased mind hatched a plan to bring things back to normal. Everyone knew Fourthy smothered her, but Father wanted to avoid a public embarrassment. The police ruled that she died of Sudden Infant Death Syndrome. But Mother, even with her mind blurry from all her pills, was not going to let this stand. She had other daughters and they needed to be protected.

Jerry Talkington was a lonely man who was estranged from his family. He had a small house and even smaller pension. After his recovery from the war, he found out he could survive but not enjoy his life. His wounds made it impossible to get a job. The family drugstore did not want him at all. Rumor was he wasn't his father's son.

Talkington was a man used to a certain lifestyle. He liked girls, even if he had to pay them to spend time with him. He needed money to battle his loneliness. Soon it became obvious to some of the less reputable people of town that Talkington was a man who was willing to do whatever was necessary to increase his income.

He quickly found other men like himself. Men who understood that they had to take chances to get what they wanted. At first, Jerry did little things like keeping watch while his friends burglarized warehouses. It was easy money. Nothing ever happened for a few years. Then everything changed and Jerry Talkington moved into the big time.

The gang decided to burglarize a jewelry store. It was simple enough to break into the back and slide all the rings and necklaces into cloth sacks. But they made enough noise that they heard someone yelling outside, "Call the cops!"

Jerry ran to the door and flung it open, oblivious to the alarm noise. He raised his Army issued Colt and shot the man dead. The one-eyed man went from two-bit crook to murderer in less than a minute.

He told his partners to keep the jewels. Keep his share. He didn't want anything to do with them. He knew the moment they were on the market the police would be on their trail. He advised them to keep them hidden for at least a year before fencing them, but his partners didn't listen and found themselves in jail.

There was no evidence against Jerry. Just two crooks trying to pin a murder on a pathetic veteran. Jerry would forever be considered an unsavory person, but he got away with murder.

"Yeah," he told Willie one night over some Canadian whiskey, "It was me that night. Stupid thing to do. Like I was back in the war, only this time, shooting at the enemy. I was lucky to get away with it."

Willie nodded in agreement, making sure to file the information away for future use, if needed. And it was needed when Rosemary died.

"Willie, we can't let this go on," Mother said, "I'm scared now, for all the girls. This boy is dangerous. And Joe will just keep making excuses for him. Now he's talking about sending him to boarding school. What will happen there? And when he's back here on the holidays?

"That boy was born evil and there's nothing more to it. Joe created a monster by not disciplining him and now we have a problem. I don't know how we can do it, but we need to fix it. Now."

"An excellent idea," Willie replied, "I know a way to handle everything. But it will cost money, and it will be permanent. Extremely permanent."

"That's exactly what I want," she said firmly, "Permanent, with no connections to us. It won't be the first time a Langston enemy got what he deserved. And if my children are in danger, it won't be the last."

"Mr. Wentworth will take him on *The Curious Virgin* to tell him about his going away to boarding school."

"Good. We can get rid of them both."

"I think that might be really expensive—," Willie said, shocked at the suggestion.

"Whose money are we talking about? Just get it done."

Two thousand dollars later, Willie met with Jerry and ironed out all the details. The next week, *The Curious Virgin* sank. Detective Trask may have gotten his man, but he never uncovered the whole story.

CHAPTER SIXTY-ONE

SURPRISES, CHANGES, AND ADJUSTMENTS

"What the *hell* kind of place do you live in?" Dad was extremely unhappy when he called two days later.

The local newspaper may have downplayed the incident, but the story was too sensational to be suppressed by the national press. The *Times* put out a half-serious editorial that they may assign a reporter just to cover Pennington in the near future.

"Well," I said, vaguely aware that I was breaking Aunt Vera's word rule, "My sisters and cousin are all nice. Poor Veronica is devastated. Jerry proposed to her just when it all happened. She was so happy. Now she's alone again."

"And you think that's a bad thing?"

"Yes," I said with a little growl, unconsciously imitating him, "Poor Veronica is as sweet a girl as you could ask for and no man ever gave her a thought at all. Hardly even the time of day. Just because she's blind. How would you like it?"

"I wouldn't," he said slowly, I think he was taking deep breaths to calm himself down, "But come on, Amy, there's a lot of bad things that go on in that house. I feel like taking the train up there and bringing you back. For your own safety."

I thought about how we were all forbidden to leave the grounds. The front gate was adjusted to close all the way. I would not be sneaking through it again. My outside activity was limited to playing fetch with Fluffy. And he preferred to play with Lisa. Going back to Faucette seemed like a nice idea.

"Now, Dad," I replied sadly, "I would love to come back with you, but I also want to stay here. They're family too. And besides, I'm quite safe. I just had a few…adventures."

"Amy, please. Try not to have any more adventures. It costs a fortune on these phone calls just to find out what's going on up there."

"I promise. Everything will be as smooth as silk. I guarantee you. I will not have any more adventures up here."

"Please don't guarantee it. Bad angels may be listening."

When the call was over, I wondered how I could ever have been embarrassed by him or anyone else in my Louisiana family. I missed them all.

Aunt Vera called a house meeting the next day and it was going to be serious. Family and servants gathered in the main ballroom. Nobody knew what was going on, but Aunt Vera's eyes were red and puffy. I never saw her so unkempt and carelessly dressed before, with her hair wild and hastily brushed. Barbara placed a mimosa in her shaking hand.

The servants all stood by patiently while family sat down in the chairs as ladylike as possible. Veronica was still in mourning and chose not to attend. I sat between Millie and Lisa, trying not to be noticed. Why aggravate her by reminding her I was still alive?

"Very good," she said to start the meeting off, "We have been avoiding some scandals and we have minimized others," she looked at me darkly, "We have been subject to newspaper gossip all summer, ever since the…ever since my brother's boat sank. But today, I have the sad duty to inform you of the worst and most unexpected scandal in Wentworth family history. And this one is nothing short of a disaster. This will affect our lives forever. Especially you girls."

She gulped down the mimosa which added quite a dramatic flourish to the whole thing.

"Well, tell us," Charity said, losing so much patience that she started her sentence with that dreaded word 'well.'

The events of the last few days matured her. It was time to start asserting herself. Like the rest of us, the carefree days of childhood were behind her. It was time to be an adult. It was time to start doing for herself and the others.

"I will. This first thing is to never start a sentence with 'well.' You always forget such important things," she got a faraway look for a moment, "Maybe it doesn't matter so much anymore."

Maybe it never did.

She softened a bit.

"Our lives are so different now. Who knows what will happen to you children? I always wanted the best for you all. I wanted you to be the most desirable wife material a man could ask for. Dainty, prim, polite. Matilda couldn't raise you properly. She was sick all the time. Joe was too busy. I had to do it. Who knows what will happen for now?"

She was rambling a bit and I thought she must have had a few more drinks before she started talking. Whatever her announcement was, it was going to be devastating. Charity knew it by now, I think, and let her take her time.

"You know, your mother, bless her soul, had her issues with her health and was always taking medicines and pain pills, which were not helpful. My brother worked long, hard days to give you everything you have. But he made some odd decisions at work and Edgar had to go figure them out."

She switched subjects abruptly now.

"Something else. Joe was turning everything into cash. He was going to buy a huge amount of stock in General Electric. Edgar advised against this, as the businesses needed the cash to invest in new products and innovations. But Joe was determined. He felt that if he became a major shareholder in GE, then he could urge them to buy Wentworth Enterprises. They would invest in the stores and factories. Since Joe was the CEO of Wentworth, his plan was put into effect.

"When Edgar took over, he saw all that cash. And he fell to temptation."

"He took all the money?" Willie asked, his face an ashen white.

"Everything," she replied, her lip quivering a bit, "It's all gone. He had a cashier's check written out to him and just left me a note. Juvenile nonsense, most of it. He didn't think he was sixty-two and wanted to live like a young man again. He even found himself a young woman to run off with. Your cousin, Bonnie."

"Bonnie," we all yelled and started whispering to each other.

I thought back to that evening when I saw them together in the foyer. I wish now that I had said something, but who would I have told?

"They're on a boat to Europe. We don't know which country yet, but Felix and Shirley are treating it as a kidnapping. I am confident Bonnie will be coming back, I'm not so sure about the money.

"In the meantime, we have no liquid assets—"

"Liquid assets?" Claire asked.

"Cash, bonds, stocks, things that can be converted into cash quickly. Edgar already drained all that. As bills come in, we can't pay them. After looking things over, Mr. Davis, our attorney, has advised us to declare bankruptcy. We will sell everything we can to pay off what we owe. We might even be able to keep some of our ventures. But for now, everything is for sale. Including the houses."

"This house?" Claire and Millie were crying and Lisa and Charity were close to it. They lived here all their lives.

"This house, the guest house, my house, everything," Aunt Vera answered.

Everyone was in tears. Zelda held me close until I recovered.

"And the servants were invited to this meeting because?" Willie offered.

"I hate to say it, but you have all been terminated. You can all stay on the premises until you find a new situation or until the property is sold, but without salary.

"Which reminds me," she went on, "You girls will be moving in with your Uncle Henry until your boarding school situation is resolved. We need to move you and your things out while we sell the house. Henry won't allow the dog because he's afraid for that damn stuffed parrot. The Palmers have agreed to take Fluffy. They say the house needs a pet to be complete."

To my surprise, no one, not even Lisa objected. Maybe they were in shock. We all went to our rooms and started packing. I knocked on Veronica's door and told her the news while offering to help her with her things. She nodded.

"Take care of yours first," she said lifelessly, "I knew there was something off with Uncle Edgar and Bonnie. I could see it plainly."

"How?" I asked. I was beginning to accept her use of 'see' by now.

"Her voice was a little happier, more adult when she spoke to him. Like she was in love. And his voice was softer, like he was encouraging her."

"That makes sense," I said, "I don't think he just 'fell into temptation.' I think they were planning this for some time now. Didn't they even think about the rest of their family at all?"

"Their family will always be their bank account."

That made sense.

"When Mother married Father, didn't all the Langston assets merge with Wentworth Enterprises? How did Uncle Henry get to keep his house?"

"The Langston fortune was divided so each heir got some pieces of it. Your mother's share was merged in with the company. The others all either kept what they had or sold it for cash. Uncle Joe wanted to sell off my share of the canning plant, but I wouldn't let him. The Hookers are in charge of it and won't do anything dishonest."

I was glad she would be alright, at least financially. I didn't have long to think about it, though. I had to pack. I was surprised at how many new clothes I had. I moved in with a small valise but was moving out with two trunks and two small portmanteaus.

Chapter Sixty-Two

My New Home

Uncle Henry lived in a fine house. I found it comfortable, though obviously not a palace to show off his status. It had all the required rooms but no ballrooms or servant quarters, which made sense since he didn't have any servants. The kitchen had a hand pump instead of a faucet, similar to what we had in Louisiana.

Although I saw a detached garage, he had no car and didn't drive. He always relied on Mother or Aunt Shirley to provide his transportation. Just Aunt Shirley now. The garage was filled with forgotten old props and movie posters from his acting days. Uncle Henry's past was more interesting to him than his present or future. That seemed to be the case with older people.

It was a five-bedroom home. Two of them were downstairs and three upstairs. Uncle Henry claimed the master bedroom, of course. Quincy had the one across from him. The bird had the most interesting room in the house. It was pure decoration, with no furniture. One wall was painted like a rain forest with tall green trees and a mountainous background. Parrots and macaws stared out at us, looking majestic and content, comfortable in their own feathers. Oddly, several jaguars were lurking below them, ready to pounce. The other three walls were murals of Uncle Henry and Quincy from their pirate movies together. The images showed a tilting ship with a noble pirate standing tall and smiling while battling an evil naval officer whose sneer was nothing short of chilling. Huge sea monsters, vividly painted in the background, attacked the sinking ship with giant tentacles, painted in disgusting yellow and green colors, pulling the vessel underwater.

Even worse, mermaids were sitting on the bow of the ship, their mouths opened wide, exposing yellow fangs as they watched the fight. By now, I was discovering that I had a serious aversion to mermaids. These sirens, however, were the worst I had seen. They had an unclean, harsh look to them, as though they were mostly used up, although still pretty enough, I supposed, with loose flowing hair. But their fish scales only covered them to their waists. Their breasts were brazenly uncovered, unlike most mermaid images. They reminded me of a word I heard back in Louisiana: strumpets. I wrenched my eyes away from this scene to inspect the rest of the room.

"Lovely, aren't they? They were modeled after my late wife. I had her old publicity photos printed and sent to the artist and told him exactly how I wanted them painted. He did wonderful, except he made the teeth too long. And the sunlight seems to have yellowed them a bit, but oh, well," Uncle Henry told us.

"Your wife was an actress?" I asked.

"Oh yes," he replied, "We met on stage. Her name was Endora Stallings, but we changed it to Langston. She decided she wanted to be with our children more than she wanted to be a star. Of course, we still found her a few bit parts and extra roles. At least until sound came out. Her voice was too breathy."

"Oh my gosh," Lisa asked, "She actually posed for these?"

"Don't you think these pictures make her look kind of…easy?" Claire added, with her usual tact.

"Of course not," Uncle Henry growled, "And it's just her head. I had a nude model pose for the body. Then the painter added the scales, for modesty."

"It seems to me that a little more modesty was possible," Millie whispered to me.

"So, the model looked easy," Claire went on, oblivious, "And quite buxom. Was Aunt Endora really that well-built?"

"Better," Uncle Henry replied, "But she would never consent to posing for something like this. Only Quincy and I saw her…like that."

"Quincy?" Claire asked.

"Of course. Quincy found women to be attractive, just like any other man. He liked to look too. He was quite the Peeping Tom."

"That's disgusting," Claire exclaimed, "It's not right for a bird to watch—"

Charity gave her a not so light cuff on the neck to keep her from completing the thought. Quincy, the stuffed parrot, was perched on a limb from an artificial tree that stretched from floor to ceiling. He leered at me, undressing me with his eyes.

However, the bird had a stately grace to it, with his wings spread out showing off his colors as though he knew he was king of all he surveyed. We all stared while we circled it, keeping our eyes off the hideous fresco.

"It's not completely Quincy," Uncle Henry said sadly,

"There wasn't much left of him. But we did rescue a few feathers and used them to dress this one up. That's all right, though. Amy and I can still see and hear the real Quincy."

The girls all looked down to suppress their laughter while I smiled, even though it took some effort. I think I preferred Quincy to be invisible.

Our rooms were upstairs. Charity and Lisa were assigned the largest room. It had two single beds with slightly frayed pink spreads and a hideous dark pink dresser pushed up against a pastel pink wall with pink wallpaper trim showing off pink parrots on pastel palm trees. Claire and Millie got the next one, which had a blue theme with blue parrot wallpaper plastered to the ceiling. Mine was the smallest. All I got was a bed and chifforobe. It was off-white with no wallpaper and (thankfully) no parrots. Uncle Henry thought that since I was the newest and knew everyone else the least, it would be better that way.

Claire, of course, had a different view on that.

"Why does she get her own room? She wasn't even here six months ago," she asked.

"It's also the smallest room and she has the least amount of things," Uncle Henry pointed out.

"But Uncle Henry," she went on, trying to be logical, "Wouldn't I be a better choice? I'm in the middle, usually forgotten—"

"You never let anyone forget you, Claire," Lisa broke in, using her sweet tone of voice that I imagined masked not so sweet thoughts.

Claire ignored her, "And Amy and Millie are closer in age and so are Charity and Lisa. I think it would make more sense with me in the smaller room."

"Could we put her in the garage?" Charity asked politely, "There's no car."

"Or maybe a cave?" Lisa added helpfully, ignoring Claire's menacing glare.

"No heat for either. It is September and it gets mighty cool at night these days," Uncle Henry replied thoughtfully, "How about this: Amy would you mind sharing a room?"

"Of course not," I answered, hoping I would share my space with Millie. She smiled at me, so I knew she was thinking the same thing.

"Very good," he said with a happy smile, "Quincy just had a wonderful idea. You can share his room. He'd be honored to have you."

I was mortified. Claire laughed out loud, but the others looked down. Millie tried to help me out of the situation.

"But there isn't any furniture there," she said, "She can't just sleep on the floor."

"Oh," he said thoughtfully, "That's okay. I have a bed in the garage we can bring in. It's lovely, really, a prop from the movie set. Follow me. You'll love it."

I hated it. It wasn't anything more than a long storage chest with drawers on the side. A safety rail surrounded the top to prevent the sleeper from rolling off. It stood high enough that I had to use a small wooden box to even get on it. There was no mattress.

"Rats got a hold of it," Uncle Henry explained, "That's why there were cats on the movie set. But all is well. We'll stuff some pillows on it so it'll be nice and soft. We'll probably want to spray it down with bleach as well. Get it as clean as possible. We don't want roaches running on you during the night."

"Can't we just move one of the beds downstairs?" Lisa asked.

"No, it's easier to move this one from the garage inside. No stairs."

We spent the rest of the afternoon hauling, lifting and cleaning. At first, it was a family project. Lisa and I dragged my luggage down to my creepy new room. We set the bed up and it was mine to clean. Lisa disappeared. I found letters from long ago in the drawers and put them aside while I wiped down everything I could reach. I found a few roach corpses and shivered as I got rid of them. Then I sprayed the inside with bleach and water. Finally, I polished the wood to a nice, if dull, shine.

The whole time I was moving around, it seemed that I was being watched. No matter where I was in the room, the people and monsters in the mural were staring at me. Following me around with their eyes. Quincy seemed to leer at me as well, now that I heard about his Peeping Tom habit. It was very unsettling for a ten-year-old.

"I'm all moved in," I heard Millie's voice a second before she entered with some pillows, "I thought I'd see if you wanted some help."

"Yeah," I replied, "You can get me a big blanket to cover up the walls."

"That won't do any good. You'll still know what's behind there. Besides," she added brightly, "If those statues in Flowerton didn't get you, you know a little paint can't hurt you at all. It could be worse, you know. I have to look at Claire in the mornings."

"Hmph," I chortled, "I thought Claire got my room."

"Lisa got your room. Charity stayed in the pink room. That left me and Claire, the two youngest, sharing a room. Claire's comments about the mermaids'…um…you know, did nothing to endear her to Uncle Henry. She offended Quincy too."

"Oh, I wouldn't complain about sharing a room. Uncle Henry could send you down here."

"I doubt it," she replied, "I threatened to fry Quincy up like a chicken a few months ago. Quincy would throw a fit if we even suggested it. Besides, I don't like your taste in décor."

"You were going to cook a stuffed bird that doesn't exist? That seems kind of featherbrained."

"Ha-ha," she said, "It was in the heat of the moment. I don't even remember what Uncle Henry said, but—" her eyes lit up for a second and I knew she thought of something good, "Whatever it was, it ruffled my feathers."

She giggled at her own joke and I smiled.

"Good effort," I commented, "But right now, there aren't enough pillows."

Indeed not. She brought in four decorative pillows that must have adorned some forgotten couch somewhere.

"That's all we could find."

"Did you ask Uncle Henry to help?"

"He's the one who found these in the attic. There were others, but the squirrels got to them. Or rats. They smelled funny."

"Gee, thanks," I said.

"But Melanie will be by later today with some more. She heard about your bed and found some soft fluffy ones. I hope."

"So do I."

"Look at what I have for you," Uncle Henry wheeled in an old wardrobe. It was quite a bit taller than we girls and covered in gray dust. He opened the doors to reveal a firm hanging rod and two drawers on the bottom.

He was followed by my other sisters. Charity and Lisa were carrying an old table that was scratched and scarred, but at least it was clean. Claire followed them in with a basin and pitcher of water.

"Maybe you should get her a dressing screen to keep Quincy from leering at her," Claire said with false concern.

"Quincy only 'leered' at Endora," Uncle Henry sneered, "And she liked showing off to him and me. Besides, even if he were so ungentlemanly, he wouldn't 'leer' at family. That would be incestuous."

They all agreed and quickly left, seeing as Uncle Henry was getting a bit cranky. And more than a little creepy.

"I'll find you some more cleaning supplies," Millie said and ran out of the room after them.

"I have all I need," I called out, but she was gone.

Uncle Henry laughed softly.

"You're the only one who's ever done any work, I can tell. That's why you have more personality. At least, I can talk to you while working because you haven't run away to do lazy things."

With that, we turned to the neglected armoire. Uncle Henry got the drawers out for me to start on and I first dusted them off quickly. After getting me a bucket of water and vinegar with baking soda, he sat down on the bed.

"Oh dear," he said after a second or two, "I'll have to go get you quite a few more pillows if you're to be comfortable."

"Melanie's coming over this afternoon with some," I replied, but he was gone, leaving me to clean the giant wardrobe by myself.

"Hmmf," I said to myself, "He's the one doing lazy things now."

The wardrobe was mostly just dusty. A few flicks of my cloth and some wood polish made it look like new. I was lucky. It had heavy duty wooden rollers on it so I could push it to the wall when I was done. I chose to cover the mermaids.

Sorry, Uncle Henry and Aunt Endora.

I was satisfied with my work and went to clean myself up. Hopefully with a nice warm bath.

"Oh no," Uncle Henry said after I inquired, "I installed a water closet, but never had the inclination for a bathtub. Seems like a waste of money. Pouring in all that water and letting it drain away. That's why you have the wash basin. When the water gets dirty, just pour it in the toilet and fill it back up."

He opened a drawer and showed me a bar of soap and sponge. At least they were new. There was a sink in the water closet that we could use for brushing teeth.

One toilet. Two sinks. Three weeks. Four bedrooms. Five girls. Even at that young age, I could see some potential for problems. And that wasn't counting the zany old uncle and dead bird.

Chapter Sixty-Three

Another Invitation

I knew how to use a wash basin. Never pour more water than you can carry to the nearest drain. Get the skin wet and then soap and rinse only small places at a time. Don't get water on the floor.

I also learned something. A privacy screen would be nice to have when a young girl shares a room with an ogling stuffed parrot. Quincy seemed quite aware of me when I was undressed and sponging down. It may sound funny, but that bird had a licentious gleam in its little eyes. It made me uncomfortable. I was really beginning to dislike that parrot.

When I told that to Millie, she understood and we rooted through the garage until we found an old wooden changing screen. After a little dusting, I set it up between my bed and Quincy. Now at least I had a modicum of privacy.

"How nice," I heard Melanie's voice call from the door, "I really like what you did to the room, especially covering up those obscene mermaids."

I peeked around the screen and smiled. She and Claire were carrying a mattress for my bed. I hurried to pull off the pillows and we fitted it on the chest. It was perfect, if a bit hard.

"Why do you have the screen between the bed and the door?" Claire asked.

"To keep Quincy from staring at me."

"You know it's not really Quincy and it's stuffed," Melanie said after giving me a quick hug, "And it's a bird."

"It still stares at me."

"It's a work of taxidermy," Claire said haughtily, "That's all it can do."

"I suppose. But it's too bad they didn't stuff it with its eyes shut."

"Veronica would like it then," she replied flippantly.

For a moment, I truly didn't like her. It must have shown.

"Poor Veronica," Melanie smoothed things over, "I feel so bad for her that her boyfriend died like that. And with her being blind and all the changes going on, how will she hold up? At least Aunt Vera found an apartment for her. But she won't have anyone looking out for her anymore. I do worry about her."

We were worried too. I think that Claire regretted her insensitivity. She left soon after.

"What I really came to talk to you about is that Ursula has invited us back to the *Sirena* this Saturday. We're going to go to Cape Town and see the whole city. She wants to take us all the way to Romania someday. She thinks you have the spiritual intensity to become a medium, just like her. Wouldn't that be grand? She wants you as an assistant right now. Of course, I'd be there with you."

Of course.

"I told her you'd consider it, given how precarious your situation is."

"Oh," I said unenthusiastically. I didn't want to go to Cape Town. I didn't want to be a medium or assistant. My instincts told me to avoid Ursula. "Wouldn't it be better if she took Claire for the ride? She might be a better assistant."

"You just want to be free of Claire for a day. Anyway, I told her you'd come. We'll talk about you being her assistant on Saturday. She already hired someone you know. Zelda is working for her as a hostess and maid. I know she'd love to see you again. Dress warm."

She was oblivious to the fact that I did not want to go anywhere with Ursula and left after giving me a quick hug goodbye.

After a couple of minutes, I realized that a trip around the cape and excellent food might not be all that bad. I didn't know what a medium's assistant actually *did*, but I doubted it would be harder than my work at the café back home. Maybe it wouldn't be so bad if I could get her to stop calling me Yvonne.

I slipped a sheet on the mattress, tossed a couple of parrot themed blankets on top and called my room done.

Dinner was clam chowder, only Uncle Henry forgot to buy clams. He also forgot to turn the flame on the stove up high enough, so dinner was essentially raw potatoes soaked in cream and milk. No wonder he always accepted Mother's dinner invitations. The other girls put on a brave show to not hurt his feelings. Even Claire made light of it.

"I always feel sorry for those poor clams, but I have no pity for potatoes," she crunched with the fakest smile I ever saw.

"Good for you," Uncle Henry smiled, "But tomorrow we'll feast. We'll have the clams without potatoes."

I nodded as I chewed through a raw potato and listened

to the moist crunch. Its hard, uncooked texture was almost enough to make me gag, but I refused to say anything that would hurt his feelings. I think it was the same for all of us. After all, there were not very many housing options for us anymore.

That night, before going to bed, I wrote to my family in Louisiana, telling them of my new situation and giving them my address. There would be no more phone calls since Uncle Henry didn't have a telephone. I shared a bedroom with Quincy the parrot, who would only have me and none of my sisters. It was generous that he was willing to share and now I had a bigger bedroom than anyone else. All I had to do was keep Quincy happy. I didn't mention the fact that he was dead and displayed on a movie prop tree. With that done, I adjusted the screen so Quincy wouldn't spy on me while I undressed and shut out the light.

I was thinking about the trip aboard *The Sirena.* Job or no job, good food or not, I just didn't want to go. Ursula made me uneasy. I knew that Melanie wanted to be her friend, but Ursula was more interested in me. Even at ten, I could see it.

Chapter Sixty-Four

Decision and Separation

The next day was Friday. It was cloudy and cold. The sidewalk was darkening in early morning drizzle. All in all, a good day to stay inside. I hoped for a storm to cancel our boating excursion.

"The clouds aren't dark enough to cancel your trip," Charity told me over a breakfast of oatmeal and cranberry juice, "But good thinking. Ursula gives me the heebie-jeebies. It wouldn't surprise me if she plans on calling up demonic forces by using you as a human sacrifice."

"Yeah," said Claire, "They tie you to a table and cut off your head and drink the blood, just like vampires."

I looked at the red juice in my glass. I didn't want to drink it now.

"Claire," Lisa exclaimed, "Don't try to be funny. Your face is all you need to make people laugh."

"Now girls," Uncle Henry said, "I don't want you fighting with each other. Unless you're fighting over me."

"I hope you were trying to be funny," Lisa said with obvious distaste.

"I hoped I was being successful."

The doorbell rang and we were spared any more awkward conversations. Millie answered it, as she was

closest and had just finished her breakfast anyway. She
came in with Aunt Vera.

The poor woman aged twenty years in the past two
days. She lost weight and her face lost its firmness. Her
back stooped, like she was carrying the weight of the world
on her shoulders. After a few pleasantries and hugs, she got
to the point.

"After much discussion," she started, "The family has
agreed to continue with the plans for finishing school." She
nodded towards Charity. "And boarding school. You will
all be taking a bus this Sunday afternoon, so you will all
arrive just before the school year starts. Your Aunt Audra
will be financing this adventure. In return, she will have sole
possession of Wentworth Founding. That way we won't
have to sell it to outsiders. If your grades are bad, you will
be removed and sent to live with me and go to public
school. I can't even imagine how bad your marriage
prospects will be after that. But you'll still be family and I'll
love you anyway."

I just bet.

"However, this arrangement does not include Amy. As
the Wentworth family knows that she failed the blood test,
they feel no financial obligation towards her. I don't have
the resources to contribute to her future. And she can't stay
here much longer."

"Why not?" Uncle Henry asked, annoyed.

"Because times have changed. There are too many
advances and setbacks in the world. I'm afraid you couldn't
raise a young girl properly at your age. There are some in
the family who are uncomfortable with you having them
already. What if you forget to feed her or something? What
if something happens? We can't have another scandal. We
just can't."

Last night's dinner was a sad testimony to poor Uncle Henry's child rearing skills. I could cook dinner. Plus, I volunteered to Aunt Vera.

"But what if he forgot to buy food?"

I had no response to that. I also knew it was a distinct possibility.

"Willie has gone to Providence to interview for a position. When he comes back on Monday, it will be up to him to make arrangements for you."

"Willie the butler?" Lisa asked, "How does he get to make the decision?"

And so the story came out. Another Wentworth scandal. As it was, my sisters were going to boarding school. I had to be content with 10,000 shares of stock in a bankrupt company.

After Aunt Vera left, we were all in shock. We were poor and living on the charity of our family. We were orphans and no longer heiresses. We were being separated. Charity was going to finishing school. My fate was unknown. Whatever happened next would affect us all differently. This would be our last weekend together as a family. I think we all went to our rooms and had a good cry.

We eventually made our way up to Charity's room and talked about our futures. What seemed so settled two months ago was completely unknown now. My sisters were not prepared for anything except marriage. I at least had some limited skills in the kitchen. If I ever got back to Louisiana, I vowed to learn everything I could to be a good cook.

The others didn't really have an option like that. Any time they did anything that even looked like work they were admonished to let the help do that. I didn't know what would become of them if they didn't marry well.

More importantly, I didn't know what would become of me. My excursion with Ursula and Melanie was tomorrow. Perhaps being a medium's helper paid enough to see me through. I could only hope. An orphanage seemed like a bleak place to finish up a childhood.

Chapter Sixty-Five

A Day on the Yacht

It was cloudy and windy that morning. It wasn't freezing, but it was close. Melanie was cheerful as always when her car arrived for me. I was wearing flannel leggings with a winter dress, gloves and a tight-fitting wool pullover hat. A nice, warm, knee length coat completed my outfit.

Melanie gave me an approving glance. She was buttoned up just as tight as I was, except she wore long brown boots that clicked loudly on the floor while we walked to my remodeled bedroom.

"I love what you did to your room," she commented, "Too bad you can't have the walls painted and the tree and bird removed. I swear, it always looks as though Quincy is staring at me."

"Me too," I said, "But what else can he do? It's not like he can talk anymore."

"Anymore? It's a stuffed animal, not actual taxidermy."

"Well," I said, afraid Quincy might tattle on me if I agreed, "You never can tell where the bird's spirit might be. I wouldn't want to hurt Quincy's feelings, you know. After all, I'm his guest."

"Maybe not for long," she replied with a curious glance

thrown my way, "Ursula is thinking of having you come live with her. Won't that be nice? Then whenever I visit her, I can see you too."

"Live with her?"

"You'll have to, if you're going to be her apprentice."

"Oh."

"It won't be any fun living here without the other girls," she told me.

I nodded. I already knew that. I also knew I wouldn't be here long, or so I hoped. Pretending a dead bird was an intelligent, living being was getting on my nerves. It was also reaching the point where it wasn't just pretend. I was beginning to think Quincy was real.

The trip to the pier was quiet. We were both in our own thoughts. I was thinking about my future. I really wasn't too excited about being Ursula's apprentice in the first place, but to have to live with her was unsettling. It wasn't just that her being a medium went against my Christian upbringing, although that was part of it. It wasn't just that she insisted on calling me Yvonne. She seemed to have some kind of plan that involved me that made me nervous.

She was waiting for us on deck, wearing a dark fur coat and winter hat. She smiled and waved when she saw us, but something in her smile made me even more uneasy. It looked like the smile I saw on Mom's face when she spung her trap on Guy the night of the shotgun wedding.

I realized that when we were on the water there would be nowhere to go if I needed to run away. And I might need to run away. I shook it off as a dumb premonition. My 'womanly intuition' was obviously not fully developed. I followed Melanie on board and we all faked-hugged each other. Boys are lucky, I thought, they just shake hands and keep a distance.

Fortuna stepped up from below deck and we repeated the same pointless ritual before going down. Andy and Bar removed the gangplank and untied the ropes. Captain Garza smiled at us from the bridge. All in all, this should be an enjoyable little voyage. But somehow, I knew it wouldn't be pleasant at all.

Andy loaded the table with shrimp cocktail, potato salad, bread, and butter. Melanie tried the shrimp and recommended it to me.

"This is simply divine," she gushed, "This is the best."

I smiled politely after trying it. It was cold shrimp in spicy ketchup. Hardly divine. It wasn't even breaded and fried. The potato salad was not to my taste either. I never had potatoes mashed in a salad before. I have always avoided it since, though, to be fair, it may not have been the potatoes' fault. The Romanian vinegar and mustard may have played roles in the disaster. Luckily, there was bread and butter. Nobody could ruin bread and butter.

The yacht pulled out of the dock and into the cape. I felt like we walked into a trap that just snapped shut.

"All is in readiness, Madam," Andy called down to us.

"Oh, good," Ursula called back, "And everything is clear in Boston?"

"It is."

"Then come down here for a moment."

Boston?

"I thought we were going to Cape Town," I said, looking at Melanie.

Melanie looked perplexed and turned to Ursula.

"Oh my, Melanie," Ursula laughed, "You look so confused. We had a change of plans, you see."

Bar came in from the side as Andy descended. Both had pistols stuffed in their belts.

"Ursula, this is not funny," Melanie said softly, through her fear. At least she could talk. I was paralyzed.

Again?

"No, dear," Ursula said sweetly, "It's destiny. We live in a strange world. My darling sister Yvonne was taken from me years ago, but here she is again, only she thinks she's someone else. We are going home to Kheronia, just outside of Bucharest, where my family still lives. I'm going to teach Yvonne all the things she needs to know to be a medium. We'll set her up in her own parlor. She'll be famous. My protégé. My sister.

"And you, Melanie? We have the opportunity to be more than friends. My dear son lost his wife a few years back and now we'll be family. You'll be my new daughter-in-law. And even though you may not have the gift like Yvonne does, you will be a serviceable fortune teller too. You will have a whole new life. Doing what you always wanted to do."

"No," Melanie was crying, as if that was going to do any good, "Ursula, I am married. I have a son who needs me. You can't do this."

"Yes, I can. Your son is being raised by your servants anyway. Your husband is a non-believer and he's embarrassed by you. You will be happier with me. You wait and see. My son will be a better match for you and you can have other children. A woman can have as many babies as she has years of youth.

"And Yvonne?" she turned to me, "We'll clear your little head of all this Amy Collins nonsense. Why would you want to be an orphan girl when you can be a Transylvanian princess? And a famous one at that. A reincarnated girl who remembers her past life. Like the Tarot card. 'The drowned girl lives on.'

"People will come from miles around to see you and hear your story. You'll continue your life from the day you died. Maybe we can exhume your grave and put the little bones next to your bed. You can sleep side by side."

She seemed a little dreamy at this point. Not to mention the fact that she was scaring me.

"You were so hard to catch," Andy said at this point, "I started climbing those stupid vines up to your room when that man started yelling. And when Zelda told us you and your sister were going to the city, we followed you to that museum, but you slipped out the back. I wanted to take you that night when Fortuna and I were in your room, but she wouldn't let me."

"Of course not," Fortuna hissed at him, "She'd have screamed her head off and we'd be caught. Zelda was supposed to give you sleeping draughts but when I heard you whimpering, I knew she forgot to give you the potion. It almost seemed like we weren't going to get you at all. But now you walked right into our arms."

"Zelda was a part of this?" I asked, disappointed and sad.

"Indeed. But I figured you would never trust her or be comfortable with her around again. So, I sent her to Dublin to wait for us. But we'll never pick her up. She was well paid. Now she is back home and whatever happens to her doesn't matter to us.

"But little Yvonne does matter, because destiny calls," Ursula said, back from her little trance. She smiled at me and reached out to touch my hair, but I pulled back.

"Ursula, if this is a joke, it's not funny," Melanie said while sitting down, looking helpless, "You can't do this."

"I can tell the future," Ursula said, changing the subject while her eyes bored into Melanie, "And do you know what's going to happen? Andy's going to tie your wrists to the chair. And if you insist on talking, we'll stuff a napkin in your mouth."

She nodded to Andy and he expertly bound her wrists tightly with smooth twine.

"Isn't it interesting? I've done all kinds of readings on my little sister and always there seems to be a mermaid in her future. Either in conjunction with death or danger. And here you both are, Amy and Yvonne, on board *The Sirena*. Do either of you even know what *Sirena* means? It's an Italian word. It means mermaid.

"And do you know what's going to happen next? *The Sirena* is going to crash into those large rocks along the coast. The wreckage will be found, but no bodies. Everyone will think we all drowned. And while they're searching for the bodies, we'll all be whisked away in my other motorboat. Sean will be waiting for us. And we will all sail away. First to Boston, then to our new home."

"You'll never get away with this," Melanie said defiantly.

"Not with you gumming up the works," Ursula said grimly, "Maybe you won't survive the crash. Maybe you'll drown. That will be such a pity. I really like you and enjoy your company. But I am taking my sister home, with or without your help."

"The rocks are in sight," Bar called out from the stairs, "Time to move."

He untied Melanie and guided us to the deck. The ocean waves thrashed across the boat and rocks. Two small fishing boats bobbed in the distance, but they were too far away to help us.

Andy fitted us with small life vests, just in case something didn't go exactly right. We watched as the monolith loomed ahead of us while we raced forward.

Another, larger ship floated nearby, moored to a glistening outcrop of granite. Our yacht sped up for the crash. Bar stood behind me, firmly gripping my shoulders. I could only watch as the boulders collided towards us.

"Pull away," Melanie whispered to me as Bar was bracing for the crash.

I lurched to my right and he lost his balance for a second. Melanie kicked him hard in his crotch. Her aim was perfect. He went rolling down the deck just as we felt the bottom of the boat rip into the rocks. I dove overboard in the confusion.

The ship lurched sideways and pitched everyone else backwards. There were a few men assigned on the rocks to assure that everyone got safely on board the other vessel, but I swam away from them to escape. Sean was there, helping Melanie into a lifesaver. I saw that she was with Fortuna and Ursula, and the men were towing them towards the other vessel. I didn't see Bar, but Andy was thrashing about, calling my name.

The water was icy cold. I was able to kick off my shoes and hat, but my coat was weighing me down even with the life vest. I only got maybe ten yards away from the boat when I felt myself being pulled out to sea. I tuned back to *The Sirena.*

The captain was searching for me with a telescope. I took a deep breath and grabbed ahold of the monolith. My shoulder scraped on a rock. The current was rushing all around me. The waves crashed over my head, preventing me from breathing. I didn't want to wash out to sea so I held on as best as I could, but soon I knew I would have to swallow the water. I thought I heard music and I felt peaceful.

Again, I was back home in Faucette. Mom was cooing to the

baby. Jason was playing with some wooden toy. Neither of them saw me. Jason looked through me and asked Mom, "Where do you think Amy is?"

Then I felt a hand grab me and pull me up. What happened after that, I don't know. I was on the beach. Detective Trask was over me. I thought he was kissing me at first (Yuck!) but I learned afterwards it was mouth to mouth resuscitation. I coughed up a lungful of water and gasped for breath. Trask then told me what had happened so far.

A fishing boat saw the 'accident' and called the police on the wireless. They hurried over and fished me out of the ocean while Ursula and her crew escaped. Trask was the closest to my location and drove like mad to get to the beach. When he arrived, I was unconscious and my rescuers didn't know what to do. He immediately administered first aid until an ambulance took me to the hospital for overnight observation.

"They put Melanie on a little flat perch so she'd be safe and took off when they saw they lost you," Trask told me, "Wherever they went after that, we don't know. They had an escape plan. Hopefully, it's about as good as the one they used to make us think their boat sank."

"I thought it did."

He laughed, "I meant to say with you on board. It was clever, though. Everyone would think you're dead. No one would look for you after a while. We'd just believe your bodies washed up on some deserted beach never to be found.

"It would have been a better plan if they put you on the other boat *then* crashed the *Sirena*. Oh well. Criminals aren't smart."

"And Melanie's alright?"

"Couldn't be better. She got a big dose of common sense today. No more occult or spiritualism. Just home and family. So, she says."

CHAPTER SIXTY-SIX

HOMECOMING

It was late when I got back Sunday night. Uncle Henry was not very interested in my adventure. He wanted to go to bed. I took a quick sponge bath and went to say goodnight, but he didn't even wait for me and I could hear him lightly snoring.

I sighed and told Quincy about my adventure, but even though stuffed parrots may be good listeners, they really don't add anything to a conversation. I stroked his chest for a bit and went behind my screen and fell asleep.

The house was quiet when I got up the next day. My sisters all left for their schools while I was still at the hospital for observation. I didn't even get a chance to say goodbye and I missed them all. Even Claire.

Uncle Henry made me breakfast that day. We had orange juice.

"The pantry is getting a little empty," he mused, "Maybe later I can send you to the store."

"The store?" I answered blankly, "The one that's downtown?"

"That's the only one I know of."

"Isn't that something like five miles away?" I asked.

"It's less than three miles as the crow flies."

"Yeah, but the crow flies over the marshes and forests."

"And a young girl needs her exercise. She also needs food."

I really wasn't hurt from yesterday. Maybe some exercise would be good. So, without any more argument, I went to my room and brushed my hair to get ready. After I put on a nice warm coat, I went back to the kitchen to get Uncle Henry's grocery list and some money.

"Twenty pounds of birdseed?" I asked.

"Quincey gets hungry."

"Quincey doesn't eat."

"He has friends."

"But twenty pounds? On top of milk and oatmeal and…that's it?"

"I have friends who invite me to dinner."

No wonder Aunt Vera was worried about him feeding me.

At that moment, the doorbell rang.

"I'll get it," I said, shaking my head.

It was Willie. We hugged for the first time. Me and my father. One of them, anyway. Then we sat down in the living room while Uncle Henry made us some tea. At least we had tea and water.

I told him all about my latest excursion on the now defunct *Sirena.* I also told him I was lonely here now.

"Then I have some good news for you," he said, "I just received an offer of employment down in Providence."

"That's wonderful," I said back, "When do we leave?"

"We don't," he replied, "My employer does a lot of confidential business dealings. He doesn't believe children are good at keeping secrets. But, on the bright side, he gave me an additional sum to provide for you a wonderful home to live in. A place where you'll be family and accepted and loved just as much as if you were with me."

I looked at him skeptically.

"It's in Louisiana. A town called Faucette."

CHAPTER SIXTY-SEVEN

BACK HOME

Melanie and Uncle Henry drove to the station with Willie and me. Willie supplied me with two boxes of stationery and instructions to write every day if I wanted to avoid execution. It was a sad farewell with lots of tears. Of course, there were no other options. Melanie couldn't take me in since she had a damaged marriage to repair. Uncle Henry couldn't really take care of himself, much less anyone else. Lettie couldn't have me because it might hurt Marvin's career. I wasn't considered to be a Wentworth, so that whole family turned their backs on me. Mother's sisters and brothers were too old to be suitable, as far as Willie was concerned. Veronica wanted me to move in with her, but Willie said no to that. He worried that I would be taking care of her instead of enjoying my childhood. My life at Wentworth Founding was soon to be a memory. It was time to go.

I left Faucette with a frayed little carpet bag. I returned with two trunks and two portmanteaus. I changed right after the train reached Hammond into my beige dress, the one that nobody liked back home. It seemed to be a good travel dress since it was still warm and I had a matching hat and gloves. I didn't wear the gloves though. I didn't want to be overdressed.

The conductor was a nice man who helped me unload my luggage at the Faucette station. I sat on one of the trunks for a moment and listened as the train pulled away. I could have gone inside to wait, but it was cool outside and the mosquitos were sleeping somewhere. What a life I might have had. Yet whenever I was in trouble, it was my family here that I wanted. We may not be as sophisticated as my family in Pennyton, but I was accepted here by the people who mattered. My imperfect but loving family. I heard my name called out from behind me and turned around. The whole family was there for me, even though it was a school day down here.

Mom hugged me so tightly I couldn't breathe. Dad was a little more formal but just as loving. Holly and Jason were chattering nonstop about how grown up I looked. Michelle hovered in the background with a happy smile as she waited her turn for a hug. Even Anna Marie seemed happy I returned.

I was too. I truly enjoyed my life of luxury up north, but here was family. They had their faults and flaws, but I realized that I did too. They didn't care about my freckles and I didn't have to measure up to their ideal of beauty. They didn't care how I talked or sat, or which fork I used (we only used one per meal). They only cared about me.

"I just love your dress," Michelle said, "Don't you, Mom?"

"Oh my goodness, Amy," Mom replied, "You look so adorable and elegant."

"Elephant?" Jason asked quizzically, and we all laughed while Michelle explained to him what elegant meant.

Gramma Morris looked at all the luggage and shook her head.

"When I was growing up, we wore two dresses. One for church and one for everything else."

"Well," I said, "Some of these I'll share with Holly when she's older."

But Holly was just as big as me now.

"Or maybe when we get home."

"Yes," Mom said, "Let's get you home. You must be tired from that ride."

I nodded, "A nice hot bath sure sounds good right now."

"Bath?" Gramma Morris scoffed, "That can wait till tomorrow. You can take one with everyone else. And don't expect maid service!"

THE END

EPILOGUE

I didn't understand why there were any questions about their blood relationship when Gramma Amy completed her story, so I asked, "Why is there any confusion? The hospital employees recanted their testimony. The blood test said Wentworth wasn't your father. Willie claimed that he was your father. You and Millie had to be sisters, or at least half-sisters."

"The next week after I arrived home there was another scandal that involved me," she smiled, "You see, Aunt Vera didn't pay to have the blood test. She paid for the results."

"The results?"

"Both of my mothers, Tillie and Cassie, were Type O. So was I. It didn't matter what blood type the father was unless he was AB. Willie and Joe Wentworth were both Type A. Hugo Landacre was Type O. Both women and all three men could have been my parents. In those days, the doctors couldn't do any better. Aunt Vera paid the doctor to say I had Type B. That doctor was caught taking bribes from all kinds of rich families to deny their paternity. Then a woman's family had a second test done. Aunt Vera was completely humiliated again.

"That's why Millie wants the genetic test. But in the end, it doesn't matter. It won't change anything. She was the best sister I could ask for. Everyone in both families was nothing short of wonderful. It's almost sad to find out which family is blood and which one isn't."

The next day, Aunt Millie was having a bad day and stayed in bed. We all went in to see her. Gramma Amy had the test results with her in a folder. There was a lot of hugging and hand holding. Maggie and I also gave her a loving squeeze. I really liked Aunt Millie after hearing Gramma Amy's story.

After a few seconds of small talk and well wishing, Aunt Millie nodded to the folder.

"Is that it?"

"It is, indeed," Gramma Amy said cheerfully.

"So, are we sisters?" Millie asked in a phlegmy whisper.

"Yes, we are," Gramma Amy said soothingly while stroking her hair, "We have always been sisters. And we'll stay sisters forever."

Millie squeezed her hand. "I'm so happy."

We all were. Although it meant nothing to Gramma Amy, she was glad everyone else was happy. And we all stayed that way until it was time for us to go.

On the train ride home, Maggie eventually asked Gramma Amy, "You said you've always been sisters, but were you blood sisters? You really didn't answer that. Besides, at best you were half-sisters."

"After ninety-two years, it's not the blood that counts. It's the love. It only mattered to me because it mattered to her."

"But was it true?" Maggie persisted.

Gramma Amy gently reached down and gave her the genetic test results. As Maggie began to examine it, I leaned over to read it, too.